THE WHITE SPACE BETWEEN

The
White
Space
Between

Ami Sands Brodoff

Second Story Press

Library and Archives Canada Cataloguing in Publication

Brodoff, Ami Sands

The white space between/ by Ami Sands Brodoff.

ISBN 978-1-897187-49-4

1. Holocaust survivors—Québec (Province)—Montréal—Fiction. I. Title.

PS8603.R63W44 2008   C813'.6   C2008-904617-X

Developmental Editor: Sarah Swartz
Design: Melissa Kaita
Author photo by Mikhail Hoch
Cover photo © iStockphoto

Printed and bound in Canada

Second Story Press gratefully acknowledges the support of the Ontario Arts Council and the Canada Council for the Arts for our publishing program. We acknowledge the financial support of the Government of Canada through the Book Publishing Industry Development Program.

ONTARIO ARTS COUNCIL
CONSEIL DES ARTS DE L'ONTARIO

Canada Council Conseil des Arts
for the Arts du Canada

Published by
SECOND STORY PRESS
20 Maud Street, Suite 401
Toronto, ON M5V 2M5
www.secondstorypress.ca

The setting of this novel is the historical reality of the Holocaust. Names, characters, places, and incidents are the product of the author's imagination, except in the case of historical figures and events.

Though this novel is a love song to Montréal, my adopted home city, I've taken the occasional fictional liberty with familiar haunts.

The YIVO standard for Yiddish transliteration is used in this novel.

For my mother, Minette Davis

And for my "other mother," Shirley Brodoff

And for my shviger, Brana Hochova,
In loving memory,

And in honor and memory of the entire Hoch family

And the millions of families like them

The Torah is written "black fire on white fire" . . . black fire refers to the letters of Torah . . . The white refers to the spaces between the letters . . . They are the story, the song, the silence.

—Rabbi Avi Weiss

PROLOGUE

1942
Auschwitz, Poland

JANA IVANOVA WAS CHOSEN: one of fifty Jewish women in the Politische Abteilung, where she worked as a typist. Each night, she typed death certificates. She processed a card with the hour of death. She was free to choose from a list of thirty-four prescribed diseases for the cause of death, to choose the time. *At 6:42 A.M. the Polish Jewish Prisoner X died of pneumonia.* The documents were sealed with the signature of an SS physician. Her cards were filled out with false accuracy—the cause of death was always the same.

One day, when the call came, Jana followed the SS man to an alcove. On his breath, she smelled chocolate and the rich odor collided with the memory of Ivanova's, her family's sweetshop, in Prague.

The colors, the smells, the plenty—prunes and sunflower seeds dipped in extra-dark chocolate, halvah studded with nuts, not to

1

mention butter mints, caramels, fireballs, licorice, and toffee. Her father, Vilem, held her in one arm, fed her butter mints with the other, teardrops of pink, pale yellow, mint green. They melted smoothly against her tongue, stuck to the roof of her mouth, as she crunched the sweet white sprinkles. The wave of memory makes her eyes burn. Days after school, Jana watched over her younger sister and three little brothers, and helped her mother in the candy shop. Nights, her father sculpted his beautiful, ferocious heads in their building's basement. Jana liked to be in the candy store, but even more, she lived for her time down below with her father. When he came into a room, he took up all the space, he was all Jana could see. The way he looked at her, the light she brought into his face made Jana feel more alive than anything.

As a secretary of death, Jana wrote the name and numbers of the people who were "selected." One day, her father's name was on the list. She begged the *Rottenführer* to spare him. "What does it matter?" he asked. "Today, tomorrow, next week?"

Jana Ivanova made a card for her father—*Herzschwäche,* heart failure. Each night, she talked to her father in her head, heard his voice, conjured the features of his face. She wasn't sure how long she could hold these beloved sounds and shapes intact, before they blurred.

The SS men called Jana and the other typists, *Geheimnisträgerinen,* secret-bearers, the troop on its way to heaven. For their secrets could only be safeguarded by their deaths. When would it come? That morning? At nightfall? The day after tomorrow? Next week?

In that way, Jana knew she was the same as the other Jewish

prisoners, her father, mother, sister and baby brothers, her grandparents, aunts, uncles, and cousins . . . but in another way, she was special, different. Jana was allowed to bathe, she got a little more food, she could wear a kerchief over her shaved skull. She lived inside daydreams, dreams more vivid than the terrors of her nights, dreams that put a sparkle in her dark brown eyes and a half-smile on her full lips. She dreamt she would give birth to a child someday, a beautiful, healthy baby who would take after her father. A girl! Why did she see this girl? The dream of a daughter sustained her. She could make it through another day.

※ ※ ※

1947
Bremerhaven, Germany

JANA IVANOVA CLIMBED QUICKLY to the highest deck of the ship. She was surprised by the strength in her legs, the spring to her step. She was alone on deck, he rested down below, as they sailed from Bremerhaven, Germany to Halifax, Canada. It was cold on deck, bracing, wind whipping off the sea. The sky above shone pale, the sea dark blue. The wind made her face flush, the sea-spray prickling her cheeks, salting her chapped lips. Her hair, choppy and chin-length, flurried about her face, into her eyes. It had grown in dark and straight, lank planes instead of curls, nearly black. Jana gazed through binoculars and watched the turbulent darkness all around, the flapping white gulls. They keened with a desperate, mournful sound that pierced her heart. She was free now, alive. Jana glanced at her arm with the tattoo number and could barely believe she was here. She willed that her suffering would fade with this new life; and she willed this, willed that she would give birth to the child she had imagined for so long, a beautiful, healthy girl.

Jana spotted the man who had saved her life—brought her back to life—climbing up on deck to join her, the camera slung around his neck. He lifted the camera and took aim. Jana stretched her chapped lips into a smile, her eyes tearing in the wind, streaming down her face. The horror was behind her. She would not turn around.

❊ ❊ ❊

PART I
HIDING

Memory Book
Winter 1968

Mama, where is you?

Willow, for me say, where are you?

Where are you, Mama?

Not here.

I see you!

Don't touch. You'll smudge the picture.

You is . . .

For me say, you are.

You are, Mama?

Jane Ives.

Why I am Willow, Mama?

Oh, lovey, the willow is the most beautiful tree, graceful, but strong,
tough. Look out in the yard, blue it looks tonight. Blue willow, silvery

blue, so strong, stronger than what, I don't know. The willow bends, lovey, but won't ever break.

Where is you, Mama. In this picture?

Hiding.

Behind your Daddy. He's so big. How old is you Mama?

Are you. About your age.

I'm four soon.

Another year, you have yet.

Why you hide, Mama?

To make people find me, maybe not find me.

Mama, close your eyes.

Willow! Come out right now! Time for bed. Willow, where are you?

ONE

January 2005
Kingston, New Jersey

A LETTER. The creamy envelope looks fresh, as if it has not even gone through the postal service, and it is addressed to "Miss Jane Ives, 7 Madison Street, Kingston, N.J., U.S.A." No zip code. Jane holds the letter, feeling its weight in her hand, the rich texture of the stationery, fancy paper with a grain like wood.

She stopped hoping for a certain letter years ago when Willow turned five. She got her answer a few weeks before Willow's birthday, not the answer she yearned for, but an answer nonetheless. For years she had waited, hoped, yearned. She harassed the poor postman—he saw her coming and cringed. She ran out into the street when he was still several houses away, nearly tackling him, tearing into his canvas sack if he was too slow for her, grabbing other people's neat stacks of mail and rifling through to make sure there was no mistake . . . But the letter never came.

Through the years, Jane kept busy, teaching kindergarten at Cedarpark School in Kingston, taking long walks each afternoon with her best friend, Sunny, attending Willow's puppet plays. Her days were full, and the yearning for this one letter receded to the background like static. She rarely received a letter. There was always mail, of course, she made sure of that—stacks of catalogs from around the globe, subscriptions to six magazines and three newspapers, but a letter, that was rare. A letter would mean trouble, no? Who would write?

Willow, now up in Montréal, called. Until her daughter's move up north to Canada a month ago, Jane had talked to Willow once, twice, even three times a day. Twenty-four hours without some contact with her daughter was hard for Jane to bear.

She had, after all, just the one child, always her child, even though Willow is now nearly forty. But with her move to Montréal, Willow had insisted on a new routine. A time, a schedule for calls. *So I'll be sure you'll get me, Mama.* Spoiled, I am, Jane thought, glancing at the fridge where she kept Willow's schedule tacked to the door with a bright apple magnet, so she could contact her any time of the day. Or night. Moved up to Montréal to take a job as artist in residence at the old jam factory, *Usine de Confiture. Usine C,* they called it now, a theater, where Willow would do her puppet plays and a little teaching. It was an honor.

Yet Jane suspects Willow headed up to Montréal for more than a job. Her heart flutters in her chest, a trapped butterfly. There are things Jane needs to talk to her daughter about.

She thumps the stack of mail on the kitchen table and sinks into a chair, her fingers trembling. She flips the envelope over: it is not from Willow, not from a person, no one she knows. It looks official. From an organization called WITNESS: THE HOLOCAUST REMEMBRANCE FOUNDATION.

Jane considers throwing it into the garbage, hiding it, tearing the paper to tiny shreds, burning them, chewing, even swallowing the bits. Making the letter not *be*.

Records, they have always: files, names, information.

Dear Miss Ives:

We are in the process of collecting and documenting testimony of survivors of the Holocaust like yourself. We are honored to invite you back to Montréal to tell your story, in your own words.

Enclosed here, you will find detailed information about our Foundation, our history, and our vision for the future. So we will never forget to remember . . .

There is more, a thick clump of literature, the catalog of the foundation with its yellow Mogen David set aflame, other images, children, parents, grandparents, old sepia photos with tattered borders, but what catches Jane's attention is a large, pink sticky note slapped onto the catalog. She adjusts her bifocals to read the handwritten scrawl.

Dear Jane,

I'm working at the Witness Foundation now. It's intense, but I'm learning a lot. Hope it's okay that I gave them your name and address. My father said it would be fine, good even. The directors are always trying to track down new survivors—sorry, that didn't come out right, but you know what I mean—while they're still—you know. Sorry I'm babbling, what else is new? Can you babble in print? Whatever.

It would be so cool if you could come up here and work with us. I don't do the interviews myself, but maybe in time, who knows? Now I'm just an assistant, girl-Friday-type person, but it's interesting. Anyway, it would be great to see you! And I'm sure Willow misses you. The theater she's at is this out-of-the-way hub of the arts, if that makes sense, and it's a draw for some top artists doing new work. Personally, I plan to see every one of her shows, maybe even take a class in marionette making. Your daughter is one talented woman, but you already know that, right?

XOXO, Shoshy

Jane sets the letter on the counter and measures grounds and water for coffee. The girl's father, Leonard Rappaport, is her neighbor in Kingston. Jane taught him at Cedarpark School and now he is a big *makher,* head of Jewish Studies at Princeton University.

Jane imagines telling her best friend Sunny all about this letter to make it feel less strange. Witness? What kind of word is that? Everyone is putting on a show these days, Jane thinks, showing off what should be private.

My name, it looks like someone else's. Not mine. My story, no one wanted to hear. Mine and not mine. Blame those who would not listen.

In the little bathroom off the kitchen, Jane splashes cold water on her face, then stares into the mirror above the sink. There she is. Round, rosy face with a cap of straight, silver hair and girlish bangs. She is just five feet tall and built like a fireplug, a perfect size fourteen petite, with a determined waddling gait, her stout arms propelling her forward. She feels solid and healthy and has no desire to slim down.

Five years ago, she survived breast cancer, and when her weight dropped with the therapy, it caused her a panic she had not felt since the war. She was disappearing. Jane has an ache in her right shoulder, even after her operation, and on damp days the pain is bad. Sometimes, she doesn't hear because of a buzzing in her left ear, but that passes too, along with the dizziness. She managed to keep both breasts and, knock on wood, has been in the clear ever since. Some days when she is anxious, alone, Jane feels her heart race, an odd sensation, clawing, an animal caught in her chest. But it always goes away. Why worry?

The aunt and uncle, all the cousins in Montréal—relatives of the man who saved her life—greeted them at the train station. Jana remembers the crowd, feels again the heat and crush of their bodies, the smell of their eager breath. Relatives and friends.

Me, no one recognized, because no one knew me.

All around her, Jana heard English and French, foreign languages. Growing up in Prague, she spoke Czech and Yiddish, as well as German, which saved her. A smattering of Hungarian in the DP camp at Belsen. Words, phrases, sentences to survive.

She remembers the tiny apartment on Jeanne Mance in Montréal, its outside staircase zigzagging upward. Weathered brick, flaking yellow trim the color of lemon pie filling. Seven they were, crowded into that flat, family and yet not.

When Jana tried to speak, they shushed her. Sha, Sha. Don't let's talk about those things. Forget the past, be glad you lived, don't make others uncomfortable.

Good news, good times! That's what everyone wanted. Isn't that what most people want? All the time?

Don't know, don't tell. Hiding again. Dress nice, speak like a Canadian, don't say words you can't pronounce well. And in America, the same. What could be more American than Jane Ives? A new life, fresh start for her beautiful baby girl. Willow. A willow bends, never breaks.

Outside her kitchen window, the January morning is sunny, still and windless, all glittering pines and deep-shadowed snow. Jane will keep to her routine, which gives shape to her day. Sipping her coffee, she leafs through one of her memory books. As Willow grew up, each night they lay, side-by-side, on Willow's bed, the heavy books spread across their laps, heads propped on pillows, leafing through them, their bedtime ritual. Now Jane does it out of habit, nearly every morning and evening. It puts her life out in front of her where she can see and touch it, where all of her losses are links in a story, where everything flows and makes sense, even looks pretty.

She is thankful for her girlhood friend in Prague, Michaela, whose family saved valuables and cherished photos and mementoes for Jane, hiding and preserving these treasures, sending them to her after the war. Dear friends are a *brukhe*, a blessing.

Jane is still transfixed by her own image, the image of her daughter, of the people and places she loves and once loved. She cherishes these bits and pieces, miniatures of reality, and can't help wondering if people expelled from their own pasts become the most fervent picture-takers and collectors. Jane is grateful to make memories; soon there will be no more new memories to make.

She picks up the phone, dials Willow's number, her hand trembling as a familiar voice rings out through the kitchen window.

"Yoo-hoo, Janey!"

She jumps, clutches her chest, the receiver still in her hand. "A heart attack, you'll give me!" She lumbers up from her chair and slides open the glass door to the windowed sunroom, putting a plump arm around her dear friend, guiding her in. Sunny brings in the fresh, bracing scent of the day—pines, wood smoke, cold air.

"Like winter, you smell. Nice." Jane strokes Sunny's hair, a glistening platinum, which complements her fair skin and teal eyes. She is a tall, strong-boned woman, with long, lithe limbs and wide, womanly hips, which come as a surprise. She's nineteen years younger than Jane, though most put her at little more than fifty-five. They became fast friends at Cedarpark School, sharing coffee and anecdotes about their students, Janey's little ones and Sunny's big fifth-graders.

"I'm antsy today," Sunny says. "I need a walk."

"It's not time yet," protests Jane. "I didn't go through all the mail."

"The mail can wait, dear. It's lovely out, I can hardly believe it's January."

"I got a letter."

"From Willow?"

Jane shakes her head.

"Nothing bad, I hope."

"Well, bad or good, I don't know."

"Go put on your coat, Janey. Let's talk as we walk."

The friends head out toward the canal, and Sunny takes Jane's arm as the light turns pearly for a moment. This morning, the woodsy path is nearly deserted, shards of sun and sky splintering through trees. The ground is hard and crunches under their feet, as they watch glints off the canal. Jane loves it in here; enveloped by the trees and sound of the water, she feels safe. They stroll alongside the canal, where a grove of white birch leans toward the slow-moving river.

Now and then, Jane picks up treasures: a pinecone, the skeleton of a small animal, a pod, or pretty stone. These she saves too, artifacts to complement the photographs in her memory books.

"So how is Willow?" Sunny asks.

"Lately, she is always with one question or another," says Jane, glancing into her friend's eyes, straining to see them through her sunglasses. "In the night, she has strange dreams, she tells me."

"It's a new life for her."

Jane clucks her tongue. "I got a letter."

"You said. How nice—from *whom*?"

"Not a whom, a place."

"Stop being mysterious Janey, what place? What about?"

"One of those organizations. Like poison mushrooms, they crop up!"

"*What* organization? A hate organization?"

"*Oy gevald!* Hate, I can handle. This is worse, curiosity, *farshteyst?*"

"Spell it out for me, Janey."

"Tell your story, my story, I'm okay, you're okay, I'm not okay, you're not okay. Like pornography, this documenting."

The wintry sun slips behind a cloud and the towpath is engulfed in a greenish dark. Sunny flips her sunglasses on top of her head. It is so still, all they hear is the crunch of their boots on the hard frozen path, the scurry of a squirrel up a dry trunk.

"Witness, they call themselves. They want me to come up to Montréal to tell . . . "

"About your life during the war? And after?"

"*Vos iz der takhles? Vos iz der khilek?* What's the difference? Now? Useless!"

"Well, I'm inclined to disagree with you."

"Why?" Jane stops suddenly and stares down her friend.

"If you don't tell your story, who will? It's something you can leave behind, for Willow, for . . . "

"I'm not going anywhere so fast."

"It's a nice excuse to go back to Montréal to see Willow. Do it while you are hale and hearty. You love that city! Like nowhere else on earth you tell me."

"Willow, she has her whole life out before her," Jane says, speaking too fast. "All the men look at her when she's passing." Jane ruffles her bangs with a mittened hand. "Not one can she stick with, Sunny, nothing sticks with her."

"Her puppets stick. She's an artist."

"Don't let's talk about it."

"You miss Willow, dear."

A winter hawk perches on a branch, chocolate-brown with a light-banded tail and black-tipped feathers. It hovers a moment with deep, vigorous wing beats.

"What I remember, I don't know. There is no beginning, no end. It will make no sense."

Sunny touches Jane's wrist, a fleshy space between mitten and coat sleeve, and Jane feels the warmth of her friend's hand, which is bare.

"Your gloves, put them on," Jane commands.

"I don't feel the cold today."

"Sunny," Jane says suddenly, "at dusk let's come out again. I want to see a snowy owl."

"Wouldn't it be lovely?"

Jane hooks her hand through her friend's arm and they continue down the wooded path, the canal glistening beside them, risen with rainwater and melting snow, the winter-warped trees lacy silhouettes against the sky. When Jane needs to rest, they stop at a bench, or a sturdy stump and sit awhile. Warm now, Jane pulls off her mittens and hat, which makes her scalp itch. She looks into the water, keeps on looking. Pearly clouds shroud the sun and a wind with the underside of winter lifts her hair from the back of her neck, where she is sweating. Without warning, she gets up and leans down to the river and thrusts her hand into the current. The water is glacial, it makes her bones ache. Jane stares down into the river, the reflection of trees shivering into a shadow world. As they walk back the way they came, they pass under a weeping willow.

"Your favorite," Sunny declares with an impish smile.

"The roots, you can't garden around. So many pests, every minute dropping leaves."

"So graceful," puts in Sunny.

"They grow quickly," adds Jane, "*anything* they adjust to, rain is all they need."

Their litany calms her, as Jane watches the shadow of the willow, black across the path, green in the water. Like two different trees, showing different colors.

That night, Jane is submerged in the dream again. Hands clawing at damp earth, nails ragged, fingers bloody. Digging, digging. Digging up or burying, she never knows for sure.

Jane cannot mention this dream to anyone—she never talks of it—not even to Sunny, whom she tells nearly everything, and certainly not to Willow. This dream is hers alone.

In her sleep, she furiously buries or digs up the menorah, the one her father sculpted for her of brass, with a candleholder modeled after each member of their family, a gift for her thirteenth birthday. Such a full house they had: mother and father, two daughters, three sons, even a puppy, Samo.

Frantic, on her knees in the moist, cool earth of the Old Jewish Cemetery in Prague. A burying to keep alive, to hide, to make safe. Or is it a digging up to salvage, find, bring back to life?

The dream changes, but at its heart, remains the same. Digging up or burying, as if her life—all their lives—depend upon it. *Will the menorah still be there, intact? Broken or stolen? Vanished?*

Digging up or burying, over and over, no end or beginning.

Jane awakens in the midst of her task. She lies very still until the icy sweat dries, her trembling stops, the afterimage fades. She has no idea what time it is, but soon, soon she must begin another day.

❋ ❋ ❋

TWO

May 1965
Kingston, New Jersey

AS A LITTLE GIRL, Willow had enjoyed hearing the story of her birth again and again. *When you were born, I lost you,* her mother always said. *Lost, you look. Lost, you can still find. Outdoors, you were born! Right here on the towpath.*

Willow liked to imagine the feel of warm, wet earth on skin, sun and cloud drifting through trees, a canopy of glistening leaves overhead. Her mother had shown her the exact spot many times, a woodsy stretch between Washington and Alexander where one can still see a great blue heron, a gangly beauty with a nest fifty feet off the ground, the smell of guano thick and penetrating, the Delaware-Raritan Canal flowing beside the towpath for miles and miles.

"Forty-four years old, I was!" her mother exclaimed every time she told the story. "Go figure. Already, I had lost two babies, years before. A secret you were, my secret."

At six o'clock that May morning, the path was nearly deserted as Jane and her best friend ambled along on their daily exercise walk. Sunny was twenty-five years old, tall and statuesque, with long honey-colored hair and dark blue eyes, the daughter of Christine Howe, Jane's first English teacher when she arrived in Montréal.

Thanks to three generations of Howe women, Jane often said, she was able to make a new life for herself in the United States. Christine, her English teacher at McGill University, introduced Jane to her mother, Emily, who was the principal of an elementary school in Kingston, New Jersey, where Jane was able to get a job teaching kindergarten. Later on, Christine gave birth to her daughter, Sunny, and—despite an age difference of nineteen years—Jane and Sunny became best friends.

Willow was not due to be born for another thirteen days, and Jane, who was punctual to an extreme, assumed that her new daughter would be as well. Sunny pointed out some bleeding hearts forming an elfin garden among the mossy rocks and mats of fern a few yards into the wood. Suddenly, Jane felt unbearable pressure. She squatted down as Sunny spread out a canvas jacket, and within minutes, Willow descended with a slithery plop. Her mother doesn't remember pain, not the agony so commonly immortalized in literature and Hollywood with such a sameness about it—the sweating brow, grunts and screams, the blood-trickled thighs. There was no time for high drama, or detail. Jane described her as "a colossal bowling ball dropping," and then, strain, heat, urgency.

Sunny did what she had to do. She'd spent many a girlhood

summer on a farm in Southwestern Ontario, where her paternal grandmother was a midwife; Sunny knew what went where.

After Willow appeared, Sunny placed her on Jane's chest and then turned to get water from her knapsack. Jane lifted her new baby and put her down again on the jacket. She stood staring, transfixed by something she saw a ways into the woods and wandered away to investigate.

"Janey!" shouted Sunny. "Where's the baby?"

"Snow," Jane whispered, gliding like a somnambulist toward her vision, as blood rushed from her and puddled on the ground. "It's snow."

"Lie down, Janey. You can't be walking around!" Sunny turned, searching for the new baby in a frenzy. There was a confused moment where the two women could not find Willow. She was lost. Misplaced. Like so much else her mother had lost.

"My God! Where's the baby?" screamed Sunny.

"Right there, I put her down," Jane said in a panic, struggling to get to the empty blood-soaked jacket still spread upon the mulchy ground. "Stolen!" she screamed and then started weeping. "Sunny, help me! My baby girl."

They found Willow. Just a short distance away from the jacket on a bit of boggy ground, hidden beneath skunk cabbage and fern. On her tummy.

Willow's mother scooped her up. Sunny grabbed the baby away from her, swabbing mud from her nose and mouth. "Thank God, she's breathing."

Resisting her friend's efforts to take her baby back, Sunny

cleaned the baby off and swaddled her in the shirt she had peeled off in a hurry.

Once again, Jane reached for the baby, and with a warning look, Sunny gave Jane her newborn daughter. Jane rocked Willow close to her chest. Willow was screaming now, red and wet with fury. Her mother rocked her possessively, as she returned to the spot where she had been transfixed a moment before.

"Snow," she repeated to Sunny. "Just like on *la montagne* in Montréal."

"It's not snow, Janey. They're trilliums. Aren't they beautiful?"

Jane and Sunny stood mesmerized by the snow-white flowers that filled the woods. Still holding Willow tight, Jane plucked a bloom growing in threes beside a fallen log. "A sign," she said with a troubled smile.

"What?"

"Three petals."

"Janey, everything about the trillium is in threes, the flowers, the leaves, the petals."

"Ach!" Jane dismissed her, as Sunny descended back to the path to look for a jogger and call out for help. Still, Jane was troubled. "Three," she said to herself. "Always, does it have to be three?" Jane couldn't bear to lose a third baby.

With Sunny's shouts for help ringing out in the distance, Jane lingered with her baby girl, staring at the steep-sided gorge of hemlock and the eye-popping expanse of white blooms rippling over the hillside. Soon Sunny heard a sound on the river and signaled the racing shell that neared shore with eight oarsmen, one coxswain, and their coach roaring ahead in a motorboat. The Princeton crew coach sped Jane Ives and her baby safely to the hospital, where they were cleaned up and cared for.

Willow believed this story of her birth. Still, sometimes she wonders where she came from. At five-foot-eleven, she towers over her mother, has fine bones, long, loose limbs and athletic shoulders, and has always been slim without effort. Her hair is golden brown, rippling and shining with amber and coppery lights over her shoulders, her eyes a near match, wide, long-lashed, almond-shaped. Her mother is dark-featured with fair skin, while Willow's complexion is a deep olive, which tans easily to café-au-lait in the sun.

While Willow was growing up, her mother hardly ever spoke to her about the war. Mostly, she spoke around it, in carefully prepared anecdotes. An eerie, mechanical voice invaded her natural one, her tone formal and distant; official. The strange staccato rhythm put Willow on edge. She learned little of her mother's experiences from these stories or their gaps, but with the memory books, magic happened. Her mother's memories became at times more real than Willow's own.

During Willow's childhood their bedtime ritual was to browse through these memory books together. Her mother told Willow stories, illustrated with captions of swirling script and yellowing photographs. "You can survive almost anything, if you can tell a story about it," she once told Willow. "You are alive to tell the tale. You create the beginning, middle, and end."

Even now, Willow remembers the candy shop, its fusty sweet

smell, remembers her grandfather Vilem's basement studio, the wild, ferocious heads, remembers the day he sculpted "Justice," a cigarette slanting white across his lips. Willow sees it all, memories that belong to other people, that she has stolen for herself from the memory books.

She remembers pain, but holding the memory books, her mother shimmers and glows, the comforting weight across their laps makes them both feel safe, and loosens her mother's tongue. Willow savors the magic of each individual scene, fixed in time, anchored in space, and if she imagines herself inside, she can walk right into each photograph, and make everything come out all right in the end.

❋ ❋ ❋

Memory Book
Winter 1970

Mama, what are those monsters on sticks? They scare me.

Heads. My Papa made them, your Zeyde Vilem.

Zeyde has a funny name.

Czech.

Check what?

Czechoslovakia. Go get your globe, lovey. There. See how far Czechoslovakia is from America? We lived in Prague. Like a fairyland it was.

Why did Zeyde make those heads?

You know what is a sculptor? Your Zeyde was an artist. That's his studio in the basement, gray floors, walls of cement. I used to stand at his elbow and watch. Always there was music, Dvorak, his favorite, a man who made beautiful music. I'll play it for you. Papa looked at me like that—in the picture there—head tilted, always a cigarette hanging from his lips. He wanted my opinion. What do you think, meydele? he'd ask. That head he called "Injustice." Look how angry, the eyes.

What's injustice?

Not being fair.

To who, Mama?

Any person.

Did people like the heads?

Nah! Ugly, they called them. Miskeyt!

Did he have hurt feelings?

Not too bad. To make people feel what they didn't want to feel—he liked that. So alive, his heads were. Like people walking and breathing.

Can I see one?

Tomorrow, lovey. Look at this picture. Here's your bube Hannah, your grandmother. See the house we lived in when I was your age? Staromestske Namesti. The South Side of Old Town Square. A narrow alley I walked through each day to go home.

A castle, Mama. You lived in a castle. Can we go someday?

Ghosts there were, Willow, in that passage. On dark, windy nights.

Like that man?

He's a statue, lovey, Saint Anthony of Padua.

Mama, what's this picture?

Ivanova's. Our sweetshop, right below where we lived.

Can we go there? Please, Mama?

It's gone, Willow.

Did you have chocolate?

Chocolate? Chocolate! More kinds than you can imagine! Oh, how

I wish you could taste our chocolate. Do you know what is dragée? Of course not! Dried fruits, even seeds dipped in chocolate. Our specialty. And licorice, hard candy, every flavor of the rainbow, toffee too. The smell got into our clothes, our hair, under our skin. Sometimes, lovey, I smell it still. Not just candy, Willow. Batteries. We sold key rings, safety pins, tiny nail scissors, aspirin, balloons, pencils. Whatever a person might need on the spot.

Will you ever take me, Mama, to your old house?

I don't know, lovey, it's so far.

I want to go to some faraway places, Mama. What is this place?

A music room we had. My mother put beautiful lamps everywhere. Light, we always had light. That one, such colors, like a mosaic of stained glass. Cloisonné they call it, and the lampshade shaped like a bell. Your bube played cello. There, you see her, a wonderful cellist. It's like a violin but bigger. See how she holds it between her legs? A sound so beautiful my teeth ache, remembering. Now bed, lovey. It's past time.

More, Mama! Please! What's that?

Who, you mean. Mr. Gregarov. Papa made him from an old sock, his eyes are buttons, mother-of-pearl. Lovey, turn the page. There is Dobrou noc: good night. That's what Papa called my puppet theater. He made it from an old orange crate. Each night before bed he did a show just for me. Mr. Gregarov always had the biggest part. I have him still. Wait while I look . . .

Here, Willow! Here he is!

Oh, he's so soft Mama, squishy.

See how his eyes glint different-colored fires?

Like rainbows! Let's do a goodnight play, Mama.

Tomorrow.

No, now. Mr. Gregarov will blow his magic whistles. One makes fire, one makes—what does it make, Mama?

Safety. The whistle makes us safe.

We are safe, Mama.

Yes lovey, we are safe. You and me together. School tomorrow.

Just kindergarten.

Just? Genig is genig. Enough is enough!

'Night, Mama. Sleep tight. Don't let the bedbugs bite!

Good night, lovey. Gey shlofn.

THREE

January 2005
Montréal

WILLOW WAS DRAWN to the old jam factory, now a theater, the first time she set eyes on the place. Even in winter, bicycles were stacked outside the old red brick hulk on Lalonde Avenue, between la Visitation and Panet streets—musical names, though the area was a bit run down and often deserted. Beside the main building, a huge round smokestack rose up like a lighthouse, a beacon in the sea of misty gray winter sky.

She's been pulled up north by an invisible cord, linking her to her mother and to the family she never knew. Though Willow doesn't let herself talk much about it, even with her mother, she is determined to find out more before it is too late. There is this urgency now that her mother is getting on, a pressure built up over years of pictures in the memory books, hearing the stories of those family members, only half-told.

Today, Willow is entrenched down below in her basement studio. She likes working underground in cave-like spaces, a connection to the grandfather she never knew, pale wintry light filtering in from the high, narrow windows, the sound of life overhead. The staff has fixed the space up for her, wood-paneled walls, worktables, even a small antique bed, in case she needs to crash for the night; an underground lair, except for the sliding glass doors that lead to a stone patio and sunken garden, now frozen over, a space where she can be inside and outside at the same time. Tonight, moonlight washes in. There are some offices down here, a large, empty room she might use as a classroom to teach marionette making and puppeteering, the theater above, with a café she looks forward to trying.

Willow sets up her workbench and a pegboard for tools. As she unpacks her puppets, tools, and props, she tries to imagine what the place used to be like, what type of jam they made and how they made it, the sound of French ringing through the factory, the smells of stewing fruit, the clink of jars. She'll ask her mother if she knows anything about the factory when they talk, though Jane often has trouble elaborating, getting to the details; other times, she is lost in details and Willow finds it hard to see the larger picture. Still it's good to be here and have space between her and her mother (it is time, she's nearly forty!), but her excitement floats on an undercurrent of fear. Her mother lived here after the war for ten years, then came back periodically for shorter periods. The father she never knew was from Montréal. There must be people still alive who knew him, who can tell her more than her mother ever could, or would.

Is it all these jagged jigsaw pieces that made her fall in love with the city at first sight? As one might fall in love with a person, a *coup de foudre . . .*.

For starters, she's in awe of the northern winter. Drifts of snow, thigh-deep, eyelash-freezing mornings, darkness and chill, the cold closing in. She loves it all because it is so much itself, a pure force.

Just wait, people say. After all, she has been here only a few weeks. What does she know of winter? Montréalers are tough, she's discovered. The city and province are confused and conflicted about everything else, but they know how to handle snow! The city rarely comes to a halt, even after a blizzard leaves several feet of white stuff or coats everything in sight with a shimmering layer of ice. Willow admires their professionalism. Yet she expects there will be mornings when snow cascades into her freshly shoveled walk or snowplows roar through the night and deposit a mini-mountain of dirty sludge in front of her apartment, mornings when she slips and turns an ankle on the ice-encrusted sidewalk and will curse the season, this city, the province, and her plan to start fresh in this cold eternal place.

Arriving in Montréal a few weeks ago, Willow drove along Laurier in the van with the movers and saw a Hasidic rabbi, a stroller on skis, a prostitute, a juggler (out for the holidays), and an artist, all within a half-block of each other. She had laughed in amazement. *I could be happy here.*

She was seeing the things her mother talked about in unexpected bursts, like a light bulb sparking then going black: the frosty glow of St. Denis Street on a winter's night; Nat's grocery, where you could still find a second-hand kettle, a romance novel in yellowed paperback, an unframed painting to decorate a hallway, a pair of boots that might actually fit; and la montagne—the mountain, looming up in the heart of Montréal, still unscarred, her mother's favorite escape winter, spring, summer, and fall.

Willow loved the casual mingling of languages, everyone stirred into the linguistic stew, and the marvel of the Montréal accent, skitterish, lightning-quick, rough, but musical in its way. So many languages, and a new language, French blending into English and English into French with seamless fluidity. *C'est okay to stay late to voir le show.* She loved the fact that it was an island, a city-island, surrounded by water. And it was a happening city, a place that cared about, well, cheese, for instance.

Where else could you buy whole-milk, unpasteurized chèvre, Oka, Parmigiano Reggiano, and Roquefort right off the shelves of any supermarket?

A throat-clearing cough emanating from the hallway jars Willow, and when she looks up, she sees an elderly man standing in the doorway of her studio, smoking a cigarette with trembling hands.

"Can I help you?"

The man steps inside, tall, angular, and lean, with tufts of yellowish-white hair springing from either side of his shiny pate. For a moment, he stares at Willow with deep-set black eyes framed by wildly unruly brows.

"Are you Jana Ivanova's girl?"

The sound of her mother's forsaken name, on a stranger's lips, unnerves Willow. She nods slowly, as the man steps further inside, not taking his eyes from hers. He has a wide-spaced, ice-stepping gait, fragile.

"And you are?"

"An old friend," he says, sucking on his cigarette, then submitting to a terrible, phlegm-clotted cough. He is breathing heavily. "I got a bum ticker!" he exclaims, then adds, "Shoshy Rappaport told me you were in Montréal. Bern Orlofsky. How do you do?"

He extends a long-fingered hand and Willow clasps it gently, feeling the bones and veins beneath his tissue-crinkled skin. "Would you like to sit down a moment?" she asks.

"How is your mother?" he demands, ignoring her offer.

"Pretty well, I'd say."

"She must have spoken of me, eh?" He cocks his head, flashes her a sidelong glance.

Willow smiles, awkward and uncertain how to respond. "Well, Mr. Orlofsky . . . "

"Bern. I knew your mother well," he says. His black eyes sweep from the top of her head down to the tips of her toes, penetrating right through her.

"How did you know her exactly?" Willow asks. "My mother."

"Jana? I'm sure she must have talked about me from time to time." He flicks the inch-long cylinder of ash onto the floor, and Willow notices his yellowish nails, yellow-brown teeth. He wears old-fashioned rubbers with black oxfords showing through.

"Well, to tell you the truth, she . . . "

"The *truth, ach!*" He takes a long thirsty drag of his cigarette, then stubs it out underfoot. Annoyed, Willow sweeps up the butt and tosses it into the bin.

"I forget my manners," he says. "Jana worked at Fairmount, I stopped in often for bagels. My shop is two doors down."

"She told me about the bagel shop."

"There you go. Well, Orlofsky's Cleaning and Tailoring is nearly beside the place. Jana and me, we talked, made a connection. We lost touch, see? Your mother was not the best correspondent. Didn't bother with the phone, letters."

The telephone rings, loud and jarring; Willow excuses herself to pick up. It is Marie-France, manager of the theater. "Got to take this," Willow apologizes, holding her hand over the receiver. "But I'd really like to talk with you."

"Talk? Sure, we can talk—there's lots to talk about! I have breakfast at Beauty's Thursdays. You know Beauty's?"

Willow shakes her head.

"Oh, you gotta try Beauty's. Mont-Royal, corner of St. Urbain. Thursday. How 'bout at ten?"

"I'll be there, Mr. Orlofsky."

"Bern. Friends—and family—call me Bern."

He turns and walks painfully, slowly out of her door and into the winter day, as Willow talks with Marie-France, who wants to set up an appointment for the following week to plan Willow's upcoming puppeteering class.

Alone in her basement studio, Willow unpacks her marionettes one by one, lifting them carefully from their wooden cases, and hanging them on their iron stands. Weird, this strange man popping up, Bern Orlofsky. The fact that her mother never mentioned him increases Willow's curiosity. Well, maybe over breakfast she will get the story, his version anyway.

Looping Mr. Gregarov's soft sock body over the post of the antique bed, Willow is anxious to see how her puppets have weathered the move. Mr. Gregarov has been a part of her life since she was five years old and holds a lost history in his mother-of-pearl eyes.

Willow crafted Ernestine when she was just seventeen, and she has improved upon her favorite little by little. Lise, Alphonse, and Trevor, she made in her thirties. There are others, two dozen boxed away and enveloped in tissue up in the attic in Kingston, an additional seven on exhibit at a new toy museum in New York City, and still others sold to eager children or given as gifts to friends.

Four pairs of eyes glow at her in the dark, their wooden limbs poised in suspended animation. Mr. G. looks at her steadily, as Willow checks each of them carefully for damage. Ernestine bats her black lashes, which are meant to curl to perfectly arched brows, and Willow notices one eyelash is missing. E sits cross-legged on her stand, her velvet miniskirt high on her shapely legs, and Willow sees with alarm that her left calf is cracked. She peels off a piece of old tape someone has left on her worktable and bandages the injury, a temporary fix.

Willow lifts her favorite with care and nestles her in the crook of her elbow like a kitten. The black cami reveals a tantalizing shadow of cleavage, as Ernestine lies across Willow's arm, her head surprisingly heavy, her tiny limbs trailing. Her leopard mini is covered with a film of dust and the cracked calf looks even more fragile with the dirty white tape bandaged around it. Willow rocks

39

Ernestine gently, the move has been tough on her, on them all. "Okay, then."

Ernestine squirms to move into Willow's lap, her voice just a girlish purr. *"Where have you been?"* Ernestine, her favorite. Smart, funny, talks a mile a minute *sotto voce*, lots of freckles, and a mane of frizzy red hair.

Willow slides Ernestine onto her right thigh, balancing her gently.

"On the mountain? A refreshing stroll."

Willow doesn't know why it comes out as a question. She needed to clear her head a bit, but realizes now her favorite five are offended, clearing her head before she's even unpacked them, set them all free. These folks intimidate her at times, her little Frankensteins.

Laughter fills the basement studio, high and tinkling, low and guttural, shrill, tender, happy, and mocking, Alphonse the loudest. He is the biggest of the bunch, as round as he is tall, built like a sumo wrestler, but with an unexpectedly high, piercing voice that goes right through you like a train whistle. *"Yeah, you and Moses, right?"*

"Not exactly." He settles on Willow's left thigh and she spreads her legs to support his girth.

"You know my mother used to stroll there, it meant a lot to her, that place. You guys don't want my whole song and dance routine, not now. It's late, we're all tired and . . . "

"Skip the royal we," quips Ernestine in her sinuous whisper. *"I know you."*

"I made *you*."

"You are a sneaky little sleuth, Willow, trying to track down clues about the things your mother never told you—and who is this Bern, anyway?"

"You go too far, Ernestine. Don't get your knickers in a twist," clips Trevor. He is seventy-three, born in London, and wears his morning coat dawn till dusk, oxfords buffed to a high shine.

Lise idles up to Willow slow and deliberate, dressed top to toe in black. *"I just want to talk,"* she says in her low monochromatic voice. *"I don't know how I feel being here."*

Willow makes room for Lise on her thigh beside Ernestine, who pulls a sour face.

"Now, now," Willow warns, "we all have adjustments to make."

Willow moves Ernestine over to a little examining table in the corner of her studio, where she has set up her conservation lab, her mini-hospital. Ernestine shrieks in histrionic fear, and Trevor, forgetting his stiff upper lip, groans audibly. Willow knows she will be awake all night and the next doing repairs, unpacking, and setting the studio up for work. Fixing a cracked skull here, a split limb there, cleaning soiled and dusty costumes and mending torn ones, not to mention untangling strings, repairing the damage from the move and from the spirited love of the children in schools where she has performed. She lets the kids touch her marionettes and try to work them; one child even made off with Trevor and took him home for the night! No doubt, the worst off are the best loved—the puppets played with the most, the ones snuck under bedcovers.

Willow lifts Trevor's oxfords one by one, checking the pieces of lead on the bottom of his shoes, designed so that the audience hears his footsteps as he walks. Willow cleans the dust from Ernestine's mini-skirt, as her favorite lets out a long sigh of pleasure, then starts her chattering.

Soon the others drown her out and their cacophony fills the basement studio until the sky blues through the sliding glass door and narrow windows. With her puppet family surrounding her, Willow falls into a sudden deep sleep, like a swoon, Mr. Gregarov watching over her from his post.

❋ ❋ ❋

Memory Book
Spring 1970

Is that my daddy, the one with the beard?

No, lovey. Remember, that's your Zeyde Vilem.

Where's my daddy? Charly has a daddy, Devon has a daddy, Lola has a daddy. Where is my daddy?

Up in . . .

The sky?

Heaven.

Can we go visit Daddy in heaven?

One day. Your daddy died, lovey.

Was he always dead? He was always dead, right Mama?

No, no lovey! First, you have to be alive, dead later.

Where did you meet him, Mama?

Montréal. Up in Canada where I used to live.

Are there polar bears in Canada?

Not too many.

What did he do, my daddy?

He was a caretaker.

A what?

He took care of the chalet, that's the little house on top of Mount Royal, a beautiful mountain we have, right in the middle of the city. In Montréal. While walking, I met him on that mountain. Every day I walked there, in every season—winter, spring, summer, and fall.

Can we go there, Mama?

Someday, lovey.

Did my daddy have a name?

A name? Everyone has a name, Willow. Your daddy's name was Roger Pelletier.

That's a funny name.

French. But good English he spoke.

Roger Pelletier. A mountain man!

A mountain man, lovey, that's right. Up in heaven, now. Sending his love down to you.

FOUR

WILLOW AWAKENS in her studio, stiff and disoriented, with no idea of the time. She stretches, gazes about at her favorite five and the piles of boxes, crates, and bags brimming with tools, scenery, props, paints, and materials. Snow is gently falling and it still looks like morning. She is thinking about the strange, elderly man who appeared yesterday—Bern Orlofsky—impatient, yet anxious about meeting with him later that week.

Rooting around inside the boxes and crates, Willow excavates the official copy of her birth certificate, which she obtained only recently from the Office of the Registrar of Vital Statistics, State of New Jersey. Feeling perverse, she tacks it up on her bulletin board in full view.

Name of child: Willow Hannah Ives
Sex: Female
Place of Birth: The Medical Center at Princeton
Date of Birth: May 7, 1965
Father's Name: Unknown
Mother's Name: Jane Ives

Willow sighs, uncertain what she hopes to accomplish by nailing this above her head to prick and prod her. She digs out her coffee pot and a pound of beans she bought at Brûlerie St. Denis, a lovely café with huge burlap sacks near the entry, open to reveal fragrant varieties of beans you can sift and let cascade through your fingers. She sets the coffee going and then splashes cold water on her face, brushing her teeth with a finger, then finger-combing her tangled curls.

She moves Ernestine, Trevor, and Lise to a back rail, keeps Mr. G on the bedpost, a few others dangling from their individual stands, and another group spanning a tight wire that she suspends from one corner of the studio to the other.

Bundling up in winter layers, Willow leaves the theater and scavenges the neighborhood for the closest *dépanneur*. Warming up inside the shop, she stocks up on some basic provisions and then ambles dreamily back to Usine C.

The day is hard and bright, without wind. Though she has only been in Montréal a short time, she knows enough not to be fooled by these glittering days that warm you through a window, buttery sun turning hardwood floors golden and hospitable to bare feet. These days are the worst: a cold that burns.

When she arrives back at the studio, Willow stands in the doorway, alarmed. A man is inside—a different one this time—about the tallest man she's ever seen, swathed in a black canvas duster, which spills like a dirty puddle onto the floor. He moves about her studio, long-limbed and sinuous, the duster flapping about his ankles, tousled chestnut curls wild about his shoulders. Now he is touching her marionettes, moving long fingers over their wooden limbs, feeling the texture of their hair, running a fingertip over the surface of their eyes.

Fear freezes her throat, makes her mute. He moves slowly, languidly, as if underwater, like he has all the time in the world, arms held loose and wide from his sides, knees bending into each step. He lifts Trevor by the flyer, then Lise, murmuring softly. His voice rises and plunges with a diver's motion. He supplants the voices of her people with his own made-up characters, using *her* marionettes as vessels, his voice booming or rising into the highest registers.

Willow charges into the room.

"What the hell are you doing in here?"

"Oh, hello."

She points out the door into the hallway. "Men's room is *that* way."

The man gazes at her with gem-green eyes, gold at their center, and heat penetrates her skin. Fear—he must be off—she likes the idea of crazy, just a little. The buzz heightens.

"Excuse me, I . . . "

"No, excuse *me*, this is my studio."

She goes to him, bolder now, and slips Ernestine and Trevor

from his grasp, hanging them back on their iron stands. "Look, don't touch," she commands, as if he is a child.

A half-smile flickers across his wide, full mouth. "I'm Noah Issenman." He holds out his hand, as she folds her arms across her chest.

She feels herself petrify, turn wooden, from the outside in. Awful, too familiar. The more she feels, the less it shows. *Any leak, a flood.* The only response others see is her numbing frost. Paralyzed as one of her puppets without a master.

Willow has heard this guy's name before; he's a playwright— in fact they're doing one of his shows at the Centaur. She can't remember what it's about, but knows she's seen reviews, some photographs of this odd person gazing out at her from the local press.

Willow plops her sack down on the old tapestry couch and starts unpacking her groceries, just for something to do.

"Willow, so how are you settling in? I wanted to give you a real welcome."

She goes about her business, her movements stiff and awkward.

"Marie-France thought we should meet," he goes on in a deep, soft voice, at once creepy and soothing. "Willow Ives, I like the sound of that, so many images . . . associations."

She glares at him, her body craving coffee, a long, hot, pounding shower. Still so much to do.

Noah nods slowly for no reason.

"I'm just setting up here," Willow says icily, "as you can see." Her face warms; she's embarrassed by her old sweats, wrinkled from the day and then the night, her unwashed hair. She finds she is curious about this guy, despite herself.

"I've never worked with marionettes," he says, sounding almost shy now, "but I've longed to." He lopes about, touching odd props, old sets, lingering over Lise in her black, and Willow can feel Ernestine bristling, not to mention herself.

"She is amazing," he says, "all of them, actually." His earnestness takes her by surprise.

Willow smiles, a hand covering her mouth.

"All these presences."

They are both quiet for a while, and Willow feels some of the tension and impatience drain from her limbs. She doesn't know what possesses her, perhaps just good manners. Finally, she asks, "Coffee?"

"A coffee is just what I need." He flashes her a half-smile, and she notices his green eyes again, downslanting, his fair skin.

"But first," he says, and already she knows what he has in mind, an odd telepathy.

"Okay then," she relinquishes, "sit down."

He obeys, folding himself into the old tapestry couch, its springs popping.

Willow lifts Lise from her stand and carries her over, sliding in beside Noah, as if he were one of her students. She moves his left hand to the flyer, his right to Lise's footbar. His hands are strong and graceful, the fingers unusually tapering for a man. He smiles and she notices dimples, making him a man-child.

"Not too tight," she cautions, holding her hands lightly over both of his.

Together, they pull one arm string, one foot string; they lower Lise's body forward, then sit her down in his lap. As she helps Noah move her puppets, Willow feels herself come back to life, such a relief to feel . . . what? Human!

"I don't know if I like this," murmurs Lise in her deep, monochromatic voice.

"Don't brood so," Willow clips impatiently. "Be here now."

Noah laughs low in his throat, as Lise makes herself comfortable on his knee.

Without warning, Lise rises from Noah's lap and breaks into a stark, interpretive dance full of contorted, violent movements, curling into herself, then erupting with arms stretched wide. When she finishes, she collapses on Noah's lap. Willow smiles, these favorites do make her happy.

"I would be down here all day," Noah whispers in a conspiratorial voice she has to lean close to hear, "just playing with these people."

Willow looks at this strange exotic man on her couch, gangly and hunched, beautiful and ugly, silly and grave, foreign yet familiar.

She unearths the painted yellow duck with three strings from one of her boxes, a simple marionette that she uses with children, placing Noah's right hand over the flyer, her hand on top of his. He has large hands, sculptor's fingers, and unusual manual dexterity for a beginner. She shows him that by tilting the flyer, he can get a bit of movement.

He smiles like a child with a secret.

Once he's mastered the duck, Willow moves on to a clown with nine strings—one to each hand, one to each leg, one to each shoulder, one to each ear and one to the spine. Noah rocks the flyer back and forth to get some motion, then practices using both hands, one on the flyer, the other holding the leg bar. Silent, absorbed, they work on head, hands, then feet. Bowing, throwing a ball, even playing a tiny guitar.

"My favorite," Noah whispers.

"You're not bad," Willow murmurs, "not bad at all."

"There's a place I want to take you," he says randomly. "Do you know Ha'makom?"

Startled, she shakes her head, eyes bowed. She was comfortable a moment before, teaching him.

"Ha'makom means, 'the place,' in Hebrew. It's this Jewish Center on Westbury, off Van Horne—they've done a few of my plays there, in English, Yiddish, Hebrew, and French. I'm active in some of their arts programs. I'm thinking, you might want to do a puppet play there." He is talking much too fast.

"I'm just starting out here," she says, remembering something she read about the place in the Jewish press. Willow thinks that if she gets to know this man better, she may pick his brain about her students' puppet play, scheduled for May. "I'm starting a puppeteering class. We are supposed to have a performance here this spring. Honestly, I have no clue what we're going to do."

"That's the fun of it, no? I'd worry if you were too calm."

"Right."

As they talk, Willow shows Noah how she cares for her worn-out and fragile marionettes, lubricating sore joints, untangling twisted strings, fixing cracked or broken limbs.

"It's weird," she says, unsure for a moment if she is talking to herself or out loud. "I'm not much of an extrovert, but I become one on the bridge."

"Yeah, yeah."

"There's nothing like choosing that right string in the dark."

He smiles at her with his whole face.

She finds two dusty mugs, rinses them, and pours coffee.

"Regular or black?"

"Regular." With utmost care, he takes Lise and hangs her back on her iron stand, freeing his hands once more.

Willow pours in cream, stirs in sugar, and hands him the steaming mug, before serving herself. She's usually much more reserved with new people, and wonders what it is about this person that makes her feel comfortable. Maybe his weirdness.

Feeling suddenly skittish, she says, "You know, I've got to get going here," waving her arm to encompass the chaos. "You can get the mug back to me later."

He nods, slipping out as suddenly as he crept in.

❋ ❋ ❋

Memory Book
Fall 1971

Mama, what happened to those pictures?

They're old, lovey. Old pictures crack, turn yellow. We can still make them out, no?

Look at those goofy guys with the mousy ears!

Hurvinek is the little one. And the tall fellow, you see his black morning coat and white collar? That's Spejbl.

They have funny names, Mama. Why are strings coming out of their heads?

They're a different kind of puppet, lovey. The puppeteer, he makes them move, dance, by pulling the strings. Here, look at this picture. You can see the puppeteer working the strings. Wait a minute. I want to find something I've been saving for you.

Oh, Mama, he's beautiful.

Very delicate, ancient. His name is Ivo and look! He has three little children hiding under his puffy pants.

"Oh, Mama, can I play with him? With the little children?"

"Very careful, lovey, they're fragile, so old. My best friend, Michaela, and her family saved him for us during the war.

Why, Mama?

Because he's special and we couldn't save him for ourselves.

I'm glad they saved him, Mama.

Me too, lovey. We had dear friends, friends are a brukhe, a real blessing. Now. Let me tell you about the time when I was your age. Each week, my Papa took me to a puppet show. See the clown? The knight and horse? Papa sculpted the heads of those puppets in his basement studio, remember I told you? In the corner there, with the heavy glasses and beard, that's your Grandpa Vilem. You remember Vilem. By the end of each day, his shirt was soaked through!

Was my Papa a sculptor like yours, Mama?

No, lovey.

Who was he?

A caretaker, remember, I told you?

Could he make magic?

Oy.

Did he do any work on that mountain?

A job, you mean?

Or magic, which?

It's in another book, I have. That one. It's heavy, let me lift it. See that lovely house on top of the mountain? They call it the chalet. It's at the very top of Mount Royal. A caretaker he was, like I told you, keeping watch of that chalet. His name was Roger Pelletier.

Do you have a picture, Mama? Does he look like me?

*I'll have to look. Buried, so much is lost, too. More pictures I
have, here and there, but not tonight, lovey, we're too tired tonight for
searches.*

Why did he die, Mama, my daddy?

He got sick. Smoking too many cigarettes, they hurt his lungs.

Did you ever smoke, Mama?

Nah!

*Not Mr. Gregarov either. Here he is! My favorite Mr. G! Mr. G! Mama,
I want to do a show for you with Mr. G. You sit there, Mama. Watch
me!*

FIVE

ON THURSDAY MORNING, Willow heads off to Beauty's to meet
Bern Orlofsky, her heart beating too fast, her mind filled with
questions. The coffee shop is bustling—no sign of Bern when she
first arrives—so she secures a window table in the back for two.
She waits, orders coffee, still no Bern. Anxious, she checks the
window, watching passersby hunkering down against the winter
wind and cold. A half-hour later, guilty to be monopolizing a table,
she orders a stevedore's breakfast, which she eats mechanically,
without tasting a morsel. When the waitress appears with her
check, Willow asks, "You know, I was supposed to meet a man
here, Bernard Orlofsky. You know him?"

"Sure, Bern. He's usually here by now."

"Said he's regular about Thursdays."

The waitress glances around the coffee shop, then says, "You might check with his daughter."

"Yes?"

"Madie has a great boutique not far from here. You know, vintage clothes, some consignment . . . she would know what's going on with her dad."

"Thanks," Willow says, as the waitress scrawls down the address of Madie's on the Main.

When Willow arrives at the boutique, the bordello-like room is abandoned, but for its treasures. She is entranced by the place with its crimson shag carpet, heavy gold and garnet curtains, and antique wardrobes and bureaus. The shop is stocked full with vintage finds and riches: tiny beaded bags, old train cases, sequined sheaths, white go-go boots, cameo brooches, fifties aprons, and cashmere cardigans with rhinestone and pearl buttons. Wandering about in a browsing trance, she feels inspired for new costumes and accessories for her puppets. Ella Fitzgerald, singing Cole Porter, suddenly breaks the silence and shortly after, a tall, buxom blond struts in.

"Good morning!" she calls out in a deep throaty voice. "I'm Madie. Looking for something special? An occasion dress? I've got some gorgeous things."

She sashays over to Willow in a tartan ball skirt, black spandex top, and gold hoop earrings, over-bleached yellow hair falling to her thick waist.

"Well, I . . . "

"*You*," Madie declares, "are a beauty. But I can tell," her voice rises playfully, "you don't give a hoot how you look!"

Willow giggles, studying Madie—inspiration for a new mario-nette. Madie looks to be in her mid-fifties or so, but it is hard to tell under her spackling of makeup and heavily shadowed eyes, dark brown, like Bern's.

Willow starts as she feels Madie's taloned fingers gather the loose fabric at her waist and crumple it in her fist.

"Now what is *this?*" Madie almost snarls. "You with the gorgeous bod are wearing clothes two—no, make that three—sizes too big."

"I like being comfortable, need to move for my work."

"Comfort, schmomfort. We have work to do." She points a finger at Willow's chest. "Did you *know,* when we girls go shopping, a *hormone* is released?"

Willow smiles. "Guess you learn something every day." She glances about the still empty boutique. "Let me explain . . . "

"We do makeovers, last Sunday of each month. You would be a great candidate."

"I don't quite know what to say." Willow takes a deep breath. "Your father came in to see me," she blurts out under pressure.

"My father?"

"Yes, he came in to see me at my studio. I'm a puppeteer, a marionette-maker. Anyway, apparently, he knew my mother."

Madie's eyes darken under the thick liner and glimmering green shadow. "*Who* is your mother may I ask?"

"Jane—I mean Jana Ivanova."

"Oh my God." Madie collapses into a delicately carved brocaded chair, which squawks under her weight.

"I didn't know Jana had a daughter."

"Here I am."

"It would kill my mother. Good thing she's already dead."

Willow stifles the smile tickling the corner of her lips. "I was going to meet your father for breakfast at Beauty's this morning. He offered to talk things over with me."

"You? He was meeting *you*?"

"I was, am, grateful actually, to have the chance to talk to him."

Madie wipes her damp brow with a lace hanky and stands with effort. "Well, Dad had a heart attack last week."

"Oh! I'm so sorry."

"He's had heart trouble for a long time. Nothing new. And he smokes like a chimney . . . but I just got a call from his doctor. He's doing well, stable for now. I'm going over to the Jewish to see him." She glances at her watch.

"I hope he's on the mend soon."

"Your mother, she still alive?"

"Very much so."

"They used to battle so over that Jana," Madie mutters under her breath, pacing the shop, arranging a necklace on a pillow of velvet, smoothing the hem of a creamy satin gown.

"Who battled?" Willow asks, her voice rising.

"My parents! Who do you think? Jana worked at Fairmount Bagel. She was always hanging around my father, or he was hanging around her, I don't know which. I was just a kid. My mother didn't like her at all. The effect she had on Dad."

"Do you know what their connection was exactly?"

"Told you, I was young. But I can imagine." Madie glances

59

suddenly at her delicate diamond watch. "You know, I should really head over to the hospital. You'll have to excuse me."

"Of course. I'm sorry I took you by surprise."

"No, no."

"Please tell your father I hope he feels better soon."

Madie turns to Willow with a smirk, then opens the door to let her out.

That afternoon, Willow sets to work again unpacking her studio, drinking cup after cup of smooth, strong coffee, musing about Bern—when he is better, she will go see him—then about the more comforting image of Noah Issenman. Her history with men is not sanguine, and she has spent the last five years alone, without the old repetitive drama, which serves only to deplete her. Willow has convinced herself there is no room for a man in her life now, with her marionette-making, puppet plays, and the care of her mother. Although she sometimes longs for someone, she isn't sure whom she longs for. In her thirties, she lived with Ilya Bernstein, eighteen years her senior, a director at Playwrights Horizons in New York, and when he passed away five years ago, she was in too much pain and grief to consider even meeting a man for coffee.

Ilya was comfortable with the bond she had with her marionettes, and left her time and space to make her puppets, to do her shows, and to teach her classes. He was busy with his own plays, so each of them remained self-contained, with a subterranean understanding of each other and their personal passions, though in the last few years, they seemed only to be living side-by-side. Still, it was a terrible shock when he died suddenly, alone, in the back row of an Upper West Side movie theater, watching *Some Like It Hot*, one of their favorites.

The men she'd met more recently seemed drained of life and color, or too clingy and intrusive, qualities she couldn't abide. A clingy man made her feel as if she were drowning in quicksand, lost to herself. She always fled in the end, or became nasty, so ugly and cruel she barely recognized herself, though it worked to set her free.

The coffee gives Willow a sudden jolt and she drags a small bookcase over to the corner furthest from the door and sets to work unpacking the torn and tattered volumes her mother gave to her as a child to develop her craft. Classic works on marionettes and puppeteering, they are now spotted with plaster stains and chocolate handprints: Bill Baird's red cloth volume, heavy and unwieldy, with its color photographs; *The Art of the Puppet* by Rossbach, Merton's *Marionettes*, and Mabel and Les Beaton's carefully diagrammed volume.

Willow pages through them, glancing at her underlinings and margin notes, little sketches, and ideas clipped and flapping from the heavy illustrated pages. She flips open Helen Fling's *Marionettes: How to Make and Work Them*, a simple little craft book she uses with students.

First, make an armature.

If only she could. All alone in her studio, she smiles to herself, warming. That simple phrase fills her with an unreasoning pleasure. With the chaos of the move and settling into her new apartment, Willow hasn't had the chance to fully unpack in the studio, yet she is itching to work again. She rummages through a half-dozen boxes before she finds the bamboo and leather reed. She holds it to her mouth and blows, listening to the long sound, and soon a wordless vocabulary of sounds.

Unwinding the handkerchief from her Don Quixote puppet, Willow gives the silk motion and life. Ripping open cartons, she finds sketch paper and charcoal; sounds lead to gestures, an expression of the eyes, then the lips. Before she makes a new marionette, she does sketch after sketch. Often she doesn't know who this new being will become and the mystery keeps her going.

Her tools are simple, collected over the years, some raided from friends' supplies; she uses many for both marionette and prop building. Slitting open boxes, Willow locates her small hand saw—ideal for cutting wood into spiral and ornamental designs—the dovetail saw, large and small wire pliers, and carbon twist drills. She digs out chisels, metal files, wood rasps, and tack hammer, then the whittling knife and hand shears, hanging them one by one on the pegboard above her workbench. Next come her clay modeling tools and the enamel bowl she uses for preparing plaster. In the bins beside the bench, she organizes wood from boxes, lengths of white pine and scraps of plywood—soft woods are best—they carve more easily and the lighter weight is an advantage.

In their own bin, she puts 1.25-inch dowels, as well as soft wood broomsticks, useful for legs and arms, and in another, she sorts pear and alder wood, ideal for hands and feet.

Willow finds the carton filled with puppet hair and sorts it into the drawers of a battered Victorian desk that has been left in the studio: wigs, curly and sleek—black, auburn, gold, purple, silver, even blue—hair of twisted yarn and shredded rope, crepe, wool and silk, eyelashes made of bias-cut buckram and fur strips. She relaxes, absorbed, burrowing in.

Her costumer turns up, a wooden base about ten-by-fifteen inches with a one-by-two upright the height of most of her puppets, a gibbet at the top for fastening the marionette. Willow finds a place for it on the oak table she's put near the sliding glass doors, where she has the best light. When she designs a marionette's costume and then dresses it for a show, she uses the costumer to hang up her puppet and see how he or she looks. A small box holds pins and needles, and attached to the base, she finds an old note to herself: *Good movement, balance bring a puppet to life—joints in a vertical line, puppet supporting its own weight, body lighter than the legs, head larger than normal—don't overdo the costume.*

Willow tries to remember where she excavated this nugget, as she opens box after box of props, wiping sweat from her face with the rag she's stuffed into one of the cartons to keep the tiny toys and furniture from breaking in transit. She arranges the contents on three small round tables beside her workbench. She loves this miniature world she can hold, whole, within her eye, unlike the real one, which never makes sense in its ever-changing, shifting fragments.

There is the Victorian lamp that took an entire day to make from the top of an old incense burner, a brass chain, and an old rhinestone brooch of her mother's, the drum she built from a hatbox, its lacing a leather thong, tiny colored beads for ornament.

Hours pass and Willow still has more to do. Soon she is grimy and sticky and, despite the chill, slides open the glass doors and pours herself a glass of water before getting back to work. The winter air is glacial, bracing. She just wants to finish, so she can begin again.

Bundling up for the cold, Willow stops by Fairmount Bagel where her mother worked so many years before. She buys a dozen, then asks one of the guys manning the counter if the owners are in.

"In Israel now," he says.

"Israel, wow. Okay."

"But his brother is in. Shall I get him?"

Willow nods. "If you wouldn't mind."

The fellow goes to the back, and in a few minutes, an elderly man appears, looking a bit younger than Bern, than Willow's mother, but not by much.

"You wanted to talk to me about something?" he asks, stroking his salt-and-pepper beard suspiciously. "Is there a problem?"

"No, not at all," Willow sputters. She steps away from the line so others can be served, asks if she could have a moment, and the man grabs a coat and steps outside with her into the bracing Montréal air.

She doesn't know where to begin, and so she begins anywhere. "My mother, Jane—I mean, Jana Ivanova—she used to work here ages ago, like I mean in the forties and fifties. Do you remember her?"

The man strokes his beard, gazing skyward. He's quiet for a long minute or two. "Oh, okay. Yes I do remember her a little. Coming and going."

"And did you talk to her? I'm sorry—I don't even know your name."

"Aaron."

"Willow."

They clasp hands for a moment, Aaron's hand strong and warm in hers.

"Willow, did I talk? I have my own business. I would see her coming and going, like I said. We exchanged pleasantries. Small talk. Small talk, I'm not good at."

"Neither is she," Willow clips. She feels a desperation rise in her throat, then seep into her voice. "What was she like then? I'm sure you can tell me *something!*"

He looks alarmed, but just for a moment, then his eyes turn tender toward her. "Something, something, let's see. Jana was a very warm person, a little sad. Lost."

Willow feels her eyes tear in the cold. "Lost, how?"

"A look in her eyes."

"Where did she live?"

"With family."

"*Family?* What family, I mean can you tell me who they were?" Willow realizes she is nearly shouting at the poor man.

"Look, Willow. When my brother returns, you should talk to him. He will know more. I'm sorry I can't tell you much, because I don't have much to tell."

"Can you tell me when your brother plans to be back?" Willow presses, her voice thin and strange in her own ears, almost bitter.

"Spring. Good evening."

"Okay then, thanks." Weary, she is reluctant to leave and stands a few minutes on the sidewalk outside the bagel shop. When her feet begin to numb, Willow finally heads back to her apartment, ready to take a long, hot bath, sleep a bit, and try not to think. She arrives at her place, dusty and tired, but with a feeling of satisfaction that she has finally set up her studio.

After her bath, Willow gazes out the window at the winter-warped trees, the pewter light. Something outside glistens, snow so stealthy it takes a moment for Willow to notice, and she knows she will awaken to pillowy drifts weighing down branches, effacing steps, turning cars, boulders, hedges into a child's clumsy, cut-outs, the pure whiteness of the snow giving off its own light, standing in for the sun. She will begin her own life here in Montréal, create her own damned history.

❊ ❊ ❊

Memory Book
Spring 1975

Who's that girl, Mama? She's smiling like she's got a secret!

Michaela, my best friend. You have Charly, I had M.

Are you my age there?

Four years older, fourteen already. Michaela's mother, Eva, was wonderful to me. I called her my other mother. My second family, even though they were gentiles. Turn, two, three pages. There! That's Petrin Hill. M and I lived there in summer, slept outside, like wild animals. Walked, daydreamed, picnicked. You see the pear and apple trees? They had soft pink and white petals. We covered ourselves with them.

What's that place?

Hvezdarna, the Observatory. See the girl by the telescopes? That's M. At night we went, traced our fingers over the outlines of Pegasus, Orion, and Cassiopeia, every dim and bright star.

Did you like boys, Ma?

Later I found a man I loved.

Roger Pelletier! Tell me more about him, Mama.

Acch! Tomorrow, lovey, we need to save something for tomorrow.

SIX

THE FOLLOWING WEEK, Willow meets with Marie-France, the theater's manager, in an office backstage, its walls painted pumpkin and adorned with posters of past productions. "We are happy to be having you here, Willow," she says, her voice welcoming, yet staccato. There are two armchairs and a small stack table in the far corner of the office, away from the door, and Marie-France motions Willow to take a seat opposite her. She is a small, pert woman with a brisk, almost martial way of moving, her black hair cut short and spiked with electric blue streaks. The short blue-and-black-checked kilt she is wearing suits her.

"Your course is already with a waiting list," she says, smiling. The phone rings and several people come and go with questions, crises, requests. Flustered by the interruptions, Marie-France apologizes, clicks on her answering machine, and makes coffee.

"We can take a breath now?" she asks.

"With luck." Willow slides off her clogs, curling long legs under her in the cushiony armchair.

"I am fielding people off, truly," Marie-France goes on. "So now this is a favor, no a question." Crossing her black-sheathed legs, she swings a delicate, booted foot back and forth. Willow listens to the comforting burbling as the office fills with the smell of freshly brewed coffee. In a few minutes, Marie-France fixes them each a cup.

"The workshop we did limit to eight," Marie-France says. "Are you able to take one or two more without . . . how can I say this, my English is rusty from little practice, *qualité compromise?*"

"How large a room have you got?" Willow asks, stirring cream into her coffee.

"*Très grande,* I'll show you. Many people are calling, pleading if this is not too much a word, to be in your workshop."

"Thanks for the publicity."

Marie-France waves her small white hands, adorned with blue-black varnish, in a dismissive motion. "This is the least we are doing for our artists."

Willow watches her sip espresso, then add a sugar cube with delicate fingers. "And so, you are to be starting the first week of *février* for the course—that is already next week! We are booking a show in . . . *mai.* And of course *le deuxième en octobre.* Is this timing good for you?"

Willow feels a rush of excitement, a flicker of panic. She has no clue what she is going to do for either show, but is hoping her students might take on the first with their own marionettes and play, while she guides and directs, saving her own play for the fall.

"Should be fine," Willow answers, sounding more confident than she feels.

"Everyone is excited to have you with us."

"Thank you, you're very kind."

"So, bring with you your coffee and I will take you around and show you the workshop room for your class."

Marie-France walks at a clip, shouting instructions and questions in French to everyone they pass. The classroom workshop is in the basement along with Willow's private studio—through a door and a zigzagging maze of hallways. It is a large, industrial space, well-equipped with tools and tables, a bit of natural light from high windows and artificial light from tracks above. Willow wonders what transpired down here in the days of the jam factory.

"This place is huge," she says to Marie-France. "I could certainly handle, let's see, up to ten."

"*C'est beau!*"

"These are puppeteers with experience, right?"

"*Oui*. We are calling this a master class, *ça va?*"

"That's it."

"So I will make two more of your fans happy today."

They wend their way back upstairs and return to Marie-France's office. The phone is ringing. A man leaves a long, complex message on the machine in French and Willow immediately recognizes Noah Issenman's voice. A smile spreads across Marie-France's small, heart-shaped face. "Pardon, Willow. This call, I must take. I will find you later."

Willow nods and slips out, longing to eavesdrop on their conversation.

All through the following week snow swirls, as Willow prepares for her master class. Though she has plenty of experience teaching, as well as performing, the concept of this master class is different, a first: A collection of experienced puppeteers will work collaboratively under her tutelage to write, produce, and perform their own show, making the marionettes who will dramatize the story. She is excited, a bit edgy. The puppeteers applied on paper or sent videos of their work, though she hasn't yet met them, and wonders how their personalities will mesh. At the eleventh hour, she is fretting about her wisdom in permitting ten people to take the class, an unwieldy number.

Willow unlocks her classroom, wipes off the long table fashioned from an old door, and sets out chairs. When the room is ready, she runs out for coffee, surprised by how nervous she feels; a brisk walk in the bracing winter air will calm her—it usually does.

When Willow returns, eight of her ten students have already arrived, some standing in clusters chatting, others settled around the table. She feels a buzz, uncertain how it will all work out, expectant.

※ ※ ※

Memory Book
Winter 1978

Mom, is that Michaela again, your best friend?

Yes, one of the last times I saw her.

How old is she there?

Seventeen, lovey, about four years older than you.

She looks grown up, a lady.

People did, then.

Did you get to say goodbye to her?

Oh, no . . .

Mama, I'm sorry.

Well, it's better in a way, I would see her again, I knew.

Maybe you will. You can, right?

Goodness. I suppose I could.

How old is she?

Oh, about like me, fifty-five years old.

You should write to her. Invite her to visit. Or we could go there! To Prague. I want to see where you grew up, Mama.

Someday, lovey, maybe someday. I want to show you something in the photo, here, look.

What a cool menorah!

Special, yes. My Papa made it. A present when I turned thirteen, your age, lovey.

Wow, he made that?

Out of brass. He was such a talented sculptor, Willow, my Papa.

Who are the figures, Ma?

Our whole family! We were a full house. Papa, Mama, of course me, my younger sister, Ada, my three little brothers, Pavel, Josef, and Jan, the baby. And our dog, Samo. Each of us could hold a candle, see?

It's beautiful, Ma.

Every year, Papa let me light a candle, even when I was just two years old. His hands he held around mine.

Like you did with me, Ma.

Just like I did with you.

Where is the menorah now, Ma?

It's not here.

Where, then?

Buried.

What?

Hidden, lovey. Hidden far away, down deep.

What are you talking about? Where?

In Prague.

Do you think it's still there, Ma? Where did you hide it? You remember?

Of course I remember.

When we go together to your old home—you promised me someday—
we can look for it.

What happens to something buried, Willow, I don't know.

SEVEN

JANE'S TAXI SHUSHES through wintry white streets, as she clutches Willow's address in her hand, straining at signs obscured by the flour-fine mist. How can this be? April already and several feet of snow! She hasn't been back to Montréal in almost forty years, since she was pregnant with Willow, but now memories come back in a rush.

"*Meshuge* weather you have!"

"You're telling me?" the driver says. "Your first time here?"

"Of course not." Jane tells the driver the bare bones of her story: how she first arrived in Montréal in 1947 after the DP camp and ended up staying ten years, though she never felt settled, before moving to New Jersey; how even years later, she was drawn back up to Montréal, as if by an invisible thread. But that was another story, a more private one.

"4155 Avenue de l'Esplanade," she reads aloud to the cabbie. "Do you know it?"

"Between Rachel and Duluth, near the Regiment, the Grenadier Guards. Got a good view of Mt. Royal and the statue. Nice."

"My daughter lives there."

"Don't she pick you up at the airport?"

Jane clucks her tongue, waves her hand in a dismissive motion. She wants to surprise Willow and hasn't bothered to write, even call, before showing up. The truth is she didn't want to be convinced not to come, or to have to think or discuss anything. Most of her life is now scheduled down to the minute, except for this surprise visit; for once, she has broken out, acted on impulse. The back and forth about coming, about participating in the Witness Foundation Program was making her crazy, one day wanting to come, the next day preferring to be eaten alive by wild dogs. She just couldn't take her own ambivalence anymore. Besides, she misses Willow terribly—it's already four months now.

Soon the cabbie pulls up beside an apartment building made of masonry blocks in gold and brown with a green, gabled roof and tiny balcony. "Like a gingerbread house!" Jane exclaims. "So pretty." Jane glances at her watch, just ten a.m. Then she murmurs half out loud, half to herself, "According to the schedule, she should be here now."

The cabbie hops out and unloads Jane's suitcase, carrying it to the building, while she opens her change purse with a click and pays the fare, giving him a good tip. Her hand trembles as she pushes the buzzer beside Willow's name. Inside, there is barking, scratching, then a long buzzing, releasing the heavy front door. Jane enters a lovely foyer with dark wood paneling and a parquet floor, adorned with a small dhurrie rug. The warmth inside is welcoming, delicious.

After a moment or two, a young man, disheveled and unshaven, appears in pajamas and opens the door, greeting her in French. He lifts Jane's case into the foyer, as a huge dog bounds out of his apartment and jumps up on Jane, nearly knocking her over. The man grabs the dog by the collar and scolds him roundly in French. The dog's tail falls between his legs.

The young man steadies Jane, asks if she is all right, keeping a firm grip on his dog's collar, with his other hand. There is something about this young man—his careless plumpness, a smell of sleep and sweat, his long-lashed eyes of pale blue, his soft voice— something that makes Jane comfortable. She reaches down and pats the dog, her shaking hand sinking into his thick black fur, soft and shining as mink. She has not felt anything this soft and warm in a long time.

"Oh," she exclaims, "a beauty, you are!" and the young man's face breaks into a smile. "I could maybe fall in love with you," Jane goes on, stroking the dog's ears. "I am looking for Willow. Willow Ives," Jane says. Her fingers curl anxiously at her sides. "I am looking for my daughter."

"Is there some emergency?" the young man asks, a kind look in his pale eyes.

"Just that I am here!" Jane answers, and again, he slips into that gentle smile.

"I did hear her going out this morning very early," the young man says. "Why don't you come inside my place and wait for her?" He gestures toward his apartment with a loose-wristed flourish. "It would be my pleasure. Bête Noire and I will keep you company."

The dog's tail wags wildly as a whip, and without a moment's hesitation, Jane steps inside the man's apartment, her heart beating fast as she thinks of Willow. She will see her daughter soon. Very soon.

🦋 🦋 🦋

Memory Book
Fall 1980

You look happy there, Ma. In Montréal.

It was beautiful. Turn the page, Willow. Again. In this book there is a picture of la montagne in winter. The long winter, which seems to have no end. April? Nah! May, not necessarily. I'll tell you, lovey, snow in May in Montréal—I have seen it. But there was something special about that winter, the snow. Turn again, keep going. A certain picture I'm looking for. There!

Is that the mountain?

See how the pines glitter—like glass—the maples with their white icing of snow, the shadows of their branches, blue, the same blue as the winter sky.

It's beautiful, Mama. Can we go visit together?

I remember, lovey, walking on the mountain, carrying you inside me. You were my secret! A good one, pure. Light and full, I felt.

Willow, turn more pages. Go on, flip. There is another favorite picture. The colors, lovey, if only you could see them! Like a blaze they were in fall, a beautiful fire. There I was, at the top of la montagne, about to start fresh, a new life.

What new life?

Ours.

Tell me something, Mama. One thing. Why did you leave Montréal?

I lost your father. He died before you were born. Painful memories I had, as well as good. I wanted to be a teacher. In Montréal, it was hard to teach; I had English, but not much French. Here in Kingston, I had an opportunity. I knew people, they knew me. A fresh start, new roots, that's what I wanted.

Why?

When you're older, you'll understand.

EIGHT

WILLOW AND NOAH stroll the neighborhood near Usine C, snow flurrying, though it is already April. Cold enough that Willow's nostrils pinch and her bare hands ache, as she wriggles her fingers to keep warm. Noah wears his signature black duster and a long, blue and red muffler wound around his slender neck. Willow, overly optimistic, is in a brown, lined leather bomber jacket, hatless and gloveless, defiant against the unseasonable weather. At Pâtisserie de Thérèse, a small café where Noah is a regular, they take a window table and watch passersby hunker down against the wind in their down and woolen layers, a hat blowing off a head, a scarf unfurling into the tenacious wind.

Lately, Noah has been popping by her studio at odd, unexpected times, and she has been teaching him to work her marionettes.

Together in the quiet of the theater's basement, completely absorbed, hours passing like moments.

As Noah lowers himself into one of the ladder-backed chairs inside the pâtisserie, his hair brushes Willow's cheek; it has a wonderful clean smell, balsam and mint. Though his hair is a jungle of curls, it is corn-silk soft. He shucks off his duster and throws it over the back of his chair, painstakingly rolling up the sleeves of his rumpled shirt. He has long, slender arms with a blue-veined strength about them. Her last lover, Ilya, was short, barrel-chested, and stocky, such a contrast to Noah—though Noah is not her lover.

"How's the workshop going?" he asks, emptying his pockets of objects: a broken fortune cookie, still in its wrapper; flyers from Ha'makom; a leather notebook with sticky-notes of every color flapping from its curling pages.

"Well," Willow answers, "my students and I are getting to know each other *very* well."

He smiles at her with his whole face, a wide-open loopy grin, unnervingly like a baby's first smile.

As they wait to order, Willow says, "May I?" and picks up the fortune cookie.

Noah nods, pulling his chair in close with a sudden screech across the marble floor.

Willow uncurls the ribbon of paper and reads the fortune: infinitesimal English on one side, French on the other. *"With greater time, effort and patience, a longed-for dream comes true."*

"Keep it," Noah says, stopping her hand when she tries to show it to him. "I can tell it's a good one."

"So. Will the language police sue these folks?" Willow waves the white ribbon of paper in the air. "Surely this falls short of the two-to-one ratio." She slides the fortune into the pocket of her leather jacket, as a waitress comes to take their order.

Before Willow can glance at the menu or inspect the pastry case, Noah has ordered for them both in beautiful French and the waitress has disappeared into the kitchen.

"Hey. I've been doing my own ordering since I was three."

He laughs low, conspiratorial. "Isn't this fun for a change," he says, a statement, not a question.

"Will you cut my pastry for me too?"

"Whatever you want." He looks at her dead-on.

Soon the waitress is back with steaming bowls of café au lait and buttery croissants topped with toasted almonds.

Willow breathes in the rich smell of coffee and croissants, as they watch the procession of mothers pulling toddlers on sleds, the occasional student or businessman yakking into a cell phone, oblivious to the sun, the sky, the day.

"I was wondering," Willow says, warming her hands on the warm bowl of café au lait, "about your play at the Centaur."

"*Freeze*. There's this photographer, a loner, who takes pictures during the monster ice storm we had here, moments that are like lifetimes. He's always outside, looking in, but something shakes him up. I don't want to give away too much, you might see it."

"How's it doing?"

"Exceptionally well. There will be a French version soon and it's nominated for a Governor General's Award."

"I'm impressed." Willow sips her frothy coffee. "I've seen

some of the photographs from that ice storm. This crystal fairy-land, where time just stops."

"That's it."

Noah gazes at Willow and then smiles with his wide mouth, a funny off-center smile, starting in one corner and then spreading slowly through his face, taking her in.

"There's something about the cold I really like, I mean, it's part of our national identity. Many try to escape it, but it's in my blood, I guess."

He bends and sips his coffee, froth sloshing over the edge of the bowl, dotting his chin. Willow wipes it off, and he is not the least embarrassed. His face has a manly roughness.

"We'll see how I brave this cold. I didn't expect it to hang on this long. You know how you can like a person right away? It's the same deal with a place."

"And you," he says, "How is it going at Usine C?"

"I've got a great group, really lucked out, though there are some tensions—competitiveness you don't expect with puppe-teers, chemistry issues."

"Ah, artists."

"We're going through with the show in May."

"Cool."

"Don't cool me so fast. *Riders on the Storm*, we're calling it. She raises her brows, bites a corner of lip. "Lots of weather, storms, a bit of an homage to you, I'm afraid, to *Freeze*. They idolize you. Homage is the polite word."

He shrugs. "This is for kids?"

"Hey, puppet plays are different from people plays. Seriously,

I kind of like their concept, it plays with mythology, new and old media, weather, maybe it's a bit over-the-top, but they can play with that. So, it doesn't bug you, storms and all?"

"Imitation is the highest form of flattery, no? Plus, we all know, no new ideas, right?" Noah takes a long sip of coffee.

She breathes out in a histrionic sigh of relief.

"So after this workshop, you have your own puppet play in the fall, right?"

"My blood pressure is rising." Willow warms her face in curls of steam.

They are both quiet for a while, concentrating on their coffee and the view of swirling snow outside the windows. Noah breaks the silence.

"It's quite a leap you took, to uproot from New York and come to Montréal. Most folks are going the opposite direction."

"My mother lived here a while, twice actually, for about ten years or so, then again about five years later for a shorter stay, about two years I think, when she was pregnant with me. In between she went to Kingston—a little town in central New Jersey, near Princeton, where she had some connections. That's where I grew up, where she is now. I've always longed to come here, but felt—I don't know what—afraid of what I might find or not find."

He nods slowly. "Other family?"

"Or not." Willow shrugs, forming a circle of thumb and forefinger. "Actually, my father is from here, you know, Québécois. He was French."

"Yeah?"

86

"A caretaker of the chalet. Never met him though. He died before I was born."

Noah looks at her steadily and Willow appreciates his response, which is merely neutral.

"Mount Royal is one of my favorite places," he says. "We'll have to take a walk up top, I'll show you the chalet. It's quite interesting. I know the current caretaker a bit, Alain Chevalier."

"Think he knows much about prior caretakers?"

Noah shrugs.

They linger a while, watching flakes settle and stick, then leave the café and walk, without speaking or planning.

"Ever feel you need time out?" Willow asks Noah suddenly, the words coming unbidden. "You know, from your life, or even your self?"

"Now." He pulls off enormous down-filled leather mittens and gives them to her.

She accepts them gratefully.

They walk for a long while and eventually find themselves near McGill, wandering the streets around the university. The snow is coming down thicker now, flakes piling into soft down on the cars, whitening the sidewalks.

"I want to show you a place," Noah says, slipping, nearly taking a pratfall on the sidewalk, Willow catching his arm to steady him.

Through the gold-lit window of an old brick storefront, Willow sees a wall of books, but there is no sign outside. She follows Noah into a homey place warmed by a wood-burning stove and an old Rudd heater, packed floor to ceiling with used and rare books.

It has a wonderful smell of old paper and must; she breathes in deep, holding the memory, preserving it. A tall, broad-shouldered man with a salt-and-pepper beard moves about the store with concentrated absorption, straightening a book here, adjusting a dustjacket there, placing volumes marked a dollar on a bench.

"I come here a lot," Noah says, "when my loft feels too empty."

Willow nods, as they browse the shelves.

"I have these days," he goes on, running his fingers over the spine of an Arthur Rackham, "when I'm running on empty, sure I've got no more characters, no more stories."

Willow starts, spooked by sharing this same fear. She brushes it off, every artist's secret terror.

"I'm cleaned out," Noah goes on, "then I come here." He lets out a long sigh of pleasure. "Sometimes I just like to look at picture books, I get inspired. Don't know why—somehow the images lead to characters, voices, even stories." He leafs slowly through the Rackham drawings. "Look at these colors," he says. "Like stained glass."

He draws out another volume. "Janet Ray does this primitive thing. Check out the eyes, the princess is like a statue. Then look at this sun, it's tentacled, alive. Her colors, the shapes, they're like Gauguin, yet her own."

Willow picks up *Once There Was A Tree*, skimming through the tale about a tree split by lightning, then felled by a woodsman so only the stump remains. Inside this small stump is a world of activity. Gennady Spirin's illustrations are earth-toned, dream-like, with a texture so gauzy, they seem spun of air.

Noah runs his fingertip over the page, the teeming world of the stump, with its beetles, ants, bird, bear, man.

"I also come here when the loft is too busy, noisy, when it doesn't seem like my own. I have this habit of bringing home strays . . . "

"What is this place?"

"Used to be a Chinese laundry twenty-five years ago. Adrian and Luci borrowed a thousand dollars and started the store. When I first came here there was a sign outside: "The Word." It was stolen and the new sign ran afoul of the language police, so for years, they haven't bothered to replace it."

"You have to stumble upon the place," Willow says, "or be taken." She wonders if her mother ever used the laundry or walked past it, if she knows of the existence of this secret book store. Willow imagines her mother visiting and introducing Jane to something *she* has discovered.

They wander about the book-filled room and Noah shows Willow a signed copy of Lorca's *Casa de Bernarda Alba* and a beautifully bound volume of Chekhov's early plays. A customer comes in, others linger among the shelves in a half-conscious state of poring and browsing.

As they walk about the shop, the bearded man rises from the depths of his focused attention and greets Noah. While they're talking, Willow wanders about on her own. An elderly, blue-haired lady with an elegant cane is reading aloud to herself from *Othello*. A young guy with shoulder-length, black hair, slick as licorice, places a saxophone case on the floor and pages through a book on Buster Keaton.

Willow feels enveloped in a startling, unexpected silence, no buzzing of fluorescent lights, no hum or tentacles of computers, phones, cells, or fax machines, no ding of a cash register, and no background music. Unlike most bookstores, there are no markers or signs to guide one to specific sections. Amidst the quiet, Willow falls into a browsing trance, moving among the Brontës, through Eugene O'Neill, settling among a stack of Russian poetry. She slides out a volume, selected poems of Marina Tsvetaeva and sits cross-legged on the floor reading, "Epitaph."

The poem has a bottomlessness. Crazy, Willow feels as if it were written for her and also for her mother, for people she has known and lost, and those she has never met. As if the words were flames, the phrases, fire.

When she looks up from the page, Noah is sitting on a crate beside her, legs stretched out. She was so immersed in the poem, the lines and the spaces between them, so caught in the midst of a private emotion, she hadn't heard him.

"Do you know much about Tsvetaeva's life?" Willow asks him.

"Not as much as I should."

"When she left the Soviet Union in the 1920s, she went to Prague, where she lived in exile for a few years. She lost her homeland, her native language . . .wrote about being outcast, as a part of being chosen."

Noah touches her hand, turning the book slowly toward him. He reads the poem aloud, threading a hand through his curly hair. "That has a familiar ring, eh?"

She puts faith in this state of being," Willow says, "Jews do that as well, I think."

"In this poem, it's like she's writing about the pull toward an empty space where there should be something. I feel that."

Willow feels a rush, a tingly warmth penetrating her skin.

"What is it?"

"I don't know."

Suddenly, Noah is far away, elsewhere. He glances at his watch. Then without warning, Willow feels his strong, slender hands under her arms, pulling her into his lap, where he sits on the crate.

"Hey!"

"You don't weigh anything."

Hearing the screech of floorboards, treads approaching, Willow leaps up, as Noah grabs onto a bookshelf and unfurls to his full height.

"One day, I want to meet the rest of your Frankensteins," Noah says softly.

She looks at him, startled, then picks up the slim volume of Marina Tsvetaeva poems, as if to break a spell. "I'm getting this for you," she says, clips to the front, pays, and meets him out on the street.

"I'll always come back to The Word," she says, "thanks for showing it to me."

He cocks one brow.

She realizes, too late, she's blowing him off.

Outside, it is still light. The whole day seems suspended and out of time, not quite real. Turning the corner onto Aylmer,

Willow has the urge to thread her arm through Noah's, as he stops suddenly, taking in the whirling snow.

"'*Mon pays ce n'est pas un pays, c'est l'hiver*'. My country is not a country, my country is winter. Gilles Vigneault. Great folksinger. The snow, the ice, the white, I miss it all when it goes. Finally."

"You're showing off."

"One day, I want to stay at one of those ice hotels. You're reduced to whatever warmth you can hold inside."

"Winter doesn't wear you out?"

"It's home."

Noah starts to walk again, long wheeling strides, and they amble through the snowy downtown streets till twilight. The April storm still has not spent itself.

❉ ❉ ❉

Memory Book
Fall 1980

Ma, where is that?

More pictures, lovey, of Montréal. Look about three-quarters of the way through. That's the first apartment I stayed in, on Jeanne Mance. Worn old brick, with bright yellow trim, and a rickety outside staircase.

Was it nice inside?

Crowded, so crowded. Seven people crammed into that flat. I had lived a quarter of my life in places more dirty and crowded, but it was still tough. There was a person I knew, another survivor of the war. His Aunt Rivka, she took me in.

Is that her?

The short, fleshy woman. Queen of the Castle. Not a relative, never would let me forget that, Willow. Never!

What did you do, Ma?

Walked. In all seasons, lovey, all weathers. Turn a few pages. Guess what that is?

A bakery?

Bagelry. On one stroll, I stood outside, hypnotized by the smell of hot, fresh bagels tumbling out of the wood-fired oven. I closed my eyes and was a girl again in Prague, where I'd eaten so many bagels—at a bris, when a neighbor was in labor, during shiva. The round shape reminded me.

Of what Ma?

A halo. Good luck, life.

You're really making me hungry, I'll put up some bagels for us. Night snack.

Just what I need!

Me too.

Whenever I eat a fresh bagel, Willow, I am a girl again with my mama and papa in Prague, and then a young woman in Montréal taking baby steps back into life. The taste and the smell make me feel all the changes from misery back to happiness that we all go through.

NINE

ALREADY, IT IS TWILIGHT. Jane doesn't know where the day has
gone, but she has whiled away the hours quite pleasantly in Luc
Chartrand's apartment with his enormous puppy, waiting for
Willow to appear. Jane and Luc have gotten to know each other a
little in these lazy wintry hours, and with Bête Noire, it has been
love at first sight.

As Jane sits on Luc's battered leather sofa, Bête Noire rests his
muzzle in her lap and she can feel his warmth and wetness through
her wool dress. His ears lift attentively, and he looks at her with
one chocolate-brown eye, the other, ice-blue.

She wonders what his breed is.

"Is he a St. Bernard?" she asks, suspecting that this is not right.
Bête Noire is more elegant than the drooling, loose-mouthed St.
Bernards she has seen. He is also leaner.

"Bernois . . . you say, I think Bernese Mountain, no? This breed, they are from Switzerland," Luc points out, "winter dogs, lying on drifts as if they were clouds, swimming through snow, taking nips out of the white waves to quench their thirst."

Jane strokes the soft fur and is soothed by the rhythmic thump of Bête Noire's tail on the hardwood floor. She has never seen a more astonishingly beautiful dog. His back and ears are lush black, his chest a creamy white, his paws touched with chestnut and white.

"Most of these dogs have two brown eyes, but Bête Noire is unique."

Jane smiles. "I like the one blue and one brown, for different moods. So big. How old is he?"

"Just nine months."

"So he will grow *bigger*?"

"My vet he say he will reach one hundred and forty pounds."

"A wonderful big companion for you."

She is charmed by this slow-moving, relaxed young man. Luc Chartrand seems to have nowhere to go, all the time in the world.

Jane has called Usine C several times, left messages, and that is really all she can do. The people who answer the phone say Willow is out, they don't know where, but will tell her as soon as she returns. Returns from where? Why is she not at work? Why is she not where she is supposed to be, according to the schedule?

This disheveled Luc comforts Jane in Franglais. Her own French is rusty. Demoralizing how quickly a language will go if you don't use it. Luc says he doesn't see much of Willow, she is always at the theater.

Jane has become more trusting in her old age, believing in her gut feelings about people. Some friends have asked her if she believes in God, and now she thinks that she believes in goodness—in love, though not necessarily the romantic kind.

"Willow will be home soon, I am sure," Luc reassures her. "Now let me make you something to eat. I used to be chef at La Colombe. You must go there with Willow."

"A man who likes to cook, a rare thing."

"And even more I like to eat! Me, I would not trust a person who does not like to eat."

"I agree, Luc. One hundred percent! What is your specialty?"

"*Figue.*"

"What?"

"Like anglais. Fig. Dessert, entrée, everything with this beautiful fruit. Do you like it?"

"On a good day."

"If you stay awhile in Montréal, I will make you dinner. You and Willow. *Ça va?*"

"You are very nice young man. If you don't mind my asking, what do you do that you can stay home all day in your pajamas?"

"I am a writer."

"Everyone is a writer!"

Now he is laughing.

"I'm sorry."

"I write poems. I have two books published in Québec, what is it you call them . . . chapbooks."

"I decorate lampshades."

"Pardon?"

"I collect beautiful lamps, all shapes. Then I cut out pictures I like from magazines."

"*Mais oui?*"

"And I cut and paste and decorate the lampshades with mixed-up patterns and shellac them. One day I will show you. Or you can look in Willow's apartment. She has several."

"Light, we need light."

"More than anything." Jane smiles at him.

"But I am also a proofreader at night. Soon I will go to work, but you can make yourself at home. Willow, when she arrives, will see your note on the mailbox."

Jane does not want to part with this nice young man, does not want to be alone just yet.

"Does she seem happy?" Jane asks suddenly.

Luc's eyes expand, and then Jane remembers that Québécois are not as blunt as Americans.

"You know Jane, I see her only coming and going, but she is . . . how can I say this, very purposeful in her activities. I hear she is a talent and I hope to attend one of her plays at Usine C."

"Me too," Jane says, her voice unnaturally clipped.

"Now if I am to make you something, I must get started. Already I have a baguette to put in the oven and some soup."

Bête Noire waddles after his master into the small kitchen, his soft furry behind wiggling this way and that. Soon Jane smells fresh coffee brewing and the buttery, yeasty smell of baking bread, and a delicious, spicy, sweet aroma she can't quite identify.

Before long, Luc brings in a tray with steaming bowls of soup, bread just out of the oven, butter, and mugs of coffee.

"A prince, you are," Jane says, as he hands her the bowl of soup. "How good it smells."

"My cream of vegetable."

As Jane takes a spoonful, blows on it, then tastes, she hears the outer door open. She places the soup on a side table so abruptly, some sloshes over the bowl. Heart fluttering in her chest, she rushes out to see who is there.

✳ ✳ ✳

Memory Book
Spring 1981

Who is that couple, Ma? In the bakery, with the chute pouring out bagels?

Emma and Myer Lewkowitz. I told you, lovey, in Montréal I escaped by walking. Turn the page, you see me outside the famous shop, smelling hot, fresh bagels. I closed my eyes, a gentle tap I felt on my shoulder. A pretty woman with a warm smile—you see her—that's Emma! Go to the next page.

She's handing you a bagel.

Brown and crisp on the outside, warm and soft inside, the tiny poppy seeds sticking to my teeth.

Who took that picture, Ma?

So the story, let me finish. Many pictures I have of Fairmount Bagel. A second home.

I want to go to Montréal, Ma. To see everything.

One day we'll go, lovey. When the time is right. So Emma, she intro-duced herself to me, Willow. And we talked in Yiddish almost every day, outside or in the shop, depending on weather.

Is that you, Ma? Oh my God!

That's me, lovey. You see, I went to work for them a few years after I arrived in Montréal. I think it saved me, got me through. Myer, there's his picture, with the black hair and nice smile, Myer taught me how to shape rings of dough.

In that picture Ma, you're making bagels.

You see me, in honey-water I am dipping them. Five minutes, it took.

Were you fast, Ma?

Me? Nah! Myer, he could twist a thousand bagels an hour!

No!

I never got that good. My hands were stiff from . . . Turn a page, look.

What are you doing there, Ma?

Adding white sesame seeds or black poppy on the shibba—the long wooden plank we used to push the bagels into the oven. We were famous. I'll tell you a little story. One night, the bakery got a call. Twenty-dozen bagels for Prince Charles!

Some kids messing around, right?

The owner says, it's Saturday night, we're busy, stop fooling around. An hour later, a British fleet pulled up.

You're making this up, Ma!

A British naval officer, he marched into the shop. I'm here, he announced, for Prince Charles' bagels. The clerk said, You'll just have to wait like everybody else. So the officer had to wait with the limousines parked outside.

And Prince Charles?

Oh, him. He was in the Old Port aboard a naval ship, waiting for Montréal bagels.

Do you miss it?

What, lovey? Prince Charles? Montréal? Baking bagels?

Everything!

Sometimes. I miss la montagne, its beauty. Emma and Myer, of course, their kindness. You see, the Lewkowitz's were my first real friends in Montréal, that you never forget. That, you miss. Friends are a brukhe. A real blessing, lovey.

TEN

THE SKY IS DARK, bored through with stars like glittering holes, leading where? It surprises Willow how many she can see right in the center of the city. She still feels the glow from her afternoon with Noah, as she lets herself into her apartment.

Willow lets out a cry of joy, fear, surprise, as she sees her mother standing there, solid and smiling, her arms spread wide to take Willow into a soft, enveloping hug. Her mother holds her out, so she can take a longer look, and her gaze turns accusing. A blot of clouds across the sun.

Willow has grown used to these sudden mood shifts of her mother's, the fear and anger that is constant beneath the kind, sweet surface, flashes of temper that come without warning. Willow has her own angry sparks, a helpless rage. Living after the fact, she wonders if she herself could have survived what her mother did. Sometimes, she goes numb, lives for days in a dead fog, encompassing her like a heavy blanket. Ilya accused her of this, and she could do nothing to prevent it; in truth, she was more comfortable on her own, a loner, but for her marionettes.

"You're too thin," Jane accuses.

"Ma. Stop."

"And so tired looking." Jane's hands are on her hips now, her dark eyes blazing and blinking with that familiar combination of fear, anger, and concern. "What's wrong with you?"

"Did you come here to criticize me?"

Jane lets out a long sigh.

"Ma, I'm fine, actually."

Her mother's admonitory look softens.

"I'm here, lovey," she says. "Back."

"So I see," Willow replies. "Is everything okay, Ma?" She is alarmed to see her mother appear on her doorstep, without warning. And yet she is relieved to see her, too, standing there solid, living and breathing. Her mother is stouter and appears to have shrunk a little in height, but has good color in her face and her dark eyes are glowing. "I'm fine, lovey. Luc and Bête Noire, they have been taking good care of me."

At that moment, Luc emerges from his apartment and greets Willow, as Bête Noire bounds out. Willow buries her face in Bête Noire's creamy chest for a moment, looks up, thanks Luc, as he hands Willow Jane's coat and luggage. She has been lucky in her neighbors here, though she doesn't know any of them well. They seem kind, polite, without being intrusive.

"Come, Mama, let's go upstairs. You must be tired and hungry."

"Tired, yes. Hungry, no. Luc fed me well."

Willow laughs, a neighing sound that always makes her mother laugh too.

"You sound like a horse."

She takes her mother's plump arm in hers, grabs the suitcase, and leads the way up to her apartment on the second floor.

"I'm almost settled in. You'll be proud of me, I actually unpacked."

"Are you happy?"

Again the hard glitter in her eyes, the sadness, the accusation. All her life Willow has felt this responsibility to be *happy* after what her mother went through. There is so much she has to make up for, so much to stand in for, so many lost relatives she never knew, the old litany tires her, even thinking about it.

She opens the door and leads her mother inside, waiting for her reaction.

"Very nice," her mother says. "I like the touches, the molding, the large windows. Beautiful wood floors. A lucky girl, you are."

"Not exactly a girl, Ma, but lucky to get this place. It was my friend Manon's, but she's in Paris, all of her furniture stored with her parents in the country, so I had a clean slate."

Willow walks her mother into the living room, a rough-hewn stone fireplace set against a brick wall at its center.

"Stone and brick together, very nice," Jane says, and Willow beams. "A fireplace, this is the heart of a home."

"Light, warmth, not to mention survival around here." And

then Willow thinks of fire's double-edged nature, fire needs a special place—a fireplace. She is a little afraid of her own fire, not to mention other people's.

Willow has an eclectic mix of furniture in her living room, a brown velvet couch, a striped wool ottoman from Peru, old armchairs of cracked leather, all with curved tops and rounded edges. She sees her mother's eyes alight on the end tables, where Willow has proudly placed two of Jane's lamps. The bases are porcelain, the hourglass shape of a woman, and her mother has decorated the shades as wild hairdos, one curly and untamed, the other in a crown of braids.

"You see, Ma, they've gotten compliments already."

"From who?" her mother challenges.

Willow holds her breath, caught. "The movers, for starters."

"Well, I want you to show my lamps to that nice Luc, once I get settled."

The kitchen is small, but Willow is not much of a cook anyway. Low winter light fills the room on sunny afternoons, and her friend Manon told her, the vine-covered arbor over the veranda softens the harsh summer light. "It's cramped, but the light is beautiful in here," Willow says. "I try to keep it uncluttered," she adds, "to make it seem larger."

Willow leads her mother into the bedroom, which is a mix of patterns, objects, and textures. She has an old sleigh bed she found at a sale in the Québec countryside and covered with the patchwork quilt her mother made for her, a colorful afghan beneath for extra warmth. Pattern is everywhere, on the walls, drapes, rugs, even in the texture of the furniture and decorative objects. And colors:

soft greens, blues, cream, and gold. There's a Tibetan rug and a black French antique chair, and on her night table, another of her mother's lamps—this one with a purple-heartwood base shaped like a tree, and a lantern-shaped shade.

Jane smiles approvingly at the lamp. "A talent you have for this," she says admiringly. "If I tried, it would be a mish-mash mess."

Willow gives her mother a hug. "I just think of the place as a blank stage, I guess," she says. "A broad neutral background, and go from there. The tassels on the pillows, echo the gold in the chair," she says in her best British accent.

A dozen marionettes are at home here, their wooden limbs poised in suspended animation, on their iron stands. Mr. G. is pulled snugly over a bedpost. Willow takes him with her to the studio every day. Though he is the oldest, he is the least fragile of all her puppets, made simply from a sock. Two dozen more are boxed away, swaddled in tissue, in various closets.

"So Ma, come into the kitchen."

"Tea with lemon would be nice."

Jane settles at the kitchen table. Willow fixes tea, then gazes into her mother's eyes, as Jane warms her face in the curling steam.

"So, Ma, what brings you here now?"

"Worried thoughts."

"I'm fine. Really."

Jane cradles her tea. "I miss you."

"I miss you too, but why not call, make a plan? These surprises . . ."

"I didn't know what you'd say . . . if the time was right. And I don't know how much time there is."

Willow feels the barb, the pang of guilt.

"Are you okay, Ma? Is there a problem with your health?"

"Nothing new." She slips plump fingers around the edge of a biscuit and puts it on her plate.

"You have your whole life spread out before you," Jane says, speaking too fast. A shadow passes across her eyes.

"Some of it, anyway," Willow cracks.

"I came here to do a job." Jane munches a biscuit in ladylike nibbles, brushing crumbs from her ample bosom and lap.

"A *what?*"

"Delicious, what kind?"

"Ma, no offense, but you're eighty-two years old . . . "

"I know how old I am."

"It's not the time for new jobs . . . "

"Says who?"

"What *kind* of job?"

"Well, it's a job to tell my story. You know, for history."

For a moment, Willow cannot speak. She is unnerved that her mother would now decide to tell her story to strangers, a story Willow has been told only in bits and pieces, fragments that don't quite fit into a whole. And yet in truth, she has been afraid to hear this story, as much as she longs and needs to, settling up here in Montréal to sleuth it out on her own.

Willow glances at her mother's arm, sees the indelible blue tattoo. She closes her eyes, crosses her legs, tucking her right foot inside her left ankle, twisted and tight as a caduceus.

With horror, she realizes she cannot recite all the numbers of her mother's tattoo or remember their order, is even unsure on which arm the brand appears. Willow thinks of a lifetime of questions, empty spaces, the eerie feeling of not being able to ask questions when she was—still is—full to bursting with them.

And then there are all the contradictions of her mother's life after the war. She never took Pelletier, the name of her Québécois husband, yet changed her own name to one devoid of her roots and identity, a *goyish* name. She reinvented herself as Jane Ives, but kept her tattoo. Named her daughter after a tree, yet gave Willow a middle name in honor of her own mother, Hannah, murdered in the Holocaust.

Willow remembers her mother's explanation for everything, for moves, for silence, whenever Willow had a question or challenge, which often erupted, as if under pressure. The litany: "*I wanted that my child will live in a free country without any experience of what I had to suffer.*"

"This job—is it at one of the universities?" Willow blurts out suddenly, her voice cracking.

"A foundation."

"Which one?"

"Witness Foundation, they call it."

Willow lets out her neighing laugh, bitter and absurd to her own ears. The hurt she feels, not to be a part of this—her mother's story, her own—is like the unexpected raw pain of touching a black and blue mark.

A streak of rage passes across her mother's eyes. "What's

funny?" She leans across the table toward Willow. "Do you know this place?"

Dead eyes, face front. The old numbness again, when she feels too much, what she does not want to feel. "No, Ma, I don't. Hey, wait a minute . . . isn't that the organization Shoshy is working for? I've heard of it, but I don't know much about the place."

"Do you think I'm doing right?"

Without warning, Willow's eyes fill, burning, but she cannot cry. She shakes her head fast. As her mother has gotten older, Willow realizes everything is not in order. How could it be? What her mother went through cannot be suppressed anymore. Physically, her mother's experience during the war is taking its toll as well. When her mother had bursitis last year, they discovered her shoulder bone had been broken. Jane had no idea how. Then she remembered, told Sunny—who then told Willow—that a guard had struck her in the camps. Jane has trouble with her inner ear, spells of dizziness, a buzzing. Willow's eyes burn like they are on fire and she cradles her mother's plump arm in her own. If she could leach out her mother's pain and make it her own, she would.

"I got a letter," Jane says. "I'll show you."

Out of her purse, her mother draws the letter and Willow skims it quickly.

"You don't think, Ma, all this will disturb you?" Willow knows how people are in their perverse interest in the Holocaust, the danger of pulling things out of her mother and leaving them—and Jane—exposed.

"Already I am disturbed."

They sit for a long while, drinking their tea, separate yet

together. Soon Willow rises and fixes the pull-out couch in the living room for herself, puts fresh flannel sheets on her own bed for her mother.

"Welcome back to Montréal, Ma," she says. "If we drive each other nuts, I can sleep in my studio."

"Tomorrow I have to go into Witness and I want to walk up la montagne."

"Slow down, Ma. Walk up Mount Royal?"

"With you."

Willow draws in a deep breath.

"I want to know what it feels like to be on the mountain with you, lovey. Now."

"It's a big day you have planned, Ma. We should both get some sleep."

"Show me again where is your bathroom. Also I want to take a hot bath." Then she murmurs under her breath. "Here they know me. Lately, I want my usual, nothing new."

Willow leads her mother into the bathroom and draws her mother's bath very warm the way she likes it. While her mother is bathing, Willow collapses on her pull-out couch and draws Mr. G. snugly over her hand.

When Jane emerges from the bath, Willow sits on her own bed, her back bolstered against pillows, legs spread, her mother inside her legs. She sweeps her mother's lovely silver hair from her brow and Jane leans back against Willow, closing her eyes. They are both peaceful, quiet, connected for the moment.

❋ ❋ ❋

Memory Book
Fall 1982

Ma, what is that place? With the flowery decorations.

Jewish Town Hall, in Prague where I grew up. On the roof, see the small wooden clock tower? The steeple was green, and on one of the gables was a second clock. Turn a few pages. There you have the gable clock.

Why two clocks?

The hands of the roof clock circle clockwise, lovey; the hands of the gable clock, the opposite. Time, it moves forward and backward, at the same time.

Is that Hebrew on the gable clock?

Hebrew goes right to left. The hands of this clock circle counter-clockwise. Keep turning pages. See the old Jewish cemetery?

What does that inscription say, Ma?

Stary Zidovsky Hrbito. The House of Life. Twelve layers deep, slant-

ing this way and that, one on top of the other. This burial ground for Jews, it was the only one. One hundred thousand people buried there. We have relatives in that cemetery. And something else is buried down deep, precious. Safe, I pray. Go forward in the memory book, keep going. There.

What does that symbol on the gravestone mean?

Scissors. Izak Ivanova, did good for himself, a tailor. Very good, Izak and Ada.

So who are they, Ma?

"Your great-great-great-great grandparents, lovey. The last person buried in this cemetery was in 1789.

What are the grapes?

Luck. In our family, we will have luck, in the future.

ELEVEN

JANE WAKES UP SLOWLY and glances around her daughter's bedroom as snowplows roar and garbage trucks beep their way down Esplanade. Through the window, she sees the men, bundled against the cold early spring air, hanging onto the back of the truck, emptying the pails at house after house and hurling them back like frisbees, careless where they careen and land. She stretches in bed, yawns languorously as a cat, surprised by how well she has slept here. A deep and dreamless sleep that has left her refreshed, no early morning nightmares.

Jane gazes around Willow's cozy bedroom, surrounded by puppets, the day outside the window a mix of sun and clouds, the temperature uncertain. She bustles out of bed, wraps her fleece robe around her, belting it tight, and slides plump feet into matching fuzzy slippers.

In the kitchen, Jane fills the coffee pot with water, measures grounds from the sack in the freezer, and clicks on the pot, savoring the rich, nutty smell. She sets out mugs and plates, then pulls sesame seed bagels out of the freezer and pops them into the toaster, setting a block of cream cheese on the table.

Thief-stealthy, she tiptoes into the living room and peers in at Willow. Her daughter is asleep on the couch, a large lumpy pillow stuffed between her legs, one knee scrunched tight to her chest, arms flung outward like wings. She is breathing deeply, snoring a little, and Jane settles gently at her side, just listening to her breathe. How she always loved the sound of her daughter's sleep, that ratchety little snore, that smell of sleep-breath, a little milky, a bit fusty. It is hard to bring herself to wake Willow.

Gently, she places a hand on Willow's back and her daughter stirs and sighs just as she did as a child. Jane can't stop herself from humming the little Yiddish song her own mother had sung to her every morning, the song that she, in turn, sang for Willow to wake her up for school, as if the familiar ditty could close the gap of years. *Zing Faygele Zing.* Sing, Little Bird, Sing.

Willow liked to hear it in Yiddish and English, then Yiddish once again.

I remember when I was a child
My mother used to sing to me
You're an angel, beautiful as all the worlds
I will bring a little star to you
Sing little birdie, sing.

Willow groans, stretches, and rolls onto her back, opening her arms to hug her mother. Jane leans down and gathers Willow to her, as if she were a little girl again, and they stay that way for a minute or more.

"Like a baby, I slept!" Jane says.

"Me too. It's good to have you here, Ma."

A sliver of anxiety runs through Jane. "Oh, I almost forgot. I have my appointment at Witness this morning."

"What time, Ma?"

"Ten."

"I'll take you over."

"But you have to be at that theater, what do they call it?"

"Usine C."

"You shouldn't be late for your job."

"I make my own hours."

Jane whistles through her teeth. *How do you make hours,* she wonders. "We should dress first, then have breakfast."

"How about breakfast first, then get dressed? You know I'm no good without my coffee."

Jane laughs. "Come lovey," she says, and they settle together at the kitchen table.

After breakfast, Jane dresses carefully in a tweed suit, brown and amber shot through with gold threads. Beneath, she wears a cream-colored blouse, and stockings with seams up the back. Of course, she has to put on snow boots and her roomy wool coat with the full sleeves, large enough to accommodate the suit beneath. She carries her pumps in a huge tapestry satchel, which opens like a doctor's bag, along with a blank notebook and pen. Jane had thought she might write things down to help her remember, but so far the book remains blank. Maybe it is better, she decides, to just talk, see what comes out. The writing is too much for her.

In a minute, Willow is ready, in tight black cords, a black sweater, and a lined leather jacket.

"Will you be warm enough?"

"I have a hat and gloves," Willow says. "Don't worry about me, Ma."

Willow shepherds Jane to Witness, and Jane shoos her off to work, though they plan to meet later for lunch and, Jane insists, a walk on the mountain.

The center is part of something called "The Jewish Campus," a phrase that rings with possibility, importance, safety, Jane thinks. She takes in the block-long community of buildings, modern and glistening in polished white stone, sparkling glass, and steel. The Witness Foundation does not open until ten, so Jane lingers just outside with the other early birds, some, by the looks of them, waiting to return books to the Jewish Library. Not only is there a library in this campus, but also a Yiddish theater, a YMHA. Such riches.

The day is confused, a scuffling of sun and shadow, with high, soiled snow banks flanking the streets, their crusts loosening to blackened snowmelt. Warmer than yesterday, Jane thinks, spring thaw in the air. The crowd on Côte-Ste-Catherine thickens, as does the noise. The air feels thick with so much breathing and talking, a babel of horns, drivers shouting, *meshugene*, these Montréal drivers! A tightness starts in her chest. She doesn't know if she is doing right, yet forces herself to stay. At last the doors open.

In the marbled foyer, a uniformed security guard gently asks for Jane's tote and politely examines its contents. Jane steels herself against this invasion, straining to remember its purpose, struggling not to confuse it with so many other invasions with no purpose but degradation. As her heavy satchel plops down on the black conveyer belt and lumbers through the X-ray scanner, the guard asks her a few basic questions and Jane struggles to remain calm.

With her satchel in hand, she smoothes her coat, sweat pooling under her arms and at the back of her neck, and boards the elevator.

The offices of the Witness Foundation are carpeted in gold and have simple teak furniture. The hall and waiting area are quiet and peaceful. Behind the reception desk, Jane sees a familiar face—Shoshy—a fine young lady now, and the sight of this neighborhood girl is so comforting, she feels she might weep. Shoshy bounces out from behind the desk and greets Jane, kissing her on both cheeks.

"The French way, both sides," Jane says, beaming. "How grown up you are." She envelops the girl in a hug.

"You came!" Shoshy answers.

Jane does not know what to say.

"Can I get you a coffee or something?"

"Juice would be better."

Shoshy returns with a tall glass of orange juice and Jane sips delicately, waiting. On a mahogany side-table, she sees a stack of glossy brochures and lifts one to examine it. An insignia with Hebrew letters too small for her to decipher, shaped into a flame. Jane feels a sudden welling of nausea at the back of her throat, swallows, drinks more juice to tamp down the feeling.

"Mrs. Korenberg is ready to see you," Shoshy says, as a small, pert woman in an elegant silver suit and pearls greets Jane. Jane has no idea how old she is, her handsome features seem ageless. When Jane enters Mrs. Korenberg's small office and settles into a brocade armchair, she finds she has lost control of her hands and voice. Her very breath seems to stop short of full, short of empty, a weight in her blood. She wants to turn back, run away, but it is too late. The woman asks Jane to call her Natasha, but insists on calling Jane "Mrs. Ives," her voice neutral, neither warm and welcoming, nor cold. Its evenness unnerves Jane more than confrontation might.

"Welcome to Montréal," Natasha says, and Jane struggles to smile. They engage in small talk for a while, something Jane has never been good at. When Natasha tells her, they won't begin her interviews until the following week, Jane feels a relief so intense, it mimics joy.

"What I remember, I don't know." Jane says, her head nodding involuntarily, a tremor.

Natasha nods back slowly, looking directly at Jane in a way that makes Jane painfully self-conscious: What does she see with her probing eyes?

"Here I am," Jane says, absurdly and laughs.

"Well, you may find things come back to you as you talk," Natasha says.

"In what order? It may be a jumble."

Again that slow nod, then at last Natasha removes her eyes from Jane's. They chat a bit more, and finally, the initial meeting is over and Jane can leave, though Shoshy makes an appointment for her with her interviewers at Witness for the following Monday, ten sharp.

Jane is relieved to leave the building and get out into the air. A breeze is blowing, stripped of icy winter chill, a teasing promise of spring. At last Jane is able to take a full breath. Willow will meet her back at the apartment for lunch, and then she has promised Jane, they will walk up the mountain.

Jane returns to the apartment with the key Willow has given her and changes into a velour track suit. She feels a burst of energy and can't wait for her daughter to get back home, so they can set out again.

※ ※ ※

TWELVE

JANE AND WILLOW choose a winding trail on the mountain, which is still deep with pine-shadowed snow. It is late afternoon, just before twilight, Jane's favorite time, and she feels fueled with energy and relief to be outside in the fresh air. As it is a weekday, there are not many people about, and for this Jane is grateful. She feels Willow's slender arm loop through her own and her daughter takes her hand.

"So Ma, you haven't really told me much about your morning. How did it go?"

"Next week I really start."

"How is Shoshy?"

"She looks good."

They walk slowly along the muddy trail, snowmelt, mulchy leaves and earth pulpy beneath their feet. Jane's boots sink down into the earth and suck free with each step. Her bad shoulder aches a bit, but she has become accustomed to the pain, no more than she can handle. Every so often they rest, so Jane can catch her breath, which comes raggedly. She is warm in her winter layers, but beneath this damp heat, feels pure joy.

So much has changed in the city she called home after the war; she has changed, but this mountain remains rising up in the center of Montréal, a comforting constant.

Pearly clouds scud across the sky, a warmish wind sweeping them away to reveal a bracing clear sky. They amble along, walk without speaking, as the breeze lifts Jane's hair from her neck.

The pine trees still have shelves of green weighted down with white, the birches stretch up Y-shaped, their papery bark glinting in the last rays of sun. Jane hears a rustling further off, the snap of a branch, a bird, perhaps a rabbit.

"I hope it won't be too hard for you at Witness," Willow says, touching the small of her mother's solid back. "Too upsetting."

"I told you," Jane says, chuckling bitterly, "I'm already upset."

They zigzag in wide bends up the slope, finding their rhythm. Jane feels her strength increase as she makes her way up, fiber in her limbs, a heat in her blood. She bends now and then to pick up treasures, a small stone speckled with mica—which she slides into her coat pocket—a sodden pod, and a silver feather.

"You know, Ma, you never talked much to me."

Jane makes a dismissive noise with her tongue, but grows uneasy. How can she explain without hurting her daughter, that it is so much easier to talk to a stranger than to her own flesh and blood? She bridged an abyss, a chasm. How could she begin to show what was below? Willow was new life, as different from death as good from evil. Pure proof that she, Jane, was alive.

"Ma?"

"I did not want to burden you with more weight," she says softly. A load to sink in, as she herself almost sank. How could she pass down a terrible history to her beloved daughter, a history Willow never lived.

"But you want to talk to strangers." Willow stops, staring at her mother until Jane looks up at her.

"You know what they say?" Jane's voice is clotted with rage. "That nothing happened. An invention, they say, of the Jews! How much more do I have to live, who can say? I have to do this! I have to leave something behind. If not me, who will?"

"I know, Ma, I know. I think it's necessary, what you're doing, but . . . "

"Also, even if they say it did happen, for most people, the Holocaust is history. Dead. History doesn't matter to them."

Willow nods.

"Good," Jane says with finality, patting Willow's arm. "You understand."

"Well, not exactly, but . . . hey! I wanted to mention, this man came to see me."

Jane feels a panic start deep in her breast. She breathes slowly, trying not to show how startled she feels, the dread. "He did?"

"Bernard Orlofsky. Told me to call him Bern."

Jane breathes out in a long, relieved sigh. "Oh, Bern!"

"So who exactly is this Bern? You never mentioned him. He thought you would have."

"A crazy kibitzer. A terrible flirt. Not my type, lovey, not at all."

"Hmm, I see." They walk slowly arm in arm. Willow hears her mother's heavy breathing and slows her pace even more.

"His wife, Golda—boy, was she the jealous type!"

"Well, did she have something to be jealous *about?*"

"Maybe, but on my part, no. How did he look?"

"A bit frail, with a wicked cough. Want to rest, Ma?"

"Let's keep going. If I stop, well, I don't know what will happen. A heavy smoker, Bern."

"Still is. In fact, he was hospitalized at the Jewish recently."

"Oh, no. I'm so sorry." Jane stops to rest, wipes her sweating brow.

"But apparently he's okay. According to his daughter."

"You *do* get around."

"She has a boutique."

"Maybe she could outfit you, Willow. Comes in handy for a single gal."

Willow takes her mother's arm and they continue on the path. "Anyway, do you think about my father when we walk up here?"

Jane is taken aback by the question, doesn't know what to say.

"This was his place, no? Caretaker of the chalet. Tell me about him, Ma. He is such a blank to me, I can't even imagine him. You've said so little."

"Oh, don't let's talk about *him!*"

"What?"

"Can we save it for later? I'm getting a little tired."

As twilight draws in, the sky deepens, and the lacy outlines of shorn trees are netting against the sky. Ambling along, Jane watches their two shadows lengthen in the snow.

"Soon it will be dark," Willow says, as they listen to the hooting of an owl from far off. They pick up momentum, Jane breathing hard and steady, her heart flooded with memory. Another day here on this mountain, nearly forty years ago when she returned to Montréal to try again. A gift. At the summit, a surprise. From his pocket, he took out a small velvet box, midnight blue, the same color as this sky. Jane hadn't had a gift, a real gift, since she was a child in Prague and her parents were still alive to make each birthday special. He motioned for her to sit down on a rock. She pried the box apart, it sprung open. Inside was a gold *fleur de lys* locket on a chain.

Open it. Inside, look and see. . . .

A picture he'd put in, the two of them together, their cheeks touching, hands entwined, eyes on one another. Where was that locket now? She'd worn it for some time, until Willow was old enough to snap it open and look inside. Into the jewelry box it went, a bottom compartment. When Willow turned five, she wrote to him, but he crushed her heart with his answer, and she locked that bottom compartment of the jewelry box, the locket safe inside. It was over. The jewelry case was hidden in the crawl space behind a trapdoor in the ceiling of her bedroom closet.

"Ma, you okay?" Willow breaks into her reverie. "Look."

Snow whirls in thick flakes as they press on, a cold wind

whipping down from the mountaintop. Jane has no idea of the time, how long they have been walking, as darkness closes in on the day, the snow blue, the lengthening shadows of the trees, indigo.

"Like butterflies," Jane says, trying to catch a snowflake in her mouth. Thickening flurries cloud their vision until the trails, trees, the mountain itself appears as a world of white, sky blurring with land, not a soul in sight in any direction.

"Which way?" Jane asks.

She hears her daughter's intake of breath. "I don't know, Ma."

They walk for a while in one direction, try another trail, which leads to a dead-end of woods, snow sucking at their boots.

Willow breaks away from the trail into a hollow nearly hidden by snow-laden pines, bushwhacking through the woods, making as much noise as possible. A knife-like wind whips down from the peak, as Jane's throat aches. She is thinking of her locket, finding it, she is thinking of all she has found and lost and found again.

"Ma, we're lost," Willow says, her voice breaking.

"Lost you look," Jane says like a somnambulist, "lost you can still find."

"Not if we freeze to death," Willow cuts in. "C'mon!" She pulls her mother up a trail, any trail.

"In this city park, nothing can happen," Jane says, oddly calm. "There are people."

"Where?"

"Hell-o!" Willow calls out. "Anyone?" Her voice echoes back at them, as they slog through snow, Willow nearly falling into a drift. Jane drags her out, surprised by her sudden strength, slaps away the clinging snow, as a blowing scud smacks against her cheek. She shakes her head hard, catches her breath. Snow finds its way beneath her scarf, discovers the gap between boot and sock, gathers inside her sleeves.

"Are you wet, Ma? Cold?"

"Not too bad."

"It can't be far, the chalet, right? That chalet at the top?"

But which trail? Jane has no idea.

They move in one direction, then another, going nowhere, or where they don't know. The snow thickens into a blizzard. They walk and walk, achingly slow, Jane panting. She knows her daughter is in a panic . . . but not her, not yet. To die here, wouldn't be bad, but not Willow, not yet, she feels the fear enter her blood at last. They rest for a bit, waiting, for what, who?

Then Jane hears something behind them and Willow whips around. A scarlet shape in the white, black hair streaming from fur earflaps, head bent to the trail. The figure passes them in long, heavy strides without stopping.

"*Monsieur?*" Jane says, as Willow calls out, "Hey!" running after this person and tugging his sleeve.

He turns slowly.

Panting, Willow sputters, "*Nous sommes perdus. Parlez-vous anglais?*"

The man stops. Willow grabs his bulky shoulder and shakes it. "*Comprenez-vous? Il faut* . . . help! My mother . . ."

He looks down at them both, a middle-aged man with a weather-beaten face.

"You'll be safe in the chalet. It isn't far. Follow me."

The man has a tough, kindly face and they follow him, straining to keep pace with his wide-spaced deliberate gait, thick arms held wide from his sides. Every few minutes, he slows, turns, checks on them both, then carries on.

Jane concentrates on each step, her breath coming raggedly. Soon they pass the cross, its lights blazing into the night, one hundred feet high. Next the familiar monuments, explorers and kings, and the carving with words Jane reads without thinking: *La Sentinelle et Les Sans-Abris.*

"In a minute, we're there," she says to Willow, and then it appears, the chalet, built atop stone steps. The joy is back, despite the cold, the wet.

"Thank you," they both say to their guide, as he shepherds them to a wooden bench inside and disappears back into the cold.

A young caretaker appears from the back of the chalet and motions that he is closing for the night. He is short and wiry with a long black ponytail. Jane notices Willow eyeing him closely, as wind rattles the panes and makes a long wailing cry, almost human.

Jane looks around, sees the tourist paraphernalia—snack bar, water fountain, pay phone—as well as the old-world paintings, framed in wood, dramatizing the founding and history of Québec and North America by the French. The space is larger than Jane remembers, adorned with chandeliers.

Again the caretaker approaches, tells them in French that the chalet is closed, they have to leave. *Tout de suite.* Jane easily understands the clipped commands; the language is coming back to her.

The caretaker turns away to tighten the latches on the windows.

"Just give us a few minutes, please," Willow says. "My mother is very tired."

Jane watches Willow rummage in her pocket for coins. "Ma, I have a friend, Noah. I'll call him, he'll come get us."

The young caretaker shrugs, resigned, makes a face, half-smile, half-grimace. With sudden, almost martial movements, he unlocks a door off the main part of the chalet, a small, enclosed room, and sets up an electric heater. It rattles to life, the coils warming from ash to orange into crimson. A few minutes later, he brings them each a steaming cup of coffee in white Styrofoam cups. Mother and daughter peel a half-moon from the lid and sip slowly from the crescent, warming their faces in steam.

"*Merci beaucoup,*" Willow says gratefully. "Ma, wait in here and warm up."

Her daughter settles Jane in the warm storage room. Jane has no desire to leave this sacred summit, which holds so much of her past intact. Not sleeping, not dreaming, memory envelops her like a shawl.

With her mother settled for the moment, Willow goes back to the caretaker. It is so strange to be here in this chalet, where her father supposedly worked. She isn't sure what she feels, but has a need to know, finally, to know something true.

"Thanks again for your kindness," she says, her voice tentative.

"It is nothing." He pulls his hair out of the ponytail, shaking it free around his narrow shoulders.

"You know," Willow murmurs, "I think we may have a friend in common."

His dark eyes flash. "Yes?"

"Noah Issenman." For some reason, Willow can't look him in the eye and the longer and more directly he looks at her, the shyer she feels. Finally, she forces herself to glance for a moment into his olive-skinned face.

The caretaker smiles broadly. "Of course, Noah! I like him. He is funny. Together we make jokes and he makes me laugh, even when I am in a black mood. By the way, I'm Alain Chevalier."

"I know—I mean I'm Willow Ives. Nice to meet you."

They shake hands formally. There is an awkward moment, when Alain moves to return to his work.

"Oh, by the way," Willow starts, looking down at the floor. "Do you know much about the other caretakers? I mean, the one before you and the one before that one?" She knows she sounds absurd, but can't stop herself.

He laughs with an unexpected delight. "I hope that I do. My father was caretaker before me and his father before him—my grandfather, Pascal."

Willow feels her ears burn. "Pascal, your grandfather, was he a heavy smoker?" Her mother told her that her own father died of emphysema, that he was a heavy smoker, died before her birth.

Alain gives Willow a quizzical look, not entirely welcome or pleasant. "Excuse me?"

"Well, did he get sick from smoking too much?" She finds herself staring at him now, one extreme or the other with her, no in-between; the smooth social graces seemed to have passed her by.

Alain laughs again, but this time, Willow's chest clenches. "My grandfather Pascal, he is as healthy as you say, a horse. No, he never smoked and does not smoke still."

"He is alive." Willow's voice sounds flat, strange in her own ears.

"Much alive."

Willow glances toward the storage room where her mother is resting, then back at Alain. He looks impatient to get back to his duties.

"I'm sorry," Willow says, touching his shoulder as he turns to go, so unlike her usual way. "When your grandfather worked here, were there others? I mean other caretakers, other shifts?" She needs this to be so, but an age-old bubble has burst within her. *Her father up in heaven beaming down his love, the old ghost-father.*

"Of course there were other caretakers. My grandfather he did not work day and night."

Willow cannot stop herself. "Did you know a man called Roger Pelletier?"

"There is a plumber by that name."

"A plumber?"

"Yes, a young guy in his twenties. But others too. It is a common Québécois name. Pelletier, there are many. Now I must return to my work, you will excuse me, okay?"

"I'm sorry to keep you," Willow apologizes, her voice clipped. She sighs deeply, a shapeless doubt given form. She never quite believed in Roger Pelletier, the mythical caretaker of the chalet.

Her mother is right here, alive, and yet to challenge, even question this age-old history feels daunting. And perhaps, a thread of possibility, other caretakers, other shifts. . . .

After years of listening to her mother's shadowy outline of the caretaker, the vivid colors of her own childhood fantasies come back in a rush: her father an Egyptian king springing from ancient tombs, an explorer with special powers who lived and ruled beneath the sea, a trapeze artist in the circus who could actually fly, a tamer of lions and tigers and boars in the African jungle, himself part lion, part tiger, part boar. Later, as a cynical teenager, Willow wondered if her father was a ne'er-do-well who would never do well, a one-night stand or a short, passionate fling her mother wished to forget—a cad, if the word still had meaning—a man who wanted nothing to do with a daughter, any child in fact.

Turning abruptly, Willow goes to call Noah, while Alain continues his work, closing the chalet for the night. While Willow waits for Noah to rescue them, snow swirls outside as her mother's past—her own—melts into the boundless white.

❋ ❋ ❋

PART II
TELLING

The Witness Foundation
Testimony of Jana Ivanova, April 28, 2005

Thank you for this coffee; it warms me up. Always now I take my coffee with cream and sugar, a luxury. In Prague, Papa always gave me milk with a stain of coffee. Later, there was none. During the war, I worked with other Jewish women in the Politische Abteilung. I was a typist with very good German. These skills saved my life. One day, an SS man left a big mug filled with coffee on the steps of the building. The mug was shiny blue and the coffee rich with cream and sugar. This I remember.

It was winter, snowing, a cold that burned, wind like a knife. I had a plan: make myself the last one to leave the Registrar, so I can take this mug. I slipped the mug inside the sleeve of my dress, under my arm. The coffee was now milky brown ice! Nervous and excited, I went inside the barracks for women. This was Auschwitz, 1944, I think. My mother and father and my younger sister, Ada, were still alive. I was twenty-one and Ada fifteen. In a circle we sat, me, my sister, our friends

135

Rebecca Ruben and Esther Mendelson, as well as other women in our barrack, and we passed this blue mug from hand to hand. A long time, we kept passing, until the warmth of our hands melted the brown ice. Then we each dipped in a finger and tasted: sweet, creamy coffee. We dipped again and again and everybody had a little. No coffee will ever taste that good to me again.

Later, they brought us gray soup in metal cans. No bowls, not a spoon in sight. So we slurped the soup out of dirty palms. Until I took out my beautiful blue mug. Again we passed it from hand to hand, this time drinking soup.

You ask me about my life in Prague before the war. When I let myself remember, it is another time, another realm, and today I am a different person. We were a big family. I was the oldest, Papa's favorite, and Ada six years behind me. Then there were my three wild little brothers, Pavel, Josef, and Jan, the baby. We had a puppy, Samo. He was a stray Papa rescued from the street. A mix of I don't know what, but he wiggled when he walked. How we all loved Samo. He completed our family! A full house. We lived on Staromestske Namesti, right beside Melantrichova Passage, a narrow alley we walked through to Old Town Square. There were ghosts in that passage on dark nights, and I loved to tease my little brothers about them, when they were naughty. At street level was our candy shop, Ivanova's, the best in the city, the heart of our neighborhood. We lived right above it.

Our house was lively. We children played and fought. Often, I took care of my little brothers when my mother was busy working in the candy shop or practicing cello. How wild and rambunctious my brothers were! You know what was their favorite game? War. Papa made them little wooden soldiers and these soldiers were always fighting. They made up different countries and these lands were at war, the baby Jan on one side, sometimes the other. Why is it little boys always play at war?

My favorite times were with my father in his studio in the basement below the store. He was a sculptor and when I watched him at work, time passed in an instant. I can still see him looking at me, a cigarette glowing from his mouth, wanting to know what I thought of his work.

Later, we were forced out of our home and herded into Josefov, the Jewish quarter. Here, on the corner of Bilkova and Elisky Krasnohorske, all seven of us lived, along with my grandparents, aunts, uncles, and cousins.

Some juice? Yes, thank you very much. I need a little break. Maybe a short walk outside, some fresh air. Fifteen minutes and I'll be back.

You ask about our property . . . what happened. What year? 1938, I think. No, that's not right. 1939. We Jews were forced to register for emigration. Left and right, our property plundered, our civil rights robbed. Our books and magazines were banned, and we were excluded. Of course, we were terrified . . . but, you know, why does no one speak of the anger? Rage! Stronger than fear.

Late one night, I crept out of my house, the whole family asleep. My precious menorah I swaddled in old hankies and then covered in a thick towel. The towel I stuffed inside a pillowcase. Finally, I put the heavy, lumpy pillowcase into a canvas shopping bag. At the last minute, I found Mama's garden spade and hid it inside as well.

This menorah was my most precious gift from Papa. He sculpted it out of brass, just for me, a surprise on my thirteenth birthday. Each candleholder he molded after a member of our family; even Samo, our puppy held a candle.

Hanukkah was a precious holiday for our family, for all Jews. The miracle of light. I thought if I could hide that menorah, with all of us gleaming, waiting to hold a candle, maybe—somehow—we too could be saved.

Out of the house I crept with my heavy shopping bag, in the deepest part of the night. It was summertime, warm, the dark air soft. Terrified, I kept my head down. Behind me I heard footsteps. I reeled around. Beneath the streetlamp's glow, I saw a boy. I knew his face. He was a neighbor, younger than me by a few years, thirteen or so, and he was following me.

"Where are you going?" I whispered, a hiss. "Go home!"

He just stared at me. I wanted to shout at him.

I broke into a run, to lose him. I knew this boy from our candy shop. He came in once, twice a week. Most customers always ordered the same thing—chocolate cherries, butter mints, toffees—but this boy, something different for him every time. His plan was to try everything we carried in the sweetshop. But he never did.

I rushed to the Old Jewish Cemetery, tossed my pillowcase over the stone wall, then clambered up and over. I was a strong girl, limber. Behind me, two seconds later, there he was. The neighbor boy. "I told you, go home! Why can't you listen?" He lowered his head, but stood fast, amidst the gravestones.

So there we were—the two of us, alone together, in the only burial ground for Jews. No space! People buried one on top of the other, twelve layers deep.

In the graveyard was a beautiful linden tree in the far corner of Hrbitova and U Stareho. I knelt under the tree and dug madly, as if my life, my family's life depended on it. The earth was moist, cool. That neighbor boy joined me, kneeling in the dirt. He was a sturdy boy, tall for his age. Silently we worked. I used the garden spade, the neighbor boy dug with his bare hands. We felt the damp earth between our fingers, under our nails, cool and spongy beneath sodden knees. Soon we were up to our elbows in earth. How far did we dig? How deep? Four feet maybe? We laid the pillowcase inside the deep hollow. Quickly we filled in the hole, smoothing it the best we could.

We did not speak. But as we stood, brushing earth from our clothes, we looked at each other. A long look. Steady. He had beautiful eyes: a fine clear gray with long black lashes.

When we got to the wall, the boy clasped his hands in a sling. I stepped into his linked hands with my muddy boot and he hoisted me over the wall, then followed.

Without turning around, I ran all the way home, breathing hard.

What happens when you hide, bury something precious? Can it exist forever, hidden, intact? Or is it lost, gone for good, because no one finds it.

In 1942, the first train took us from Prague to Terezin, less than an hour's journey from our home. I was nineteen, my sister Ada thirteen, and sickly with asthma. Pavel was ten, Josef, eight, and little Jan, six-and-a-half. Terezin was the last time we were together, all seven, a family.

There was a second train, two years later, which took us to Poland. On this train, a soldier passed through the packed car and promised my brothers candy and toys. My little brothers and the other children were taken off the train.

For years and years, I expected to see my little brothers, Pavel, Josef, and Jan, just how I left them—young, wild, and strong. I never saw them die, never witnessed their murder. And so I could imagine them alive. Hidden in barns, running through forests. Even now, I am an old woman, eighty-two years old, and I dream of Pavel, Josef, and Jan, just how I left them. Healthy boys, with shining dark eyes, playing war.

THIRTEEN

THE FOLLOWING MORNING, Willow's bell rings. No one appears, just a balloon bouquet bobbing skyward in multicolored splendor, and the sight of these dozen balloons in their paint box colors buoys her spirits, however puzzling their arrival. She tugs the strings that hold the cluster, each balloon different—an elephant, a cloud, an airplane—feeling their taut pull upward. It is midmorning, the last day of April, and she has been savoring her coffee alone, watching the birds gather in a pond of melted snow.

Willow holds her balloon bouquet, fumbling with the small white card. Balloons wouldn't occur to her mother. Marie-France? Willow hasn't performed a hit play or done anything special at the theater. Sunny? Maybe they're for her mother. Sunny might do balloons.

Wherever I am, you appear
—Noah

Willow feels a rush, the same warmth penetrating her skin that she felt in the bookstore, sharing their finds.

One of the dozen balloons is scarlet like Pascal's in *The Red Balloon*, her favorite book as a child. She tugs it down, releasing the others to bob and float along the ceiling.

Inside the red balloon a small object settles near the tie; through the shiny translucence of plastic, Willow tries to make out what it is. From her desk drawer, she takes out a pin and punctures the balloon with a burst. Into her palm rolls an old brass compass the size of a quarter. She's always loved the look and feel of a compass, the fluid play of the needle, and this one feels good in her hand. It has heft.

Looking up, she springs back from the window. Down below in the street, Noah Issenman is gazing up at her. This midmorning time is more intimate than night and her favorite puppets stare at her wondering what she'll do. She's carted them back home from her studio, as she hoped to spend the day planning her October play. She has an idea, unsure where she will go with it. In her head, Ernestine, Lise, Trevor, Mr. G. and Alphonse are gossiping about her, at first softly, then in a roar, as she hears Noah's feet on the staircase, a rumbling thunder.

A knock on the door, gentle, insistent. Her favorite five burst into a cacophony of laughter, mocking, delighted.

She opens the door, hiding half-way behind it.

"You've heard of the telephone—it's this great new invention."

A tittering behind and around her. She feels herself begin to freeze up. Her features tighten, only her eyes betray her, shining with feeling.

"It's gorgeous out. Finally. I thought of you. Maybe we could walk, have you been along the Lachine Canal to the Atwater Market?"

Noah is talking too fast and she feels a stab of tenderness toward him, combined with age-old caution. His face is pale, eyes thick-lashed as a child's, heavy-lidded, while his hair nearly reaches his shoulders. He has on sweats and a jester's layers beneath that flapping black duster. His lanky body with its odd tortuous grace makes her imagine beneath the layers . . . is there any softness, perhaps at the waist? She hates this longing, wants to shed it like used skin.

Willow closes her hand around the compass, too personal a gift to respond to, while inside her apartment the balloons bob against the white ceiling, torn scraps of red littering the floor.

"I can't, today there's this . . . " Willow doesn't know what she is saying, just plunks a block of words between them.

He looks at her with tenderness and something else—could it be pity? "Can't there's this today," he says neutrally, and she laughs as he laughs, a moment of communion.

"Hey," he says softly. "Don't make too much of it."

"It's just that I'm here, trying to work and . . . " Now she is babbling and can't stop herself. "I have to keep my focus."

"Yes?" He peers in, smiles as he sees her marionettes.

"And my mother is staying with me."

"Oh." Noah glances around.

"She's not here now," Willow says, grabbing a light jacket. "I'm trying to figure out what to do for my fall show."

"A walk'll do you good. I always think better in motion. We'll brainstorm."

His arm is around her in an enveloping sweep, and Willow thaws slowly within its warmth.

They head down Esplanade, their sides brushing, the day warm, gauzy sun filtering in and out of the clouds.

"Why a compass?" Willow asks, looking at him, then away.

He takes her hand in his. "I know you."

"Excuse me?" The sun hides behind clouds, the light turns silver. "Don't be so sure of yourself."

He lets loose a laugh. "Trust me, I'm not."

She is anxious suddenly about her mother, how she'll feel after her session at the Witness Foundation, what she'll want to do. Willow had promised to meet her mother there. "I don't have much time," she says, remembering her mother might want to visit an old friend after her appointment at the foundation.

"Time for a walk," he says, "a bite of lunch maybe. We'll bat around ideas."

They break into a clip, the sun warm on their faces. Noah opens his coat, then peels it off, stuffing it into his knapsack. Willow unbuttons her jacket, letting it flap free in the early spring breeze.

Without warning, Willow blurts out, "My mother is at that Witness place, you know it?" The words just walk out of her mouth, unbidden.

"Sure I do." The light goes out of his eyes, the glint that

promised a joke, that made the world a place where nothing existed that didn't have a lighter side.

"Well, they contacted her in New Jersey. That's why she's here now, supposedly. Probably, she couldn't bear to be away from me for long, we're joined at the hip, you know?"

He chuckles uneasily. "It's a solid organization. I know someone who gave his testimony there. This guy's a bit difficult, defiant, but the most loving person I know. He's the one who runs Ha'makom, the Jewish Center."

"Yeah," Willow glances at Noah, "you mentioned it."

"I'll take you there one day."

"You know, you're talking way too fast."

He holds up his hands. "I do that."

As they cross Sherbrooke and head down toward the Lachine Canal, Willow goes on, "Like I said, my mother is giving her *testimony*." She lets out a spurt of trapped air. "What a word. I mean, I'm in awe of her. I doubt I could have survived what she did, but living after the fact is hell." It's a relief to talk freely, somehow, she senses a kindred spirit.

He looks at her without speaking.

"I mean my mother is a wonderful, warm person; she has this fierceness about living." Exhilarating, a bit scary too, she thinks to herself. "But she also has these sudden rages—they come out of nowhere—and yet not, these crying jags. Who wouldn't? Crazy stuff, I'm telling you."

She looks up as the sun passes for a moment behind clouds, turning the sky to steel. "Growing up, if I scraped my knee, didn't finish my potatoes, went off somewhere without telling her, the fear and fury, I'm telling you, a force of nature."

Her way of loving me. Willow runs a hand through her thick waves and remembers her mother's strong fingers brushing her hair hard till it rippled and shone over her shoulders or gathering it into so high and tight a ponytail that her scalp ached. Such fierce love in her mother's hands.

They walk for a while in silence.

"She almost becomes . . . someone else," she goes on, half to Noah, half to herself. *Beyond herself.*

Willow thinks of the warning signs she buffeted as a child, the two of them alone together in their heated intimacy, two against the world, her mother's hectic color, livid blotches on each cheek, a tautening of her voice. The terror of stillness in that moment—her mother's lips parting, flash in her dark eyes, the trembling that passed through her.

Once when her mother was in a rage, Willow told her that she hated her and ran away. She was only five. The second time she left home to flee the anger she was thirteen.

Her mother's terrifying commands: *Stand still. Don't move.*

Willow remembers how the blood rushed and dropped to her feet, her rag-doll collapse, the sharp tug, every cell in her scalp on fire. Terrifying to upset her mother, to make her scared, to make her mother suffer after everything she had lost, after everything she had already been through. Willow became like one of her own marionettes before life was breathed into them, before the gift of speech, movement. Frightening how her own lips barely moved, only twitched and fluttered. Her mother there and not there. Nowhere, everywhere.

Why couldn't she speak? Why couldn't she move?

"You okay?" Noah asks, touching her shoulder.

Willow sees the canal, sun sparkling off the water, the trees leafing out and beginning to flower. They walk arm in arm and Willow feels she is both with Noah and alone; she cannot stop thinking, remembering.

"Often the terrors came after her bouts of anger," she goes on, and he listens, his hand taking hers, their arms still entwined, just as she walks with her mother.

And Willow remembers bad nights, a different side of her mother, a secret between them. Willow awakes with a start to her mother's cries, goes to her, holds her like a baby and whispers, *Mama, I'm here. Everything's going to be all right.*

Sometimes, her mother smiled in her sleep, the strain melting from her face with the stroke of Willow's hand. She passed from terror into another dream, one that she would not remember well enough to tell Willow. Other times, Willow climbed into bed and curled inside her mother's stout legs and arms, as her mother spooned her body around Willow and they slept, holding each other until daylight.

Willow and Noah walk without stopping, the path nearly empty. For so long Willow has felt a numbness, a cold dead fog enveloping her like a sodden blanket, apart from the life swirling around her—except with her puppets. She has had to be so careful. Terrible things have happened to her mother, so terrible her mother didn't want her to know about them.

"She wouldn't let me go on class outings, field trips, even though she taught in the same school! Afraid there would be a bus crash or something. I couldn't go into the next room without her shouting, 'Be careful!'"

Noah smiles, rueful.

"And this unbearable pressure to be happy, do you know what it's like to have to be *happy?*"

He shakes his head. "Enough to make me miserable."

This, Willow thinks, is the greatest weight of all. "You know, everyone in her family died, the only place to hold a reunion is Death."

"I'm sorry," he says softly. "It must be terribly hard for you."

"For me?"

"Yes, for you. And of course for her—that goes without saying."

Willow kicks stones along the path, watches a mother going the opposite direction pushing a stroller, her baby swaddled in pale blue blankets. "I'm thinking why give her testimony *now?* And yet I get it. Pretty simple, right?

The tears pour out of her, hot, stinging, and he sits her down on a flat rock by the water.

"I'm sorry," he says. "It's going to be okay."

"Okay? Who do you think you're talking to? A kid who scraped her knee?" She thinks of her mother's rage, which sometimes enters Willow's own veins and rises like lava within her.

Noah holds his hands up, palms out. "I'll just shut up."

They watch a snowy rabbit hop from behind a patch of trees, stand frozen for a moment, then disappear into the park.

"I haven't been able to talk about this stuff with anyone, but I feel . . . "

"What?" He strokes her face, then rubs her cheek with his. She closes her eyes.

"What?" he says again. "Say it."

Her eyes fly open. "That you can take it."

He laughs softly, low in his throat. "That's the most flattering thing anyone's said to me all day, all week, in fact." The sun shines full on them, hot on their faces, the back of their necks. "I think you're right," he says.

"I know almost nothing about you," Willow says. "Your family and stuff."

"My own parents, they're from here, but I lost them young. My mom died of breast cancer when I was eleven, and then my dad, he had a heart attack while we were walking on the street together. I was thirteen years old."

They walk again, quietly.

Then Willow asks, "So who took care of you?"

"I went to boarding school in England," Noah says, "then I was on my own."

The long canal and the light sparkling on the water remind Willow of the Delaware-Raritan, though here the dense woods are lacking, the wildlife mostly hidden.

"What about your father?" Noah asks. "You don't speak of him."

"He died before I was born," Willow says mechanically.

"Was he an American?"

"No, I told you. Remember? He was Québécois. Caretaker of the chalet, supposedly . . . "

"What?"

"I'm not so sure, now. I spoke to your pal on the mountain, Alain is it? Apparently his family has been caretaking that chalet through the generations."

"Oh yeah?"

"Shit, I don't know." Her mother's words come to her all at once: *don't let's talk about it.*

"Roger Pelletier," she says randomly after an awkward pause. "That was supposedly my father's name."

"Good solid Québécois name, for sure."

How strange the name sounds in her own ears, disconnected and unreal as her phantom father.

"When I was a little girl, I saw fathers everywhere. At school, in the park, at the community pool. My friend Charlotte's father, weird how well I remember *him*. He had these big pale arms, freckles all over, blue eyes he didn't take off his little girl. At the park, I used to watch them together, how he hoisted her into a tree. She rode his shoulders, licked ice cream that dripped down into his red hair. He used to tell her, 'Charly, it's dripping, let me fix it' and licked all around, making it smooth, before he passed the cone back up to her. At the pool, he threw her up and she exploded in this geyser of water."

Noah listens, waiting.

"At five, he let her jump off the high-dive. My little friend Charly, who couldn't even doggie-paddle. Having a Dad makes you fearless, I guess. He was right there, waiting below."

Willow looks at Noah and he strokes her face.

"You can't miss what you never had, right?" she says.

"I don't know about that."

Willow doesn't know what it is about Noah, but he turns her usual reticent self into a chatterbox.

"Let's head over to the Atwater Market," he suggests. "You can help me choose flowers for my windowboxes, and we can get some lunch there, maybe eat outside."

They stroll the market, savoring the jewel-like colors of fruits and flowers overflowing their bins, the smells of cheeses and chocolates, smoked sausage and freshly baked bread. Noah peruses the flower stalls, decides to return later, since they have no car to lug the pots back to his place. There is a densely packed crowd in the market, the stalls bustling. They line up at a small café and order take-out lunches of fresh bread, cheese, salad, grapes, pastries, and then wait at the liquor store for wine. After lingering and browsing the market for a half-hour, they head out to the canal for a picnic.

A breeze has picked up off the water, but it is a warm, moist wind, spring finally in the air. Noah spreads his black duster on the grass and they sit down, as Willow opens a bottle of merlot, filling their plastic glasses to the brim. Enjoying the mild air, they share bread and cheese, munching on red and green grapes.

"I can't stay," Willow says abruptly, her eyes darting this way, then that. "I'm picking up my mom at the Witness Foundation."

Noah nods, offering her a turnover stuffed with raspberry jam. "You said before she had some plans . . . "

"I'm worried about what they're pulling out of her, you know?"

Noah listens, watchful.

Willow takes a deep, painful breath. "My mom, she's strong, yet fragile." She sips her wine. "It's just been strange for so long, not being able to ask questions when I've been bursting with them."

"Maybe," Noah says carefully, "she's doing this for you."

Willow sighs. "As my mother says, 'Don't let's talk about it.'"

"Your play—you wanted to brainstorm ideas."

"Let's do it another day. I need to talk this out with . . . " She stops herself.

"Yeah, I bet your Frankensteins have their own ideas."

"Always do."

They sit, finishing their lunch, then head for the foundation. Before they part, he gathers her into him, and Willow feels as if she is recharging her battery through Noah's embrace.

❧ ❧ ❧

The Witness Foundation
Testimony of Jana Ivanova, April 29, 2005

Today I bring in something to show you that I saved. You see, it is a little autograph book, a gift for my twenty-first birthday from my friends Rebecca Ruben and Esther Mendelson, who worked with me in the Registrar in Auschwitz. Please! I'll hold it, because the paper is fragile. I keep the book in plastic. Do you know how many times I have taped it back together? Look how beautiful, delicate. A heart shape now, but when you open it, a flower. This color I call "love red." Very dear, paper, even a pen to write with . . . but Rebecca and Esther were able to get both at the Registrar where we all worked as typists. A surprise for my birthday.

I'll open it so you can see. So tiny, messages in three languages: Czech, English, and French. Listen. I'll translate and read them to you.

"To dear Jana—You have a big heart. Keep it beating strong on your

birthday." —Rebecca Ruben. "Hope, freedom, these are my wishes for your birthday." —Esther Mendelson. And the French: "We're blessed with your friendship when all we have is friendship."

I'll refold the little book now and put it away. So precious to me after so much time.

You ask me about the DP camp after the war. I met a young man, actually I found him or he found me. One day, he gave me a loaf of bread. The feel of it, heavy and light, its smell! Fresh bread, can you understand, I had not eaten this for years. He tore off a small piece for me, then dipped it in milk. "Jana," he said. "Jana, eat." He had to open my mouth for me. And he talked and talked. We knew each other, you see, he recognized me. This was the same neighbor boy who helped me bury my family menorah, the one who lived near me in Prague, the boy who bought a different candy each time he visited our sweetshop. There he was. His words filled me up, warmed my soul. What he said, I barely knew. And then another day.

That day, the first day we found each other, this young man combed my hair. Gently, he worked his comb through my long, tangled hair till it fell smooth. To have a comb! Still, I can see it—wood, with thick, widely-spaced teeth. I remember the feel of it pulling through my hair, tugging my scalp. This man pulled the wooden comb out of his tattered pocket like a magician!

In his touch was forgiveness.

Forgiveness for what?

Living.

When everyone I loved, ever loved, was dead. How could I survive?

Why?

My daughter, I need to talk to her. Yet, I don't want to make more weight. To talk or not, this is a tightrope walk for me, and my balance is no good.

Most of my life, I've hidden to survive, hiding natural as breath. Yet hiding bends you into funny shapes. Cripples. Hiding, I could only crawl. Never run, not even walk. Hiding made me numb to life, so death was less—less what? Terrible? Permanent? Less fearful of death, I was less alive.

Hiding, I could walk over my own grave.

Still alive!

Free?

Why?

Oh, goodness. My daughter, she is waiting for me outside. I am late! I must stop now. Later, I will go on. I must go to my daughter, to Willow.

FOURTEEN

OUTSIDE THE WITNESS FOUNDATION, Willow waits for her mother. The day is warm with a gentle breeze, drenched in spring sunlight. Jane is fifteen minutes late and Willow is worried.

As she waits, Willow flips through *The Gazette*. In the obits, she reads that Bernard Orlofsky passed away in his sleep at the Jewish General Hospital. She is surprised at the sudden pain she feels, the odd sense of loss. Now she will never know for sure who he was, what he meant to her mother, unless her mother opens up herself.

Waiting, Willow daydreams, back in the same city where her mother made her own home after the war. Her mother walked these same streets, heard the same colorful tangle of languages that Willow hears now. What was it like for her? She was young, just twenty-four years old, not much more than half of Willow's age now but had lived through the horrors of the war and had lost everyone and everything, including her youth. Willow wonders what her own life would have been like, their life, if her father had lived. The yearning for a father has been with her for so long it has become like an ache she barely notices because it is always there. Being here, building a life of her own where her mother lived, feels like a circle going around and coming round.

All at once she spots her mother leaving the building. "Ma!"

Her mother gathers her into a crushing hug; how warm she feels, how plush.

When Willow lifts her head, she can see her mother's eyes are wet, red.

"Mama, you okay?"

"A movie of my life! Once, no one wanted to hear my story, now they preserve me for posterity. Do you think anyone will watch it?"

"Oh, Ma, I've always wanted to hear your story. Even though I knew it would be hard, I . . . I have so many questions. Can we talk?" Willow longs to ask her mother about her father again, to tell her what she discovered on the mountaintop at the chalet. She wants to find out more about Bern Orlofsky, details, not headlines. "My father," she starts, "I talked to the caretaker at the chalet, Ma, remember when we hiked up there? Apparently, his father and grandfather . . . "

"I'm tired, lovey, all talked out."

Something within Willow collapses. She is alone. For a moment, a terrible flare of anger heats up—squeezing at her temples—which she tamps down hard.

"Do you want to go home and rest?"

"Nah, I want to walk. I feel a little dizzy, this fresh air will clear my head."

She wonders if she should tell her mother about Bern's death, but the time is not right. They make their way to the park along Westbury and pause there, watching the children play on the swings and seesaw, running wild, throwing their winter layers on benches or into their mothers' laps.

"This I remember," her mother says. "How spring, you feel it will never come, but then it does. And everyone rejoices!"

"Yes."

"You don't have to fight—you can let the air out of your chest."

Willow brushes off an empty bench. "Let's sit, Ma."

"The sun, I want to feel it on my face."

Willow watches her mother collapse on the bench, sighing with pleasure, plump hands clasped in her lap. She opens the buttons on her coat with stiff fingers and lets it fall loose on either side of her solid body. Willow settles in beside her mother, feeling the warmth of her hip. Eyes closed, both raise their faces to the sun, soaking in its warmth and light. For a few moments they don't speak. There is no need.

All at once, the bench shakes, breaking the spell. A little boy with long hair and *peyes* scurries under the bench for a lost ball, his mother almost loses her hat as she drags him out by the coat collar, scolding him in Yiddish.

"To hear Yiddish on the street, what a comfort now," Jane says. "I felt the same when I first arrived in Montréal. My English was not so good then."

"How did you manage, Ma?"

"I took English lessons. On a bulletin board at McGill, I saw the pink sign. And you know who taught me."

She did not wait for Willow's answer.

"Christine Howe, Sunny's mother! Christine was a beauty, like Sunny, tall, slender, and elegant. Together we worked twice a week in the late afternoon at the university. I remember the little room. The language lab, they call it now. So white and clean. Outside the window was more white, snow shaped by the wind. A world of cold and white. After my lesson, we sometimes went out for a bite at Schwartz's. Always I ordered the same thing, smoked meat sandwich and coffee."

"You're making me hungry."

Jane laughs. "I am hungry, always hungry." She clears her throat raggedly. "After these talks at Witness, my stomach goes crazy. I feel a weight there, then a fluttering. A terrible nausea, a fierce hunger. I don't know if I should eat or throw up!"

Willow puts her arm around her mother's shoulder. "Let's go then, Schwartz's."

"A little fresh air first, lovey."

"Okay, Ma, but I'm still thinking about the taste—salt and spices, garlic and pepper. Hey, how come they don't call it pastrami in Montréal?"

Jane shrugs. "I have no clue. They say it's different . . . "

A gaggle of children and their mothers approach the bench. Willow gets up, Jane scrunches over to make room, then rises too. "We'll walk a little," she declares.

Arms linked, they stroll the perimeter of the park along with a red setter and his blond teenage owner, pants barely hitched up on slim hips, the smooth-muscled plane of her stomach in full view, a flash of red thong, as she passes.

Jane clucks her tongue, as Willow spots a stately Great Dane, nearly taller and stronger than his slight owner.

"Maybe I should get a dog," Jane murmurs and Willow laughs, delighted by the idea, however crazy and impractical.

"Ma, tell me about Christine. What was she like when she was young?"

"Oh, she had a beautiful voice, clear and strong, an American girl from Kingston, New Jersey. Always she told me stories about her hometown, showed me pictures. And I too dreamed of living in that town of kings! Slowly, step-by-step Christine led me in my lessons. Diction, reading, grammar, everything I needed to take up teaching again—as I had taught in the DP camp in Europe." Jane sighs deeply.

"Christine made me stand in front of a mirror and showed me where to place my tongue. For an r sound, curling behind the roof of the mouth. Then she had me try. I practiced and practiced. Some days, words flew off my tongue. Others, I was hopeless and took refuge in Yiddish."

"It was Christine who got you the job at Cedarpark, right Ma?" Willow knows this part of her mother's story, but hopes to keep her talking.

"Christine's mother was the principal of Cedarpark School. Christine wrote her about me and I got a job teaching kindergarten. Always, I loved the little ones, just starting school. So many memories come back in a rush!"

Willow imagines into her mother's early life in Montréal. She's glad to be here, finally, in the place where her mother made a new start. Why has it taken Willow so long to get here?

"Secretly," Jane goes on, "you know what I did? I bought records of American and English actresses doing Shakespeare or I went to see films."

"Who were your favorites, Ma?"

"Bette Davis. I saw every one of her movies. And you know what? I mimicked her diction, her tone. The words she punched out, as if under pressure. She had a way of speaking, Willow, no one could meddle with."

Willow smiles. "I love her too; she made people stop and take notice."

They pass the swings and Jane breaks free of Willow's arm and settles into the creaky wooden seat, her ample bottom a tight squeeze, her hands holding the chains. The children and their mothers glance at her, giggle and smile, then look away, absorbed in their own fun.

"Push me, lovey. Push!"

Willow stands behind her mother, raises her slim, strong hands and pushes. Her mother is so solid, heavy, that it takes work to get her moving. At first, it is just a gentle rocking back and forth, but soon she is arcing high into the air and careening back, stretching her plump legs out like a child, pumping to go higher and higher.

"Ma, you're a wild one!"

"Why not?"

Jane swings and swings until the sun passes behind clouds and a breeze picks up in the trees.

Willow lets her slow down and helps her mother out when the swing has nearly stopped.

"Oh lovey," Jane says, catching her breath. "I almost forgot to tell you, but this talk of Christine reminds me. Sunny called, she misses me. She wants to visit."

Willow feels a weight lift, a relief she doesn't quite understand. "That's great, Ma. You can both come to my puppet show, you know, the one my workshop is doing."

"We'll be there with bells on."

"You two can stay in the apartment, I have plenty of room at my studio."

"Can't we girls all squeeze into your apartment?" Jane asks.

"We'll see, Ma."

"You go about your business, Willow. Sunny and I will look after each other."

Willow thinks of Noah, longing for some time alone with him. It has been so long since she has connected with a man.

"Anyway," her mother goes on, as if reading her thoughts, "I need time to think. Also, I want to look up some old friends. See if they are still alive! Sunny can join me for moral support."

"Ma, I've got a bit of sad news. . . ."

"What?"

"Bern Orlofsky passed away."

"Oh, no."

"I'm so sorry, but I thought I should tell you." Willow takes her mother's hand in hers. "Was he very important to you?"

They head slowly out of the park, the day cooler now and windy, with a pearl-gray sky, sun peeking in and out of the clouds.

"He was part of my old Montréal life."

"Yes?"

"The butterflies are gone. I'm hungry now."

"Good, Ma. Come." Willow imagines filling her mother with hot, salty soup and an overstuffed smoked meat sandwich, *babka* for dessert. Maybe with her stomach full, she will have more to say. "I have a little news of my own."

"What? Don't be so mysterious."

"I have a man in my life." She feels she is giving her mother a gift, all wrapped up in fancy paper and ribbon.

Jane claps her hands together. "*Mazel tov!* I want to hear all about him."

"You've already met him, Ma. He came to rescue us on the mountain. Noah." Willow leads her mother out of the park and they head off for a feast at Schwartz's Deli, as Willow girds herself for her mother's loving inquisition.

※ ※ ※

The Witness Foundation
Testimony of Jana Ivanova, May 31, 2005

A few weeks it's been, no? I needed a break from talk. I am spending time with my daughter and living life. My friend Sunny is visiting me, her mother taught me English at McGill, so many years ago. Now she is gone, but I have Sunny.

I remember, I was telling you about the Bergen-Belsen DP camp after the war. My mind is crowded with pictures. Among the unburied dead in Belsen. Thousands hovering in that in-between place, not life, not death, not here, not there. Stacked like cords of wood, or strewn about, broken and twisted logs.

You are free! Captain Derrick Syngton of the British Army called out. You are free! The loudspeakers blared to the sick, to the dead, to the dying—and to me.

Others gathered in the temporary kitchen near the old barracks. From my bed, I would not move, could not. Could not speak, could

*barely blink. The others were so determined! To help themselves and
each other. Even my friend Esther Mendelson who was still alive, Esther
who had given me the heart-shaped autograph book for my twenty-first
birthday, who had survived along with me, at the same cost. Esther was
among them, the determined ones. Determined to clean up the camp,
to improvise a bath in the primitive pool, to take their first walk outside
the barbed wire fence, to do forgotten chores, laundering, sewing. But
I could do nothing. How can I describe to you what it feels like to have
nothing left inside? To become hollow.*

*Other survivors, women, bathed me. My hands were so weak, they
could not do my bidding. They tried, these women and my friend Esther,
to help me into a dress. My limbs were wooden.*

*Then they were carrying me. Was I napping, they must have
wondered, or asleep forever? I ended up at the Rundhaus, the former
German headquarters, converted into a hospital. The place was crowded
with hundreds like me. Thousands more died here.*

*For months, I could not live, would not die. Not here, nor there.
That same man I told you about was with me. The one I knew in Prague
as a boy, our neighbor who helped me bury the menorah on that dark
night in the Old Jewish Cemetery. I was all alone, except for him. One
day when I was too weak to dress, to eat, even to speak, he said to me,
'Jana, now you fear life as you once feared death. You are more afraid
of life than of death.'*

He spoke the truth. And with this truth, he saved my life.

*Yes, we built a life in Belsen, but it was temporary. We were all waiting,
expectant, desperate to get out of Germany. Everything we did, thought,
created was for elsewhere in the future: a new place, a fresh start, a*

different life. The trade school, the machine shop, the fisherman's kibbutz, the young organized halutz groups, our schools. I taught at the Hebrew Folks School and the Secondary School, preparing children to emigrate to Palestine. We made this place of death not a place of death alone.

In March of 1947, I left by train with a group from the DP camp including the man who saved my life. I was twenty-four years old. Masses of people, young and old, came to see us off. The train was leaving from the same ramp where just two years before the Nazi death trains unloaded thousands from Auschwitz and Buchenwald to be flung into the furnaces of Belsen.

We thought we were going to Palestine; we all sang Hatikvah.

But it was not to be. Not for us.

Near the Palestine shore, we were seized and brought back by force to Germany. When we returned and disembarked in rage and despair, the first thing we saw were thousands of survivors besieging the Hamburg dock in protest.

We did not have much longer to wait, thank God. In the spring of 1947, after two full years in the DP camp, Alan Rose, a Scottish-born Jew arranged for our admission to Montréal, where the man who saved my life had relatives.

In truth, my feelings about Canada were very mixed. I did not trust this country back then, did not believe in it as a sanctuary. For us. My Papa had tried to get us into Canada during the thirties when Hitler was in power, but the doors were firmly locked against us. Canada's reputation was so bad that in Auschwitz, we called the place where our valuables were stored Canada: a barred-off haven of riches, from which we were excluded.

But the tide changed. It often does, no? Even when it is too late. Canada finally opened its doors to Holocaust survivors. And then a new chapter began for me and the man who saved my life.

It is now time I stop. Soon, I will go on with my story.

FIFTEEN

THE AUDITORIUM at Usine C is nearly full and the puppeteers in Willow's workshop are set up and ready to perform, as she settles into the front row flanked by her mother and Noah, Marie-France beside him. Willow is sweating and shaky, more nervous than if she were doing her own show, perhaps because she feels responsible for everything, but at this point, it's out of her hands. Literally.

The curtain opens on a two-level set, ramps on either side of the stage linking them. Above, a stylized TV studio also suggests a brothel, with décor loosely inspired by art nouveau, rosy-red lighting, the walls painted gloss red. Below, on the lower deck is a dungeon, the lighting dark and menacing. Tall wooden cabinets contain "imprisoned" puppets and are arranged in a semi-circle. A backdrop of a yellow sun, blue sky, and green lawns and topiary adorns the TV studio, while a forest scene is the background behind the dungeon. As the full set is revealed, the audience breaks into applause.

Evilyn, the meteorologist, stands centre stage on the top deck, predicting and decreeing the weather as clear, fair and sunny, with blue skies and no wind or precipitation today, tomorrow, next week, next month, next year, *ad infinitum*. She has floor-length, black hair forming her cloak, a golden E emblazoned on her chest, black eyes with golden centers, her skin ghostly. Cadaver-thin and moving with an imperious jerky stiffness, Evilyn has taken over old media, new media, and controls the world's weather. She not only states the forecast from here to eternity as fair, these weather predictions and dictates are broadcast across her pale white body in black print, as if on a computer screen.

Storms of any kind are outlawed and imprisoned down below in the dungeon, as per Evilyn's orders. Each imprisoned puppet depicts a different storm, incarcerated in separate tall cabinets.

Meanwhile, the population of Provenance represented by five various citizen puppets—scattered on the ramps linking the top and lower decks—is becoming listless and depressed, losing all motivation to do anything, bored by the tedium of unvarying weather.

Ice is composed completely of pebbled acrylic glass, while Rain's body also functions as a continuous fountain. Wind is equipped with tiny electrical fans within her diaphanous costume, and Snow is huge, white, and mountain-shaped, her enormous skirt molded into drifts.

As Evilyn holds forth, the storm puppets plot schemes to defeat her and restore normalcy to Provenance. Wind frees the storms from their separate prisons, and they join forces with the citizen puppets to create a new type of storm—evoked with a light and sound show—which wipes out Evilyn.

Each storm then returns to its true nature and the country of Provenance once again enjoys all kinds of weather. The Doors classic song, "Riders on the Storm" rings out as the natural order is restored. *Riders on the storm. Riders on the storm. Into this house were born, Into this world were thrown* . . . .

The play runs without an interval. Of course there are mishaps, such as a tangling of Wind's strings, but Willow suspects that she and Noah are the only ones who notice them, the audience is so caught up in the story.

After the final curtain, Willow's mother embraces her.

"What a talent, you are!" she exclaims. "But I have questions."

"Okay, Ma. Come to the after-party."

Over sushi and saki at a downtown restaurant, Willow's mother barrages her with questions until Willow can't take it anymore. She introduces her mother to her students and lets them explain their inspiration and techniques in exhaustive detail. At around eleven, her mother is tired, and Willow runs her home. When she returns, the after-party has geared up into a wild affair, complete with the marionettes, friends, and family drinking and dancing. Noah embraces Willow, holding her close to his chest, whispering, "I knew you'd be great," as they celebrate into the blue dawn.

✻ ✻ ✻

The Witness Foundation
Jana Ivanova, June 12, 2005

So many questions without answers. You asked me about before the DP camp, what happened. Now I'll tell you.

They called us the Himmelfahrtskommando, young women like me who knew German. Now, no one hears a German word pass my lips; I choke on the sounds. But my bube on my mother's side was German, so I learned to speak and later to write the language. My Jewish school in Prague was wonderful—we even translated the Bible into German. Knowing German saved my life. I will say this again and again.

My little sister, Ada, was not so lucky. One night in winter, she choked on her own breath. We screamed for help, but her asthma got the better of her. My little sister, not yet sixteen, died in my arms.

Not long after in Auschwitz, marching, I saw my first cousins Eva and Tamar through a window. They were inside the Schonblock because they were sick, with feet so sore they could not walk. They told me they got good food there and didn't have to work. Eva, she urged me to come too, but I couldn't. I was always healthy. Not one of the Schonblock sick survived, not even Eva or Tamar.

Secretaries of death. Chosen. We were the Geheimnistraegerinen, bearers of secrets, Himmelfahrtskommando, the squad on its way to Heaven. How could they protect the secrets we knew? Only by killing us.

But this I must tell you. Some prisoners I was able to save, collaborating with my friends Rebecca Ruben and Esther Mendelson, who worked with me in the Registrar. You see, only prisoners who were sent with transports could be gassed. Those women who were classified as Gestapo or Kripo were returned to their blocks. We could not do it often, because if we were caught, we would have been killed. Once, we managed to report six women as Gestapo, instead of RSHA, and saved their lives.

Every night, I typed death certificates. The hour of death, the cause—we had a list of thirty-four diseases we could choose from—we chose the time. What evil power!

At 6:42 a.m. the Polish Jewish Prisoner X died of pneumonia. The documents were sealed with the signature of an SS physician.

I did a card for my beloved father—Herzschwäche, heart failure—and a card for my mother, tuberculosis. Phony accuracy. Of course the cause was always the same. Those medical words poured out of me like blood.

One night in dead of winter, 1945, a group of SS jangling keys rounded up two dozen of us girls. (I was an orphan by then, twenty-two years old, the only surviving member of my family.) Before a lamp-lit gate we stood—it looked like the entrance to a fairy-tale palace. The gate opened. A rancid sweet smell enveloped us in a shroud, clinging to our skin, wafting into our noses and mouths . . . I could not breathe. Rebecca fainted, Esther tried to lift her.

Another room, with large chimneys. Outside, trucks idled. A door opened. Inside were wooden shelves, neat rows, as if for books. Instead thousands and thousands of urns. A ladder led upward.

We lined up. A chain we made, from the ladder to the door where the trucks waited. The urns we passed from hand to hand. A terrible clattering! Bones. Naked bones. Esther was hysterical, laughter burst from her body like a scream. Rebecca fainted again, this time I tried to lift her. The SS men took down one urn after another. They were heavy and my arms ached, then burned. In the urn, I saw my father's face, his dark brown eyes like mine, and my hands shook. The urn fell from my hands, shattered, bathing me in shards of bone, flurries of ash.

I am here today. Now. Some days, I cannot believe it. Why?
Walking, this keeps me healthy, sane.

Walking—this is how we rested on the final death march in January, 1945. In snow, wind and cold, without water, food, or shoes. Rebecca, Esther and I developed a plan. We would run to the front of the column, and then wait, mark time, rest a little until the others had passed and we were at the back. This way, we could catch our breath and stay a little warm.

On the train, we were packed in together, could not move a leg or arm on that journey. No water or food. When we arrived at Belsen in the final transport of women from Auschwitz, we lay in snow, washed *in snow, and licked the mounds to quench unbearable thirst. We were Jews from many lands: Poland, Hungary, Germany, Czechoslovakia, Lithuania, and Greece.*

Running forward, falling back.

My pain grows. Only my daughter and my friend, Sunny, keep me from going crazy. How could I go on as Jana Ivanova? Not with those human bone chips stuck to my feet. Not with ashes coating my hands. Not with this stain on my heart.

SIXTEEN

WILLOW'S STUDENTS PLAY to sell-out performances, thanks to good reviews and publicity. Marie-France is happy, and after every performance, Willow parties with her class till late, surviving on drinks, long talks, and a few hours of restless sleep. Willow's mother is proud of her and for days speaks of nothing else, corralling everyone they encounter to come to the old jam factory to see *Riders on the Storm*.

Noah keeps out of sight, and Willow is surprised by her longing, as she strains not to think about him.

Then she collapses, deflated by the let-down that follows a show, a vacuum that can only be filled with work: parts for her favorite five, plans for new marionettes, voices, a fresh story to tell. For a week, Willow sleeps twelve hours a night, awakening into obsession.

She does not contact Noah, there is no need. Willow goes about her ordinary life like a sleepwalker, carries on an interior dialogue with him. In her free time, she wanders Montréal during the remains of a dark, damp, windy May, exploring Noah's haunts, his neighborhood, inhabiting Montréal through his being. She feels a fierce wave break over her head, which leaves her breathless and sputtering, a current of water pulling in the opposite direction of the surface, an undertow, the glittering pressure of something about to happen.

So submerged is she with Noah, Willow is barely aware of thinking of him, until like the glimmer of a dream remembered, it comes to her, *yes, I am thinking of him right now, Noah Issenman,* going under once again.

Nothing bothers her, not the incessant rain or spring darkness, not the shadow of her mother's life during the war, not the empty space of the father she never knew, the extended family she did not have. Not the fact that she has found out virtually *nothing* about her mysterious roots, save the niggling doubt surrounding Roger Pelletier. Though she longs to confront her mother, to let loose the artillery of questions she holds in under pressure, it feels like a violation of the lifelong pact between them.

And so her own puzzle-pieced life catapults her into sleuthing Noah out, an anticipation like sex, this heat of discovery: her obsession, in truth, detective work.

Finally, Noah calls her. Willow does not pick up the phone. She's missed him so much that now that he is there, she doesn't know what to do, how to be.

He calls twice more in the coming weeks, but Willow still

doesn't pick up. She knows she's acting weird, maybe crazy, child-like, but there it is, that doesn't change anything.

On a Thursday in June while her mother is off with Sunny on an excursion to Lake Memphremagog, the weather turns, becomes summer, and Willow trails Noah, her obsession an escape—from the new play that will not come, from her mother's life and past, from her own loneliness. She cannot stop herself. She is going over the edge.

Willow sets out and wanders near an apartment on St. Viateur, where she last caught sight of Noah. From there, she walks until she reaches the cobbled streets of Old Montréal, with their tall flowery streetlamps glowing in clusters of light, and strolls along the pier beside the river. Here is where Noah lives, in a loft near the Old Port.

Willow stands around until the light fades and she spots Noah heading down the street toward home. She feels the blood drain from her face, is about to bolt, when he calls out to her.

"Willow!" Noah catches up with her. She sees the green glare of his eyes as he holds her shoulder.

"What's up with you?" he asks, anger hovering beneath the simple question.

Willow shrugs, as his grip tightens.

"Hey, you're hurting me." For a moment, she's frightened. "Let me go."

"Let *you* go? Why're you following me around? What's up with this craziness?"

Willow doesn't know what to say, strains under his clenched grip.

"Well," he says, anger in his voice, "is this some kind of game?"

Willow is startled, yet sees what it must seem like to him. "No, no, it's not like that."

"I called you, what, three times? If you want me to get lost, just tell me, okay?" At last he lets go of her, but Willow still doesn't know what to say, can't find the words she needs.

"I don't get you, Willow, really," he goes on more softly now. "Ignoring me one minute, trailing me the next. You're scaring me a little. Should I be scared?"

"Maybe we should end things."

"*End* things?" His eyes expand and he bursts out laughing. "*End things!* Hey, there must be something going on between us that I don't know about."

Willow feels her ears burn.

"No. Don't. I'm not . . . " It's as if she's newly found language, has no idea how to use it. "I've been missing . . . " she starts, unable to look at him, ashamed of her fantasies, baroque and private. She feels like a teenager, the young girl she never had the chance to be.

His face turns gentle. He says, "You're with me all the time."

I believe that. Willow isn't sure if she says the words aloud or just thinks them to herself.

Noah leans his lanky frame against the wall of the building.

"Why haven't you . . . " he starts.

"I wanted you to come to me."

"But I did."

His being here—now—in a place other than her imagination

brings Willow up short. The grave look in his eyes, his intensity, unleavened by humor or irony is new, unexpected. Imagining their conversations and his replies, dreaming up encounters, she doesn't know what to say, how to be. It is so much easier with a ghost-lover than a real one. She imagines the scent of his skin.

He grips her arm again with a force that surprises her. "We should get away," he says.

"Away? Where?" *We?*

He pulls her into him with that signature shepherding sweep that makes her melt. "One of my favorite places in the world."

Willow smiles just with her eyes, her lips together. "Which is where?"

"Let me surprise you."

"Oh, I don't know." But she does suddenly, knows better than anything. She has to take this chance.

Early the next afternoon, Willow and Noah pack their belongings into the trunk of his acid green Plymouth convertible. Noah puts the top down, she climbs in, and they speed toward the airport. Willow's mother is staying the full week at a B&B with Sunny, and for once, Willow can let the air out of her chest.

She feels like a tumbler, just tumbling down block after block, their hips touching, wind whipping their hair. Summer sneaks up on you here, catches winter-jaded Montréalers unawares. Is it just weeks ago that they had that April blizzard? The day is hot with a dense, languid humidity.

"Two seasons," Noah says, as if reading her mind. Willow feels the newness of heat on her face. "Winter and summer. Spring, even fall, forget about it."

Marie-France had told Willow that you go from parkas, toques, and mittens straight to halters and short-shorts.

Driving through downtown, balconies and well-kept gardens are a riot of color, the black-speckled blaze of tiger lily, the fuchsia and creamy white of lady's slipper, the rosy begonia and purple lupine. Through the open window, Willow smells apple trees, their rose-tinged blossoms carpeting the road, white petals and cottony puffs blowing like summer snow.

"I feel like I've stepped from black and white into color," she says, glancing at Noah, who just smiles, meeting her gaze.

The sky is electric blue, the light turning churches gold and dappling downtown streets—a carnival atmosphere, Mardi Gras mania. At last, light, warmth. Summer.

Willow hears the brass of horns and sax, the beat of drums, the ribboning of flute. Bookstores, cafés, and shops are packed: business people, shoppers, students, mothers, children, all enjoying an afternoon break. Clowns with stars for eyes and tinsel hair brighten the outdoor markets. They speed by a street musician applying white-face in the reflection of a Porsche's side mirror.

Noah fits right in. Long khaki shorts, Hawaiian print shirt, red basketball sneakers, and a floppy canvas hat. Usually goofy takes the edge off sexy, but not with him, not for her.

On Highway 20, the car shuddering with speed, Willow thinks there is no better place to be with someone you want all to yourself than in a car; you can be alone together, moving, no one can get in there with you (if you don't want them to), and speeding along there is no way out. She doesn't want the ride to end.

Inside the airport, Willow savors the anonymous hum, the feeling of time out of time, where anything is possible. She and Noah show I.D. at the ticket counter and an attendant motions them through. Noah takes her hand and tugs her toward Security, then to the gate at Air Alliance. He presents their boarding passes, as Willow catches a glimpse of the sign: Îles-de-la-Madeleine.

Inside the plane, the flight attendant greets them as a couple and they settle into their seats just ahead of the wing. Willow huddles by the window, gazing at the view of sky, as the engine roars and they rise toward the clouds.

🦋 🦋 🦋

SEVENTEEN

June 2005
Îles-de-la-Madeleine

THEY TOUCH DOWN on an island Friday afternoon. Another world, Willow feels immediately different. The air is cool and moist, a fresh salt wind prickling her cheeks. As far as she can see, islands and sand blend, come apart and stretch out as if flung and molded by the sea. The islands are tiny masses—soft green valleys, golden dunes, and long wild beaches butting up against the startling red sandstone crags and cliffs.

"Where are we?" she asks. Looking out to sea, Willow has never seen so many blues, reflecting colors from the sky. At the harbor, lobster boats compete with luxury yachts and sailboats for space at the dock.

"Like I told you, my favorite place on earth," Noah says, linking her arm through his and enclosing her hand; Willow is a girl again, lost inside one of the stories she makes up to escape her self.

"*You might have brought me along,*" Ernestine whines. "*I never get to do the fun stuff!*"

"*Some places you go,*" intones Lise with her usual darkness, "*you can never turn back.*"

Noah glances at her, brows peaked.

Willow hears the voices of the others burbling just beneath the surface of her consciousness and strains to silence their voices.

"Sorry. I'm talking to myself—selves."

Noah chuckles, a deep and secret sound. "I do that."

He lets her move in and out of her imaginative world, entering it with her when she lets him. Willow wonders how long this will go on, Noah accepting her foibles instead of trying to change her. Then she snaps back. "So tell me, mystery man. Where are we *exactly?*"

"Île du Havre-aux-Maisons," Noah says, telling her a bit about this archipelago rising from the heart of the St. Lawrence, as they climb sandstone cliffs at the southern tip of the island, sea and gulf before them. Walking along a path that descends toward the sea, Noah guides Willow around washouts, places where the trail skirts dangerously close to the waves, the staleness of the flight melting away. Overhead, Willow spots the brilliant blue of a kingfisher, watches him plunge into the water for his next meal, crested feathers like a spiked haircut.

"We're in a different time zone," Noah says.

Sea water washes over Willow's sneakers, drenching them. "Ahead or behind?"

"Ahead, just one hour."

"That's all I need."

They clamber up the embankment and walk over dunes through salt-marsh, sun warm on their shoulders.

"How far away are we?" Willow asks. "From Montréal?"

"As far as you want to be." He smiles, full lips closed.

Together, they stroll through Île du Havre-aux-Maisons; the landscape stark, a mix of cedar-shingled and brightly painted houses scattered among winding roads.

"Look," Noah says, pointing out a cottage, nearly fuchsia with shell-pink shutters. "That sailor can see his home from the sea."

In town, they stop in at the Le Vieux Couvent, an old convent converted into a small hotel with sea view rooms at its corners. At the Chez Gaspard bar, they share a lunch of clams, French fries, and ice-cold ale. The waitress, bartender, the owner all greet Noah.

"So you're a regular."

"Whenever I need to get away."

He dips a fry in ketchup, nibbles in small bites. "Why did you trail me?" Noah stares at her, gold flecks in his eyes.

Willow feels her ears burn. "Because I wanted to know you." She breathes out audibly.

"Why not ask?" says Noah softly. "Why not just *get* to know me?" He puts his hand on her forearm for a moment and she feels electricity where he touches, warmth. "It's actually okay," he says.

"What?"

"To be watched by you."

Now she notices his pale skin warming.

"I mean, I wondered what I looked like through your eyes.

Me. My life. Made me more conscious, not sleepwalking through my days."

"You do that."

He laughs low, embarrassed. "Quite a bit."

"Not a bad thing."

As they finish their lunch, Noah says, "Ever gone sea kayaking?"

Willow shakes her head. "Oh yeah—but on a lake, at camp. I was about twelve."

"It's the best way to see this place. You look like an adventuress."

She can't stop the smile that spreads across her face.

After a stop at a dépanneur for provisions, Noah rents a double sea kayak and gives Willow a quick lesson on land and the old camp experience comes back to her. He shows her how to get in and out dry, wet, using her paddle behind her as a stabilizing bar; how to paddle with her whole body, not just her arms, so they won't cramp and tire. He demonstrates strokes, the scull, how to lean into a breaker, and what to do in case of a capsize.

She's impressed, but thinks *too much too soon*. The spray skirt alarms her; it seals water out, but also seals her *in*.

"What if I have to get out? Quick?"

"To escape from me you mean?"

She laughs, "Something like that."

Noah calmly demonstrates how to release the skirt, pulling the grab loop forward, then up. Of course, they have life-preservers—Noah also shows her the bailer, an old bleach bottle with its bottom cut off, the top sealed on—a Freon-charged horn, and emergency flares.

"You're a veteran," Willow says with relief. She feels safe, ready for anything.

By late afternoon, they set out on the sea, Willow at the bow, Noah the stern. They coast along, the only sound the rush of the paddle, wind, waves, and the subtle whisk of their kayak as it slices the water—so low, close to the sea and its motion, that Willow soon becomes a part of it.

As they glide along, Willow stows her paddle for awhile and leans back, gazing up at the sky, feathered with white clouds on pale blue as if painted by a brush. Now and again, red sandstone cliffs rise up, like nothing Willow has seen before, one the shape of a medieval castle, another a lion, a third, a woman's torso, cinnamon-colored crags and cliffs, each sculpted into their own shapes by the whims of the sea.

They float, bobbing, buffeted by wind and waves.

"Why do you write plays?" she asks.

"I've always told stories. My father made up a new one for me every night, I was always the hero, of course."

She cranes her neck, nods.

"The way my dad told them, all in different voices. Like a play. I love voices, they seem the key to a person. Yours is quite lovely. Soft, yet definite. You pronounce every syllable, you make a person lean close to hear."

Willow enjoys listening to him speak of her, to see herself through his eyes.

"So more about me. I wasn't too social as a kid, kept to myself. What was inside was always more interesting—or taking what was outside and making it new."

"Sometimes what's inside is more frightening."

"That's it."

Willow's ideas for her new show are just glimmering, trying to find a shape. "When I'm not working, I get a bit crazy."

They both stop paddling and drift.

"In the past I was really secretive about the inner workings of my shows. It really bugged the hell out of people."

They paddle again, in sync.

"I used to hang a curtain, a wall of canvas around my backstage elements to keep everything private."

"And now?"

"I'm changing, becoming part of the magic on stage. Being seen, creating the characters. It adds something I can't quite put into words."

Willow's arms ache, she rests a moment. "I remember when I was a girl, maybe eight, my mom took me into New York City to see a puppet show—Peer Gynt. Everyone's clapping and cheering, on their feet, shouts of encore! And I streak backstage, I don't know how. I was right there, inside the dark. I crawled on my knees behind the hanging marionettes feeling them one by one. I still remember the bony sharpness of the troll king's antlers, the softness of his beard. I never wanted to leave that magical place."

"And so you never will."

The kayak glides into shallow water; Noah hops out with a

sudden splash and pulls the boat on shore with a forceful tug. Already it is twilight. Willow hears the gritty scrape of the boat's bottom and climbs out, her feet sinking into wet sand.

They tug the kayak up onto the beach, leaving their backpacks and provisions on a rock higher up on the shore. Together they stroll among the dunes in bare feet, the sand holding its warmth deep down, cool toward the surface. On the sunbaked slope, Willow spots the scribes of nameless creatures—snakes, lizards, maybe ants. Abutting the dunes is a thicket of shrubs, pitch pine, and loblollies, branches low, crowns clipped by the island's strong winds.

Willow's arms are sore, her legs cramped from hours in the kayak. All day, the sound of the water, its smell, the light reflecting off its surface. Ahead of Noah, she runs down to the water's edge, strips off her clothes, except for a bandanna taming her wild hair. With Ilya, she undressed in the dark, half-covered by bedclothes, a closet door, a bathroom shower curtain, but now she is just standing there. With Ilya, she made love in the dark, every move, thought, crowded with consciousness. Eyes open or closed, they didn't see each other, the habit of living, being together, a kind of blindness. Their movements gulped to fill hunger, rarely tasted.

Willow feels Noah behind her; he turns and bends his head, leaning in, but she just brushes his lips, then ties the kerchief over his eyes, knotting it tight. Then she peels off his shirt and shorts in a swift motion, hurling them to shore. Willow takes his hand, leading him into the sea.

The water is bone-chilling, blood-stopping cold. She gasps

as she steps in, feet and ankles aching. A hard shell scrapes her toe, the salt water prickles her skin. They run in and out. A sudden hollow, the sea chest-high. Willow loves the sensation of water under her arms, her breasts buoyed by the waves, water between her thighs, inside her mouth. But it is too damn cold! She leaps away from the oncoming waves, dashing back toward shore.

At the edge, the rush of surf surrounds them. A sharp wind whips the bandanna from Noah's eyes and blows it out to sea. He and Willow dash back into the waves.

Willow loves the sound of sea, a sudden rearing up, pouring down with a wild pitching crash. She tumbles to bottom, inside a wave's vortex, not sure which way is up or down, surfacing or drowning.

"You okay?" Noah lifts her against his hip, its sharpness like a blade. He is a man with a secret strength, muscles you can't discern through his clothes; now she feels them in his arms and thighs.

"We better get out of here," Willow calls out. "We'll freeze!" The bandanna is a bright spot of color in the distance.

Another plunging breaker; the wind peaks, spilling scuds of foam over their faces. Willow gasps. Noah's real voice, his actual touch, is like stepping out of one of her miniature sets into a living breathing landscape. He holds her in a body lock so tight her blood stops. And then her breath comes.

They climb from the surf, their blood throbbing, the warm air a relief. The darkness of sea melts into blue-black sky. Willow shivers with cold as the wind picks up; they pull on T-shirts and nestle in a hollow on the dunes. Noah builds a fire from scattered driftwood and unpacks a camping mattress and sleeping bag.

They sit, warming up by the fire.

"I've been almost afraid to ask before, but . . . do you have someone special back in New York?" Noah asks.

"I have special people, no one special person."

He smiles at her.

"I was with a man for a while," she says.

"Was?"

"He died about five years ago. A heart attack. He was quite a bit older than me. Ilya Bernstein, a theater director."

"Ilya Bernstein? From Playwrights Horizons?"

Willow feels a strange fluttering in the pit of her stomach; she nods slowly.

"I knew him a little. We were in touch some time ago, a decade maybe. He was thinking of doing a play of mine called *Seasleeper*, but nothing came of it. Quite a powerhouse, I've heard."

Willow nods. "Maybe that was our problem."

"How so?"

"He'd jump in, tell me what to do, when I just needed someone to . . ."

"Listen." Noah strokes her forearm gently. "You've never asked me, but I want to tell you now. I was with a woman for twelve years," he says quietly. "We ended three years ago. She was, still is, an actress, Gabrielle de la Montagne. She works in French, do you know her?"

Willow shakes her head, relieved.

"Well, she's quite well known here and in France."

"We like our make-believe." Willow holds her hands out in front of the fire, crossing her legs beneath her. "So I'll be nosy, what happened?"

Noah laughs softly. "Well, I adored her. She's a major talent, but quite fragile."

Willow thinks sourly. *Aren't we all?*

"I loved seeing her on stage, bringing these characters I'd created to life. But inside, she was a mess. She suffered from manic-depressive illness."

"Was she on medication?"

"She didn't like to take it; never found the drug that worked and let her be her full self." He sighs deeply. "Toward the end of our relationship, I was mother, father, psychiatric nurse, shepherding her to different doctors, nursing her through sleepless nights and manic episodes, chasing her all over the globe to make sure she was safe. For five years, I didn't get any writing done."

Willow looks at Noah, his green eyes are cloudy. "So, what became of her?"

"Eventually, she went to Paris where she has an older sister and an aunt that she's close to. She's living more quietly now. Makes me sad sometimes. She's the real thing."

"Do you still . . . "

Noah touches Willow's hand. "I care about her. We e-mail now and then, call each other occasionally." Noah grabs his backpack and excavates cheese, bread, grapes, a bottle of shiraz, and they share a supper beside the warmth of the fire, its heat on Willow's face and chest, wind and waves at her back.

Noah looks at her with a slow, unflinching gaze, holds her there a moment, then lets go. Willow smells the wood burning, the smoke mixed with the briny smell of the sea. In the distance, she hears the hooting of an owl, a mournful sound.

"So, now that we've finally had True Confessions, where are we?" Noah asks.

Willow doesn't know what to say. She's brought the compass with her, has been carrying it around since he gave it to her. She draws it out of the inner compartment of her knapsack. "Look what I always keep with me."

"Okay." Noah holds her gently in his arms.

"Where are we really?" Willow asks. "Geographically."

"You want geography? Some small, uninhabited isle. Ours."

There is no one, nothing, but an abandoned fisherman's shed, but they decide to stay outside. Willow leans back, lying between Noah's legs, her head against his chest. With great tenderness, he strokes her wet, matted hair, finger-combing the waves. With long fingers he parts and plaits it. She is both sleepy and aroused at once, a swelling in her blood, a leap in the pit of her abdomen.

Willow shuts her eyes tight, closes her ears, willing her mind into white silence.

Turning over, she closes Noah's eyes with her palm, running her tongue over his lids and lashes, tasting sea salt. She slides downward, feels the sharpness of his hip as he presses against her, then the fuller hardness between his legs burrowing into her belly. Straddling his thigh, she rocks and sways, shattering into pieces, her toes curled and clenched tight.

"Wait a minute," he whispers, taking a condom from his

backpack. She slips it from his hand, tears open the foil wrapper with her teeth, and glides it smoothly over him.

Willow slides her hips up and Noah enters her. Holding his shoulders hard against the sand, she uses her thighs to move higher, faster until she hears his low, throaty growl and feels a knot unfurl inside both of them.

Willow leans backward, falling into the sand, pulling Noah on top of her where she can feel his long sighs against her neck. They doze awhile.

Sometime in the middle of the night, Willow awakens and doesn't know where she is, panics, hears the waves crashing, feels the wind, the sand burns on her legs and the soft place on her forearms, sand clotted in her hair, her mouth.

Her eyes are wet, stinging. What's she doing here? Always an ache for what she doesn't have, this *need to know,* a restlessness. Willow is shivering, chilled. Concerned all at once for her mother, where she is, what she is doing. She'll call her.

Noah stands awkwardly, bleary with sleep. He staggers over to the camping mattress and stretches it out smooth, tugging Willow on top of it, stretching out himself, then covering them both with the sleeping bag,

"Everything's going to be okay," he whispers, pulling her close against him. She is soothed by the intense warmth of his body, like a sun-warmed rock. She curls sideways, nestling against him, her face on his chest, and drops into dreamless sleep.

※ ※ ※

The Witness Foundation
Testimony of Jana Ivanova, June 15, 2005

My life in Montréal was very hard at first. We were seven people crowded into that flat on Jeanne Mance. A quarter of my life I had spent in places more dirty and crowded—yet it was still hard. You ask about the man who saved my life? Immediately he went to work in his uncle's engraving shop, using the trade that kept him alive in Auschwitz. That was not his dream, but soon he would find another path.

His aunt Rivka. Acch! A short, fleshy woman with a thin, cruel mouth. She treated me like a servant, thought he was too good for me. So virtuous taking me in, not a relative, never would she let me forget her charity. That woman I hated more than some of my tormentors in Germany! One of my own—yet not. "Family."

Cheek to jowl with people who were not relatives, not friends, I escaped by walking, in all weather, often with the man who saved my life. The mountain at twilight, in every season, we walked and walked, our only time alone together.

Soon, he promised me, there would be enough money for our own place; he wanted to marry me. He had big plans to found a Jewish center—for refugees, immigrants, and Montréalers—a haven for Jews of all backgrounds. And when this man had a vision, nothing could stand in his way. Like a force of nature he was, is.

That was his dream and he found a way. One of the Bronfmans was a customer at the engraving shop where he worked. He provided the financial backing. This man would be the creative force, the leader. Me, he assumed, his right hand. But this was not my dream.

My dreams were simple, ordinary. A child, I wanted, a daughter, my own family. Simple ordinary things, because of the simple things I had lost. I needed to make life.

EIGHTEEN

June 2005
Îles-de-la-Madeleine

WILLOW'S EYES FLY OPEN before dawn to an overcast sky, a pewter sea. The wind is wild, billowing the sleeping bag like a sail, pitching the waves that spill scuds of foam along the beach. Sand stings her cheeks. Noah tugs the sleeping bag over their bodies to their necks. For a moment, the wind holds its breath. Beneath the weight of down, Willow is sweating.

Black grackles fight the wind, gulls hunch in the sand, their bodies clenched tight. Beach grass etches arcs, then scribbles in the sand. A curtain of thunderclouds moves across the water; they hover in the morning darkness. All at once, rain blasts down, cracking like shots, pocking the sand, the ocean roiling.

"C'mon!" With a swift motion, Noah gathers sleeping bag, backpacks, provisions and tugs Willow toward the abandoned fisherman's shed.

Through warped beams, they watch the waves. Wind shakes the shed, as rain hammers the flimsy roof, beating out a rhythm and Willow thinks about how the elements, just weather, blot out everything, all our trivia and silly humanity.

"So," she says, "what's on the agenda for today?"

"Watch the sea empty its belly, the sand shift."

When the rain and wind quiet, they stroll about the shore, examining the remains of the storm. Seaweed is flung about like tangled beards; smashed clam shells glimmer in small pools.

Noah pulls Willow into his chest, then lifts her chin. He kisses her and she feels the pressure of his lips, the motion of his tongue echo throughout her body. With Ilya, kissing was the first to go.

"'*Exultation is the going of an inland soul to sea,*'" he whispers.

"I love that poem," Willow says. "Emily Dickinson."

"Doesn't surprise me."

In the backpack, they find the remains of their provisions. "You okay?" Noah asks.

Willow shrugs. "Think we can brave it?"

"I want to get to Grosse Île. I know a place we can stay the night."

Willow nods. "Anyway, you know what you're doing, right?"

Noah laughs, mischievous, a little scary.

"In your dreaming days of me—you stalker—you found out everything, no? Brave and brilliant playwright, storyteller, expert kayaker, why not?"

"Stop. I need to be going somewhere." Working quickly, they pack up their things and stow them in the kayak.

"Will I be your secret, then?" Noah asks.

Startled, Willow doesn't know what to say. Secrets have ruled her life for so long.

They finish loading up the sunny yellow kayak and push off, out to where gulf meets sea. The water is choppy, but they make headway in the wake of the storm.

The water is blue, the sky gauze. They glide through the tunnel in the middle of a sandstone cliff shaped like a medieval castle. Willow knows she will always remember these crags. They're like nothing she's seen before.

All afternoon, they paddle through the waters, which grow calmer, a play of light as sun tries to emerge from clouds. Looking over the side, Willow spots the flash of minnows, a radial of light and motion. In the distance is a lighthouse painted white and red, greenish-brown land visible from afar. They are both lulled by the sea, the kayak an extension of their bodies, ripples whirling slowly beneath their paddles.

Suddenly, everything changes.

The water turns to iron, wind spinning them like a top. Through a split in the fog, Willow sees surf crashing against rocks. If a breaker hits, they'll be swept against crags. A wave breaks beyond them, another catches them from behind, and they are on the wildest ride of their lives. Willow swerves, leaning away from the next breaker. One moment breathing air, the next, water.

The sudden chill of the sea makes her gasp and she loses hold of her paddle, watches it bob and spin, then disappear. There is a muffled yell she can't make out. She tries not to think, just to stay steady, treading water, but the cold aches. They have no wetsuits, no paddling jackets, just shorts and shirts over bathing suits. Treading, she drifts further away from Noah, from their kayak. Noah tries to get out of the kayak to help her, but the spray skirt holds him fast; he pulls and releases the strap and slides out of the boat clutching a lifejacket.

Waves break all around them, as Noah, fifteen feet away, holds onto the kayak, and tosses Willow the life jacket. He still has his paddle. "Just hold on!" he shouts.

Willow struggles with the lifejacket, but can't get it on, while Noah fights his way up wind to her, pulling the kayak behind him by a rope. When the boat reaches Willow, she tries to hang on, but the hull is slippery and the wind blows her back down. She swims back to the kayak and holds on for dear life.

Again and again, Noah fights to right the kayak. After a half-dozen tries, he gets it upright and slides in on his stomach, crawling forward toward the cockpit. When he is over the cockpit, he sits up with both legs spread for balance. Then she watches him slide his legs in and lower his bottom into the seat.

Using his paddle to help her, Noah pulls Willow in toward the kayak and she clambers back into the boat, nearly capsizing it again. Bumping and sliding into the bow, she is freezing, exhausted—sitting now in a pool of water.

"Bail!" Noah shouts. "Start bailing, fast!"

He hands her the old bleach bottle. Shivering, Willow fills and empties, fills and empties, as more water sloshes into the boat with each wave. She feels like Sisyphus, but keeps going.

Noah sets off two sky-blazers one minute apart. The flares seem dim, a match in wet dark.

Willow keeps bailing, filling the bottle, emptying it into the sea. Noah launches a third flare, insignificant against the wild wind, waves, the whitecaps.

Waves surf them, as Noah sets off the final flare. For several minutes, nothing.

Then a sailboat appears. In a minute, they are on deck.

That night and the next, they recover in a B&B as far as you can get away from the ocean, the driest spot in the islands.

On the plane back to Montréal, Willow leans into Noah. As they roar off, he reaches for her hand and she feels that roller-coaster lift in the pit of her belly, feels his eyes on her, though he doesn't speak. His gaze warms her from within and she wants this flight to last forever, to be suspended inside the roar of the plane twenty-five-thousand feet above the earth by nothing she can see or understand.

❊ ❊ ❊

NINETEEN

JANE RUSHES OUT of Witness into the mild summer afternoon. Before she can stop herself, she heads around the corner, up two blocks to Ha'makom, pumping her arms as she goes, swaying slightly side-to-side. She is determined to do this; she won't be around forever. Time, life, is short. Willow is away for a few days with this new man of hers and Jane wonders if the connection will stick. With her daughter, nothing adheres, except her puppet family. Jane knows from her own experience that, in the end, you make what you can of your life. Still, she would like to see Willow with someone to love.

Jane remembers the location of Ha'makom, even though she has not been inside its doors since 1964. Chaim had big dreams. Ha'makom, The Place, a center that would become the hub for the Jewish community, a model for Canada and the world. This was his vision.

Now Jane stands in front of the sprawling facility hewn from polished stone and glass, stretching across several blocks and adjacent to a leafy park and dog run. She is breathing heavily, sweat pooling under her arms, at the back of her neck, her palms sticky. She can't find the door, the place is formidable.

A gaggle of teenagers burst out of a wall of glass, dressed in gym clothes, speaking Hebrew, laughing and jostling one another. Inside, a uniformed guard talks into a pager.

She looks up and sees an immense Star of David adorning the entry, molded of twisted brass and studded with seven Eilat stones—one on each point of the star and the largest at its center— each blue-green jewel gleaming its own varying shade.

Jane touches the shoulder of one of the girls who is wearing a tiny tank top that leaves a smooth swath of brown midriff exposed, low-slung shorts hanging precariously from sharp hipbones. She cannot believe what children wear nowadays, they might as well go naked. The girl looks up at her, surprised.

"Please can you tell me where is administration?"

The group of kids stop, stare at her as if she has just landed. Well, in a way, she has. For a moment, everyone is silent. Then one of the boys switches to English, talks of going around the corner, up two blocks, down a third, entering an archway, going up stairs . . . or a quicker route through this door, around left, then right, up an elevator, through a passageway, down a short flight. The words blur, heat fills her; Jane is confused, panicky. *So Ha'makom is a fortress. How will she find him?*

"Wait," a boy says, looking directly into Jane's eyes, his own nearly black, pupil and iris melting into a warm shining darkness.

"Who are you looking for?"

The glass doors whoosh open and a group of people her own age amble out slowly, as if they are walking on ice, step by careful step. They are chatting in Yiddish about what they will do for dinner, and if they should see the play at the Sadie Bronfman. Jane snaps back to attention. It takes all of her concentration to collect her thoughts and put them into words. She steps on the wrong spot and the doors open, whoosh closed, open for no reason. A trick door. Magic.

"Here," the boy says kindly, gently moving her away from the magic spot. The doors remain closed. "Now tell me, where do you need to go?"

"I came now from Witness. A movie they are making of my life. Now I'm finished. I think I have nothing left to talk about with them. I'm here with my daughter, Willow Ives." Jane's eyes sting, watering in the sun. She knows she is babbling, not making much sense, but can't stop herself.

A pall comes over the group of kids, they stand frozen as statues. One of the girl's eyes contract with light, then darkness. Another looks at her with pity, her head tilted to one side, lips downturned. How Jane hates that look! As if they know her life, its details rummaged through like the private contents of a spilled purse.

The boy with the beautiful black eyes touches her shoulder gently.

"Who are you looking for?" He is young, but he understands some things. What would her life have been if she had a beautiful boy like this? A grandson maybe . . . he is just the right age.

Embarrassed, she stops herself, what good are these fancies, she has the life she has, that's it.

"Chaim. Chaim Rosenblum." The words run on. "The big makher who runs this place!"

The boy laughs. "Of course," he says. "Let me take you to him."

"Oh, thank you," Jane says.

"I'm Ari," he says.

"Pleased to meet you, Ari, I'm Jane, Jana, but you can call me Janey. That's what my friends call me, I mean. When . . . " She breathes in sharply, then sighs, able to stop the babbling this time.

Ari looks confused for a moment, then pulls himself together. "Okay Janey, this place is huge, a maze if you're not used to it." He takes her arm and Jane breathes out in a sigh of relief. "Come," he says, "it's not far."

Inside, Jane shows identification to the guard and he riffles through her pocketbook. She stands very still, mute. She remembers searches. Then she just surrenders to this beautiful boy. Air conditioning blasts down from side and ceiling vents and she basks in the cool air, the sweat drying on her skin.

When they get to Chaim's office, the panic is back, worse now. Ari speaks to a receptionist in an outer office. He comes back, asks Jane for her full name. She can't stop the sweating now, despite the air conditioning.

Ari looks at her, concerned.

"Thank you," Jane says to him. "You are a *mensch*!"

He smiles, blushing darkly beneath his olive skin.

She takes his face in her mottled, plump hands. "You go," she says, "find your friends."

He smiles at her, turns and disappears into the labyrinth of Ha'makom.

Jane waits less then a minute and Chaim appears. He is still a colossus, with long, silver hair streaming straight back from his high forehead.

She made him smaller in her mind. That made it easier somehow. He stands a good foot taller than she, and Jane remembers how comforting his height was to her that day they reunited in the DP camp after the war, the day he brought her the loaf of bread. She remembers his hands, tearing off a piece for her, large hands, but so thin, she could see every bone shift as he moved. Chaim lifted her to eat and she put her arms around his back. How could it be? He felt strong to her though his frame was like the poles of a tripod thrust into clothes. He tore off a piece of bread—the smell of it—heaven, dipped it in milk, opened her mouth for her. And they talked and talked.

Now, they just look at one another. She has not seen him face-to-face for forty years, since she conceived Willow and fled. She had already lost two growing babies in the womb, his children. One she lost early, the second close to term. She could not let it happen again. Jane knew she must flee, start fresh, be someone new. Kingston offered her this chance.

Jane looks at Chaim, keeps on looking. Chaim gazes at her, a gentle smile playing in his full lips. His bulky shoulders, barrel chest, and hard paunch strain the material of his denim shirt; she sees he has put on weight, though he was always a husky man, once he'd recovered from the camps. The sleeves of his shirt are rolled up to reveal powerful forearms and strong, large hands. His eyes are still beautiful and intense, a clear blue-gray that turns to teal in certain light.

"Jana, you look well," he says, his deep voice rough from pipe smoking.

"Liar," she says, and they have a laugh together, puncturing some of the shock, the tension. "How is your health?" she asks.

"Knock on wood," he answers. "You?"

"I've been better. And worse!"

He pauses and stares at her. "I can't believe you've come. So many years, Jana, so many years you didn't come." Suddenly, he springs into action. So what are we standing here for? Let's go to my office. No, no, we have too much to talk about! We'll leave here, go to Schwartz's, our old haunt."

They take Chaim's rattling old shuttle bus with Ha'makom emblazoned on its side, and its logo in English, French, Hebrew and Yiddish: "Your Home Away from Home: A Place You Can Be."

He speeds through Snowdon and around twisting downtown streets, like a crazy person, forcing everyone to make way for him. Up front, she feels every rumble and rattle in her bones. Her breasts bounce and she folds her arms tightly across her chest to contain them. The shuttle bus is noisy, clackety-clacking down the city streets, making it hard for them to talk, let alone think. On his sharp turns right, then left, Jane slams against the window, then careens into Chaim's muscular shoulder.

"A rollercoaster I'm on!"

He chuckles. "Enjoy the ride, Jana!"

"Alive I am, alive I want to stay."

"Accch!"

"You're a typical Montréal driver," she accuses and he just laughs again, this time with pride.

"Got to be on the offensive," he booms. "Or you get screwed. Fast."

"You haven't changed," Jane shouts above the din of the bus, the traffic and beeping horns, as well as a radio program.

"Why should I?" Chaim booms back. Without slowing down, he zooms into the final straightaway, a quick jolt forward, then back, the screech of the safety brake and they are there.

As Chaim gathers his things, Jane tugs down her skirt, smoothing her hair and bangs with a few staccato pats. She steals a glance in the sun-visor mirror, pinching her cheeks and applying a streak of lipstick. *Acchh. What am I thinking?*

Chaim goes around to Jane's side and helps her out. He still possesses the wide-spaced, deliberate gait she remembers, arms held loosely from his sides, bouncing on the balls of his feet like a prizefighter.

It is a long way down from the seat of the shuttle bus and Jane tugs down her skirt once more for good measure, tries to be graceful, light on her feet, as he lifts her and whisks her to the sidewalk, as if she were a feather.

As they stroll down St. Laurent, Jane recognizes bits and pieces of the old neighborhood tucked in between the trendy boutiques and elegant cafés and restaurants—scattered fragments of the world she once knew along the Main. What was once Schreter's wood-floored dry goods store, now carries suits, jeans, sweat-shirts, shorts, and shoes.

Chaim stops in front of Schwartz's Deli with its faded red and white candy-striped awning, a row of teenagers lining the bench out front, in shorts and crop-tops, jewels glimmering from the bellybuttons of the girls, a gold ring piercing the nose of one of the boys. Standing beside them is an older man, hump-backed, leaning painfully down to pat his dog, a mangy mix Jane can't identify. The dog rolls in bliss, as the man scratches and strokes his matted coat.

In big block letters, Jane notices the newly painted sign out front:

CHARCUTERIE HEBRAIQUE
de Montréal, Inc.

"We're in luck, Jana," Chaim says. "No line."

"It's early, yet," she replies, her mouth dry, not with hunger, but with the scratchy rasp of memory.

He holds the door open for her, then takes her arm, as they pass through the curtain of smoked meat. Brisket cured with salt and spices, then smoked and steamed. There is the framed tribute she knows so well:

WHEN I DIE
I WANT TO GO TO SCHWARTZ'S

They both smile as they pass by and Jane glances across the street at Berson's Monuments, its granite tombstones polished and blank, waiting to be carved.

"Convenient, eh?" Chaim winks at Jane.

A waitress greets Chaim, "Mr. Rosenblum, how are you today?"

"Well Vilma, you?"

"Okay . . . I hope."

"All of us, no?" he says, laying open broad palms.

"Your usual table?"

Chaim nods, puts a firm hand on Jane's lower back, as they follow the waitress to the back.

"Privacy, we'll have, "Chaim says gently. "So we can catch up."

We need more than privacy, Jane thinks, as they settle in at their table near the very back of the restaurant.

"I like your hair," Chaim says, his eyes gazing steadily at her in a way that makes Jane feel exposed, newly shy, and she runs her fingers through her shiny silver bob, hanging straight and curving slightly inward to her ears. A tide of memory floods her. Hair, lank, dirty, tangled in knots.

The first day Jane saw Chaim in the DP camp at Belsen, the same day he fed her fresh bread, tearing it in small pieces and softening them in milk, as if she were a baby, his own child—that day, out of his tattered coat pocket, he pulled that comb! Such a luxury to have this comb; she wondered where he'd gotten it. Gently, Chaim worked that comb through her long, tangled hair, holding it away from her scalp so it wouldn't pull. So tender, patient, Chaim had worked through each knot and tangle, until the mass of brown hair fell smooth. The feel of his large hands, the memory of that touch, makes her scalp tingle, then ache.

The waitress comes, "Mr. Rosenblum, your usual?"

"For the lady," Chaim says, "water, sparkling, with a pinch of juice. Orange juice. And for me the same."

"You remember," Jane says, touched. "My summer refresher."

He taps his temple. "Everything, farshteyst?"

When their drinks come, Chaim orders for both of them. "Two smoked meat sandwiches, medium fat, with fresh coleslaw and sour pickles. And coffee from a fresh pot. Later, we'll choose dessert."

"What if today I want something different?" Jane teases.

"Our usual, nothing new," Chaim says, his eyes grave.

Jane nods, smiling with a gentleness that surprises her.

"Everyone knows," she says, "*you* wouldn't have it any other way!" reverting to her ironic tone, laced with affection, to keep him in his place—as if anyone could—to prevent him getting too full of himself, which he already was!

Ten long years they were together here, after the war; they were together and yet not. He was always so sure of who he was, what he wanted, what needed to be done. The larger vision he had, while it took her four years to gain back even a semblance of the health she enjoyed as a young girl in Prague. Four years to put on some flesh, to sleep through the night, to eat without her mouth tasting sour and full with nausea, without feeling sick at heart. Four years to get through a whole day without shaking and weeping, a full day free of daymares and night terrors.

Chaim's vision and dream, this place Ha'makom, held him anchored and safe, while her own longings made her shaky. Could she ever feel whole, give birth to a healthy child, be part of a family?

She lost the first baby in the DP camp in 1946, twenty-three years old and a skeleton, ill in her body, sick at heart. How could such a body support another life? Yet, she wept for weeks when she passed the clots and blood that would have been their child. Later, in Montréal she became pregnant again with Chaim's child. She was twenty-seven, already three years in Montréal, but in the seventh month, she had sudden unbearable cramps, and on the way to the hospital, continuous bleeding. When she arrived at the Jewish, they told her she had lost the baby. Again.

The despair she suffered this time was beyond bounds. Chaim too was heartbroken, but threw himself into work, so as not to think. They didn't speak much about what had happened. She thought it was a bad omen, a curse on them, a sign. He became more driven, domineering, obsessed with Ha'makom. He spoke of nothing else and was rarely home.

Chaim's power was a wave breaking over her, carrying her with it, rolling her in its inescapable momentum, pulling her under. She was always forced to assent to his pronouncements, even when she was not altogether in accord. Once in a blue moon, she put herself in complete opposition to him, just to hold on to some sense of herself. And then they would fight over any small thing, shouting and breaking things. Yet she was grateful to him, grateful and resentful at once. She owed him too much.

She remembers his extraordinary words to her in the DP camp

when she was neither awake nor asleep, here nor there, alive nor dead.

"Jana, now you fear life as you once feared death. You are more afraid of life than of death."

Truth.

Sometimes throughout the long years, with him, without him, she wondered: why her? There were so many dying . . . but of course there was this recognition between them. And so he devoted himself to *her*, breathing life back into *her* heart, soul, and body. He became everything to her.

Jane always wanted to ask him why he had followed her late that night to the Old Jewish Cemetery, just a boy of thirteen. Why he mutely dug a hole in the earth and helped her bury the menorah. Yes, they were neighbors, but she didn't even know his name; she'd never paid him much attention, serving him in the sweetshop as she would serve any other customer.

That night, when they'd finished her mission, he had looked at her directly with a focused intensity. It was a quality of attention she had only experienced before with her father. As if she alone were the most important person in the world, in that moment, the only person.

"I knew you were here," he says, breaking into her thoughts, as if reading them, looking at her steadily with his clear, gray eyes. "At Witness."

"So?"

"I decided to wait. For you to come to me."

"How did you know I would?"

"I knew. One day, before it was too late."

The waitress is back, laden with food. She sets their plates before them and Jane just inhales the heavenly smell of smoked meat, fresh rye, steaming coffee. Her head spins, and she realizes she hasn't eaten all day. For balance, she sets her elbows on the table and smoothes her napkin in her lap.

"Eat," he commands. "Start, Jana."

"Bon appétit," she says, then waits a moment before picking up her sandwich, delicate and ladylike, conscious of Chaim watching her. She eats with fine, small motions, though she is ravenous. She senses it pleases Chaim to watch her.

Chaim sits with his arms on the table, large and sun-browned, pushed forward toward her. Even at his age, they are still attractive, manly.

"I sometimes think about that buried menorah," she starts, hesitant. She wonders if he will know what she is talking about, but he doesn't miss a beat, as if what happened, happened yesterday, instead of a lifetime ago.

"It's safe, I bet," he says, looking up at her, "deep in the ground under the linden tree where we left it."

"You think?"

He nods, two beats.

"I want to go back. Home."

"Oh, Jana, home is in New Jersey—or here in Montréal, if you want."

"To take Willow. I want to show her where we lived, grew up. The Old Jewish Cemetery. Maybe, as you say, the menorah it is still there!"

"And so it should stay."

"I dream about it sometimes, digging it up again. Burying it. Over and over, these dreams I have." She is startled by what she tells him and feels her face flush, turn hot.

"It's your family, Jana, that you are thinking about."

"Dr. Freud, thank you."

He looks at her steadily, keeps looking, takes her plump hand in his. "If you go back now, nothing will be the same."

"Why should that stop me?"

He shrugs. "My life is here. Now. I have no desire to go back to Prague. Or Budapest where I was born."

She extricates her hand from his. "We are not talking about *you.*"

He chuckles good-naturedly. "So, eat Jana, don't waste away on me."

Now it is her turn to laugh.

❊ ❊ ❊

TWENTY

CHAIM GLANCES AROUND the restaurant, greets a few people he knows. Jane thumps on the table with her knuckle to reclaim his attention. "We've yakked enough about the distant past. I came this time to talk to you about Willow," she says. "Your daughter."

He looks away, scratches his nail along the plastic placemat, as if to remove a speck of dirt.

"She is in Montréal," Jane goes on.

She can see his discomfort. He begins to chew his full lips, tapping now on the table, a wish to bolt, escape. Jane won't let him; she is the strong one now. Perhaps she will torture him just a bit. To get back.

"You know, I brought her here for a meal. Poor deprived girl, she'd never had a meal at Schwartz's! Ever."

He attacks his food now with a vengeance, as if it is to blame.

No one can speak while he is eating. She waits. He devours half his sandwich, the pickle, wipes his mouth with a slash, sips coffee. Then he looks up at her.

"My girl, how is she?" Chaim asks.

"*Your* girl? You call her *girl!*" She is surprised by the force in her voice, the fresh hurt and rage. "*Your* girl, whom you've never met. Who doesn't know you exist! Your *girl* who turned forty this year!"

His eyes look suddenly sad, defeated, and Jane stops herself. They are quiet for a long while, slowly sipping their coffee. Jane's hands tremble as she holds her mug. He touches her wrist.

"A day doesn't go by that I don't think of you, Jana," he says softly.

To save herself, she jokes, "But what do you think? Nothing good I'm sure."

"Be serious," Chaim says. "These are serious matters."

"Okay, only *you* can be the *kibitzer,* only you have the right."

They set to work finishing their sandwiches, eating with pleasure. "When we lived," he says, wiping his hands on the napkin, "survived, this is what I mean . . . when we started fresh together in Montréal, everything was good. We had a life. I was sure we would always be together. We went back so far."

Jane sighs, takes a delicate sip of her coffee.

"I think it was easier for you, Chaim. Everything was clear. Aunt Rivka and Uncle Zoltov accepted you, you were their blood. I was the outsider. Always they thought I wasn't good enough for you."

"Nah!"

"Virtuous Rivka, for taking me in. And she never let me forget that!"

"A silly woman."

"You know what I say is true!" Jane argues. "The woman is dead. Why can't you admit the truth after all these years and say it out loud?"

"You had me, what did anyone else matter?"

"You, I hardly saw. I was alone, too much time to think, remember."

"I had my work to do. Not just for me, for you, for our community."

Now he sounds like a slogan. Jane remembers how she longed for Chaim, how she missed him, waited for him, to feel the closeness she had felt for him in the DP camp. When he was with her, he enveloped her in warmth and care, but then the wave moved back out to sea. For days, weeks, she wouldn't see him.

"I was there," he says now.

"There was no there *there* for *me*," she snaps. Though she understands now that the loss of two babies made them both despair, grieve in different ways.

"I wasn't strong," she says, out of the blue.

But he picks up her thread.

"After we lost our babies, I didn't want to think. Work kept me busy," Chaim adds.

Before she can stop herself, Jane puts her hand over his. "Broken, we both were—with you, no one could see it."

"Now, we can look back."

"Then, we were in it," she agrees.

"Sometimes, I would visit you at Ha'makom," she says, "during the fifties when you really got things cooking."

"I loved it when you came. I was proud, wanted you to be a part of it all. I took so much pride in showing you around, showing you off."

"Excuse me, mister."

"What?"

"I came by, you couldn't see me. You were busy. You were on the phone. You were in a meeting. Always a meeting. And always with Rachel Goldstein, your right hand."

"She was a great help to me," he admits, looking away, a flinch in his gray eyes.

"Acch. More than a help!"

Jane remembers this Rachel Goldstein—a beauty—Chaim's age, but a different type altogether from Jane. Rachel was a native Montréaler, privileged and wealthy, from a prominent Westmount family on the hill. Her father owned several clothing companies that were succeeding, not just in Canada, but in the U.S. and Europe as well.

Rachel was tall and slender, nearly Chaim's height with auburn hair, fair coloring, and large, blue eyes. There was a delicacy, almost a floweriness to her form, and a lack of pain and suffering in her eyes that made her pure. She was another species altogether. A vacation from their shared past.

Jane remembers the way Rachel looked at Chaim, with those naked, blue eyes, recalls her long, fair throat and slender wrists, her straight, small features. How Jane hated her!

Before long, Chaim and Jane were merely sister and brother, Rachel his helpmate and lover. By 1955, Jane was starting to make plans for a new life for herself in New Jersey. She was improving her English, getting stronger, and earning her teaching certification from McGill. She loved children and wanted to teach them, even if she couldn't have her own, she could have a whole classroom.

Now she had her own vision. In 1957, at age thirty-four, she left Montréal and started her new life as Jane Ives.

When Jane returned to Montréal for a visit in 1962, she discovered from Chaim that Rachel had left him and moved to Israel. Chaim had never married Rachel, though they had been lovers for many years. She sees the contraction of light and dark in Chaim's eyes, the pain. "For me it was always you. You were meant to be the mother of my child."

Jane can't speak for some moments. She holds her fresh cup of coffee, which is too hot to drink, adds cream, then sugar.

Jane remembers now how strong she felt coming back in 1962, even beautiful, and how the passion rekindled with Chaim.

"When you came back to me, I felt it was *beshert*. I was sure we would start over and it would work."

But when Jane knew she was carrying Chaim's child, she was terrified of another loss. She was already past forty, her body a fragile vessel. The single-mindedness he poured into the Ha'makom, she poured into her pregnancy and her dream of a daughter. It became her secret and she fled Montréal for the second time.

"When you left me suddenly, Jana, without warning, I traced

you, wrote you, called you. I wasn't going to give up. I tried for three years. Nothing. It was the kind of hurt you don't get over. Betrayal."

"I did get in touch."

"Five years late!"

"I told you we had a beautiful daughter. I asked you to come see her, to celebrate her fifth birthday, to be a part of our life. By then, I was no longer so scared. My child had survived. She and I were strong. Together."

"The shock was terrible. That you would have had our child, alone, after all we'd been through. That you would keep her a secret from me—her father—when we had already lost two babies. I was furious with you. Forgive you? Not then. I wasn't ready."

"Once you turned her down, that was it. I didn't want my little girl to think her father didn't want her."

"What did you tell *her*? Who does she think is her father?"

"Dead, I told her."

"Dead? You killed me? After all we survived!"

They have a crazy laugh together.

The waitress comes by, and without asking Jane, Chaim orders a selection of desserts.

"We're not finished talking," he declares. "We need some sweetness."

When the plate comes, he cuts a piece of chocolate babka, feeds it to her, and her eyes burn, though she can't cry.

"Listen, Chaim," she says after washing the sweet, chewy cake down with coffee. "Willow is here in Montréal for awhile. She's a marionette-maker and puppeteer. A real talent."

"My daughter."

"*Our* daughter. She's guest artist at Usine C for the year."

Jane sees the look of anxiety in his eyes, the sheen of sweat on his brow. He mops his face with a linen handkerchief.

"What do I do? What can I say?" he asks. "If I were her, I would hate me."

"Look," Jane says, taking charge for once. "I'm coming back to Montréal in the fall. She has a show then, her own show, which now she is writing, making the marionettes from scratch, her own characters. I'll be back for that show. You'll have a little time over the summer to get used to the idea. Don't approach her yet."

"No, not yet."

"I'll talk to her first, this summer. Everyone then will have a little time to get used to the idea. And then the three of us we'll meet in the fall. Before the show. Maybe she'll want you there, too. I'll be there when you meet. It'll be alright."

"An earthquake for her," Chaim says. "Her papa sprung to life. From the dead."

"Magic," Jane says. She feels anxious, and breaks out in a sudden sweat. Before she can find her hanky, Chaim has his ready and reaches across the table to gently wipe her brow.

"My God," Jane says, "what will I tell her? How to begin?" After years of hiding, of weaving a past, a white lie, so as not to cause pain. "What should I do?" she beseeches him. "What should I tell her?"

He looks her straight in the eye, his gray eyes full.

"The truth."

Jane lets out a long sigh that seems to take everything out of her. She sips the cold water, gathers her strength, tries to belly up to the idea. The truth.

✳ ✳ ✳

TWENTY‑ONE

WILLOW AND NOAH return to his loft in the heart of Old Montréal, a refurbished sweets factory, overlooking the pier and St. Lawrence River. Buoyed by their time on the islands, she feels a pleasant buzz from their adventure, a story in itself.

"Not where I pictured you," she says, glancing around the cavernous living space.

"But you *knew* where I lived, my sweet spy."

She feels her ears burn. "True, but . . . "

"What?"

"I see you in one of those charming row houses on le Plateau, close enough to smell the *poutine* cooking next door."

Noah laughs, low in his throat. "Go on."

"Your house painted lavender or flesh‑pink with turquoise trim, a front yard of gravel, rickety rusting outside staircase up to your flat on the third floor where you sit with your favorite pen and a sheaf of crisp, white paper, glancing at life on the street, as you look from within, where no one can see you."

"You're more original than that," Noah says, smiling gently.

Willow lets out a sigh.

"I used to live like that," he admits, thumping their bags down in the foyer, lingering a moment, surveying his loft. "I got an amazing deal on this place, quite a while ago. It was still very much the derelict candy factory, but I've got some handy friends and we fixed it up. Got a roommate, actually."

"Where is he . . . or she?"

"Mitch is in California doing a film, plans to move there for a job. One of the best 3-D animators in the business. I guess I'll be on my own for awhile."

"I'm so used to that."

"Mitch, he's more of a brother."

"Think you'll miss him?"

Noah nods. "I'd be working on a new play and check in with Mitch, who was bringing a graphic novel to film. We'd pass our stuff back and forth. In a space like this," he spreads his arms to encompass the loft, "you're never behind closed doors. Anyway, I don't need the cork-lined room." He shrugs, smiling at her. "Eventually, it becomes communal, no?" he asks. "Plays."

"You're right."

"Make yourself at home," he says, putting things away as Willow strolls about the place, still finding him out.

She sees he's created virtual rooms with groupings of furniture, and that he likes leather—a Corbusier chair in black, a red leather sofa. In every space are pens, pads, snatches of dialogue, sketches for scenes and stories.

He sneaks up behind her, wraps his arms around her waist and gazes over her shoulder as she studies a bit of dialogue with a doodle of a girl's face.

"You do work *anywhere*."

"Ass in the chair doesn't work for me. Some days I just stroll around with a pad to museums, galleries, restaurants. Got to keep moving."

Noah stands close beside her, pointing to the ceiling. "I picked this up in Europe," he says proudly, twirling a chandelier that doubles as a mobile, messages, notes and ideas clipped to its wire tendrils.

He unclips a slip of paper and pockets it. "So."

"I'm having dinner with my mother. She wants to go to La Colombe."

"Their lamb shank cooked in duck fat . . . don't get me started."

"Join us," she says, without thinking.

His face lights up. "I'll bring some nice wine."

"Could I take . . . a bath?" she asks. "I'm feeling sort of grubby."

"I like grubby," he says, reeling her into him.

She tugs gently away.

He cocks an eyebrow, then disappears for a moment, returning with a fluffy terrycloth robe, crumpled from the dryer. Willow takes it and lifts the fabric to her face, breathing in its fresh, soapy scent.

She's never seen anything like his bathroom, a huge Romanesque tub encased in limestone. Willow lights the candle she finds on the shelf and fills the tub with near-scalding water, lowers the blinds, clicks off the lights, and sinks into hot, frothing suds. She lies back and soaks until she feels her bones dissolve, her body become part of the water.

Nearly asleep, she hears Noah approach. She leaves the steamy bathroom wrapped in his robe, her legs wobbly as jelly.

"I have something for you," he says, holding out two fists, a treasure hidden in one. She taps the left, he turns his wrist, reveals an empty palm. She taps the other; inside is an antique watch-chain. "For the compass," he says, "so you never lose it, never get lost."

She fingers the lovely old chain, alternating gold and platinum braiding.

"I've made it into a chain you can wear at your neck," he says. "Let's try it."

Noah takes the compass from Willow, strings it onto the chain like a charm and fastens it around her neck. She holds it in her palm, feels its dense weight. How long can this honeymoon phase last?

Noah brings them cold ginger beer from the fridge and fixes a cheese platter; they sit, enjoying the lazy summer afternoon.

Then all at once, she feels edgy. "I should go," Willow says suddenly.

"See you later?"

"Around nine." She leaves him quickly, without an embrace.

When Willow arrives at La Colombe, holding her mother by the arm, Noah is already ensconced at the window table. She has changed into a high-necked white blouse and long, black, gypsy skirt, silk inlaid with lace, and black lace-up espadrille sandals. The high neck covers the compass pendant. She doesn't want her mother asking questions.

Noah stands quickly and waves to greet them, kissing Willow lightly on both cheeks, enclosing Jane's hand with both of his.

Willow watches her mother flush with pleasure or exertion, she's not sure which, as they settle into their table. The waitress arrives with the menus and takes the wine from Noah, opens it, and fills their glasses. They sip while discussing the menu.

"Too rich for my blood," Jane comments.

"The snapper is lovely," Noah suggests. "They can prepare it very lightly for you."

"Good," Jane says, smiling at him, as Willow looks on.

Noah chooses a peppered chèvre salad with nuts and orange as an appetizer and the lamb shank. Willow orders escargot and duck in orange sauce. It's a bit awkward before the wine kicks in, and Willow wonders if she's made a mistake. Noah lifts the breadbasket, opens the linen napkin, and offers Jane and Willow the warmed rolls.

"Very tall, your boyfriend is," Jane comments, as Willow and Noah giggle.

"Yes, he is tall," says Noah in a conspiratorial whisper, "tall and gangly and sinister!"

"How tall?" Jane asks.

"Six four," Noah says, "in his stocking feet."

"I like tall men," Jane says, setting off a fresh round of

laughter in Noah and Willow. "You know, they often choose short women."

Noah swings his arm around Willow, pulling her against his shoulder. "Not me," he says. "I like mine Willow-y."

He can be such a goofball, but it suits her mother; Willow relaxes a bit.

"So," Jane says, her voice resolute and staccato. "What do you do, Noah?"

"I'm a playwright," he says.

"Your ideas, where do they come from?" she presses, as Willow delicately pries the plump seasoned snails from their shells.

Noah taps his forehead. "Oh, I don't know. There's always this flow between inside and outside. God, I sound like an a-hole, don't I?"

"Too many public radio interviews," Willow says.

Jane sets her arms on the table, taking a rest from her green salad. "Me, I like crafts."

"Yes," says Noah, brightening to have the onus off him for a moment. "What type do you do—you know, I don't know what to call you. Miss Ives?"

"Jane. Or if you want, Jana."

"Which do you prefer?" Noah asks.

She looks confused, tormented for a moment, and Willow sees Noah's face fall.

"Janey," her mother puts in quickly. "Some people call me Janey."

Willow can see Noah is touched. "So Janey, what crafts are your thing?"

"I like two." Jane nods vigorously, her voice stronger now, more confident. "I find lovely old lamps and their shades. I go to yard sales, antique shops, flea markets, what have you. And I snoop around till I find what I like. I look for different shapes—and materials from all places in the world, every period."

"So you collect them, then," Noah says, spreading his peppered chèvre onto a toast triangle.

"I remake them new," she says. "I look in magazines, for all kinds of crazy pictures. I cut out what I like and paste and cut and shellac . . . "

"There's wit and humor in her designs," Willow says, "The way she juxtaposes things."

"What?" Jane asks.

"I'm just tooting your horn, Ma. Getting as pretentious as him!"

"Stop, you're embarrassing me."

"You stop, you're too old to be embarrassed. They carry her lamps in some wonderful boutiques in Kingston and Princeton. I'm going to show them around here in Montréal. With your permission, Ma. What do you think?"

"Whatever you want," she says, with resignation. "It's the doing I like."

Noah beams. "Always comes back to that."

The waitress clears their starters and refills their glasses.

"I have another craft I do too," Jane goes on, her tongue loosened by the wine, by the novelty of her daughter having a man in her life.

Willow watches Noah look at her mother with receptive

eyes. She thinks how beautiful he is, this gentleness with her mother.

"The other one I do," Jane goes on, "is my books."

"You write?" Noah asks.

"Nah. Just the captions. These are my books of memory. Everything that happens, I have pictures, souvenirs. I write a little about it, this I do for Willow." Jane looks at her daughter and Willow is embarrassed; the memory books are private, a miniature world shared by her and her mother alone.

"As long as we're living," Jane proclaims, "we're making new memories. Every day."

Noah nods slowly. "I never thought of it that way, Janey," he says.

"And when we're dead," Jane continues, her dark eyes on Willow. "We have no new memories to make, but our loved ones share these old ones forever in books."

No one says anything.

Blessedly, the meal arrives and they concentrate on their food.

As they rest, sipping their wine and water, the waitress clears.

"Nice," Jane says suddenly, "both of you doing drama."

"Yes," Noah says, "much in common."

The waitress passes the dessert menu and they order a *tarte tatin* for Noah, the chocolate gateau with the melting hot chocolate center for Willow, and a cheesecake for Jane.

"Are you married?" Jane asks Noah suddenly.

"Ma!"

"No," he says politely. "Not married."

"Not yet?" she persists.

He smiles at her, "Marriage, Janey, is not for everyone."

Willow sees her mother smile now. "Truer words were never spoken!" she says.

Noah insists on treating them to the meal and Willow says good-bye to him on the street. They kiss, right in front of her mother, and he embraces Jane.

"A nice man, you have," Jane says in front of Noah. "You be good to him," she warns.

Noah laughs.

"And I'll take good care of her," he reassures Jane.

"I don't need taking care of," Willow snaps back, "but thanks for the thought."

Jane tells Willow she wants to stroll back to Esplanade, "to walk off dinner."

"Are you sure, Ma?"

Jane nods vigorously and they walk arm in arm in the cool summer evening, enjoying the breeze on their bare arms and necks.

"Such a nice boy!" Jane exclaims.

"Hardly a boy, Ma, at thirty-nine."

"I have a surprise for you." Jane stops under a streetlamp and riffles through her purse, tugging out an envelope.

"Oh-oh," Willow groans, worried.

"Two tickets to Prague!"

Willow just stares at her mother.

"I made you a promise once—and I keep my promises!"

Willow hugs her mother tightly. "I've always wanted to go, Ma, you know that. I'm here in Montréal for a reason, you know?"

"I know," Jane murmurs, but does not offer anything more.

"But are you sure you want to go? It's been so long."

Jane nods resolutely. "I need to—with *you*."

"Won't it cost a fortune?"

"Well, at Witness they helped me. A relative of one of the women who works there—Ilana Cohen—she has an apartment she rents out in Prague, right in the Old City. So I got a good deal for a place to stay."

"You're something."

Jane nods proudly.

"Well, I have this fall show coming, but we've waited . . . "

"A lifetime."

And Willow thinks to herself but her mother says it aloud: "Now or never, farshteyst? I don't know where is home, anymore," her mother murmurs, "here or there or . . . "

They stroll slowly, digesting dinner, the conversation about the prospect of the trip.

"So," Jane says, "We better start packing. We leave the day after tomorrow."

"Mom!"

Jane takes Willow's arm in hers and breaks into a clip. "And when I come back in the fall—for your show, Willow—I want you to meet some people."

Willow feels her blood surge.

"Old friends I ran into here."

"*Which* old friends, Ma?" She leads her mother across St.

Denis, lined with lovely boutiques and restaurants, lit by tiny, white fairy lights to celebrate warmth and summer, life itself, though she is distracted now, on edge.

"People. I thought maybe they were gone, dead, but they are still very much alive."

"Why not tell me about them now, tonight?" she presses.

"Tonight, I'm tired, lovey. Everything in time."

Willow sighs. Her mother has kept certain memories to herself for a lifetime; perhaps she'll take them to her grave.

❋ ❋ ❋

TWENTY-TWO

June 2005
Prague

JANE STROLLS THROUGH the heart of Old Town Prague floating in a sea of strangers, leaning into Willow for balance. Families, lovers, friends, all inhabiting private worlds, spill out onto the cobbles in the square, lounging at cafés under confetti-colored umbrellas, sharing coffees and pastries, chattering away. Jane knows no one, is known by no one. The summer morning is luminous with sunshine, a pleasant breeze in the air, the sky pale blue. The shimmering brightness of the day mocks Jane, leaving a metallic taste in her mouth; she has not felt this lonely since she lost her entire family in the concentration camp.

Now she strains to hear threads of her native Czech in the roar of English, occasionally a bit of French or German, a phrase in Italian or Spanish peppered through the buzz, which threatens to drown her. Throngs crowd the Old Town, free of traffic, but for a few picturesque horse-drawn carriages for the benefit of tourists. Jane feels Willow's lean arm sweep around her shoulder and she relaxes into her daughter's strength. They have this unspoken communion—it's come back—from when Willow was small, an understanding without words. Jane sighs, less hollow than before. No, she is not alone in this place that was once her home, effaced of connections, she has a beautiful daughter to ground her wherever she travels.

"Ma, you want to stop for a cold drink?" Willow asks. "Rest a bit?"

Yes no yes no yes no . . . She has not been back to Prague, what is it now—sixty-three years, since 1942, a lifetime ago. Jane longs to find some sinew of connection to what was once her home, perhaps there is nothing left. Everyone gone, everything lost.

"Let's have a lemonade, Ma," Willow breaks into her thoughts. "It's hot, walking."

Jane lets her daughter lead her to an empty table under a striped umbrella. As they wait for service, Jane's thoughts boomerang wildly, a pinball caught in a machine. *Is Michaela still alive? The menorah, is it where we buried it? Papa, Mama, Ada, Samo, the Witness Foundation, Chaim, life, death, life.*

"Ma!"

Jane looks up, nonplussed. "Yes?"

A young waiter stands before her. He speaks to Jane in Czech. How painfully beautiful the language sounds in her ears.

"Ma, you okay?"

"An irritation, lovey. Do you have a tissue?"

Willow drags a packet of tissues from her satchel and gently wipes her mother's eyes.

The young waiter stands by, patient and gentlemanly, as Jane digs and reaches for words. She exchanges pleasantries with the waiter in Czech, rusty against her tongue.

Their tall, iced drinks arrive quickly and Jane finds herself revived by the tart sweetness.

"Later, I will show you my house, lovey."

"I want to see it, Ma."

"Where we lived and had the candy shop, Ivanova's, the treasure of the neighborhood."

Willow squeezes her hand, holds it for a moment in her own. "Yes, Mama," she murmurs. "Just as you promised me."

"And Michaela's. Michaela—alive, do you think?"

"Gee Ma, I don't know."

"Maybe we will stop by her house."

"Of course."

"It's near ours, mine I mean."

They finish their drinks and walk through the Old Town street by street, arm in arm, Jane pointing out the sights, linking them to her girlhood, Goltz-Kinsky Palace with its pink and white stucco facade, crowned with statues of the four elements, now an art gallery; Old Town Hall, with its famous astronomical clock and its crowd of visitors every hour; the Carolinum, with its carved Oriel window, where Kafka studied.

At a sidewalk shop, Jane and Willow pore over hand-painted Russian dolls, Communist memorabilia, and an array of watercolors illustrating the city and its sights. Jane bargains aggressively for a miniature painting of Old Town Square, her plump hands strident in the air.

Triumphant, she pays and hands the tissue-wrapped treasure to her daughter. "A copy of Vaclav Jansa, lovey, a nineteenth-century painter. See how little it's changed in one hundred years! Despite all that's lost."

Willow holds the painting, as if it is precious, then kisses her mother.

They stop in at a bookshop and Willow buys an old map of the Jewish Quarter. "For Noah," she explains to her mother.

Jane nods. "Don't let him get away."

As they near her old street, draw closer to what was once her home, Jane feels her body trembling and cannot stop.

"Ma, are you sure you want to do this?" Willow asks, stopping motionless in the street. "Take a moment to think about it."

Jane breathes heavily, but presses on. They reach the south side of Old Town Square, the block between Celetna and Zelezna Street.

"Lovey, here is Melantrichova Passage. . . . "

"The alley you walked through, Ma, I remember from the memory books. There is that statue you told me about, St. Anthony of Padua! It's just as you said."

"Yes, yes." She is unnerved that so much has changed, been blotted out, and yet Old Town Square is so well preserved. Obscene, it seems.

For a moment, Jane is dizzy, disoriented, as she tries to find her old home. But then she sees it. A different color now, blue with green trim. There is a café, it looks like, where the candy shop once thrived, and her home divided into—what is it? A tourist information center and gift shop. All around them, tourists are snapping pictures and Jane feels as though she might be sick.

"Ma, sit down: here's a bench."

In her daughter's eyes, Jane sees the burning wetness of her own. Jane tries to swallow the nauseating metallic thickness in her throat, to press down the fullness that threatens to rise up and out of her into a scream.

And then she hears the comforting sound of Willow's voice.

"Close your eyes, Ma."

Jane obeys.

"Tell me what your house was like."

"Cream with gold trim. So elegant. For the sign at our sweet-shop, Papa painted the letters IVANOVA'S in chocolate brown. He decorated the sign with candy, all kinds. Red, yellow, and green lollipops, like a bouquet of flowers, bonbons, and sweets tied with twists of gold and silver paper."

"Was there a sign for his studio?" Willow asks. "So people could come and view his work? I want to picture everything."

"People just knew."

"Which was your room, Ma?"

"Top floor. That's what I liked, Willow, being up so high. The eldest, I needed to protect my privacy. From my window, I could see our little back garden. Together, Mama and I tended it. Ada in the next room. My little brothers, snug as bugs, on the main floor beside my parents. Their room connected with Mama and Papa's."

With her eyes closed, the clamor on the street dimming in her ears, the interior of Jane's childhood home comes to her clear-edged and whole. She is inside, each room lit up golden in her mind, perfect as a dollhouse.

"Where did Samo sleep?"

"On my bed, if I let him. Or up against Mama and Papa's bed. Sometimes with my little brothers. He liked his freedom, to move from room to room."

"I can picture it, Ma."

Jane smiles. "Summer nights, Michaela and I would go up to the roof and lie on our backs. Stargazing, sharing secrets, our crushes mostly. Always, I had a crush on one boy or another and I couldn't stop talking about him. Them!"

The sun is hot on Jane's face; behind closed lids, the heat shimmers in rainbow colors. In a moment, other images intrude. *Soldiers ransacking the house, shattering her father's sculpted heads. The sound, terrible. Her father's face. Both her mother and father's faces, when they took her little brothers off the train . . .*

"I need to walk," Jane insists, her eyes flying open, sweat gathering between her heavy breasts and at the back of her neck. Willow takes her arm and they stroll a bit, wending their way through throngs of tourists.

"A walk will do us good," Willow insists.

But Jane cannot go far. She finds herself being drawn back to the home of her best friend, as if by an invisible thread, on the very same block, just a few doors down. Sure enough, there is her building, unchanged with its barrel vaulting painted a sage and forest green.

"Michaela, I want to see her," Jane declares.

Willow stares at her. "Ma, are you sure?"

Jane has already rung the bell. They wait silently for a few minutes, which feel longer. At last, a teenaged girl with a shining blond ponytail and lively bottle-green eyes answers the door. The eyes are Michaela's, the wide high cheekbones and narrow glittering eyes.

"Michaela!" Jane throws her arms around the young girl, burying her face in her shirt.

Gentle hands pry her loose.

Jane talks rapidly in Czech, the words coming fast, running into each other. "Do you know Michaela Lasenka?"

The girl's eyes soften. "That is my grandmother. She passed away three years ago."

Jane's heart collapses, as her own hot eyes meet the cool green ones, then rest on the denim mini-skirt, which hugs slender thighs and hips.

"You look like her," Jane continues in her mother tongue. "For a moment . . . "

The young girl smiles. "You are not the only one who says this."

"As girls, your grandmother and I were best friends."

Jane sees a light in the girl's eyes. Her face brightens.

"So you are Jana Ivanova?"

Jane nods slowly.

"My grandma talked of you often. She told me so much about you!"

"And this is my daughter, Willow."

"I'm Veta," the girls says, switching now to English. "Please do come up. My parents are away, but I can offer you some tea."

Jane looks at Willow and, without speaking, they follow Veta upstairs.

Veta motions to a soft tapestry couch and Jane sits down carefully, smoothing her skirt, then wiping her damp brow and neck with a clean hanky. She watches her old friend's granddaughter, this Veta, move around the room with vigor, straightening the spines of a few books on the shelf, snapping a throw smooth, whisking dust from a pigeonhole desk. Her movements have an energy and precision so much like Michaela's, it both comforts and spooks Jane. When Veta pulls out her ponytail and shakes her hair loose, as if she has just emerged from a swim into the shining sun, the likeness to Michaela is so striking, Jane feels a deep pain in her chest.

While Veta disappears into the kitchen to make tea, Willow puts her hand on her mother's shoulder. They sit close together, waiting. Since returning to Prague, Jane has longed for some connection to her vibrant life here, to her family, but there is so little left. All seems lost. But here is Veta, granddaughter of Michaela, and her own Willow.

Soon Veta returns with a steaming pot of tea and pastries, which she sets on a low mosaic table.

"My grandma, she was a wonderful baker. Try these. She taught me to make them."

There are fruit dumplings with melted butter, powdered sugar, and ground poppy seeds; a round yeast pastry with red currant jam and whipped cream; and a cherry strudel. Veta pours the tea and passes the pastry platter, then reaches for two dumplings, eating rapidly, motioning for Jane and Willow to do the same.

Jane takes a dumpling on her plate and eats slowly, the familiar taste so delicious, her mouth and teeth ache. She sips her tea, very hot, in a crystal glass with handles.

"These are delicious," Willow says to Veta. "You are an amazing baker."

"Like Michaela," Jane says. "She never had to worry about her figure, lucky girl!"

"Ma, how did you first meet Michaela?" Willow asks. "You never told me."

Jane's mind is wandering, her daughter's voice far away, and she doesn't answer right away.

Instead Veta says, "Ivanova's, you know, the sweetshop. My grandma came in for buttercrunch. That was her favorite."

"What, Ma, is buttercrunch?" Willow asks. "Remind me."

"Ah, buttercrunch. Chocolate-coated crunchy toffee. In squares, with chopped nuts on top. We filled ribboned bags with a half-dozen pieces. Michaela ate buttercrunch day and night."

Veta smiles at Jane with the same teeth-caught smile as M, a girl with a secret.

"After the war," Veta says, "my grandma, she didn't know if you were . . . still alive, but then she got some letters from you, from Montréal. She rejoiced that you were well. I think we still have your letters somewhere among my grandma's things. I know she sent you some of your belongings from before the war.

Jane feels a wave of exhaustion wash over her; she must lie down for a rest. "Later, we'll talk more," she says. "Now, I am tired."

"You've been so kind," Willow breaks in. "I think my mother needs to go back to our flat, you know?"

"Of course," Veta answers.

"But we'll pass by before we return to Montréal, to say goodbye."

"I hope so," Veta says.

Jane embraces the young girl who feels so light, her shoulder blades like wings, a ghost.

❀ ❀ ❀

TWENTY-THREE

BACK AT THE FLAT, Willow settles her mother into bed for a nap, covers her with a cotton blanket, lowers the blinds, and turns on the ceiling fan. All morning, wandering the streets of Old Town Prague, Willow tried to imagine what life had been like for her mother and her family before the war. It came to her in sudden flashes, a sense, an image, and then slipped away, like quicksilver. Today, with the streets free of traffic, except for a few horse-drawn carriages, and ringed with historical buildings, Prague seemed a fairyland, unreal as a stage set. The city was full and crowded with tourists from all over the world, but Willow didn't want to feel like—to be—merely one of them. Walking about with her mother, she tried to imagine Jane when she was young, thirteen, walking these same streets, browsing the stalls, her arm linked through Michaela's, both of them ready for anything; her mother, who gazed out at her from so many old photographs in the memory books, with dark flashing eyes and a boldly raised chin, adventurous, mischievous. Willow still sees glimpses of that pluck.

As Jane sleeps, Willow tries to read, then fixes a light supper for the two of them. At dusk, Willow hears her cry out, then mumble in a garbled language. Willow rushes to her bedside and strokes her mother's hot, damp forehead.

"It's okay, Ma, only a bad dream. I'm here."

Her mother sits up, the bed springs creaking under her considerable weight. Willow bolsters her back with pillows.

"The dream, I had it again," Jane says. "But now, we must go find it. It's there, here! I'm sure."

"What, Ma? Find what?"

"No, let's get ready. Now!"

"I have a light supper—"

"No!"

Her mother pushes Willow's comforting hand away and dresses quickly. In a moment she is out of the flat, Willow following behind. They make their way at a clip to the Old Jewish Quarter. The summer evening is soft and mild, the sky a deep blue—electric, the trees lacelike, inky black silhouettes. Willow stops to look at the Jewish Town Hall, a pink and white building in the flowery style of the late Baroque. On the roof stands a small, wooden clock tower with a green steeple and on one of the gables is a second clock. The hands of one move clockwise, the hands of the other counter clockwise, just as her mother had always described it. Time is moving both forward and backward at the same time, as it surely is for the two of them now.

"Come, Willow! We must hurry!"

Jane hustles Willow along the Parizska ulice, the street that practically divides Josefov in half, and then they navigate a tangled mesh of streets until they reach the Old Jewish Cemetery.

Willow and Jane enter the cemetery through the open gate, which has the inscription, *The House of Life.* Willow is startled by the snaggle-toothed tombstones, ornately carved and covering the uneven ground, slanting this way and that, some peaked, others jagged, rounded or squared, leaning up against one another in gray slate, black and mossy green. Low bushes thrust up between the headstones, a few sparse trees mark the perimeter of the cemetery. There is an unearthly quiet, they are alone here, but for the dead.

"Twelve layers deep," Jane mutters to her daughter, to herself. "This ground for Jews, it was the only one."

Willow examines some of the headstones in the glow of the streetlamp, each decorated with symbols: blessing hands, a pair of scissors, a leaping stag, bunches of grapes, the Star of David, a goose.

"How many?" she asks.

"One hundred thousand people. Right here," Jane says, tearing off toward the corner of the graveyard, where U Stareho intersects with Hrbitova, her plump arms pumping hard, Willow in tow.

"My tree! Where is my tree?" Jane cries out in despair, her voice cracking, as if she has lost a dear friend.

"What tree, Ma?"

"The linden tree. Right here." She stomps her foot on the damp, mulchy ground.

Before Willow can stop her, Jane is on her hands and knees, digging madly in the wet brown earth. She digs as if her own life depends on it, as if turning over this earth will save her. Willow tries to reason with her mother, to still her churning hands, now covered with earth, grass, and mud.

"I buried the menorah right here! To be safe, always hidden. Under the linden tree. Alive! No one would dig a grave beneath a green and growing tree."

Willow watches her mother shoveling up earth with her plump hands and tossing it aside, digging a deepening hollow. She remembers the picture of the menorah in the memory book, the one her grandpa made for her mother, with the figures of each family member—even the dog—as its candleholders. The whole family, intact, in that beautiful brass menorah.

Without thinking, Willow sinks to her knees and joins her mother. She claws up the wet, dense earth, flinging it aside, then grabs more by the handful. Both are in a fever, digging.

Suddenly, Willow feels a hot white glare shining on them. She sees it is nearly full dark. A policeman approaches, pointing his flashlight in their faces and shouting in Czech. Willow regrets never learning her mother's original language, but for a spattering of catch phrases suitable for tourists.

Jane shouts back, tears streaming down her face.

The policeman softens and bends down with some difficulty, helping to pull Willow's mother up from the hollow she has dug in the earth. As she stands, he winces in pain, then steadies Jane.

"Do you speak English?" Willow asks him, standing upright,

her arm in a protective sweep around her mother, who is panting heavily and still crying.

"A little. I understand well."

"My mother buried a menorah, a candleholder, here years and years ago. Under a linden tree that stood right here in this corner of the graveyard, apparently. She was just a teenager then. Maybe it was 1939? I'm not sure, exactly. This menorah was a family treasure. Her father, my grandfather sculpted it out of brass for Hanukkah, a special holiday for us . . . "

The policeman puts a gentle hand on Jane's shoulder and speaks laboriously in English.

"The tree you speak of, the linden tree, died."

"No!" Jane shouts.

"Well, madam, I'm afraid that it did die about five years ago." He sweeps back his thick, silver hair and presses his lips together. "They found some things here in this cemetery."

"My menorah?" Jane wails.

"The details I don't know well. Some things were found, I believe. Everything was placed in Klausen Synagogue. There is a small museum now."

Willow takes her mother's arm.

"I need to close the cemetery for the night," the policeman says. He holds out an arm, motioning them to leave. Willow supports her mother's weight as they leave the Old Jewish Cemetery and walk slowly, as if to a funeral, back to their borrowed flat.

They both awaken very early the next morning and Willow cooks them a hearty breakfast of eggs, toast, sausage, and coffee. Without planning or speaking, they set out together for Klausen Synagogue in a gray pelting rain.

"This place," Jane says, "is built on the ruins of small Jewish schools and prayer houses. *Klausen*, they were called."

Klausen is a high baroque temple with a fine, barrel-vaulted interior and rich stucco decorations. "Was this your synagogue, Ma, where your family worshipped?"

"Yes, lovey, it was."

Together they move slowly through the synagogue and Willow marvels at the perfectly preserved artifacts, relics, and sacred objects displayed within its walls. Hebrew prints and manuscripts, a Hebrew lettered alms box with an outstretched hand dating from 1800, and an exhibition of Jewish traditions and customs.

In an adjoining building, which looks like a tiny medieval castle, they find a museum with children's drawings from the Terezin concentration camp.

Willow holds her mother while she weeps and talks and talks, an outpouring, bringing back to life her mama, papa, Ada, and her three lost brothers, and for the first time ever, Willow can visualize real people, and then, their bodies.

As they are about to leave, they see a long glass display case against the western wall of the museum, and gaze inside. A long sound comes out of Jane's mouth, a moan.

There, behind glass, is the menorah Willow has heard about for so many years. A deep blackened brass, now greenish in places, with the sculpted figures of Jane's mother and father on either end, Jane next to her father, Ada beside her mother, and the three brothers, Pavel, Josef, and Jan, even the dog Samo. The figure of

Jane's mother is bent and part of the *shames* is curved instead of straight, but there is the menorah, safe, intact.

"Oh, Mama," Willow murmurs

Her mother is silent, wistful, in a private world all her own.

❋ ❋ ❋

TWENTY — FOUR

July 2005
Kingston, New Jersey

JANE IS HOME three weeks now, the Kingston summer in full heat and bloom. She likes mornings and evenings best when the fresh breeze washes through the open windows and the grass smells sweet.

It is morning and Jane sits at her kitchen table, enjoying coffee and a roll with butter. Lined up on the counter are three lamps and shades, two she found when she was in Montréal visiting Willow, one at a flea market, the second in an antique shop in Outremont. The third is from her childhood home in Prague; Veta had presented it to her to take back home.

Hours she spent in her workroom, cutting, arranging, then pasting and decoupaging, until the effect was just right. One lampshade is shaped like a candle flame—when she discovered it in a pile of old junk at the market, Jane couldn't believe it! She had never seen anything like it, the shade made of a combination of linen and silk. Jane decorated it with old black and white photographs of her own family, her mother, father, brothers, and herself in Prague—at their home, in the candy shop, and below in her Papa's studio. She didn't deliberate before deciding to decorate the lampshade this way. Since she'd arrived home from Prague, she'd been sorting through the old photos Michaela had saved for her. She just began, without thought. And once she started, it seemed right, though she wept each day as she worked, tears dripping onto the worktable and old images, tears that felt like a spring rain, washing her clean. To make something new and yet old, to keep her family alive with light, helped her heal, just a little.

She pours herself another cup of coffee, stirs in a swirl of cream and several teaspoons of sugar. She is quite pleased with her handiwork. Maybe she will give the newly made lamp to Willow in the fall.

In early October, she will return to Montréal. She's been in close touch with Willow since her visit, but misses her with a constant ache. It was nice living in her apartment, meeting the man in her life, spending time together in Montréal, then in Prague. Willow says she and this Noah are still going strong. A miracle!

More and more, Jane thinks of Chaim, dreams of him, images and scenes from their shared past in Prague, the DP camp, Montréal. She awakens many mornings, uncertain of where she is, young and lost, in love with Chaim Rosenblum, or fighting him off tooth and nail. She realizes as one grows older, the past becomes more real, more vivid, than the present.

She dreams of her brass menorah, but not of digging it up or burying it deep. Instead she sees her whole family, all seven of them lighting the candles on Hanukkah, the flames burning bright, visible inside and outside their home.

She will reclaim the menorah and save it for Willow. Surely this is what her father would have wanted, to keep the menorah in the family, to have the candles lit up bright and burning each Hanukkah. And it is what Jane herself wants. Now she is sure, clear.

As soon as she returned home to New Jersey, she enlisted the help of Chaim and the Witness Foundation with all the paperwork and bureaucracy. They got the wheels turning. Both had clout! Any day now, she hopes she'll see that menorah on her mantelpiece at home here in Kingston, so she can light the candles with her daughter next Hanukkah. A *mitzvah*.

After breakfast, Jane goes to her bedroom and finds the tiny gold key to her mother's old jewelry box, which she keeps in the back of her underwear drawer. She slips the key into one pocket of her cotton housedress, fills the other with paper clips and rubber bands, and makes her way upstairs to her bedroom and into her walk-in closet. She cranks open the step stool and drags it underneath the crawlspace. Slow and steady she climbs, pushes open the trapdoor, and steps inside the small eave space, not large enough, really, to call an attic.

During Willow's childhood, she told her child there were bats in here, and Jane kept the trapdoor locked. Inside, is an old wooden cabinet, a jewelry box, and ancient hatboxes from Prague filled with loose photographs and letters. Jane knows she needs to get ready for her fall visit, to prepare Willow for the shock of meeting her father. She wonders if she is doing right, but knows it would be far worse for Willow to discover the truth after her death, to feel a betrayal by her own mother that Jane would no longer be able to soften or explain. Every decision of her life since Willow's birth has been to protect her daughter, to keep her safe, to keep her life from being dark or heavy with the weight of a terrible history that she had nothing to do with and could never fully understand.

With a shaking hand, Jane pulls on the string cord and the old bare bulb illuminates the skeletal wood of the eave space with a brownish glow.

First, Jane opens one of the boxes, which is full of letters— many from Chaim. It is painful to look at these, to see his small, neat script. Jane can feel the words like Braille and imagines what he must have felt, given her stony silence.

She gathers the letters into a stack, binding them with a rubber band. In the dim light, she goes through old photographs. So many pictures of her and Chaim, a shared history that does not exist for Willow. Jane puts the pictures in piles, trying to organize them, grouping them together, some with paper clips, others with rubber bands.

Finally, she picks up the mahogany jewelry case—her mother's—preserved by Michaela's family, and sent to Jane after the war. Her hands are stiff with arthritis and it is difficult to open the bottom drawer, but finally her fingers do her bidding.

In one of the tiny compartments, lined in lapis velvet, she finds the gold locket shaped like the fleur de lys, Chaim's gift to her on the mountain, a photograph of the two of them inside. She tries to pry the locket apart. At last, the two halves spring open. There is the photograph of the two of them, cheeks touching, hands entwined, eyes on each other.

Though the picture is tiny, Jane thinks she looks well in it, glowing and happy. Her face is full with good health, her eyes shining, her chin nestled toward his. And Chaim looks handsome, with the large, gray eyes she loves, the strong, square chin, the full and resolute mouth. So she won't lose the locket, Jane fastens it around her own neck.

All morning, she takes things down from the crawlspace to her workroom: the letters, the photos. Then the hatboxes filled with other pictures, more letters, the whole jewelry case, which she wants to go through at her leisure. Everything she sets up in her workroom.

Later on, she locates two beautiful scrapbooks she's been saving, one of brown leather, the other a deep wine color, with a floral pattern burned into the leather. She sets herself up, makes a full pot of coffee, and begins to work on a new memory book.

Cutting and pasting, writing long notes in the margins and on separate pages, she passes the summer night. As dawn blues the sky, she is not yet finished, but feels a weight in her blood, a numbness down her side. Before the knife-like pain cuts through her chest, she stumbles to the phone and calls Sunny.

"Sunny dear, I've overdone it," she says quietly to her best friend. "I think I'm having a heart attack."

❀ ❀ ❀

TWENTY - FIVE

August 2005
Princeton, New Jersey

AS SOON AS WILLOW gets the emergency call from Sunny, she takes the first plane home. Her mother is being cared for at Princeton Hospital on Witherspoon. In a cool yet sunny room, her mother sits up in bed, her lovely silver hair disheveled. Willow embraces her mother gently and sits on the edge of the narrow bed, her side against her mother's hip.

Jane is in the "Life Care" unit, and though it has only been a few weeks since they returned from their Prague trip, Willow can see that she has failed a great deal.

"I'm not happy," Jane says.

"What, Ma?"

"This hospital johnnie, I have no dignity. Go home and get me my nightie, the pink one with ivory lace."

Willow takes one of her mother's gnarled hands, smiling down at her, "Still a bit of the coquette, Ma, eh?"

"Go, Willow."

"Later." Willow is afraid to leave her mother's side, but doesn't know what to do. "Give me a chance to catch up with you, okay?" Jane nods, a toxic look in her dark eyes. "Always, you know best," she snaps.

"You look tired, Ma," Willow says. "You should nap a bit."

"As a corpse I'll nap!" she cries out, trying to raise herself higher on the pillow.

Willow lifts her mother gently in her arms, surprised by how light she feels, nearly weightless. She takes her mother's comb and fixes her silver hair until it lies smooth against her cheeks, just as a stocky black nurse with salt-and-pepper braids comes in to check on her.

"Don't be getting your mother all riled up, now," she warns Willow. "She needs her rest."

"That's just what I've been telling her," Willow says, shooting her mother a warning look.

"Lil here, she bathes me and dresses me, changes my sheets, and makes sure I eat. A queen I am!"

They share a laugh together, as Willow notices the golden locket shaped like the fleur de lys.

"Ma, that's pretty." She leans in close to her mother and takes the delicate golden flower between her fingers. "I've never seen it before."

"Open it," her mother says. "It's hard for me now."

Willow pries the delicate charm apart and sees the photograph. She looks close, examining it for a long while.

"That's me," her mother says, looking into Willow's eyes, "with your father."

Willow looks closer. "You are so beautiful, Ma."

"I felt very happy at that time."

"He doesn't look older than you, Ma, not at all." She stares at her mother. "He's handsome."

"Still is," her mother slips, biting her lip until it bleeds.

"What?"

Jane snaps the golden locket closed. "Willow, I need a tissue, I'm bleeding."

Willow feels the echo of a nameless reverberation deep in her blood, like vibration before sound. Perhaps her mother is not right in the head, confused, the past melding with the present. She is afraid to question her right now.

Just then, Lil wheels in a dinner tray. Tepid chicken puree, applesauce, and tapioca adorned with some peeled grapes, which resemble eyeballs. Willow feels her stomach jump with nausea.

"Nice 'n easy on the stomach," says Lil. "Bon appétit."

Jane shoves the tray away, like a petulant child.

"The cuisine is not worth the money," she says. Willow is pleased that she still has her sense of humor.

When Lil leaves, Jane says suddenly to Willow, "You've got to get me out of here!"

"You're recovering from a heart attack, Ma."

"I'll have another one if I stay here."

She looks near tears and Willow gathers her into her arms. Though it's been only a few weeks, she has dropped so much flesh that Willow can feel her bones beneath the flimsy hospital gown.

"Do something for me, Willow," Jane says, her voice stronger. "Take off the locket."

"Of course, Ma. Is it annoying you?"

"No, no."

Willow removes the locket carefully, cradling the fleur de lys in her palm.

"Put it on," Jane commands. "I want you to have it."

Willow fastens the locket around her neck and lays it carefully against her chambray shirt. She pulls out the compass, which nestles in the hollow of her throat and exposes the two necklaces together, outside her shirt.

"What's that?" her mother asks, eagle-eyed as always.

"A gift from Noah. You remember him, Ma."

"Of course I remember. Your nice young man, the playwright."

"That's him, Ma."

"What is it? Let me see."

Willow leans down and her mother fingers the compass on the heavy gold and platinum chain. She examines the chain for a long while, then the compass.

"A funny gift, he gives you. The chain is beautiful. Very old."

"So I'll never lose my way, Ma."

"Nice," her mother says, smiling, a glow in her dark eyes. "You hold onto that Noah. Don't let him slip away. Please, lovey."

Willow nods, reassuring her mother. She has so many questions, a terrible pressure within, but is afraid of pushing her mother too hard when she is so frail.

"From home, Willow, I want you to bring me a few things."

"Yes, Ma, I'll make a list." Willow takes out the small black leather notebook she keeps in her purse. "The white lace nightie . . ."

"You're not listening ! The pink nightie with the ivory lace."

"Okay," she gently squeezes her mother's hand, "got it."

Her mother has a look of great relief in her eyes, as she requests a few more items from home. "Good, it's settled, then. You go home, lovey. Get my things. I'll nap a little."

"Yes, Ma," Willow promises. "But I want to sit with you while you fall asleep, like you used to sit with me."

"So the witches, they wouldn't get you," says Jane, a smile passing across her lips, eyes closing slowly.

"The witches and the green glittery monsters," adds Willow.

"And the bad men," murmurs her mother. "The bad blue men with eyes in the middle of their foreheads, and tentacles like octopi."

"And the men who . . . "

"One thing I'll tell you about men," her mother begins, but her voice trails off and Willow can hear her gently breathing, then snoring into sleep. She sits with her mother, not wanting to leave. Her mother naps awhile, opens her eyes, asks for her nightgown.

"I've not gone yet, Ma, but I will, soon. Promise." She takes her mother's hand, cradling it inside her own. Her mother smiles at her, dark brown eyes on Willow's and then she peers at the compass pendant and the fleur de lys locket. These seem to please her and she nods to herself.

They sit quietly, tranquil, Jane's eyes once again on Willow's.

In a half-hour or so, Willow feels her mother's hand go limp inside her own and when she releases it, her mother's arm drops like a weight over the edge of the narrow bed.

Willow looks into her mother's eyes, now flat slate buttons, leached of life.

Gently, she lifts her mother's arm back onto the bed and squeezes in beside her, spooning her long slender body around her mother's, holding her mother's head in her arms, its shape perfect in her hands.

❀ ❀ ❀

PART III

KNOWING

TWENTY — SIX

August 2005
Montréal

FROM THE MOMENT OF DEATH, Willow watches over her mother in a vigil. Her death is not real and Willow is afraid to leave her alone. If she leaves her mother now, the worst—which has already happened—will close in on her.

Her mother's wishes, written clearly in her will, are to be buried in Montréal. Willow is taken aback, New Jersey is her mother's home, but then she remembers Prague, the war, all of her losses, Montréal, then Kingston, then Montréal—the endless back and forth—and wonders what home means.

Willow waits in the small, white waiting room of the funeral home during the careful cleansing and dressing of her mother's body. She imagines the trickling of water, the shushing of sponges and soap, soothing sounds. Her mother will be dressed in a full set of clothing, white linen, with an enveloping shroud, a mixture of egg white and vinegar dabbed on her forehead, the traditional way of identifying a Jew. Earth and broken pottery from Israel, according to her mother's last wishes, will be placed in the casket along with her body.

At Back River Memorial Gardens, the old cemetery at the corner of Berri and Sauvé Streets in Montréal's northeast end, a small cluster of mourners, many from New Jersey, some from Montréal, gather to pay tribute to Jana Ivanova. The thrum of voices surrounds Willow, Yiddish, Hebrew, Czech, Hungarian, French, and English, the voices of people who worked with her mother at Cedarpark School, friends and neighbors from Kingston and Princeton, the staff at the Witness Foundation, fellow Holocaust survivors, Willow's neighbor Luc Belanger, and of course Sunny and Noah, both of whom stay close to Willow, one on each side, throughout the ceremony.

The late summer day begins with a patter of rain, soft, persistent, settling on the cemetery, a twilit blanket of greenish dark. Rabbi Elihu Zamir, a handsome, flushed-face man with a long, reddish beard, distributes a sole black ribbon to Willow, Jana Ivanova's only immediate living family, and Noah helps her pin it to the lapel of her black silk suit. Willow watches the rabbi as he nicks her ribbon with a small knife to make a tear, a symbol of the tear in Willow's heart. He recites the prayer:

Barukh atah Adonai . . .

"I need a ribbon, too."

Willow hears a deep, booming voice resonate in the quiet. She sees a large, tall man with thick silver hair brushed straight back from his forehead. His broad shoulders and barrel chest strain the seams of his black suit as he approaches her and the rabbi with a slow resolute gait, arms held wide from his sides. Willow knows his name is Chaim Rosenblum, director and founder of Ha'makom, whom Noah has mentioned. She and Noah look at one another, then at Chaim, bewildered.

Chaim lays a hand on Willow's shoulder, claiming her. His large, sun-browned hand is heavy, his touch firm.

Willow stands frozen in the damp summer rain. She lets it fall on her neck, face, and hands. For a moment she longs to be away from here, anywhere, alone, back in her basement studio, safe with Mr. Gregarov, Ernestine and Trevor, Lise and Alphonse, surrounded by her miniature made-up family.

She looks into the clear, gray eyes of Chaim Rosenblum and he looks back at her, a sudden flinch. Willow glances at Noah; he tightens his arm around her shoulder, while Sunny holds her hand. Chaim looks directly into Willow's eyes, willing her to look at him. "I am your father," he says.

"My father died before I was born," Willow says now, speaking too fast, her voice toneless. "I never knew him."

"It's my fault you never knew me," Chaim says, glancing away.

Willow feels a moment of disbelief, then nausea. She leans against Noah to steady herself, sees that he knows nothing of this either. Willow finds herself unable to stop looking at this strange man, Chaim; though he is elderly, he seems full of life and strength.

"I'm sorry," Chaim says softly. "Your mother only wanted to protect you. It was for you, she lived."

Willow nods, tugging down her black silk jacket, smoothing her skirt, but it is as if another woman is doing these things, a double, disconnected from her body, soul, and spirit.

"We'll talk later. I'll come to see you."

Willow cannot reply.

"We'll meet. I have so much to explain."

"I have to go back to New Jersey," Willow says dully. "My mother's things, I need to go through them. I know she left me some letters, books," Willow goes on, fingering the compass and locket at her throat.

Willow sees Chaim's eyes alight on the locket and a sudden glow warm his face. "You are wearing it," he says.

Willow lifts the locket, pries it open, strains to gaze down at the tiny black-and-white photograph.

Chaim looks at the picture, then at Willow. "I remember that day, though it was years ago, better than some things that happened to me yesterday! How happy we were on that day."

Rabbi Zamir clears his throat, impatient to proceed.

Chaim glares at him, "I need a ribbon," he commands.

The rain beats on. Willow feels breath fill her chest. She knows Chaim's eyes are on her, as if eyes could touch, but she cannot look at him. There are the rabbi's hands, pinning the black ribbon on Chaim Rosenblum's lapel, the sound of the grosgrain ripping with the slash of his knife and the whole world stands still for Willow.

Ankle-deep ruts fill with water, some of the pathways, overgrown with weeds and grass, show the ravages of time, neglect. Willow notices century-old headstones weathered by

the harsh Montréal winter toppled off their eroding bases—rows
and rows of immigrant Jews like her mother, many who died
as children, teens, or young adults— graves in pathways, some
at right angles to one another, others like afterthoughts, just
squeezed in. It reminds her of the Old Jewish Cemetery in
Prague.

Rabbi Zamir continues his interrupted prayer:

"*Barukh atah Adonai eloheinu melekh ha'olam, dayan haemet.*
Praised are you, Adonai our God, Ruler of the Universe, the true
judge."

The day is quite warm, a steady drip from the trees, but Willow
feels a chill. She clings to Noah and Sunny who stay by her side,
supporting her, one on each arm and Willow thinks, disbelieving,
in a moment she has found her absent father and he has found
her, just as she is burying her mother.

Willow feels, in this moment, that she would give anything
to have a little more time with her mother, to hear the truth from
her lips. Her mother came so close to death as a young woman, it
is hard for Willow to conceive of anything overcoming her now.
Then in an instant, no more breath.

She has so many things she wants to ask her mother, questions
she's saved up for a lifetime. Part of her feels like she is waiting
for her mother to come to her, to speak.

The questions, some of them maybe this Chaim Rosenblum
can answer, others she knows, will remain open-ended. This will
be the way she will miss her mother, through what she doesn't
know and can never understand.

Already, she is carrying on a conversation with her mother in her mind, as she does with her puppets. Some of her questions are filled with hurt and fury.

Why did you never tell me? About my father? My real father, who is living and breathing! Why did you wait so long to tell him about me?

So many people surround her at the cemetery, people she knows and loves, strangers too.

"God is good," intones Rabbi Zamir.

Willow doesn't think this way, did her mother? Does her father? And what about Noah? No, her mother did not believe in a kindly white-bearded man in the clouds—or woman for that matter—or a sky full of care and concern. How could she?

And yet.

"Before life on earth," Rabbi Zamir chants, "Jana Ivanova existed within her mother's womb, Hannah Ivanova. At birth, she left her mother's womb and entered the womb of earth, the source of sustenance. And now she enters the womb of creation. Jana Ivanova's life was a bridge connecting birth and death."

The rain lets up to a faint drizzle, weak sun filtering through the clouds, an eerie greenish light permeating the cemetery, alchemical light.

"Jana Ivanova has passed," continues Rabbi Zamir, "but her *neshama* hovers around her body. This neshama is the essence of Jana Ivanova, her consciousness, thoughts, deeds, experiences, relationships, love, her Being. Jana Ivanova's body was its container and the neshama, now on its way to the eternal world, will leave her body once it is buried in the earth."

As the rabbi blesses her mother, Willow finds herself bargaining with God, a God she is not sure she believes in, over what she would sacrifice to have one more day with her mother, a walk down the street, their arms linked.

And then Willow turns and looks at Chaim Rosenblum, his silver hair soaked with rain, his broad, craggy face glistening, his gray eyes wet.

Willow watches Chaim Rosenblum take a shovel, hands trembling, and fling the first heap of earth onto the lowered casket. Others join in, working together, filling the grave until a mound is formed. Without Noah's hand, Willow feels anchorless. She sees Noah and Chaim standing together, their sides touching, then Sunny's arm is around her back.

Willow gently frees herself from Sunny's embrace and kneels to the ground, searching for a stone to place on her mother's grave. A stone, you put a stone. She rakes her hands through the muddy earth, searching in the muck, in the puddles, and then she finds it, mauve-colored, shaped like a kidney bean. Willow rinses it in a pool of rainwater and sees the twisting vein of blue-black mica glinting.

Rabbi Zamir says Kaddish, and family and friends make way for Willow.

She lays the stone on her mother's grave and leaves with empty hands.

✻ ✻ ✻

TWENTY – SEVEN

August 2005
Kingston, New Jersey

WILLOW IS ALONE in the white, green-shuttered Victorian on Madison Street, her childhood home, surrounded everywhere by her mother's absent presence. Awakening in her old room, buttery sun streams through the windows and warms the hardwood floors, a gentle breeze billowing the lace curtains, as Willow girds herself for the task ahead. She feels she has tapped into a shaky place in a mineshaft; everything she thought she knew about herself and her mother caving in at once.

Stretching in bed, Willow thinks of Roger Pelletier, caretaker of the mountain chalet, the phantom father her mother created for her half-heartedly and with so little imagination—a few sketchy brushstrokes, amorphous images that could never coalesce into a whole—while her real father, Chaim Rosenblum, stood living and breathing, larger than life right there in Montréal.

Willow peels off the sweaty shorts and tank she's slept in, opens her suitcase to find an oversize T-shirt of Noah's, and slips into its worn comfort. In the folds of a shirt is Mr. Gregarov, her first puppet, made by the grandfather she never knew, and she realizes Noah must have slipped him in there for her. He wanted to join her on this trip back home, but Willow knew she had to do this alone. Now, she clutches old Mr. G. in her arms, his sock body soft and pilled, his button eyes, cracked mother-of-pearl, still glinting their rainbow colors. She stares into those button eyes, straining to imagine her Grandpa Vilem, the sculptor who made puppet heads and manned the famous sweetshop, as she slips Mr. G. over her bedpost, his familiar haunt.

Willow craves the familiar, but the house is strange without her mother. She wanders slowly from room to room, as if her mother might magically appear at any moment. The house is alive: parlor windows open, doors ajar, a vase of drooping flowers shedding their velvet petals in the center of the dining room, notice of an antique lamps show, a fund-raising picnic for Cedarpark School, a scribbled recipe for strawberry shortcake, all tacked to the fridge door with fruit magnets alongside photos of her mother, Sunny, and herself. The simple quotidian world.

The old house breathes, contracting around her, a slightly musty smell, threaded through with the last of her mother's cooking. She always ate heartily, as if she might never eat again.

Willow opens six windows—the house has an extraordinary number of them—and slides the glass sunroom doors open to the day. She fixes herself coffee and a glass of orange juice, drinking it in one swallow at the sink. Then she takes her coffee out to the yard, where she spent so many summer evenings with her mother. The garden is in bloom, colorful displays of marigolds, zinnias, scarlet sage, and other annuals. Sunny taught her mother about flowers and she'd become good with them, tending her garden with Sunny's advice. Willow has never believed in her mother's death, in her not being here, as if she were immortal, and life, eternal.

Willow assumed her mother had been protecting her all these years from a loser, not a strapping, lion-maned survivor and leader who had built a center for Jewish life in Montréal.

From the house, Willow hears the shrill ring of the phone and lets it trill on. When she finally steps back into the house, the answering machine has clicked on and her mother's voice fills the room, the shock of her nearness colliding with the fact of her death.

Other calls come in, one after the other, and Willow listens to her mother's voice, as if in those carefully modulated sounds lie the clues to who she really was, who Willow is.

Willow goes into her mother's small workroom. Everywhere are her lamps, some scattered memory books, stacks of magazines, scissors, glue. On the worktable is a heavy book with a design of vines and flowers burned into the wine-colored leather. Willow sits down in her mother's chair, the book heavy on her lap. When she opens it, she finds the two pockets in the front and back covers stuffed with letters and mementoes. Some of the letters are in her mother's familiar handwriting, light, swirling script, large on the page and slanting upward. Others are in a different hand, small and very dark, pressed hard into the page.

If only her mother were here, Willow thinks, her fingers working on their own to free the letters tucked into the back pocket, she could explain it all. A hollow in her chest, Willow knows that her mother might not, but then she remembers that her father is well, alive. He can speak for himself.

The doorbell rings, its familiar chimes echoing through the house, and Willow is startled from her reverie. She freezes, shuts the covers of the book, as she hears Sunny calling out for her, striding through the house until she finds Willow in her mother's workroom.

Taking Willow firmly by the arm, she tells her she stood outside ringing the bell for five minutes, then just opened the door with the extra key Jana had given her years before. In her brisk manner, Sunny leads Willow back into the kitchen and fixes her a tall glass of lemonade with sugar and empties out the coffee Willow had brewed earlier.

"Have you eaten anything?" she asks Willow, a concerned look in her eyes.

"I can't."

"Dear, you must." Sunny fixes a small plate of biscuits spread with lemon curd. While Willow nibbles a biscuit, Sunny moves through the house like a relief worker, setting it to rights, jotting down phone messages, wiping the counter and cleaning out the fridge, emptying trash, watering the plants.

"What time is it?" Willow asks.

"Nearly four-thirty."

"I lost the day."

Willow feels as if she has fallen through a fissure in time; maybe she will lose more days, whole weeks, months.

Sunny hands her another biscuit.

"My mother left me some things I need to go through," Willow says.

Sunny nods. "You have time."

"Did you know much about Mom before she came to New Jersey?" Willow asks.

"A bit, I didn't pry."

"Do you know she left me some letters and photographs, an album?"

"She mentioned she was trying to put some things together for you."

"She had this other life, this other self." *And now, so do I.*

"The truth has a fabulousness about it," Sunny says matter-of-factly, "from time to time."

Sunny offers to spend the night. Willow sleeps in her old fluffy canopied bed surrounded by her first puppets, Mr. Gregarov watching over her from the bedpost.

For hours, she tosses and turns. Sleep is out of the question. Sweating and restless, she throws off the bedclothes and pads down the hall to the bathroom, splashes cold water on her face, listening for the rumbling sounds of Sunny's snores from her mother's old room; she knows it is going to be a long night.

Down in the kitchen, Willow brews tea, and takes it to the workroom, dragging her mother's favorite rocker in from the den.

Settling into the chair, Willow opens the memory book, imagining her mother's plump hand moving across the thick pages, as she reads her words.

✻ ✻ ✻

Memory Book
July 2005, Kingston, New Jersey

Where to begin, lovey, I don't know, but begin I must. Now or never.
These books, I want to leave for you, Willow. At least this you will have.
The pictures, my story.

I am very tired, Willow. A different kind of tiredness. Finding and
collecting these old pictures, letters, has taken a lot out of me, and now
I paste them into this book for you.

Your whole life, lovey, you've asked about your father. Who he is.
I've said little; it's been too painful. Easier to tell you that he was a
nice man, Québécois, Roger Pelletier, a name I saw once on a sign! In
a pinch, that name came to me.

A nice man I made up. Older than me. French-Canadian. Caretaker
of the chalet on the mountain I loved so much, a smoker, who died from
black lungs. Someone who loved you. I wanted you to feel that love, to
be whole. Maybe your poor father was dead, but still, he'd wanted you.

You wouldn't have a hole in your heart. You would have the glow of his love, imagining it anyway.

Forgive me, Willow. A liar, I am not. Call it a white lie, to protect, to safeguard. To make sure you would not ache for a father who did not want you, who could not be a part of your life.

Now I think maybe I didn't do right. Each person has their own side to a story. My hope is, you will understand mine.

What am I saying?

Your real father is very much alive. His name is Chaim Rosenblum. Chaim means life.

My life, he saved once. Breathed life back into me, when I was not here, not there, not dead, but not living. I owe him my life. Without him, I would not be and you would not exist.

Chaim is your father, Chaim Rosenblum. A beautiful name, no? And in some ways—many—a beautiful person. I hope now you will discover this for yourself.

We kept missing each other. Two people, Willow, who speak the same language, who come from the same suffering, still sometimes can't talk. It makes me sad, these missed connections.

Now I see the situation from inside his skin, as well as my own. I am no longer filled with fear, hurt, and anger. I am too old for this nonsense.

I have rachmones for Chaim now, rachmones.

I am so sorry for the pain I caused you, Willow. Looking back, I see things differently than when I was inside each moment.

Your father, I want you to meet your father. It is late, but not too late. Willow, where there is life, there is hope, no? For you, lovey. Always, everything I do, I do for you.

TWENTY — EIGHT

August 2005
Montréal

WHEN WILLOW RETURNS home to her apartment in Montréal, she finds a fusillade of messages from her newfound father. She knows he will not allow her to ignore him, will not permit anyone to rob him of his existence. Despite the long years of absence and silence, he won't be turned away.

She is home only forty-eight hours when Chaim appears at her doorstep.

The day is very hot, humid, and Willow can see he is sweating, his broad face shiny, as he wipes it with a monogrammed handkerchief. He is wearing jeans, sneakers, and a T-shirt emblazoned with a Mogen David and the logo for Ha'makom, which says beneath it, "Our Place on Earth." In one arm, he is carrying a bulky package.

"My calls—why didn't you return them?"

Willow holds her breath, she doesn't know what to say. "I've just gotten back from Kingston. There was a lot to do there, and there's more. I'll have to sell the house."

He looks kinder now, a tender look in his eyes. "Yes, it's very hard."

Willow stands shielded by the half-closed door. She's embarrassed, wearing Noah's T-shirt as a nightie, still in her dressing gown.

"Are you going to ask me in?" Chaim demands. She realizes she's being rude, can't stop herself from smiling. "You stayed away nearly a lifetime, what's the hurry?"

Willow notices that funny flinch in his eyes. "Time is the hurry," he says. "We've lost too much already. It does not go on forever, or maybe it does, but not for us. You only have one father."

Willow snorts. "Two actually," she says, feeling the sarcasm creep into her voice, like a sour taste. "The real one I never knew, and the ghost-father I lived with, in loving memory."

He pulls the door open and she loses her balance for a moment. There is something so forceful about him that he scares her a little. "Excuse me," she says, with that snarky tone that eats into her voice when she is uncomfortable or caught off guard.

"No, excuse *me*. I don't like to barge in."

"I see," Willow says, anxious to get back to her marionettes, the studio. She has much to prepare for the fall show.

"You're tough," he says, "you get that from me."

Willow laughs, softening a little. She sees now where she comes from, at least a little. Her height she clearly gets from him, the shape of her eyes, and her strong straight nose is rather like his.

"A late riser you are," he says. "The day will get away from you."

"You call eight a.m. *late*? Come," Willow offers. "I'll put on some coffee. You sit and relax, while I get dressed."

He enters her apartment and places the bulky package on her floor.

"What have you got there?"

"Get dressed, then I'll show you."

Willow settles him on the couch in the living room. She brews coffee and dresses quickly. When she returns to the living room, Willow finds Chaim at the stone hearth, holding the brass menorah her grandfather sculpted so many years before, the one she and her mother glimpsed through glass at Klausen Synagogue in Prague.

"Jana knew the menorah would be returned to her family, she believed in that. We spoke about it."

The subject of the menorah had not come up again between Willow and her mother after their trip to Prague.

"She asked for my help," Chaim goes on, one powerful hand on the base, the other gently touching the sculpted figure of Jana as a young girl. "The Witness Foundation assisted us in the quest. The bureaucracy we had to go through! Acchh. At last, this beauty is back to its rightful owner."

Chaim holds the heavy, yet fragile, menorah out to Willow, an offering she accepts gratefully, cradling the treasure. They look at each other for a moment, then Willow turns suddenly and sets the menorah down in a place of honor on the mantle. She disappears into the kitchen, imagining next Hanukkah, lighting the candles, wondering who will be with her. In a little while, she returns with a mug of coffee for each of them.

"Did you have something urgent you needed to talk to me about?" she asks.

He shifts about on the couch, looks away, then out the window to the park. "Just everything," he says finally, and she smiles at him.

"Oh," Willow says, "by the way. I was going through things my mother left for me, and there are some letters of yours."

He sits up, looks her in the eye. "What letters?"

Willow stirs cream and sugar into her coffee, takes a long sip from her mug. "To my mother."

Chaim gets up from the couch, upsetting his mug, which shatters, spilling shards and coffee onto the floor.

"Sorry!" he booms. "I am clumsy today. Let me clean it up." He kneels down, picks up the pieces in his large palm, then goes to the kitchen for a sponge before Willow can get there.

"Careful," she warns, "don't cut yourself." She takes the sponge from Chaim's hand. "Let me take care of that."

In a few moments, the floor is clean. She pours Chaim a new coffee and they resettle themselves in the living room. "I didn't read them," she says suddenly. "I can give them back to you."

She can see the pain register in his eyes. "Listen, Willow." It is so odd for her to hear her name on his lips; it sounds so personal, intimate. "I want to talk with you, to catch up. We could go out."

"I have to work today."

"Tomorrow then," he declares, a statement, not a question. "Your mother, maybe, would want me to take you to Schwartz's. We had a meal there when she was in town."

"We went."

He seems at a loss.

"Anyway, she says suddenly. "Let's go somewhere new." She thinks to herself, a place that is new for us. "I don't want to go anywhere that you went with my mother, or that I went with her."

His eyes look puzzled, his thick, black brows peak. "You want a new place, then."

"Yes."

They are quiet for several moments. Then Chaim starts a little tentatively, "The weather is nice, in the country especially. Have you been to the country?"

"Not really. Not the Laurentians or the Townships yet."

"Good! We'll go. I have a new bicycle."

"A bicycle?"

"Yes, that's what I said. You have a bicycle?"

"Sure."

"We'll go to Val David in my Jeep, bikes on the back. We'll cycle, maybe make a picnic. And I'll show you One Thousand Pots."

"One thousand what?"

"Pots! A ceramic fair, all local potters. I will replace the mug I broke."

"Okay, then," she says, warming a little to him.

"And we will have all day to talk."

"Lots to catch up on," she agrees, trying to be companionable.

He rises quickly, carries his mug to the kitchen. "Tomorrow, then," he says, leaving as abruptly as he had appeared.

He drives like a madman up to the Laurentians, veering wildly in and out of lanes in his old Jeep Cherokee, not bothering to signal, tailgating.

"You are just the kind of driver who gives Montréalers a bad name. Do you want to get us killed?"

He chuckles, a deep mischievous sound. "My own death, I don't believe in," he says.

"I *do* believe in mine!" she shouts above the whipping wind.

In Val David, they find a parking space beside the bike path and Chaim insists on taking the bikes off the rack single-handedly; in a stall beside the trail, they buy cold water and set off. The day is warm, but not too hot, and there is a nice breeze off the river.

Now and again, they ride side by side, but when there is traffic coming in the opposite direction, Chaim pedals ahead. Willow is impressed, but not surprised, by his strength and vigor. They ride for some time without speaking, just the rush of wind and river in their ears. In a half-hour or so, there is a lovely view from a slight rise, and they take a water break on some craggy rocks overlooking the river.

"This reminds me so much of Kingston," Willow says.

"Your home?"

"Where I grew up, anyway." She takes a long sip of water, suddenly realizing how parched she is. "There is a towpath just like this along the Delaware-Raritan Canal. This reminds me of it."

"I've never been."

"Where did you grow up?"

"I was born in Budapest. When I was ten years old, we moved to Prague to be with my mother's family. Jana was our neighbor. A big lively family they were. What a beauty she was! I admit I had a bad crush on her."

Willow laughs quietly.

"Ivanova's—their candy shop—once or twice a week I went, indulged myself. Of course I had a sweet tooth, still do." He winks at Willow. "But candy was not all I was after."

Willow stretches out her legs. "Tell me more about your family."

"Your family too."

Willow flinches. It all seems so unreal to her; she wonders if this feeling will last forever or fade with time.

"My mother ran a flower shop, Agi's, nicest on Vaci Utca. The awning was decorated with blooms. I had a baby sister, Tovah, I don't know . . . "

"I'm sorry to pry—this must be hard for you."

Chaim shrugs, looks into the river, and sips his water. "Moishe, my father, was a master steel engraver. Magic hands. I learned that trade from him, and it saved my life. Later, in Montréal, engraving gave me a way to earn a living until I could do what I really wanted to do."

"Build Ha'makom."

"Right. At home, I have a steel box with some of the things I've engraved, my pirate's chest!"

"Will you show me?"

He nods. "The letters, you have . . . "

"Like I told you, I didn't read them."

"Jana, she never answered me. Again, we tried to make a go of things, but she ran away from me. I knew nothing about you, I had no idea she was pregnant."

Willow tilts her head to one side. "I guess she was afraid to tell you."

He shakes his head slowly, a sad, wistful look in his eyes.

They sit without speaking, just watching the river rush past, the groups of cyclists, couples and families with young children towed behind in caravans or on double-cycles pedaling with their mothers or fathers.

They walk their bikes to the next town and decide to shop for a picnic. Together, they choose bread, a selection of cheeses, some peaches and pears, chocolate chip cookies and a bottle of wine. They find a spot near the river, a bit distant from the bike path and settle on the grass as Willow sets out their lunch.

"So," he says resigned, "she broke my heart when she left me that last time. I thought we would finally work things out."

"But you knew nothing about me? Ever?"

He waits a long time before answering. "Later, she wrote to me. A birthday you had. Five years old."

"And?" Willow slices a pear with a plastic knife and hands Chaim a wedge.

"Too little, too late," he says, case closed.

"What do you mean?" She presses.

"I felt hurt, betrayed, angry that Jana had disappeared from my life and told me nothing about you. I was stubborn and fighting mad. Do you know how it feels to be told five years too late that you have a daughter who has been kept a secret? Always the timing was wrong. I should have come when she invited me to your birthday party. I was a schmuck!"

Willow smiles. "Who knows what would have happened if you had come?"

"Jana would have had to join me in Montréal again."

"And maybe she thought her life was in Kingston."

"But geography now, is trivial to me." Chaim takes a long sip of wine, draining his glass. He refills Willow's glass until she holds her palm over the rim, then pours himself more wine.

"Remember, *you* have to drive. And you drive like a madman *sober.*" Willow tears off a piece of bread. "Oh, and don't forget, we've got to cycle back to the Jeep without tipping over on our heads."

"Why did Jana keep you secret? I'm not a criminal. I'm not a madman or a crook!"

Willow looks up at him. "She did give you that chance."

"Too little, too late," he repeats.

"Too late?" Willow sighs deeply. "That was thirty-five years ago and here we are. How would you feel if I told you it was too late now? For *me*."

"I wouldn't let you."

"What would you do?"

"I'd follow you, I'd call you, I'd come around. I wouldn't take no for an answer!"

Chaim is as unrelenting as a breaking wave at sea—once he makes his mind up about something—and he has clearly made up his mind about her. There is something like love in that force, a love he won't let her escape from now, and Willow feels a strange free fluttering in her chest, a heady sense of fear and possibility. She has a father! At forty, she is somebody's girl.

They cycle back slowly, and as the path is less crowded, they are able to ride abreast. At the Jeep, Chaim fastens the bikes to the rack, while Willow puts the remains of their picnic away, getting rid of the trash.

"Now," Chaim says, "One Thousand Pots."

They stroll to a little hill in the center of town, where potters have set out their wares. The day is a mix of sun and clouds, a keener wind picks up. There are mugs and bowls and platters for everything imaginable, all in exquisite shapes and colors, even a bit of jewelry. As they browse, Willow feels a pang, missing her mother, wishing she could be here with them.

Chaim picks out a set of four mugs with a glaze of turquoise, lapis, indigo, and cream, which he has packed up for Willow.

"Thank you," she says, suddenly shy, leaning in for a half-hug.

On the drive back, they are both quiet, awkward.

"I'll never call you father," she says provocatively, "or Dad. It doesn't feel right." Never will, she thinks bitterly.

"I don't give a damn what you call me."

"Promise me one thing," she says tentatively, as he weaves in and out of traffic, racing past the speed limit. "Your story, about your life, who you are . . ."

"What about it? You know," he says suddenly, "I gave my own

testimony at the Witness Foundation years ago. I was one of the first. I'll get for you permission—tomorrow if you want."

Something within Willow collapses. "No! That's just it."

"What?"

"Promise me, you'll tell me your own story. Yourself. In your own words, to me."

He is quiet for a long while.

"How much time do you have?"

"As long as it takes."

"I promise," he says, bearing down on the gas pedal, as they speed back to Montréal.

※ ※ ※

TWENTY-NINE

AS SUMMER SWELTERS, Willow hibernates in her studio, immersed in work on her show, carrying on conversations with her mother in her head, grabbing sleep and sustenance in snatches. It is a relief to be solitary, trying to deal with her lost and found family, as she imagines her new puppet play and the beings that will inhabit the story. For so long, she has lived with missing pieces, a vague longing waiting to be filled, so that her life story—her mother's—would make some sense.

The new play begins for Willow with an image. Two puppets stuffed into a dusty toy chest in a warehouse on the outskirts of Prague. Tangled strings, awkward positions, an abandoned old toy factory. She names them Evuska and Razi. The time is 1945, the war ending as the play begins.

Willow knows these two marionettes, along with three others, were the best-loved toys of a Jewish boy, Ilan—now thirteen years old, if he is alive—only seven when the Nazis invaded his home. Ilan's best friend in the neighborhood is a little girl, Dela, who is a Christian. The play begins when a Russian soldier appears in the warehouse, looking for toys to plunder for his own children. He opens the trunk, spots the two marionettes, one's feet jammed against the other's face. He examines them, sees how beautifully they are crafted, and hides them in his rucksack. He hears a truck outside, and goes to investigate. A high-intensity light shines on the rumpled rucksack.

The girl puppet, Evuska, discovers that she has the power to move by herself, without a puppeteer manipulating her strings. Razi, can move on his own too, so with careful fingers, they struggle to untangle themselves from each other.

Once in the streets, they realize that the war is over and they try to make their way back home. They want to find out what's become of Ilan, the boy who owned and loved them, and the other three members of their puppet family: Mr. G., the old sock puppet Ilan has had since he was a boy, Tov, and Yael. As they return to their old home, Evuska and Razi wonder if Ilan is dead or alive, and what's become of the others.

Willow takes rapid-fire notes and sketches the characters. When she starts imagining into the play, her ideas come faster and faster. Will she use a real boy for Ilan, a real child for the girl who helps them out in their search, or will the children be marionettes?

Willow sees alternating scenes between Evuska and Razi searching for Ilan, and Ilan and Mr. G. in hiding somewhere. She envisions the sets. The warehouse of the toy factory, then later Ilan's hiding place—a cellar or barn—and the Red Cross shelter.

Evuska and Razi are taking shape in Willow's imagination, their look, sound, dress, gait. The boy, Ilan, is slowly coming into focus as well. Mr. G. will still be Mr. G, a sense of continuity and connection there, but what about the other two? She knows they will come to life, if she is calm, and gives them time to take shape in her mind.

Now and then, Chaim or Noah pops by the studio; they both have this habit of simply appearing, without warning, unannounced, a relic of a simpler world and time. Chaim comes with plastic-lidded containers of coffee and juice, Noah with steaming trays of curry from the local Indian place or delicious noodle soup from the Vietnamese kitchen. Ordinarily, the interruptions would be an annoyance, but Willow finds she is happy to see each of them. She always has more questions for Chaim; it is a newfound feeling to be free to bombard him with questions and to listen to the answers she longs for and needs to know. With Noah, Willow talks out the story and characters of her play, much as they have been doing all summer.

Sometime in the deepest part of the night, Willow sets to work crafting the marionettes that she has visualized in her head. She finds that she has endless energy when she is working on new puppets and a new play. Time passes in an instant.

Willow waits until she has all of her measurements for Evuska and Razi, until she has thought through every detail, before setting to work on Razi's head, modeling and casting in plasticine. To model and cast gives her more latitude; it's easier to make adjustments, and a solid wood head, she finds, can be rather heavy.

She measures out a two-pound block for Razi—she's a stickler about this because she finds her heads tend to grow in her hands as she models them, and before she knows it, they are huge! Usually, she wants a puppet about twenty-four inches high with a head four-and-a-half inches from forehead to chin, but she envisions Razi lean and sinuous, so he will stretch to twenty-eight inches in length, and his head will be six inches from forehead to chin.

Roughing in Razi's features first, she works on fine-tuning his character. He is angular and sharp, with bold features that will carry all the way to the back of the room. She uses planes to create high, strong cheekbones and shadows, his brows thick and straight, his neck unusually long and slender for a man. A thin spread of petroleum jelly smoothes his head; his hair will come later.

Next, Willow prepares plaster in a large enamel mixing bowl. She loves the feel of it between her fingers, first powdery, then pasty, finally like cream. She always adds plaster to water rather than water to plaster; this helps prevent lumps. Drawing one finger across the surface—there is a faint trace—she is ready to pour.

The next morning, Willow gently pulls out the mold. She mixes up her special composition recipe in the blender, and molds the head she will use for the marionette. It has to dry still, but in her mind Willow can see that his face is a perfect oval, with a dimpled resolute chin and straight Roman nose. His eyes are downslanting, his mouth wide. Willow sees his hair, blue-black, cascading down to his slender shoulders. He will wear a leotard and tights.

Or, he could don the costume of a clown or jester, his body made of leather and wood strips to make him floppy, his hair of bright twisted yarn, or better yet, shredded rope.

Usually, Willow finishes one marionette before going on to another, but now she works in a fever, sketching out the figure of Evuska, as if her vision will vanish if she doesn't get it down immediately.

She works for three days and nights running; in a week's time, she has the heads of her marionettes ready for painting, makeup, and hair—her favorite part. She uses oil colors to paint faces, a mix of white, yellow, and ochre with a touch of vermillion. Razi is more sallow, so she adds blue, and to Evuska's skin, burnt sienna. Evuska's lips are a mix of red and flesh with lacquer to give them gloss and fullness. She shadows her eyelids with silvery-blue. A fleck of white on the pupils makes their eyes come alive. She never varnishes her puppets' heads; reflected light ruins their definition.

For weeks, Willow works, submerged in her studio, as Noah visits to check on her progress and to offer suggestions. Willow needs a title for her play and they spend a late night brainstorming ideas. Finally, it's settled: *Family Strings*.

※ ※ ※

Memory Book
August 2005, Kingston, New Jersey

Willow, your father Chaim Rosenblum was, is, with me all the time. How do you talk about the nose in the middle of your face? The foundation you stand on?

Here you see me, Willow, wearing my fleur de lys locket. I want to tell you the story of that necklace.

One day, at the summit of Mount Royal, your father surprised me with a gift. It was summer, 1964; I had returned to Montréal to be with your father, to make another go of it. We two could not live together, but could not live apart! He was no longer with Rachel Goldstein, the other woman in his life. As much as I tried to forget your father, I couldn't. He was with me every day, a presence, even from a distance.

Already I was forty-one years old! Chaim, just thirty-eight, handsome and vigorous with shining black hair and clear gray eyes. I too, was still beautiful then.

My figure was full, a bloom to my cheeks. My hair was long and thick, as yours is now. A handsome woman I was; everyone said so. Making my own life in Kingston, being a teacher, had made me strong, self-sufficient. With everything I had accomplished, I hoped I could hold my own with Chaim at last.

There you see our picture on Mount Royal; we asked some strangers to take it. How happy we look on that day! A humid day, glittering with heat. I thought it might rain and the rain would bring relief. From his pocket, your father took out a small velvet box, blue. Always something special from his pocket, like the comb, the bread.

Willow, I hadn't had a gift since I was a child in Prague, when my father made each birthday and holiday special. Chaim motioned for me to sit down on a rock. I pried the box apart. Inside was the gold fleur de lys charm on a beautiful chain.

"Open it," he said. "Inside, whatever you want put in."

But he had already put in a picture of the two of us together.

He helped me fasten the clasp.

Just as the rain started, Chaim proposed marriage.

All at once, rain poured down on us in bursts, the sun in and out. We made our way down the mountain, slipping on the wet ground, soaked to the bone, covered with mud.

When we got home to Chaim's apartment, it was empty and quiet. The place was almost never empty because of his entourage—people working at Ha'makom, friends, and neighbors always stopping in, camping out, talking and working till all hours, staying over, sometimes for weeks!

The quiet, the stillness surrounded us, stark and unexpected. He helped me peel off my wet things. We bathed and he dried my body with great tenderness. We hadn't been together, made love, for some time.

Now we had the whole place to ourselves—the bedroom, living room, kitchen, the fire escape—but he drew me into the upstairs storage room, stacked with linens, towels, and cleaning fluids.

Without thinking, I closed the door.

It was dusky inside with a bare bulb on a string cord, little light. In a few moments our eyes adjusted to the dark. The shelves were lined with towels, sheets, bars of soap; the closet smelled of wood fiber, bleach, and strong detergent.

"What will happen?" I asked him.

"Again, we will begin," he said.

His words made me ache. Already, we had lost two babies together. One in the DP camp when I was ill and sick at heart, a second not long after we settled in Montréal.

"Too much is lost," I said.

"Lost, you look," he said, stroking my face. "Lost, you can still find."

We tried to go back to life together, but nothing was the same. It was fall, Mount Royal a blaze of color at twilight. Your father was working as always at Ha'makom. I was alone, walking on the mountain. At the summit, I rested and dreamed. I was very still, could hear myself breathe. And with the breathing came a feeling inside, a bubble bursting in my belly. I drew in my breath and the bubble disappeared.

The wind picked up, an edge in the air. When it stopped, the feeling came again. Stronger now. A butterfly deep in my belly, fluttering.

There you were, my beautiful daughter, the daughter I had dreamed of and longed for.

Willow, you were a parachute, freefalling through space! The world tipped away as I imagined you—your beating heart that I could not yet hear, the beginnings of your fingers and toes. Blood and bone. I began to talk to you, baby girl, sleeping under my heart. And I thought, my life is in you.

EPILOGUE

NOW THAT HER MOTHER is dead, she is with Willow all the time.

Willow's greatest fear is white silence, hollowing out, the loss of her mother's voice—truly the key to her—to them both.

The fall day is bright, glistening with that northern sun Willow has come to love, a sun independent of heat, the Montréal sky impossibly blue. She walks at a clip, head bowed, to the Witness Foundation. She treads the same path her mother trod last spring. Week after week, Jana sat in a darkened room and told her story to strangers. Easier, safer, perhaps, than telling it to Willow. Maybe her mother had her in mind when she spoke; maybe she was telling her story to Willow after all.

After her appointment, Noah will meet her. Willow has no idea how she'll feel after listening to her mother's testimony, but knows that she wants Noah with her.

She enters the shining building that houses the Witness Foundation, sun glinting off freshly washed windows. Willow holds her breath, as the glass doors whoosh closed. The elevator rises swiftly floor by floor, nearly soundless, and she feels a rising leap in her belly. Her mother's amazing life, her suffering and survival. This story will live on in the world after her death. Her mother's story possesses life, has a beating heart all its own.

Stepping into the foyer of the Witness Foundation, Willow closes her eyes for a moment and sees her mother's dark and glowing eyes. Soon, she will hear her mother's voice once again, the grit in her throat that comes with flashes of anger, the break that comes with tenderness or hurt, as if this voice alone can hold Willow up, sustain her, her mother speaking directly into her ear.

🦋 🦋 🦋

ACKNOWLEDGMENTS

My special thanks to Yaddo, the St. James Cavalier Centre for Creativity in Valletta, Malta, and The Virginia Center for the Creative Arts for the gift of time and space in which to work. Crucial parts of this novel were written during fellowships at these retreats.

I am grateful to two inspiring Canadian puppeteers: Pier Dufour of Kobol Marionettes and Ronnie Burkett and his stringed troop. Thank you Pier for meeting with me and offering a window into the magic of your craft and creations. Ronnie Burkett, fearless provocateur, your dark comedies and characters burrow in; keep on dazzling. Thank you both for immersing me in your worlds.

I would like to acknowledge The Jewish Public Library in Montréal and The Montreal Holocaust Memorial Centre, resources invaluable to me in the writing of this book. Two sources were particularly illuminating and helpful: *Holocaust and Rebirth: Bergen-Belsen 1945-1965*, published by the Bergen-Belsen Memorial Press of the World Federation of Bergen-Belsen Associations, N.Y., 1965 and *Secretaries of Death: Accounts by Former Prisoners Who Worked in the Gestapo of Auschwitz*, edited and translated by Lore Shelley, Shengold Publishers, N.Y., 1986. The scene depicting women prisoners in Auschwitz forming a human chain to load urns onto trucks was based on the historical testimony of Irene Schwarz, nee Irka Anis, which was included in *Secretaries of Death* and originally published in *The Root and the Bough*, edited by Leo W. Schwarz and published by Rinehart & Co., N.Y. 1949. Jana's autograph book was inspired by the beautiful autograph book of Fania Fainer, exhibited in the Montreal Holocaust Memorial Centre.

I am grateful to the tenacious network of Jewish Day Schools in Montréal for giving my children opportunities to learn about our heritage, and for keeping Jewish history, language, and legacy alive.

I feel blessed to put down new roots with our family and am grateful for the joy our two children, Tobias and Rosamond, bring us each day, and even for the *tsuris* that keeps us on our toes!

Margie Wolfe, you are a dynamo; thanks for being in my corner. I'm fortunate to have had Sarah Silberstein Swartz as my editor.

Carla Hagen, *amiga de mi alma y mi corazón*, what would I do without Minnesota getaways and café lattes, not to mention the chance to be an outlaw Mom every now and then? Most of all, I'm grateful for the gift of your friendship.

Finally, my love and thanks to Michael Atkin, muse and believer. Though this is a work of fiction, your memories of your mother and our lost extended family, the words, the silences, the pieces and the missing pieces, were invaluable to me in inspiring this book. My novel is dedicated in loving memory to my mother-in-law, Brana Hochova, and to the memory of the entire Hoch family, and to families like them: the hunted and the hidden, the lost and the found, the murdered and the survivors, the children of survivors, and our children.

—Ami Sands Brodoff

AMI SANDS BRODOFF is an award-winning novelist and short story writer. Her volume of stories, *Bloodknots*, was short-listed for the Re-Lit Award and an excerpt from her previous novel, *Can You See Me?* was nominated for The Pushcart Prize. She has contributed to *Vogue*, *Self*, *Elle*, *The Globe and Mail*, and Montréal's *The Gazette*. She serves on the executive of the Quebec Writers' Federation and has won fellowships to Yaddo, The Virginia Center for the Creative Arts, The Ragdale Foundation, and the The St. James Cavalier Centre for Creativity in Malta. Ami makes her home in Montréal with her husband, children, and Bernese Mountain dog.

"Linda brilliantly and biblically shine
promised gift of peace for the crippli... ... .
life. Packed with prayer and promises, this book will free you to
experience the power of God's peace."

—Lysa TerKeurst, *New York Times* bestselling author of
Unglued and president of Proverbs 31 Ministries

Praise for *When You Don't Know What to Pray*

"The book's strength is Shepherd's heart for prayer and tenderness for her readers. Recommend to people who are struggling through difficult circumstances and to pastors and group leaders."

—*CBA Retailers + Resources*

"Linda has used powerful prayer to overcome the worst of circumstances, and you can too. She does not share pat answers, she shares truth that will transform your life. Are you ready to learn her prayer secrets? Bow your head and pray your way through this book."

—**LeAnn Thieman**, coauthor, *Chicken Soup for the Christian Woman's Soul* and *Chicken Soup for the Christian Soul 2*

"This book is a must-read for anyone who desires a stronger prayer life. Linda speaks from experience, and her stories compel the reader to pray more."

—**Carole Lewis**, national director, First Place, www.firstplace.org

"Linda Evans Shepherd is a woman of prayer, and in a world of crisis, change, and constant challenges, what woman doesn't need to learn more about the praying life? Pick up this book to gain an encouraged and equipped heart."

—**Pam Farrel**, international speaker; relationship specialist; author, *Men Are Like Waffles, Women Are Like Spaghetti*

Praise for *Experiencing God's Presence*

"If you long for a relationship with God that is deeper, richer, and more intimate than you've ever known before, read this book. In *Experiencing God's Presence*, Linda Evans Shepherd reveals the secrets of learning how to listen to God during your prayer times. Each chapter is filled with practical, biblical tools that will enrich your prayer life and draw you closer to the heart of the Father."

—**Carol Kent**, speaker and author, *When I Lay My Isaac Down*

"*Experiencing God's Presence* will transform your prayer life! Please buy this book."

—**Elaine Miller**, Splashes of Serenity

The
Stress
Cure

The
Stress
Cure

PRAYING YOUR WAY
to PERSONAL PEACE

LINDA EVANS SHEPHERD

Revell
a division of Baker Publishing Group
Grand Rapids, Michigan

Published by Revell
a division of Baker Publishing Group
P.O. Box 6287, Grand Rapids, MI 49516-6287
www.revellbooks.com

Printed in the United States of America

Library of Congress Cataloging-in-Publication Data is on file at the Library of Congress, Washington, DC.

ISBN 978-0-8007-2283-8 (pbk.)

Published in association with the Books & Such Literary Agency, 52 Mission Circle, Suite 122, PMB 170, Santa Rosa, CA 95409-7953.

To protect privacy, some details and names have been changed.

14 15 16 17 18 19 20   7 6 5 4 3 2 1

In memory of my dad—

James Leroy Evans.

A godly man, a wonderful husband, and a dear father.
No daughter had a better daddy.

Contents

9

Acknowledgments

Thank you, dear family, for your love and support as I wrote this book. I want to thank my dear husband and my son, as you are always there for me. I'm also sending a special thank-you to my daughter—Miss Laura—who stays joyful no matter her challenges. You are an inspiration.

I'm also sending a shout out to my wonderful praying friends in the Advanced Writers and Speakers Association (AWSA) and my precious prayer partner, Carole. Also, a special thank-you to Team Shepherd for all you do. I so appreciate you all.

Also, a special thanks to my editor, Vicki Crumpton, and my agent, Janet Kobobel Grant, as well as all my wonderful friends at Baker Publishing Group. It has been such a blessing to partner with you in publishing this much needed message.

And finally, thank you, dear readers, for opening this book. The thing I most loved about writing it is that it helped me go deeper into the mysteries of God's joy, peace, and presence. My prayer is that this book will do the same for you.

I love you all very much!

Introduction

The Problem of Stress

Peace be with you.

Luke 24:36

A clock would make a poor bank. No customer would ever be able to deposit a moment to save for later because, at the end of the day, every second would be spent and the clock would be bankrupt.

While it's true that each day gives us twenty-four hours to spend, those hours have to be divided into moments driven by the demands of our to-do lists, not to mention our problems, worries, families, and jobs. It seems that our minutes evaporate no matter how fast we rush to meet them. The ticking of the clock is one of the reasons why, according to *Psychology Today*, 39 percent of Americans claimed their stress had increased over the past year. The article continues with unsettling news: "More alarming, only 29 percent reported that they were doing an 'excellent' or 'very good' job at managing their stress."[1]

13

We'll get up tomorrow with a brand-new set of twenty-four hours, a new day that will give us another chance to catch up, find solutions to our challenges, and—hopefully—calm down. Yet, by the end of tomorrow, many of us will fail to find solutions to our stressors. A recent survey shows that most people hear alarm bells when it comes to money (75%), work (70%), the economy (67%), relationships (58%), family responsibilities (57%), family's health (53%), personal health (53%), job stability (49%), housing (49%), and personal safety (32%).[2]

If we can't find a way to quiet these alarms, we could be in for even more stress, which eventually impacts our health. Web MD explains:

> If stress happens too often or lasts too long, it can have bad effects. It can be linked to headaches, an upset stomach, back pain, and trouble sleeping. It can weaken your immune system, making it harder to fight off disease. If you already have a health problem, stress may make it worse. It can make you moody, tense, or depressed. Your relationships may suffer, and you may not do well at work or school.[3]

Not only that, but stress contributes to conditions such as fatigue, poor concentration, irritability, a quick temper, obesity, cancer, stroke, heart attack, and even death.

Yikes! The thought of the effects of stress is enough to stress out anyone.

Before I start to tell you the secrets to taming stress, let's define it. Wikipedia defines stress as "a negative concept that can have an impact on one's mental and physical well-being,"[4] while the World English Dictionary describes it as "mental, emotional, or physical strain or tension."[5]

Besides the mental and physical impacts of stress, stress can also impact our spiritual well-being with what I call "soul blocks." These include such things as harboring offenses, the feeling of being overwhelmed or out of control, continually striving for more, frustrations, burdens, hopelessness, offenses, anxiety, bad attitudes, distractions, and depression.

But I have good news! I've felt the effects of these negative consequences more than a few times, and I've discovered powerful solutions that can help you build bridges over your stressors so you can journey on to peace, as well as to "love, joy, . . . forbearance, kindness, goodness, faithfulness, gentleness and self-control" (Gal. 5:22–23).

Though it's true that we all get twenty-four hours each day, we can choose to spend our time filled with anxiety, or we can push toward God's peace that passes understanding. Building a bridge to peace involves gaining a better understanding of God and the tools he's given us, which include prayer and God's Word.

As for me? I would love to tell you that I've eliminated all stress from my life, but as a fellow traveler who happens to be married with kids, I often get opportunities to test God's solutions of peace in my own crazy life, which includes a profoundly disabled daughter, the recent death of my father, and book deadlines. So, yes, I know the taste and feel of stress. Yet, I've also tasted and felt God's peace. I've learned to use the tools of prayer and God's Word, tools we will use together throughout the pages of this book.

A Stressful Day

Not long ago, I heard a radio preacher say, "If you have stress, that means you're not trusting God." I was having a stressful day, so I didn't particularly care for this remark. I silently argued, *Why of course I trust God. My problem is I'm having a day that won't let me "phone it in."*

My stressful day started the morning I had to drive fifty miles to get to a live radio interview in another town. As the clock ticked down to the time I had to leave, everything started to go wrong.

I suddenly remembered I needed to get a tax report in the mail, and then my college son called to tell me the registration tags on his car had expired six months ago. He needed me to run down to the county clerk with my checkbook in hand, as he lived out of town and couldn't take care of this errand himself.

While racing to finish the tax report, I made a call to the county clerk to see if I could pay the car fee by phone. "You can't phone it in because it will take a month for your son to get the new registration sticker," the clerk admonished. "His car could be impounded by then. Come in today and, if possible, bring cash."

As I felt my stress level rise, I got another call telling me my office payroll was late, a payroll I had to sign before I left town so my assistant could buy groceries, a habit she didn't like to break. By the time I finished the tax report, signed the payroll, and paid the car fee, my stress was running high, as I was now running late for the radio interview, an interview I could not phone in.

So I hopped in my car and, with sweat trickling between my shoulder blades, raced through freeway traffic for fifty miles. When I arrived, I had to park a block away before sprinting to the building to catch the elevator. When the elevator opened at the top floor, I dashed down the hall and slipped into the chair and head-phones as the radio station's mike went live. The host barely managed to whisper, "I was beginning to think you wouldn't make it!"

Though we can't control all the things that happen to us, we can, with God's help, control our reaction to them—trusting God even when we're stressed.

By the time I got back home, I was exhausted. The next morning, instead of feeling relieved that the stress was over, I found myself reliving it. That's when a friend called and asked, "You sound stressed. What's wrong?"

Happily, I rattled off my list of yesterday's woes, a list I was sure would cause Sara to gush, "Oh, Linda! I can hardly imagine."

16

Instead, Sara replied, "Is that all? I have four of my five kids on the couch with the stomach flu, each with their own bucket!"

"Oh, Sara!" I cried. "Your stress trumps mine!"

We shared a laugh, but after we hung up, I wondered why I'd allowed yesterday's stress to block God's peace, peace I could have had today. I hated to admit it, but that radio preacher had been right in part. Though we can't control all the things that happen to us, we can, with God's help, control our reaction to them—trusting God even when we're stressed.

The Story of Peace

Throughout this book, I'm going to share stories based on God's Word and told through my imagination. For example, when I think of the disciples, frightened and hiding after the crucifixion of Jesus, this is how I imagine the scene.

The disciples sat in the upper room with the window shuttered against the bustle of a bright Jerusalem day. They sat quietly, hardly daring to move lest their footfalls or voices be overheard by a passerby. Even so, they occasionally muttered things like, "And we thought he was the Messiah."

One of the shadows belonged to Mark. He shifted a bit and said, "But did you hear that the women reported his tomb was empty and . . ."

Another shadow wrung his hands. "That's just proof that they're mad with grief."

Peter, from a darkened corner, added, "And fear. I saw the tomb myself, and it was empty, the body probably moved."

"Quiet. I hear the sound of soldiers in the street," Andrew whispered.

Luke rose. "Have they found us so soon?" He peeked through a crack in the wooden slats, then announced with relief, "They've passed us by."

"For now," Peter said. "Perhaps we should have gone to Emmaus with Cleopas and his cousin, at least until things cool off."

"But what about the women's report?" Mark asked. "Mary seemed to believe. What if Jesus did rise from the dead?"

A soft knock sounded at the door. No one spoke, until a muffled voice called out, "It's me, Cleopas, and my cousin. We have news."

Peter sprang to his feet and unbolted the door to let the men slip into the room. He asked, "Then we're to be arrested?"

Cleopas announced, "We've seen . . ."

Peter fingered the sheath strapped to his belt. "The soldiers are on their way?"

"The Lord!" cousin Ethan blurted. "We've seen the Lord!"

Cleopas explained, "Earlier tonight Jesus walked home with us and . . ."

"Our hearts burned within us as he explained the Scriptures, about why he had to die and . . ."

"We didn't recognize him, until . . ."

"Until he broke bread with us. That's when we saw his wounded hands and . . ."

Not only did Jesus walk through the wall of the upper room, but he can also walk through your walls of doubt, fear, and stress and bring you peace. But first you have to invite him into your life.

Suddenly, a brilliant glow filled the room and Jesus appeared. He held out his nail-pierced hands and spoke his first words to his disciples since his death. "Peace be with you."

The men, minus Thomas, who'd slipped away to buy bread, stood stunned, doubting their very eyes until Jesus showed them the wound in his side. The men were soon filled with joy, for they understood. Jesus had walked through the wall of death and into life, just as he had walked through the walls of their doubt to bring them peace (based on Luke 24:13–39).

Not only did Jesus walk through the wall of the upper room, but he can also walk through your walls of doubt, fear, and stress and bring you peace. But first you have to invite him into your life. You can start with a prayer like this:

> *Dear Jesus,*
>
> *I need you to walk through the walls of my doubt and unbelief. I choose to believe you are alive! Give me supernatural belief so that I can see you more clearly. You died on the cross for my sins and came back to life again. Because you took my punishment, I can now walk with God.*
>
> *I turn from my sins and turn to you, to follow you and to trust you with my whole heart. Please forgive me for my past and let your Spirit come inside me so I can learn how to walk in your peace.*
>
> *In Jesus's name, amen.*

It's good that you prayed this prayer, for although Jesus can walk through walls, he's a gentleman and never goes where he's not invited.

Shalom, my friend. Throughout the pages of this book, I will help you unpack the prayer tools of peace Christ has given to us. But for now know that his words to his disciples are also his words for you: "Peace be with you."

You'll see. Everything is going to be all right.

1

The Key to Peace

Finding More of God's Presence

> The mystery in a nutshell is just this: Christ is in
> you, so therefore you can look forward to sharing
> in God's glory. It's that simple.
>
> Colossians 1:27 Message

My Introduction to the Prince of Peace

When I was nine years old, a group of girls from my church and I
piled into my mother's car and went to our church camp nestled
beside a cow pasture near Newton, Texas. In between splashing in
the swimming pool in the sweltering heat, singing campfire songs
under the balmy stars, and hanging our tempera-painted crafts
from a clothesline, we listened to the speaker for the week nightly
implore us to come to faith. After his message, the young pastor
would extend an invitation to all those who wanted "Jesus in their
hearts" to come forward. I would stand with my row and sing the

old hymn "I Surrender All," watching repentant girls make their way to the front of the meeting. As we sang, I also watched my mother, who stood with her head bowed as she fervently prayed for my soul.

One morning, the older girls in our group cornered me outside the dining hall. "Linda, your mother told us that you aren't saved. We want you to know we're praying for you."

My cheeks burned. "My mother told you that?"

Donna, the oldest girl at about thirteen, said, "Don't be mad. It's just that your mom is very worried about you and asked us to pray." The girls tried to blink back tears. "Linda, won't you please come to faith in Jesus at the meeting tonight?" they pleaded.

"I've been thinking about it," I admitted. "But tomorrow night is our last night at camp, and with tomorrow being my birthday, I'm thinking of waiting until then."

Before the girls could hug me, I warned them, "But you can't tell my mother. If you tell, I won't go down for the altar call, and that's a promise."

Their heads bobbed. "Don't worry, Linda, we won't tell."

I felt relieved. I so wanted to go forward, but this had to be my decision, not my mom's. I breathed a sigh of relief and skipped off to arts and crafts, knowing that if these girls kept their word, I would soon know Jesus as my Lord and Savior.

But the next evening, just before the start of the service, my mother hugged me and gushed, "Linda, the girls told me you are coming to faith tonight. I'm so proud."

My heart stopped. "But the girls promised they wouldn't tell."

"Honey, they just wanted me to know, and I'm so glad."

I felt like crying as I tried to explain, "This is something I need to do by myself. Now I won't be able to go forward tonight."

I hated the hurt look on my mother's face, but I couldn't help it. This was a decision I wanted to make myself, without her influence. So during the altar call that night, as two hundred girls sang "I

Surrender All," I crossed my little arms and set my jaw and didn't surrender a thing. If the girls wouldn't keep our agreement, neither would I. Despite the quiet weeping of Donna and her friends, and even though I desperately wanted to bolt to the front of the camp meeting to get Jesus into my heart, I stood my ground. A promise was a promise.

The next morning, I begin to realize the impact of my obstinacy as the older girls shot me looks of disappointment as we packed our suitcases for home. Though they had nothing to say to me, their swollen eyes and sad expressions spoke for them. How could you refuse Jesus? How could you hurt your mother like this? That's when it began to dawn on me. What a bad little girl I must be!

The disappointment of the older girls was nothing compared to my mom's. As we drove home in silence, I felt my mom's profound sadness hover over the car. Now, for the first time in my life, I felt the weight of my sin.

I continued to feel this weight, especially during the altar calls at my church every Sunday morning, Sunday evening, and Wednesday night for the next several months. I longed to go forward but couldn't bear the thought of surrendering to my mother before I surrendered to Christ.

Still, I worried what would happen if I was killed in a car crash and went to hell. Our pastor had described hell as such a frightening place. I knew I didn't want to spend eternity burning in the flames of God's wrath. Plus, I was worried about what my pastor called the rapture, the day Jesus would come back to earth with a shout and take all the believers to heaven, leaving only those of us who had refused to come to faith to face the terrible plagues at the end of times. That's why, whenever the house got too quiet, I would rush to check on my family to see if Jesus had somehow taken them and left me behind.

It wasn't until early November, when my church held an evening Vacation Bible School, that I finally saw my opportunity. That first night of VBS class, my fifth-grade teacher passed out printed note cards and stubby pencils. The cards asked if we wanted Jesus to come into our hearts; check yes or no.

Without the prying eyes of my mother, I was more than relieved to check yes.

The next question asked if we would like to talk to the pastor. I checked yes again, never dreaming that the pastor would soon be on the phone with my mother to arrange a home visit.

So the following afternoon after school, with my mother hovering in the kitchen listening in on the conversation between me, our pastor, and the visiting evangelist, I prayed the famous sinner's prayer. "Dear Lord, I repent of my sins. Please forgive me. I invite Jesus to come into my heart, to be Lord of my life. In Jesus's name, amen."

After I said the prayer, the men looked at me expectantly, but I felt disappointed. This was the same old prayer I'd silently prayed almost every Sunday and Wednesday since I was six. I'd expected to feel relief and joy, yet I felt nothing but embarrassment at the overwhelming joy of my mother.

But later that night at church, after my VBS class and during Evangelist Bob's sermon, I was surprised when he told the church congregation, "Just this afternoon I saw a young junior girl come to faith."

My heart skipped a beat. He was talking about me! And the thing that so impressed me was that Evangelist Bob had *seen* me come to faith despite the fact that I hadn't felt anything when I'd prayed. That's when I knew it must be real! Jesus was in my heart at last.

At the end of the service, the moment I'd dreaded came. It was finally time to do the one thing I'd so far failed to do, to surrender everything—including my stubborn will—and to give the Lord the lordship of my life. Evangelist Bob extended the invitation for all those who had made decisions to follow Christ to come forward as we sang, you guessed it, "I Surrender All."

This time I didn't have a choice, and though my mother was watching, I pushed through the row of kids from my class to the aisle, where I finally made my way to the front of the auditorium to surrender everything and to make my profession of faith public for the first time. But something unexpected occurred. As I walked to the front of the auditorium, my wall of stubbornness burst and the Holy Spirit rushed into my soul. I was so overwhelmed that despite my embarrassment I broke down into sobs that wouldn't stop, not even after the hymn ended—and not even after the people of the church had all shaken my hand to congratulate me for joining the family of God.

> *I believe God's Holy Spirit touched my soul as I became a new creation in Christ, an actual dwelling place for the Lord's presence.*

I've long thought about that moment, when in a flood of tears that final wall of pride that had held me back from the full presence of God fell away. I believe God's Holy Spirit touched my soul as I became a new creation in Christ, an actual dwelling place for the Lord's presence.

The Temple of God's Presence

Does God really enter into our spirits like that? Yes. The second chapter of Ephesians says, "Together, we are his house, built on the foundation of the apostles and the prophets. And the cornerstone is Christ Jesus himself. We are carefully joined together in him, becoming a holy temple for the Lord. Through him you Gentiles are also being made part of this dwelling where God lives by his Spirit" (vv. 20–22 TLB).

I believe I was "saved," "born again," or "pardoned for my sin by God" perhaps even the first time I secretly called upon the name of Jesus when I was only six. However, I also believe that the moment I was able to push past my pride and go public with my decision, the final wall came down, and I was transformed from a stubborn ten-year-old to a person filled with the Holy Spirit. Today, decades later, the Holy Spirit still resides within me, and I am indeed a new creation in Christ, as 2 Corinthians 5:17 explains: "Therefore, if anyone is in Christ, the new creation has come: The old is gone, the new is here!" The Living Bible reads, "When someone becomes a Christian, he becomes a brand new person inside. He is not the same anymore. A new life has begun!"

Did you know that until Christ's resurrection from the dead humanity endured a great rift with God that started back in the Garden of Eden? The garden's inhabitants, Adam and Eve, once had such access to God that they walked with him unashamed, clothed only in their innocence.

The rift between God and this man and woman started when this couple broke God's only rule: not to eat the fruit from the tree in the middle of the garden. Not realizing the fruit would poison them with sin, the two bit into trouble. It was in that moment that Adam's and Eve's eyes were opened and they saw that they were naked. In their shame, they did something they'd never done before. They hid from God.

Humankind has been hiding from God ever since, unworthy to be in the presence of such an awesome, holy being. To help remedy this rift, God's people turned their stone altars red with the blood of bulls and goats as they followed God's directive to cover their sins with the blood of their sacrifices. Still, their efforts to hide their sins from God dissolved each time they failed to follow each of God's laws to the letter. Their constant failure kept the people slaves to a law they couldn't keep. It wasn't until Jesus's death on the cross that the rift between God and humankind was finally bridged. Now, through Jesus's sacrifice, his blood covers our sins, breaking us free from the law of sin and death.

God's very presence has become available not only to clothe us in the righteousness of Jesus but also to enter into our very beings.

In fact, when we call out to Jesus, his righteousness descends on us like a garment, and his Holy Spirit dwells within us, transforming us from the inside out.

But just who is this Holy Spirit? Jesus described him in John 14:17 when he said, "He is the Spirit, who reveals the truth about God. The world cannot receive him, because it cannot see him or know him. But you know him, because he remains with you and is in you" (GNT).

It is the Spirit who helps us tear down our walls, makes miracles of our messes, comforts our heartaches, and leads us to breakthroughs.

Jesus introduced the Holy Spirit to his disciples this way: "But I am telling you the truth: it is better for you that I go away, because if I do not go, the Helper will not come to you. But if I do go away, then I will send him to you" (John 16:7 GNT).

Max Lucado explains:

> If I were to ask you to tell me what Jesus did for you, you'd likely give a cogent answer. But if I were to ask you the role of the Holy Spirit in your life . . . ? Eyes would duck. Throats would be cleared. And it would be obvious that of the three persons of the Godhead, the Holy Spirit is the one we understand the least. Perhaps the most common mistake made regarding the Holy Spirit is perceiving him as a power and not a person, a force with no identity, such is not true. The Holy Spirit is a person.[1]

As Lucado reminds us, the person of the Holy Spirit helps us (John 16:7), he convicts the lost to turn to God (John 16:8), and he leads us in all truth (John 16:13). It is the Spirit who helps us tear down our walls, makes miracles of our messes, comforts our heartaches, and leads us to breakthroughs. Lucado believes that God's Holy Spirit is already at work in our lives. He says, "By the way, for those of us who spent years trying to do God's job that is great news. It's much easier to raise the sail than row the boat."[2]

This *is* great news, because we have the Helper, the Counselor, living inside us. All we have to do is let the breath of God fill our sails to power us through our stressors and into the peace of God.

I have spent so much time explaining the Holy Spirit in this chapter because we will be using his tools to help us tear down the fear, stress, worry, and heartbreak that have walled us from the peace that Jesus came to give us. Jesus explained in John 14:27, "Peace I leave with you, My peace I give to you; not as the world gives do I give to you. Let not your heart be troubled, neither let it be afraid" (NKJV).

It's in fact the Holy Spirit who can give us the supernatural peace of Christ that will help us de-stress. But what must we do in order to enjoy this peace?

To get our first clue, let's go back in time to the day the Comforter arrived. Here's how I picture the scene.

The Story of Peace Continued

Peter looked around the table at the surviving apostles, plus Matthias, serving as Judas's replacement. Peter cleared his throat. "My friends, do you realize it's been fifty days since we broke bread here with Jesus at Passover?"

Thomas walked to the window of the upper room and looked down at the street through the slats of the tightly closed shutters. He turned to face his brothers. "It's so hard to believe it's already Pentecost. But the streets never lie; they are teeming with people who've come from near and far to celebrate the holiday."

"What I want to know," Andrew said, "is how much longer we are to wait here."

Peter responded, "What does it matter? If Jesus told us to wait, we wait!"

Thomas interrupted, "Agreed, of course. But what exactly are we waiting for?"

Matthew looked up from writing on a scroll and reminded the group, "Jesus said not to leave Jerusalem until his Father baptized us with the Holy Spirit."

Thomas shook his head and strode back to the table. "I don't get it. When a man has been baptized in the Jordon River, he can wring water from his beard, but how will a man know when he's been baptized by this Holy Spirit?"

The silence that hung in the air shattered as the shutters slammed open with a great blast of wind that whirled through the room, extinguishing the candles on the table.

As the candlewicks trailed smoke, the men gasped as a flame appeared over each of their heads, as if they were *human* candles on fire with the Spirit of God.

Thomas was the first to speak. His voice lifted in the babbling tongue of a Mede, a language that he, a man of Galilee, had never learned. Thomas's voice was soon joined by that of John, who was speaking fluidly in a tongue of Egypt. The babbling grew as one by one the disciples began to speak in a language they had never known before.

As God's Spirit joined with their spirits, they were emboldened and rushed down the stairs and into the street, each calling out in the language they'd been given. In moments, clusters of passersby surrounded every disciple, shouting questions in the same tongues in which the disciples proclaimed.

The roar of voices soon generated a mob. The voice of a man could be heard yelling, "They're drunk!" and many heads nodded as if to say, "What else could it be?"

In answer, Peter climbed up on a nearby cart, then motioned for the crowd to be silent. He spoke to them in clear Aramaic. "These men are not drunk. It's only 9 a.m. after all."

The crowd blinked back surprise at the discovery that Peter's words were not slurred with wine. A tall Roman merchant shouted out, "Then what's happening here? I can see that these men are locals, nothing but uneducated fishermen. Who taught them to speak in our own tongues about the things God has done?"

Peter's face glowed as he exclaimed, "It's happened as the prophet Joel predicted. God is pouring out his Spirit on all people—men and women alike. Our sons and daughters will prophesy, young men will see visions, and old men will dream dreams. The heavens will show signs and wonders, as will the earth with signs of blood and fire, clouds of smoke, and the sightings of a red moon, all before Jesus returns. But those who call upon the name of the Lord will be saved."

"What does it all mean?" a man with a Judean accent shouted.

"Don't you see?" Peter replied. "It's all about Jesus, the holy One who lived among us, who was endorsed by God to do signs and wonders, as you well know. He was the One who died in the horror of the cross—the holy One, who as King David predicted, would not rot in the grave but would instead make his enemies his footstool."

"Are we then his enemies?" a dark-skinned Libyan called to Peter.

"God has raised Jesus from the dead, and we are his witnesses. But do you not understand?" Peter motioned to the crowd. "You have crucified our Lord the Messiah!"

A Jewish farmer cried out, "What should we do?"

Peter answered, "You must each repent of your sins, turn to God, and be baptized in the name of Jesus Christ for the forgiveness of your sins. Then you too will receive the gift of the Holy Spirit."

The crowd responded to Peter's call, and that day three thousand men were baptized by the disciples in both water and the Holy Spirit (based on Acts 1–2).

Shine the Light of the Word

Just as those Galilean disciples were ignited with the flame of the Holy Spirit, we too should be filled with the Holy Spirit. It's like Billy Graham explained:

The first truth we must understand is that God has given us his Holy Spirit, and that he dwells within us. If I have accepted Christ as my Savior, the Spirit of God dwells within me. Remember—I might not necessarily *feel* his presence, but that does not mean he is absent. It is the *fact* of his presence we must understand. God has promised that his Spirit lives with you if you belong to Christ, and God cannot lie. *We must accept this fact by faith.*[3]

I agree with Graham that when we come to faith the flame of the Spirit of God mingles with our souls, making us new creations filled with the very presence of God himself. But having his Spirit inside us doesn't necessarily mean we know how to yield to him. And this yielding could very well be the key to experiencing less stress in our lives.

Before we pray a yielding prayer, let's look at what Paul says about the Holy Spirit in Galatians 5:25: "Since we are living by the Spirit, let us follow the Spirit's leading in every part of our lives" (NLT). Note that this verse indicates that we *can* live by the Spirit, meaning that it is possible to tap into the power of God, not to control God but to be controlled by God.

Pray, "Lord, open my eyes to see your truth as I read Galatians 5:25 again."

Let's yield to the presence of the Holy Spirit through prayer.

Yielding Prayer

Dear Lord,

How glad I am that you've redeemed me for yourself. Thank you! Thank you also that when I came to faith your Holy Spirit touched my very soul to indwell me. I am now a new creation in Christ, your temple filled with your presence. Lord, I invite more of your presence. Teach me how to yield to your Spirit so I can follow your leading in every area of my life—including my stress. Teach me the secret of having more peace in, through, and despite my circumstances.

In Jesus's name, amen.

2

Overwhelmed

Finding Relief When the World Closes In

> And let the peace that comes from Christ rule
> in your hearts.
>
> Colossians 3:15 NLT

Have you ever seen an episode of the A&E TV show *Hoarders*? It's a show about perfectly normal-looking people who live in perfectly normal-looking houses who become overwhelmed by their possessions. Their problems start when what appears to be an innocent collection of baseball cards takes over the attic. Meanwhile, a pile of magazines stashed in a closet forces its way into the hallway before claiming the living room. But that's nothing compared to the sacks of bargains—beautiful new clothes with the price tags attached, shiny red blenders, and Star Wars figures still in their boxes, all of which conspire to push the car out of the garage and into the front yard. Add in a few bags of trash that can't find their way to the curb for pickup, and the next thing anyone knows, the people residing in the house are trapped. Most end up sleeping on top of a pile of dirty clothes because they can no longer find their beds. Of course the situation wouldn't have gotten so bad if their army of non-neutered cats hadn't continued to spawn new litters of kittens.

Before the occupants knew what happened, their house became a mewing, mildewy, macabre mess, a mess you'd think they'd love to be rescued from, but no! When a concerned family member tries to remove so much as a cobweb, the trapped inhabitant protests, "But that's Sylvia, my favorite spider. I couldn't possibly part with her. Her work has been hanging on my walls for years!"

But by the end of the show, after a professional clean-up team sorts through the massive contents of the house, clears away the carcasses of a few expired pets, and hauls away the trash, a miracle happens. With their belongings no longer piled to the ceiling, the homeowners walk from room to room admiring the fact that, yes, their house does have a floor, and even a couch you can sit on! One woman gushes, "I have so much space that I can now open my refrigerator door!" while a man admits, "With the hallways passable, I don't have to use the outdoor toilet in the backyard." Another amazed homeowner looks around at her now livable space and says, "I had no idea I'd let things get so bad."

Really? You didn't notice the smell of your dead pets or that you had to climb over a mountain of clothes and newspapers to get to the kitchen?

Somehow, I believe their admission of blindness because I've seen this same blindness at work in my own life.

While my family is not buried under a pile of old newspapers, my office has been known to contain so many piles of books that you'd think the local library had opened a branch on my desk. Being a book lover and a card-carrying member of the media, I receive books in the mail every week—beautiful books, signed-by-author books, and books I absolutely love and could not possibly part with. That is, until my piles of books got so big that my office became little more than a book storage facility.

Afraid that a pile of books could fall and hurt someone, I finally decided to do something about it. Two of my friends and I spent an entire day sorting my books—some to keep but the majority to give to a prison ministry. The good news is that by letting go of so many of my treasured books not only was I able to encourage prisoners and their wives, but I was also able to reclaim my office. How wonderful it was to return to my desk and work on my projects.

It seems to me that life is about figuring out which things should be discarded and which things should be kept and put in their rightful place.

So as someone who's had her own struggles with hoarding, I feel somewhat of a connection to those A&E hoarders and therefore feel I have the right to discuss their issues. It seems to me that life is about figuring out which things should be discarded and which things should be kept and put in their rightful place. This same wisdom can be applied to the things that overwhelm us.

I think a lot of people are paralyzed by worry, grief, and fear, or, in other words, they've reached the point where they are overwhelmed.

According to my research, the word *overwhelm* has several meanings. Tap your finger next to any that apply to how you are feeling:

1. To overcome completely in mind or feeling.
2. To overpower or overcome, especially with superior forces; destroy; crush.
3. To cover or bury beneath a mass of something, as floodwaters, debris, or an avalanche; submerge.
4. To load, heap, treat, or address with an overpowering or excessive amount of anything.[1]

Most of these definitions could be applied to the hoarders we discussed earlier as well as to ourselves as we struggle to sort through our own messes.

Trying to deal with your messes may be what inspired you to pick up this book. You're looking for power to help you cope or even to change your circumstances. If so, I'm really excited for you. You're headed for a breakthrough—a breakthrough where you'll clean up your soul by learning how to let go of your toxic emotions and yield to the peace of the Holy Spirit. But it's going to take some work on your part, as you're going to have to:

- clean house
- let go of your control
- learn how to be dependent on God

Clean House

As many a reformed hoarder can tell you, housecleaning is not without its rewards. As we dig out of our messes, we might even find a treasure or two. For example, as I was rearranging my remaining books on my bookshelves, I found a solid gold coin that my son had placed on that shelf fourteen years earlier.

Jim and I had studied coin collecting the one semester I'd homeschooled him when he was nine years old. The lesson on coins had led to a field trip to our town's coin shop, where we'd placed a low-ball bid on this coin in an auction. To our delight, we won the coin for a song. But somehow, instead of putting it away when we got home, we placed the coin on the bookshelf and forgot about it. Fourteen years later, I uncovered the treasure, now worth hundreds more than what we'd paid for it.

Cleaning out our lives is a lot like my experience of cleaning out my office. Not only will taking out your emotional trash give you more "livable" space, but you'll also discover forgotten treasures like peace, a treasure far more valuable than a gold coin.

Another treasure I gleaned from cleaning out my books was the knowledge that I'd put idle resources to good use—investing my dusty books in the lives of men and women who needed them. In fact, the ministry soon wrote to say, "Linda, you should have seen the faces of the wives of the prisoners when we handed out the books and CDs you sent to them. Each resource was a perfect fit for the one who received it."

I'm wondering what resources and treasures have been locked inside you because of the emotional congestion in your heart and soul?

Don't be afraid to invite Jesus in to take inventory of your life, to sort through your difficulties, and to sweep out the cobwebs. Like the professional cleaners who rescued those hoarders on A&E, Jesus comes to remove our trash—our sins, shame, stress, and feelings of being overwhelmed by our present troubles and trials.

The good news is that we are about to start the process of cleaning out our toxic emotions in our upcoming times of yielding prayer. As you pray with me, not only will you find the treasure of supernatural peace, but you'll also experience supernatural joy as you fully trust God to lead you through your difficulties.

Let Go of Your Control

"But," you might complain, "don't you see? I would never have to deal with toxic emotions if I could control all of the troublesome areas of my life."

You do have an interesting point. Imagine what it would be like if you *were* in perfect control of all that concerns you. Whenever you wanted to drop a couple of pounds, the extra weight would vanish by lunchtime. Or you could instantly cure cancer with a knowing smile or create an extra payday just by wishing. If you could accomplish these things by yourself, do you think your abilities would lead you to trust God more deeply, or would you be tempted to trust more fully in yourself?

Perhaps the reason we aren't the answer to our every problem is that we would never discover the truth behind Romans 8:28: "And we know that in all things God works for the good of those who love him, who have been called according to his purpose."

Think about it. If everything always went our way, how would we ever discover that God can flip our difficulties into good, like the time a cancer patient didn't find his complete healing until he discovered he was cancer-free in heaven? Or the time a jilted fiancée discovered her true love to be someone she met *because* God ignored her original prayer to be reunited with the one who broke her heart?

So perhaps instead of kidding ourselves into believing we can become the boss of our own circumstances, much less the boss of God, we need to learn how to trust God more deeply than we ever thought possible—even when we don't understand what God is doing or why.

So perhaps instead of kidding ourselves into believing we can become the boss of our own circumstances, much less the boss of God, we need to learn how to trust God more deeply than we ever thought possible — even when we don't understand what God is doing or why.

Sarah Young shared wise words in her devotional *Jesus Calling*, written from the perspective of Christ. "When you start to feel stressed, let those feelings alert you to your need for Me. . . . Thank Me for the difficulties in your life as they provide protection from the idolatry of self-reliance."[2] In other words, it's like Jesus said in John 15:5: "I am the vine; you are the branches. If you remain in me and I in you, you will bear much fruit; apart from me you can do nothing." If we are "in Christ," not only will we not be overwhelmed by our trials, but we will also be fruitful and victorious.

Learn How to Be Dependent on God

We were created to be continually dependent on God, yet we often strive for our independence. We're like a toddler who manages to aim a gallon jug of milk at a small glass on the edge of the kitchen table. When her fingers slip, this little one unleashes an ice-cold tidal wave that cascades across the table, down her dress, and into her tennis shoes before sloshing across the floor. If only this child had allowed her loving father to help, she could have tasted the milk instead of wearing it.

God is our loving heavenly Father who's standing by, ready to turn our messes into miracles.

This little girl reminds me of us as we desperately try to control our own lives with an "I can do it myself" mentality. But too often our circumstances slip from our grasp to splatter into a massive mess, and we're left to mop up. That's when we look up to ask the Almighty, "Were you just standing there watching when my life turned into this mess? Don't you even care?"

Instead of scolding God, we should humbly seek more than his help; we should seek to become dependent on him. After all, God is our loving heavenly Father who's standing by, ready to turn our messes into miracles. However, when we seek his guidance, we'll avoid the messes altogether, just as when a child allows her dad to pour her milk.

We need to be like the psalmist David, who cried, "In my distress I called to the LORD; I cried to my God for help. From his temple he heard my voice; my cry came before him, into his ears" (Ps. 18:6).

The Story of Peace Continued

Take a moment to go back in time, as David's life became a nightmare.

David bent toward the low mouth of the cave, then scrambled in on his hands and knees. Long moments passed until he found room enough to sit up and lean against a damp rock. He blinked in the inky darkness, barely believing it had come to this—crawling into what could easily become his tomb. David pulled out a small harp from the sack he'd lugged along and strummed his thumb over its strings. A jarring chord echoed on the walls around him, and suddenly he felt overwhelmed.

It hadn't even been a year since he'd lopped off the head of the giant Goliath to win a much needed victory for the Israelite army. But the trouble had started as he accompanied King Saul on their victory march back to the palace. In every town they entered, Saul would hold up Goliath's head by its hair as the women danced in the streets and sang, "Saul has slain his thousands, but David his tens of thousands." At first King Saul only laughed at the lyrics, but as the song became the unofficial anthem of the people, a cloud fell over his face, a cloud that continued to darken.

Sometime later, after Saul had called David back to the palace, the storm finally erupted as David played his harp for the king. As David sang, Saul closed his eyes and listened until his smile twisted. The king's sword struck the wall as David leapt, barely escaping death.

Three more times the king missed his mark. But when David learned of Saul's plot to kill him, he knew it was time to run for his life—to retreat to this old hiding place, only a stone's throw from where he'd faced down Goliath.

How far he'd fallen!

As David pondered these things, he tuned his harp, confident he was far enough into the cave so as not to be heard. The tuning complete, David closed his eyes and sang from his heart:

I cry out to the LORD;
    I plead for the LORD's mercy.
I pour out my complaints before him
    and tell him all my troubles.
When I am overwhelmed,
    you alone know the way I should turn.
Wherever I go,
    my enemies have set traps for me.

David wiped his eyes on his sleeve and continued to sing his sorrow:

I look for someone to come and help me,
    but no one gives me a passing thought!
No one will help me;
    no one cares a bit what happens to me. (Ps. 142:1–4 NLT)

David's thoughts wandered to all that had happened since he'd become the hero of the land. His own family had pulled away from him, in part because they felt his success should have belonged to his older brothers. Then, in his flight from the palace, he'd been forced to leave his best friend, Jonathan, behind. It would not be fitting for the son of the king to go into hiding with him.

Then there was the beautiful Michal with her dark, flowing hair and her liquid green eyes. She was Saul's daughter, whom David had taken as his wife—despite the fact that he'd known his betrothal to her was merely one of Saul's baited traps. Saul's face had registered shock when David had strolled into his court with the demanded dowry, bloody proof that he had indeed slain one hundred Philistine men as a payment for his bride.

But now, despite all his triumphs, he was alone, with only his Lord to talk to. David continued his song:

Then I pray to you, O LORD.
    I say, "You are my place of refuge.
    You are all I really want in life.

Hear my cry,
> for I am very low.
Rescue me from my persecutors,
> for they are too strong for me.
Bring me out of prison
> so I can thank you.
The godly will crowd around me,
> for you are good to me." (Ps. 142:5–7 NLT) (based on
> 1 Sam. 18–19, 22)

What a prayer! In the lowest place in his life, a place where David admits to being unimaginably overwhelmed, he calls out to the Lord to thank him for his goodness. Don't you think that if David could find this kind of peace despite his circumstances you can too? Yes, and we'll work toward this goal of peace together. But in the meantime, you may be wondering what ever became of David as he hid in the cave.

It's good news. God heard David's prayers and moved on his behalf. His family came to be with him—their relationship restored. His parents and brothers were soon followed by four hundred mighty men who wanted to stand with David against Saul. This meant that later, when he hid in the caverns and strummed his lyre, he sang not only to praise God but also to encourage those God had sent to stand with him.

Shine the Light of the Word

While David became the leader of a small army, he stayed on the lam for many years, managing to stay just out of King Saul's grasp. But throughout his troubles, he began to notice a pattern. Whenever he called upon the Lord, the Lord showed up—freeing him from whatever trap Saul had set. David continued to lament his trouble before the Lord, but he always ended his laments with strong statements of praise and trust, as he did in Psalm 31:24: "Be of good courage, and He shall strengthen your heart, all you who hope in the LORD" (NKJV).

You too can take David's hard-learned truth to heart, but first pray, "Lord, open my eyes to see your truth as I read Psalm 31:24 again."

Write down your thoughts and impressions regarding how this Scripture passage might apply to you:

Review what you gleaned and thank God for these truths.

Now we are going to pray not only a prayer of hope but also a prayer that will help us yield all of our feelings of being overwhelmed to the Holy Spirit. In this way, we will exchange our stress for the supernatural peace of Christ. After all, Jesus is the Prince of Peace who came to give us peace. It's time that we learned how to receive this peace through the workings of the Holy Spirit.

Yielding Prayer for the Overwhelmed

To start the process and to yield to the peace of the Holy Spirit, we're going to use prayer. Much like the A&E hoarders, we're going to call on someone outside ourselves (in this case God, who is a pro at this sort of thing) to declutter our hearts and to remove the piles of stress that threaten to overwhelm us.

Shine the Light

Dear Lord,

Please turn on your light of truth over me and my feelings of being overwhelmed. Show me which attitudes you would like to set me free from so we can clean my soul and make more room for you and your peace.

List the situations that have overwhelmed you:

_____

_____

_____

_____

Yield

Put your hand over your stomach and pray the following:

> Dear Lord,
>   I yield all these things, including my feelings of being overwhelmed, to your peace through your Holy Spirit.

With your hand still on your stomach, take deep breaths and start to relax as you repeat the prayer above until you feel God's peace drop into your spirit.

Forgive

> Dear Lord,
>   I'm not strong enough to let go and forgive myself, you, and those who have caused me distress in any of these areas. Still, I choose to forgive. Therefore, I ask that you, through your Holy Spirit inside me, forgive all. I acknowledge that you, Lord, are without sin. Though you may have allowed these difficulties, you will use them as seeds for miracles. Thank you!

Give It All to God

> Dear Lord,
>   I cast these situations at the foot of the cross. Now they are your problems, not mine. Thank you for setting me free from feeling overwhelmed.

Pray for Healing

Dear Lord,
    Please heal the pain caused by my feelings of being overwhelmed. Thank you for your supernatural peace.

Exchange the Enemy's Work for God's Peace

Dear Lord,
    Please forgive me for allowing my circumstances to overwhelm me instead of trusting in you. I close all the doors I have opened to the enemy in this area. In addition, I cancel any plans the enemy has for my life. I cast out any power or influence from any evil spirits trying to overwhelm me. I pray this in the power of the name and blood of Jesus.
    I exchange the enemy's work for God's peace. Send the river of your peace not only to me but also to those overwhelmed by these same influences and circumstances. I pray this also in the power of the name and blood of Jesus.

Praise God—You Are Free!

Thank you, Lord! I'm free!

Pray this prayer whenever you need a redo.

3

Stuck

Finding Release from the Cares of This World

He makes me strong again. He leads me in the
way of living right with Himself which brings
honor to His name.

Psalm 23:3 NLV

As the lambs leapt about, the fat ewe looked up from the rich clover she'd been munching, then wandered toward the shady oak for a nap. As she nestled her pregnant belly on the cool earth, the weight of her wool and the slope of the ground caused her to roll over, her four legs scrambling at the sky. Try as she might, she could not flip over. She was stuck on her back!

The old English shepherds would say this sheep was "cast down." This sheep's compromised position put her in danger of being attacked by a coyote. But even if a coyote failed to attack, the ewe and the lamb she was carrying would be dead in a matter of hours because of the pressures of the gases building within her, a terrible loss to the shepherd.

Perhaps you can relate. You know how it feels to be cast down or stuck—rolled over and pinned down by the pressures of this world. If you feel as if you've fallen and can't get up, let me encourage you to *look* up, because the Good Shepherd is on his way. You don't need to press a panic button. All you need to do is call out to Jesus. He is never too late. He will arrive in time to help get you back on your feet.

Phillip Keller, who wrote *A Shepherd Looks at Psalm 23*, was once a shepherd himself. When he tended sheep, if he saw a vulture's slow circle, he knew that one of his sheep was in trouble, and he'd immediately race to the rescue. When he found a cast down sheep, he'd gently roll it over on its side to relieve the building gases. After a while, he'd stand the sheep upright and rub circulation back into its legs until it could take a wobbly step. Then, after the sheep revived enough to regain its equilibrium, he would watch as it dashed away to join the others.

> *If you feel as if you've fallen and can't get up, let me encourage you to look up, because the Good Shepherd is on his way.*

Keller says:

Many people have the idea that when a child of God fails, when he is frustrated and helpless in a spiritual dilemma, God becomes disgusted, fed up and even furious with him.

This simply is not so.

One of the greatest revelations of the heart of God given to us by Christ is that of Himself as our Shepherd. He has the same identical sensations of anxiety, concern and compassion for cast men and women as I had for cast sheep. This is precisely why He looked on people with such pathos and compassion.[1]

Keller is right. We have a Good Shepherd who cares if we're cast down or entangled by the traps, snares, or cares of this world. But when you're stuck, it can be hard to know what to do to get back up. If you should find yourself in such a predicament, you can find God's freedom when you:

- till the soil of your heart
- look for God's peace
- shine the light of God's truth into your situation

Till the Soil of Your Heart

The cares of this world—like problems, the constant pursuit of more, the sting of loss, as well as unending busyness—can be as dangerous to us as thorns are to a sheep that becomes cast down in thorny brambles.

Jesus told a story to warn of thorny dangers when he spoke to a crowd gathered along the shore of Galilee. As he used the stern of Peter's boat for a pulpit, he told of a farmer who went out to sow his seeds. Jesus explained:

> And as he sowed, some seeds fell on the path, and the birds came and ate them up. Other seeds fell on rocky ground, where they did not have much soil, and they sprang up quickly, since they had no depth of soil. But when the sun rose, they were scorched; and since they had no root, they withered away. Other seeds fell among thorns, and the thorns grew up and choked them. Other seeds fell on good soil and brought forth grain, some a hundredfold, some sixty, some thirty. Let anyone with ears listen! (Matt. 13:4–9 NRSV)

At these words, Peter probably raised an eyebrow at the other disciples as if to say, "Whatever is the Master talking about?"

Later that evening, probably as the men poked around the campfire they had built on the beach, the disciples asked Jesus to explain his story. Jesus said:

49

When anyone hears the word of the kingdom and does not understand it, the evil one comes and snatches away what is sown in the heart; this is what was sown on the path. As for what was sown on rocky ground, this is the one who hears the word and immediately receives it with joy; yet such a person has no root, but endures only for a while, and when trouble or persecution arises on account of the word, that person immediately falls away. As for what was sown among thorns, this is the one who hears the word, but the cares of the world and the lure of wealth choke the word, and it yields nothing. But as for what was sown on good soil, this is the one who hears the word and understands it, who indeed bears fruit and yields, in one case a hundredfold, in another sixty, and in another thirty. (Matt. 13:19–23 NRSV)

According to Jesus's explanation, not everyone who hears the Word is able to receive it, hold on to it, or grow in it. The problems that can prevent a person from doing these things include:

- lack of understanding the truth
- not allowing the Word to take root
- giving in to the cares of this world

But those who do receive the Word and grow in it can produce a harvest that helps others. How does this happen? According to Jesus's parable, it has to do with the quality of the soil.

With your permission and cooperation, God will work the soil of your heart, and your life will become a lovely garden for him.

What's the quality of the soil in your heart, your dwelling for the Holy Spirit? Are you pursuing truth and allowing it to take root, or are the thorns of stress, worries, and striving for riches preventing you from yielding to the peace God is ready to supply? As Paul said in Philippians, "And the peace of God, which transcends all understanding, will guard your hearts and your minds in Christ Jesus" (4:7).

To prevent soil problems, till the soil of your soul so that God's Word can take root. Then his peace will help you grow and reproduce, no matter the floods or storms that come your way. Dig up the stones of unbelief as well as the thorns of stress and desires for riches. With your permission and cooperation, God will work the soil of your heart, and your life will become a lovely garden for him.

God's Peace

Proverbs 4:23 says, "Keep your heart with all diligence, for out of it spring the issues of life" (NKJV). I love this Scripture passage because it reminds me that though God freely gave me the gift of forgiveness through his Son as well as the indwelling of the Holy Spirit, he expects me to diligently keep my heart—yielding my messes to the Holy Spirit so I can live a more powerful, stress-free life.

One of my favorite quotations from the devotional *Dear Jesus* is, "I have poured My very Being into you, in the person of the Holy Spirit. Make plenty of room in your heart for this glorious One."[2] Making more room in our hearts for the Holy Spirit will empower us to live in peace.

But don't be fooled. Peace is not passive; it's powerful. The enemy cannot stand against us when we are standing in the peace of Christ. When we take away the enemy's weapons of fear and stress, he has little left with which to attack us. Plus, standing in the peace of God will give us the power to shine the light on the barrier of darkness that the enemy tries to place between us and the Holy Spirit.

Shine the Light of God's Truth into Your Situation

I read an article about how scientists were impeding light to mask objects and events. It wasn't until I chatted with a friend that I came to understand the deep spiritual implications of this research.

Kathi told me about the great spiritual darkness in the town where she lives. She said, "There's so much spiritual darkness in this area that it seems to mask God's truth," and the light dawned.

I returned to the article I'd read in *Nature, International Weekly Journal of Science* to review the report that scientists at Cornell University had in essence created "invisibility." They'd been able to impede part of a beam of light so that it bent to cloak an event, if only for a nanosecond.[3] Journalist Katie Drummond described the results of this experiment this way:

> Masking an object entails bending light around that object. If the light doesn't actually hit an object, then that object won't be visible to the human eye. . . . Where events are concerned, concealment relies on changing the speed of light. Light that's emitted from actions, as they happen, is what allows us to see those actions happen. Usually, that light comes in a constant flow. What Cornell researchers did, in simple terms, is tweak that ongoing flow of light—just for a mere iota of time—so that an event could transpire without being observable.[4]

I think that's exactly what the enemy, the ruler of darkness, does to us—he impedes the light of God's truth in our lives, even if only for a nanosecond, just enough to distort or hide God's grace, mercy, joy, peace, and love from us. Although these gifts are constantly available to us, when God's light is impeded, we may not see them.

But thank God that we can turn on the light when we focus on Jesus. Second Corinthians 4:6 says, "For God, who said, 'Let there be light in the darkness,' has made this light shine in our hearts so we could know the glory of God that is seen in the face of Jesus Christ" (NLT).

Now you know why we start our yielding prayer time by praying that God's unimpeded light will shine over the situations we are bringing to him. We know that the light of Christ will prevent the enemy from cloaking even an iota of God's truth so that the enemy cannot hide any of the gifts God has for us. As God's light shines in our lives, our blind spots disappear, and unlike the A&E hoarders, we'll be able not only to see the mess we made, but we'll also be able to see God helping us clean it up. We'll be set free from darkness as we enjoy even more of God's presence and peace in our lives.

Plus, God's light will help us see a great truth that the enemy wants us to miss, namely that God is a God we can trust. Hebrews 10:35 says, "So do not throw away this confident trust in the Lord. Remember the great reward it brings you!" (NLT).

The Story of Peace Continued

It was the peace that comes from trusting in Jesus that Peter and the disciples lost while in a terrible storm.

Peter and his brother Andrew set the sails of their boat and caught a breeze that whisked Jesus as well as the disciples away from the throng on the beach.

Peter gave a worried glance at the Master, who'd spent the day teaching in the blazing sun. Peter pointed to a protected place on the stern. "Master, why not rest as we set for the far shore?"

Jesus smiled and gave Peter a nod before laying his head on the cushion Peter had placed there. Jesus was soon asleep, despite a sudden sprinkle of rain.

Peter watched as the setting sun turned the bellies of the heavy clouds ablaze with pink and orange and said to Andrew, "I don't like the looks of that sky."

Andrew kidded him. "Where's your mustard seed of faith that the Master spoke of this afternoon?"

Peter's brow furrowed. "I have no need for a mustard tree at the moment, but a clear sky and a calm sea would give me all the confidence I need."

As the darkness deepened, the clouds began to crackle with flashes that lit them from the inside out. The crackles soon turned into jagged streaks of lightning, while booms of thunder beat the sky like a drum. Peter felt his boat shudder as the wind churned the sea to swells. He gave a quick glance at Jesus. How could he sleep through this?

The storm turned ugly as the boat ascended a high crest before plunging to the bottom of the swell as a mighty wave splashed over the crew.

"Shouldn't we wake the Master?" Andrew asked Peter. "The boat's taking on water."

"Why haven't you wakened him already," Thomas called above the wind as he stumbled toward them. "Don't you think Jesus would want to know we are all about to *die*?"

Peter shook the Master. "Why are you sleeping? Don't you care that we're going to drown?"

Jesus sat up and looked out at the blackened sea as the wind and rain pelted his face. He stood and held out his hands and simply commanded, "Peace, be still!" The wind stopped, and the boat glided into a great calm.

Peter was stunned as he looked at the placid sea.

Jesus turned to his disciples. "Why are you so afraid? Don't you have any faith?"

As the men went back to their duties, Andrew's voice was laced with fear as he whispered to Peter, "Who is this man who can calm the wind and the seas?"

All Peter could do was shake his head and wonder, "Who indeed?" (based on Mark 4:35–41).

Who is he? Simply put, Jesus is Lord! He's the One we can trust as we give him not only our lives but also our concerns. Jesus can calm our storms and give us peace, as he demonstrated inside the storm.

Shine the Light of the Word

We, like the disciples, can get stuck in our fear when we do not trust God in our storms. Let's see what Philippians 4:6–7 has to say to help us break free: "Do not be anxious about anything, but in every situation, by prayer and petition, with thanksgiving, present your requests to God. And the peace of God, which transcends all understanding, will guard your hearts and your minds in Christ Jesus."

Say this simple prayer: "Open my eyes to your truth as I read Philippians 4:6–7 again."

Write down your thoughts and impressions regarding how this Scripture passage might apply to you:

Review what you gleaned and thank God for these truths.

Yielding Prayer for the Stuck

If the traps, snares, and cares of this world have such a grip on your life that you feel stuck in stress and worry, it's time to turn on the light of truth. In this light, you can see that you serve not only a God you can trust but also a God who is waiting to give you gifts of peace, favor, and joy.

Shine the Light

Dear Lord,

Please turn on your light of truth over me and my stress. Reveal any areas where I doubt your provision or plan for my life or areas where I am striving outside of your peace.

List the situations of unbelief and strife that the Lord is revealing to you:

_____

_____

_____

_____

Yield

Put your hand over your stomach and pray the following:

> Dear Lord,
> I yield all these things, including my focus on the trap of the cares of this world, to your peace through your Holy Spirit.

With your hand still on your stomach, take deep breaths and start to relax as you repeat the prayer above until you feel God's peace drop into your spirit.

Forgive

> Dear Lord,
> I'm not strong enough to let go and forgive myself, you, and those who have caused me distress in any of these areas. Still, I choose to forgive. Therefore, I ask that you, through your Holy Spirit inside me, forgive all. I acknowledge that you, Lord, are without sin. Though you may have allowed these difficulties, you will use them as seeds for miracles. Thank you!

Give It All to God

> Dear Lord,
> I cast my cares at the foot of the cross. Now they are your cares, not mine. Thank you for setting me free from striving and stress in these areas.

Pray for Healing

Dear Lord,
Please heal the pain caused by the trap of the cares of this world. Thank you for your supernatural peace.

Exchange the Enemy's Work for God's Peace

Dear Lord,
Please forgive me for bowing before the trap of the cares of this world. I close all the doors I have opened to the enemy in this area. In addition, I cancel any plans the enemy has for my life. I cast out any power or influence from any evil spirits trying to trap me in my striving to satisfy my desires instead of trusting in God. I pray this in the power of the name and blood of Jesus.

I exchange the enemy's work for God's peace. Send the river of your peace not only to me but also to those with whom I've been striving regarding my cares, needs, and wants. I pray this also in the power of the name and blood of Jesus.

Praise God—You Are Free!

Thank you, Lord! I'm free!

Pray this prayer whenever you need a redo.

4

Frustrated

Finding Contentment in Difficulties

> But let patience have its perfect work, that you
> may be perfect and complete, lacking nothing.
>
> James 1:4 NKJV

If I asked you if there was ever a time you felt frustrated, perhaps you'd say, "Yeah, try my entire life."

Life *is* frustrating. It seems we spend a lot of time annoyed or upset because we cannot change our lives or achieve all that is in our hearts because of our limitations, difficult people, or circumstances.

Trust me, I know. I've been there too.

When my then eighteen-month-old daughter was injured in a terrible car accident, even before the ambulance arrived, I knelt beside her in the middle of the freeway and prayed to God for her life. I begged God, "Please bring Laura back to me. Don't let her die!"

It seemed as if God not only ignored my cry but was also determined to give Laura neither life nor death, for Laura hovered for days, then weeks, and finally months in a state of unconsciousness.

But I had hope. The doctors in the Texas Catholic ICU told me that the doctors in Colorado had a coma-stimulation program that would surely pull Laura back to the land of the living. So when we arrived in Denver by air ambulance, three months into our ordeal, I was excited to see how God would answer my constant prayers.

The next several weeks were busy as the staff poked, prodded, and gave my daughter every conceivable test. Then came the day of the big reveal, and I was anxious to hear the plan. But instead of telling me how they were going to wake my daughter up, twenty-six health care professionals surrounded me to say, "Laura's not in a coma; she's in a vegetative state. She'll never wake up."

Their prognosis?

Hopeless.

One doctor put it this way: "Your daughter could live in this vegetative state until she's eighty years old."

I was so shocked that when the meeting ended I walked out of the room as if I were a zombie. But in the coming days, my shock turned to determination. I would continue to call out to God for help. My only comfort was the knowledge that my God was bigger than the hospital staff's prognosis.

A week later, one of the doctors slipped into Laura's hospital room to confide in me. "I have good news. Because of your daughter's head injury, it's unlikely she will grow taller. She will stay about the size she is today. That means she'll be easy for you to manage."

My face flamed with frustration. "Number one," I said, keeping my voice low and steady, "what makes you think this is good news, and number two, scientifically speaking, you can't tell the difference between a coma and a vegetative state. So if we put God in the equation, how do you know Laura won't get better?"

The doctor kept his eyes locked on mine as he backed toward the door. "Oh, I didn't know you were in denial," he accused before he turned and fled.

That's when the hospital chaplain got involved. She soon knocked on Laura's door. "Come in," I said, glad she'd finally come to pray with me.

The chaplain said, "I understand that you think your daughter can get better."

I answered cautiously, "Yes, I do."

"Can you tell me why?"

I tilted my head toward my sleeping daughter. "Have you seen her? She can't get much worse."

The chaplain frowned but looked determined to get me under control. "I understand that you think your daughter can get better because of God. Is this true?"

That's when it dawned on me. The chaplain and I weren't playing ball for the same team.

I gave my chin a slight jut. "Yes."

"And you're basing that on the Bible?" she asked, as if ready for a debate.

"Yes," I answered again.

Her eyes held me prisoner. "Can you tell me exactly where in the Bible?"

I broke her spell as I crossed my arms and said, "Try the whole Bible."

The gleam in the chaplain's eyes told me she thought that I was a lot worse than she'd suspected. But she wasn't through with her intervention. Her visit was followed by social workers who all seemed bent on making me recant my "My daughter can get better because of God" theory. But as frustrated as I was with the ongoing crisis, I wouldn't recant.

Yet, in the dark days and nights that followed, I continued to hover over my precious child and saw very little evidence to validate my stubbornly held position. Except for an occasional smile or a flutter of an eyelash, it seemed as if my daughter had left her body and was visiting some place very far away from her hospital bed.

Into the wee hours of the night I would cry out to God in frustration. "Why won't you answer my prayers? Why won't you return my daughter to me? Don't you love me? Don't you care that the entire staff of this hospital thinks I've lost it?"

Hopefully, you've never had a loved one in this kind of situation. But I share my story with you so that you'll know I really do understand what it means to be frustrated. Before I tell you the rest of this story, I want to take a break and explore how you can tame your feelings of frustration and live with contentment regardless of your circumstances. Take a deep breath, then consider that you can:

- give God your frustrations
- trust God in your frustrations
- develop a grateful heart

Give God Your Frustrations

One of Max Lucado's readers asked him, "Why talk to God about my troubles? He can't understand."[1]

Lucado referred this man to Hebrews 4:15, where it says, "For we do not have a high priest who is unable to empathize with our weaknesses, but we have one who has been tempted in every way, just as we are—yet he did not sin."

Yes! Even when I felt alone in my daughter's hospital room, not only was God with me, but he also cared and even understood how I felt.

If you've ever wondered if God cares or understands your feelings, consider this Lucado remark:

Every page of the Gospels hammers home this crucial principle: God knows how you feel. From the funeral to the factory to the frustration of a demanding schedule, Jesus understands. When you tell God that you've reached your limit, he knows what you mean. When you shake your head at impossible deadlines, he shakes his head too. When your plans are interrupted by people who have other plans, he nods in empathy.

He has been there.

He knows how you feel.[2]

Lucado is right. God not only knows how we feel but also cares. Plus, God knows how to help us and give us strength. Philippians 4:13 reminds us, "I can do all this through him who gives me strength."

When my daughter was hurt in our terrible accident, I was a young mom who'd never stood up to an authority figure. But God empowered me to stand against the will of an entire hospital. Looking back, I can tell you that God was with me, keeping me strong even though my heart was breaking.

Today, I can tell you that when your heart is breaking, when you are feeling harassment or the pain of frustration, God wants to help.

> *He wants you to place the weight of all that you're carrying, all the pain that you're feeling, into his loving hands, which undergird your own.*

He wants you to place the weight of all that you're carrying, all the pain that you're feeling, into his loving hands, which undergird your own.

Pray this simple prayer:

Lord,

I believe you do know how I feel and that you care. As you can see, my hands are full of so much that frustrates me. Thank you that your hands are beneath mine, holding my hands up, even giving me the strength I need to overcome. I now drop the contents of what

I've been trying to carry myself into your capable hands. Thank you that I can rest in you.

In Jesus's name, amen.

Trust God in Your Frustrations

I knew I was in a terrible dance with the hospital staff. If they could get me to admit that God was not a party to our situation, that my daughter's fate rested solely in my own hands, the conclusion would be simple: euthanasia—allowing my daughter to die by starvation.

Help me, God! Help me stand up to this threat. Lord, if you want to take Laura home to yourself, you have my permission. I trust you to make that decision on Laura's behalf.

Sometimes I would place my lips to my daughter's ear. "If Jesus asks, it's okay to stay in heaven with him. Mommy will be okay." But somehow, despite the ever present threat of death, Laura continued to survive.

You may be wondering, *In the midst of such frustrations, how is it possible to trust God?*

Billy Graham once said, "Doubts are a normal part of life. We doubt things on earth, so it's easy to doubt the things of God. Yet God's promises are His promises. What He has said in the past remains true today. God never changes or goes back on His Word. If He did, then He wouldn't be God."[3]

Trusting God is a choice, and once we choose to trust him, God himself will guard that trust. It's like Paul said when he wrote Timothy about his own trials, "That is why I am suffering as I am. Yet this is no cause for shame, because I know whom I have believed, and am convinced that he is able to guard what I have entrusted to him until that day" (2 Tim. 1:12).

But you might ask, "What about the times God fails to answer that which I've trusted him to do?"

Graham put it this way: "It's true that God often doesn't come through in the way and timing you expected, but that's not a flaw in God; it's a flaw in your expectations."[4] In other words, God has his own ways of doing things, ways that will lead to miracles you may not have anticipated. The key is to trust him to do the thing that will bring the most good, even when you don't have a clue what he's up to.

Pray this:

> *Dear Lord,*
>
> *I choose to trust you, even when you're not doing things the way I've asked. When this happens, despite all appearances, I know you are working a greater miracle. I also know that you will guard my trust and help me through.*
>
> *In Jesus's name, amen.*

Develop a Grateful Heart

Stormie Omartian shares about the time she and her family moved to Tennessee from California and experienced what she was later told was a one-hundred-year ice storm. Ice coated everything—streets, houses, cars, and unfortunately power and phone lines. Stuck inside their house, her family wasn't going anywhere, except to huddle around the fireplace. Their ordeal stretched on day after day. In her fear, she sought the Lord. "Lord, help us. We need to know You're here."

She said, "I immediately sensed that instead of despairing over the misery of the situation, I was to embrace the experience and find His goodness in it. As I did, the results surprised me. I thanked God that He had kept us together as a family, instead of having someone stranded elsewhere and not knowing if they were safe. I was grateful that He had prepared us with a good supply of food and bottled water. I appreciated our fireplace and warm clothes that kept us from freezing. . . . Our bodies were cold, but our hearts were warmed by the light He gave our souls."[5]

Omartian got it. She was able to discover the miracle within her ordeal by being grateful.

Oftentimes, God keeps his ways a secret, but when we have a grateful heart, God may open our eyes so we can see the joy we might have otherwise missed.

The best way to develop a grateful heart is to learn how to walk in step with God.

The best way to develop a grateful heart is to learn how to walk in step with God. Omartian explains, "Walking step by step with God requires embracing the moment for all it's worth. When you are tempted to become fearful, frustrated, uncertain, or panicked about what is happening in your life, stop and see that God is in it. And with Him, you have everything you need for this moment. Here and now."[6]

Let's pray:

> *Dear Lord,*
>
> *Remind me that you are in the moment, even the moments that frustrate me. Help me to learn how to walk in step with you so I can develop a grateful heart and see you at work. I choose peace and contentment regardless of what I'm going through.*
>
> *In Jesus's name, amen.*

The Story of Peace Continued

The biblical story I am about to share is about a woman so frustrated by her circumstances that she tried to bypass God and take matters into her own hands. See how her hard-won lessons apply to you.

My arms longed for the baby my husband, Abraham, told me the Lord had promised me. For years I waited, watching as our herds and slaves produced enough offspring to repopulate the city of Ur, yet my arms remained empty. As I was long past my child-bearing years, I felt frustrated. How could God fulfill his promise that Abraham would become the father of many nations unless I myself intervened?

That's when I decided to do what a lot of women in my situation did. I gave my husband Haggi, my own attendant. My plan was to raise the child of their union as my own, but as Hagar's belly swelled, she was not so easy to convince. She explained in my tent, "Sarah, you forget that I am the mother of Abraham's child, not you."

I blinked back tears as Haggi swept away a lock of her dark, silky hair and declared, "By the right of my child's birth, I will no longer be treated as a slave in this household. You will soon honor me as I stand with my child beside Abraham."

With Haggi trying to take my place, I was more frustrated than ever and furious that my plan had backfired. I blamed my husband for this mess and told him so. "You are responsible for the wrong I am suffering. I put my slave in your arms, and now that she knows she is pregnant, she despises me. May the Lord judge between you and me."

How relieved I was when Abraham took my side. "Do with her what you want," he'd instructed.

I treated Haggi so harshly that she did what I'd hoped; she ran away into the desert. I thought I'd never see her or her offspring again, but she returned, though with a better attitude about her place as my servant.

The years ticked by, and her son, Ishmael, was thirteen years old when my husband entertained three strangers in our tent. As I stood near the tent flap, I heard one of the guests tell Abraham, "I will surely return to you about this time next year, and Sarah, your wife, will have a son."

I closed my eyes and covered my mouth with my hand, trying to shoo away the laughter that begged to dance into the evening air. I guess our guest hadn't a clue I was in my nineties.

My giggles stopped when one of the guests asked, "Why did Sarah laugh and say, 'Will I really have a child, now that I am old?' "

This stranger had read my thoughts. Then he stunned me by saying, "Is anything too hard for the Lord?"

Despite my years of barrenness, God's words proved true. Here, let me lift the blanket. See how peacefully he sleeps? Isaac, the child of my laughter, born out of years of frustration, the spiritual heir of both my husband and myself. Here is the child of promise—at long last (based on Gen. 16–18, 21).

Manipulation, blame, anger, deception, and cruelty were key parts of Sarah's story, but none of these behaviors got her what she wanted. It was the word of the Lord combined with her long-suffering patience that finally produced the miracle she so longed for.

Her story reminds me of James when he said, "Count it all joy, my brothers, when you meet trials of various kinds, for you know that the testing of your faith produces steadfastness. And let steadfastness have its full effect, that you may be perfect and complete, lacking in nothing" (1:2–4 ESV).

The one thing the Lord produced in me, after all the months of waiting on my daughter, was steadfastness, or patience. And what joy when almost a year after the accident I placed Laura's newborn brother into her arms. That was the very moment when little Laura finally woke up.

Then came the day I, with the help of a friend, packed up Laura and her purple wheelchair and her baby brother and his stroller and headed to the hospital to meet with one of her doctors for a checkup.

Upon seeing Laura's bright smile and hearing her spoken hello, this doctor, who'd sat in the council of the original twenty-six, stated, "Your daughter is not a vegetable. There's no doubt. She is awake."

A few minutes later, while my friend stood in the coffee cart line with my kids, I slipped down the hall to the hospital chapel. I found it empty, so I walked up to the front and stared at the stained-glass depiction of what appeared to be the pagan child-god of prosperity juggling vegetables. So help me, in my maturity, I shouted at that god, "Ha, ha, ha! I was right and you were wrong."

I tossed my head and turned on my heels to head back to my kids. Just as I cleared the chapel's doorway, I heard the sound of a sliding door. What? Was the chaplain's office behind a panel in the wall? I strode several steps before turning around. There stood the chaplain in the doorway, staring after me. I turned and with a bright smile waved back at her.

Her expression said it all. She couldn't deny it. My God had proved bigger than my circumstances. How glad I am that I waited on him. As it turned out, God was far more powerful than anything the doctors could pronounce. Despite my frustrations, all I needed to do to see God's faithfulness was practice a little patience.

Though Laura came back to us changed, she is still our daughter, and despite her disabilities, she continues to live at home as our beloved child. Oh, and by the way, Laura is five foot four inches tall, the same height as her mom.

Shine the Light of the Word

When we are strengthened with God's power, it's difficult to remain frustrated, as Colossians 1:11–12 explains: "We also pray that you will be strengthened with all his glorious power so you will have all the endurance and patience you need. May you be filled with joy, always thanking the Father" (NLT).

Say this simple prayer: "Open my eyes to your truth as I read Colossians 1:11–12 again."

Write down your thoughts and impressions regarding how this Scripture passage might apply to you:

_____

_____

_____

Review what you gleaned and thank God for these truths.

Yielding Prayer for the Frustrated

What if you could wipe away all your frustrations and relax in God's peace? You can, but it will take some work through prayer and yielding to the Spirit of God. These kinds of prayers can lead to the gift of peace Jesus meant for us to have all along. In fact, Jesus said in John 14:27, "I am leaving you with a gift—peace of mind and heart. And the peace I give is a gift the world cannot give. So don't be troubled or afraid" (NLT).

Shine the Light

> *Dear Lord,*
>   *Please turn on your light of truth over me and my frustrations. Reveal the anger, pride, or frustration that might be hiding inside me.*

List the areas the Lord is revealing to you now:

_____

_____

_____

_____

Yield

Put your hand over your stomach and pray the following:

Dear Lord,
> *I yield all these things to your peace through your Holy Spirit.*

With your hand still on your stomach, take deep breaths and start to relax as you repeat the prayer above until you feel God's peace drop into your spirit.

Forgive

Dear Lord,
> *I'm not strong enough to let go and forgive myself, you, and those who have caused me distress in any of these areas. Still, I choose to forgive. Therefore, I ask that you, through your Holy Spirit inside me, forgive all. I acknowledge that you, Lord, are without sin. Though you may have allowed these difficulties, you will use them as seeds for miracles. Thank you!*

Give It All to God

Dear Lord,
> *I cast these frustrations at the foot of the cross. Now they are your frustrations, not mine. Thank you for setting me free from my frustrations and from trying to control my world instead of trusting you.*

Pray for Healing

Dear Lord,
> *Please heal the pain caused by my frustrations. Thank you for your supernatural peace.*

Exchange the Enemy's Work for God's Peace

Dear Lord,

Please forgive me for entertaining my frustrations. I close all the doors I have opened to the enemy in this area. In addition, I cancel any plans the enemy has for my life. I also cast out any power or influence from any evil spirits trying to frustrate me. I pray this in the power of the name and blood of Jesus.

I exchange the enemy's work for God's peace. Send the river of your peace not only to me but also to those with whom I've shared my frustrations. I pray this also in the power of the name and blood of Jesus.

Praise God—You Are Free!

Thank you, Lord! I'm free!

Pray this prayer whenever you need a redo.

5

Burdened

Finding a Way to Lighten Your Load

Then Jesus said, "Come to me, all of you who
are weary and carry heavy burdens, and I will
give you rest."

Matthew 11:28 NLT

I climbed up the steep mountain road alone, miles from where
we'd left our 1975 red Nova sedan. I was tired, thirsty, and
wondered what had happened to my young husband, Paul, as well
as to our friend Gordon, who'd recently served as Paul's best man
in our wedding. It had been hours since I'd last seen them.

The day had started with the thrill of adventure. The three of
us, all barely adults, had driven two thousand miles straight from
Texas to the base of this southern Colorado mountain range. We
would have driven even farther if our sedan hadn't bottomed out
on the rocks on the winding dirt road. That's when we'd parked it

and decided to hike our way into an upper valley of the Sangre de Cristo Mountains, where we planned to pitch our tents. The high valley would serve as our base camp for the next several days as we tried our hand at scaling a few of the fourteen-thousand-foot peaks that surrounded it.

At first, I enjoyed the mountain beauty, but after walking for miles beneath the burden of my backpack, I began to feel drained by the hot sun as well as the lack of oxygen at this higher altitude. Despite these difficulties, I wasn't prepared for what the man I'd married only a few months before said to me. "Linda, you're not keeping up. I think it would be better if Gordon and I ran ahead to set up camp. But don't worry. I'll come back for you soon. Okay?"

"I don't know, Paul," I said, frowning.

"I won't be gone long. I promise."

My frown deepened, and Paul gave me one of his charming smiles. "I'll even carry your backpack when I return. All right?"

Though I wasn't thrilled with their plan, I gave in, mainly because I loved the idea of my strong husband carrying my heavy burden.

I watched the guys disappear over a rise in the road as I called after them, "Don't be long, okay?"

The scenery was entertaining for a while, but the isolation that hovered in the mountain air began to feel creepy. There was not a living creature to be seen. One side of the road swept up into woody cliffs, while the other side careened into a steep drop-off, the kind that could hide a body forever. I bit my lower lip and hoped the men would return soon.

They didn't.

Hours later, I was breathing hard in the thin air as I continued my slow upward march. Suddenly, a bloodcurdling scream filled the air.

A mountain lion!

I had no doubt that the nearby cat was planning to drop off the cliffs and onto my back, tearing his fangs into my too-tall backpack stuffed with too much gear.

I wanted to run, but I was too exhausted. I only had the strength to lift my hands above my head, a trick I'd heard would make the predator think I was a larger creature. Besides, there was no place to go but up the narrowing trail, one foot after the other. So that's what I did until the shadows lengthened and blended into the enveloping darkness.

Night fell, and it had been six hours since I'd seen the guys. I was no longer sure I could go on.

I wiped at a stray tear. Why hadn't Paul returned?

I was cold and shivering when I came upon a group of rowdy men drinking brews around a campfire. I stood beyond the reach of the flickering light and wondered if it would be safe to stumble into their camp, a young woman lost, exhausted, and alone.

But the trail had ended. How could I go any farther in the darkness?

I pulled off my backpack and started to unzip it. Maybe I could pull out my sleeping bag and climb inside right where I stood. It almost seemed like a good idea, except I was hungry and thirsty and there was a mountain lion on the prowl.

Suddenly, I heard noise coming from the brush, and a flashlight beam hit my face. "Linda?"

It was Gordon!

I gasped, "Where have you two been? Where's Paul?"

Gordon lifted my backpack and began to carry it to our camp, which was located just through a tangle of trees and only a thousand or so yards from where the trail had ended. Gordon explained, "I guess this high altitude was too much for us flatlanders. Paul passed out from what must be altitude sickness, and I'm just now well enough from barfing to find you."

A few minutes later I reunited with my sweetheart. "I'm so sorry!" he said as he tried to stand. He took only a couple of steps before he collapsed back to the ground. It seemed he was in much worse shape than I was.

However, I was glad to be found and gladder still that we'd been reunited. It took some time, but we were able to set up camp, cook freeze-dried stew on our portable stove, and sip some of the water we'd ported in before we slept in the safety of our tents.

Perhaps you know exactly how I felt the evening I was burdened and lost. Maybe you too are straining under your own heavy burden and you're wondering where God is. You want to know how to:

- find God, his help, and direction
- find relief from your heavy burdens

Find God, His Help, and Direction

One of my best moments on that long-ago evening was the moment Gordon found me in the dark.

If you're worried about being found, let me assure you that you *have* been found. It's as Psalm 46:1 says: "God is our refuge and strength, an very-present help in trouble" (KJV). God knows right where you are, just as he knew my exact location as I hiked that winding mountain trail those many years ago. In fact, God was my constant companion that day. In between my panic, fear, and anger that the boys had left me, I shot off several earnest prayers like, "Lord, help me!" God not only heard my prayers but answered them.

Think about it. I passed only yards away from a screaming mountain lion. In Colorado, the occasional mountain lion will sometimes attack a stray hiker. Could it be that God shut this predator's mouth just as he shut the mouths of the lions in the den where Daniel spent the night (Dan. 6)?

I don't know, but I do know that not only did I survive my walk up the mountain without falling prey to either the lion or the sickness that plagued my companions, but I also found my party in the dark, only a short distance from where they had collapsed with altitude sickness.

God is with you. He's at work in your circumstances now.

Are you still feeling alone? Perhaps what you really need to do is realize who your traveling companion is. Romans 8:26–28 explains his presence this way:

> Meanwhile, the moment we get tired in the waiting, God's Spirit is right alongside helping us along. If we don't know how or what to pray, it doesn't matter. He does our praying in and for us, making prayer out of our wordless sighs, our aching groans. He knows us far better than we know ourselves, knows our pregnant condition, and keeps us present before God. That's why we can be so sure that every detail in our lives of love for God is worked into something good. (Message)

Let me ask you a question. How would your perception of your current struggles change if you knew for certain that God was with you, constantly working to turn your dilemmas into good?

Good news. God *is* with you. He's at work in your circumstances now. Perhaps it's time to acknowledge God's presence and care.

Dear Lord,

Sometimes I feel like I'm stumbling up a mountain trail in the dark as my enemies watch, waiting to pounce and devour me. Open my eyes and help me to see that you are with me and are constantly creating solutions to my dilemmas. Thank you that when I pray, "Help me," you hear me and answer. Thank you that everything is going to be all right as you work out everything for good.

In Jesus's name, amen.

Find Relief from Your Heavy Burdens

Now that we've established who your traveling companion is, I have a question. Imagine Alec Baldwin in his famous credit card commercials asking, "What's in your backpack?" What burdens are you carrying? Tap your finger next to all that apply:

- financial concerns
- job woes
- housing issues
- lack of provisions
- family dilemmas
- marriage trouble
- loved ones in crisis
- transportation difficulties
- relationship troubles
- health concerns
- not being understood
- depression, grief, or heartache
- disasters past, present, or future
- worries and fear
- stress and anxiety
- uncertain future
- _____ (fill in the blank)

Wow, I have to hand it to you. That's some list. And you've been trying to carry the weight all by yourself? No wonder you feel stressed! What you need is for someone to come along and carry your backpack for you.

Good news. Jesus said, "Come to me, all you who are weary and burdened, and I will give you rest. Take my yoke upon you and learn from me, for I am gentle and humble in heart, and you will find rest for your souls. For my yoke is easy and my burden is light" (Matt. 11:28–30 NIV).

Jesus himself wants to give us rest from our burdens. But maybe we need to read the fine print. It seems to me that Jesus is actually offering to add yet another burden onto our shoulders, the burden of his yoke. Is this some kind of divine "gotcha"?

What we have to understand is that Jesus is not offering to make our problems disappear; he's offering to give us rest for our souls while he does our heavy lifting.

What we have to understand is that Jesus is not offering to make our problems disappear; he's offering to give us rest for our souls while he does our heavy lifting. Otherwise, why would he say, "My yoke is easy and my burden is light"?

My friend Janet Holm McHenry explains the passage this way: "Behind the invitation is God's perfect love—his desire to meet my needs, his anticipation to bless me abundantly, and his longing to fellowship with *me*. At times, after I've laid all my praise and requests at his feet, it's as though God says to me, I will take care of all those needs—just 'Be still, and know that I am God' (Ps. 46:10)."[1]

Jesus wants to help us find rest from our burdens. We can find his rest when we simply come to him. When we recognize we are connected to his presence, we can relax in his loving care, knowing he's going to work things for the good, as Romans 8:28 says: "And we know that in all things God works for the good of those who love him, who have been called according to his purpose." If you are in Christ, meaning you've accepted his forgiveness and desire to walk with him, then you have been called to his purpose. God will work out your difficulties in answer to your prayers, or he will use your difficulties for a greater miracle. And what should you do in the meantime? Stay in his presence, trusting him with everything.

Whether or not we see (or even understand) the good that will come out of our crisis is not the point. The point is to rest in Jesus, trusting that he's moving in his own way, a way better than we could ever imagine. He's God after all, and that alone should be reason enough to let him move any way he wants. Let's talk to him about this in prayer:

Dear Lord,

I acknowledge that you are calling me to come to you, and so here I am standing in your holy presence. I accept your yoke, which connects me more closely with you. As I allow you to put your yoke across my shoulders, I relax in your peace. Thank you that together we will get through my difficulties and that you will lead and guide me. Your strength will get me through. Thank you!

In Jesus's name, amen.

The Story of Peace Continued

There is a way we can be free from our burdens, live into every promise of God, and win every victory through him. If you don't believe me, listen to this story of a Bible great as he might describe it.

> *God will work out your difficulties in answer to your prayers, or he will use your difficulties for a greater miracle.*

One evening, after a late supper, I gathered my grandchildren around me and told them my story, a story I warned them never to forget. Their upturned faces glowed beneath the full moon and stars that winked over our meadow. And in that moment, I felt blessed that all of God's promises had come to pass.

I told my grandchildren, "Even as a child, I followed Moses through the desert. In fact, I was only a young man when I heard Moses tell of how God spoke to him through a burning bush. He said, 'And God told me that the Promised Land, the land of Canaan, was a good and large land, a land flowing with milk and honey.' "

My grandchildren giggled, partly at my imitation of Moses's gruff voice and partly because they knew well his words had proved true. So I continued, "After forty years of wandering through the desert, our people finally came to the Jordan River, the only thing that separated us from our land of promise."

I paused, looking into the eyes of each of my heirs. "You'd think our tribal leaders would have been ready to wade through this river to see this Promised Land for themselves. Instead, they grumbled, 'Why should we lead our flocks away from this lush grassland? If we cross this river, who knows? We might well be entering a land of war and trouble.'

"I was amazed. How could these men have such little faith? But I was equally surprised when Moses took their worries to heart. 'I'll pray about your concerns,' he told them."

I implored my wide-eyed descendants, "But what was there to pray about? Hadn't God already said the land was ours?"

The children nodded, and I continued, "After prayer, Moses was happy with the answer God had given him—to send spies, one from every tribe, into our land.

"So when twelve brave men were honored with this task, I was glad to be included. However, I was surprised that Moses charged us, 'See if the land is good and if the people are strong.' "

I stopped my story and lifted my hands toward heaven. "How could he ask such a thing of us? Moses knew that God himself had said the land was good. And if God promised this land to us, what did it matter if the people were strong? They would soon be defeated, not because of our strength but because of God's."

I continued, "The twelve of us spies spent forty days discovering that, indeed, the land was as good as God had promised. To prove it, we lugged back an abundance of pomegranates and figs as well as a cluster of grapes so heavy that it took two of us to carry it.

"But even as we journeyed back to our people, I could hear my companions complain, 'The men are giants, so tall that we could never reach them with our swords before they cut us in half.'

" 'Friends,' I implored, 'if we go into the Promised Land with our God, why would we need to rely on our own reach to win the battle? Is the arm of God too short?'

"But they would not listen, nor would our people when they heard the complaints of the spies who whined, 'The land may be good, but compared to the inhabitants, we are like grasshoppers.' "

I folded my arms and looked at my grandchildren. "So? I ask you so?"

I stroked my gray beard and continued, "Only Joshua stood with me as I tried to calm the people. I said, 'We should go up and take possession of the land, for we can certainly do it.'

"But our leaders wept and grumbled. 'We should have stayed in Egypt,' they cried, rolling on the ground. One leader stood up and even implored the twelve of us, 'Who of you will lead us back to Egypt?'

"What was the result of their disbelief in the promise of God? God was so angry that he sent a plague that killed the ten spies who would not stand with him. Then God forbade our people from entering the land for forty years. In fact, my dear children, Joshua and I are the only ones left of that generation who are still alive."

The children looked from one to another, as they already knew that I was one of the eldest of our people.

"And when the day came for us to enter the land that God had given to our descendants, we crossed the Jordan ready for battle. Yes, there was war. But it was a battle easily won through God's strength."

I pointed to our sheep, which were bathed in the twilight's glow as they stood grazing upon the rolling hills that surrounded us. "This good land is exactly what God promised Moses."

"Grandfather," five-year-old Nun asked, "God is a faithful God?"

I nodded. "Yes, Nun. And never forget that when God makes a promise to you, he *will* keep it."

Young Jepth turned his face toward mine. "Grandfather, then God's promises are like a gift."

I smiled and pulled the child into my lap. With one hand on Jepth's head I said, "It blesses me to see one so small wiser than those foolish tribal leaders." I smiled down at my grandson. "When God makes you a promise, it is a gift. You must take hold of it and never let go. To do otherwise would be a great disrespect, a disrespect that could prompt God to give your promise to someone who will be glad to receive it" (based on Num. 13–14, 32).

You may be wondering why I told the story of Caleb, a man who carried no burden of fear or doubt either time he entered the Promised Land, first to spy on it, then to take it by sword.

The story is about more than Caleb and his friend Joshua. It's about the people who refused to trust God and had to carry the burden of their fear, doubt, and even defeat. Not only did they bear the weight of these difficulties, but they also died before they could see God's promises fulfilled.

How was it that Caleb, this man without the burdens of fear and doubt, was one of only two people of his generation to taste the land of milk and honey on his own parcel of the Promised Land?

It was because, although Caleb faced the same giants as his people, unlike them he believed God. Neither Caleb nor Joshua was afraid to go into battle because they knew they followed God into victory.

You may be thinking, *It was easy for Caleb. He had God's promise. But in my case, God hasn't promised me a thing. So of course I'm stressed and burdened. How could I be otherwise?*

Don't be so sure that you are without God's promises. Here are seven promises of God that apply to you right now:

1. You have the victory—"But thanks be to God, who gives us the victory through our Lord Jesus Christ" (1 Cor. 15:57 ESV).

2. You are forgiven through the blood of Jesus—"And the blood of Jesus, his Son, cleanses us from all sin" (1 John 1:7 NLT).

3. You have the strength of God—"I can do all things through Christ who strengthens me" (Phil. 4:13 NKJV).

4. God guides you—"In all your ways acknowledge Him, and He shall direct your paths" (Prov. 3:6 NKJV).

5. The peace of God is yours—"GOD makes his people strong. GOD gives his people peace" (Ps. 29:11 Message).

6. God provides for you—"And my God will give you everything you need because of His great riches in Christ Jesus" (Phil. 4:19 NLV).

7. You can live worry free—"Give all your worries to Him because He cares for you" (1 Pet. 5:7 NLV).

These seven promises are only a few of the thousands of promises you can find in between the covers of your Bible. All it takes is a little digging to find the gifts God has already given you. Once you find a promise to lean on, the only thing left to do is to believe God will do what he's promised.

Yes, giants always prowl God's Promised Land, giants of doubt, fear, discouragement, lack, disease, and more. But you can be assured that when you believe God's promises he will empower you to slay the giants, win the victory, and enter the Promised Land.

Shine the Light of the Word

This business of living a burden-free life is serious business, as Hebrews 10:35–38 explains:

Do not let this happy trust in the Lord die away, no matter what happens. Remember your reward! You need to keep on patiently doing God's will if you want him to do for you all that he has promised. His coming will not be delayed much longer. And those whose faith has made them good in God's sight must live by faith, trusting him in everything. Otherwise, if they shrink back, God will have no pleasure in them. (TLB)

Say this simple prayer: "Open my eyes to your truth as I read Hebrews 10:35–38 again."

Write down your thoughts and impressions regarding how this Scripture passage might apply to you:

Review what you gleaned and thank God for these truths.

Yielding Prayer for the Burdened

If you are ready to give God your burdens, yield to the presence of God through the following prayers.

Shine the Light

> *Dear Lord,*
> *Please turn on your light of truth over me and my burdens. Reveal to me the burdens I need to give to you.*

List the burdens the Lord is revealing to you now:

Yield

Put your hand over your stomach and pray the following:

> Dear Lord,
> I yield all these heavy burdens to your peace through your Holy Spirit.

With your hand still on your stomach, take deep breaths and start to relax as you repeat the prayer above until you feel God's peace drop into your spirit.

Forgive

> Dear Lord,
> I'm not strong enough to let go and forgive myself, you, and those who have caused me distress in any of these areas. Still, I choose to forgive. Therefore, I ask that you, through your Holy Spirit inside me, forgive all. I acknowledge that you, Lord, are without sin. Though you may have allowed these difficulties, you will use them as seeds for miracles. Thank you!

Give It All to God

> Dear Lord,
> I cast these burdens at the foot of the cross. Now they are your burdens, not mine. Thank you for setting me free from straining under these burdens that now belong to you.

Pray for Healing

> Dear Lord,
> Please heal the pain caused by my burdens. Thank you for your supernatural peace.

Exchange the Enemy's Work for God's Peace

Dear Lord,

Please forgive me for holding on to my burdens. I close all the doors I have opened to the enemy in this area. In addition, I cancel any plans the enemy has for my life. I also cast out any power or influence from any evil spirits trying to burden me. I pray this in the power of the name and blood of Jesus.

I exchange the enemy's work for God's peace. Send the river of your peace not only to me but also to those with whom I've shared my burdens. I pray this also in the power of the name and blood of Jesus.

Praise God—You Are Free!

Thank you, Lord! I'm free!

Pray this prayer whenever you need a redo.

6

Hopeless

Finding a Light in the Dark

Why, my soul, are you downcast?
>Why so disturbed within me?
Put your hope in God,
>for I will yet praise him,
>my Savior and my God.

Psalm 42:5–6

When I was five years old, I had a fluffy, white kitten named Snowball, whom I loved with all my heart. One day as I was cradling my tiny kitten in my arms, it wiggled free and ran toward the closed gate. That's when I saw them: two large dogs standing just outside my yard. I ran, screaming, "Snowball! Stop!"

But Snowball didn't stop, and just as I reached for her with my chubby fingers, she slipped beneath the bottom of the gate and into the waiting teeth of the snarling dogs.

A neighbor who heard my screams was the first on the scene, and she ran the dogs off with a stick before whisking the lifeless body of my kitten away.

This memory is one I'd like to forget, but it's one I once again encountered a few years ago at a dog obedience class with my new puppy, a miniature Labradoodle named Max.

The class was held in an old barn, and for several weeks, my classmates and I had walked our dogs through routines to sit, stay, and heel. But this day, the instructor told us, "It's time to take the dogs off lead and give them some time to socialize with one another."

I was surprised by this order, but I obeyed. Still, I eyed the German shepherd and the Akita across the circle from us. These two animals had continually snapped at each other for weeks, and it had been only the owners' tugging at the dogs' leashes that had kept the dogs from tearing into one another. So I wasn't too surprised that as soon as these dogs were unleashed they turned on each other with bared fangs. As the fur flew, all the other dogs ran for their lives except for one. My little Max ran directly toward the dog fight. I barely had time to breathe a prayer as I screamed, "Max! Stop!"

But Max didn't stop.

I knew what would happen next. After all, I'd seen this scene played out once before. These two attack dogs would soon turn their fangs on my puppy, and once again that would be it.

However, Max seemed undaunted by his impending fate as he bounded toward the battling dogs. Even the dog trainer gasped as my puppy leapt toward the clash. Time melted into hopelessness, and all I could see was the terrible end that had befallen my kitten.

But instead of leaping *into* the dog fight, my bright-eyed puppy joyfully leapt *over* it. He soared over the snapping jaws, then gleefully bounded back to me.

I'm telling you this story because, like me, perhaps you've encountered situations that ended badly. Now, because of your past hurts, you're fully expecting more calamities, like getting laid off from your new job, being hurt and betrayed by friends, or never catching that much needed break. Or maybe you're in the middle of a difficulty you're certain will have no happy outcome and you're feeling the weight of your hopelessness. Let me inject a thought. Maybe things aren't as bad as they seem, especially when you consider the God factor found in Jeremiah 29:11: " 'For I know the plans I have for you,' says the LORD. 'They are plans for good and not for disaster, to give you a future and a hope' " (NLT).

Wait just a minute! What's all this about a future and a hope? Isn't God going to give us the punishment we all deserve?

We are under the blood of Jesus. Our tab was paid in full by Jesus when he died on the cross for our sins. But not only did Jesus die for our sins, but he also came back to life with the resurrection power of God.

What if you were able to apply the resurrection power of God to your own circumstances? If you could do that, don't you think your hopelessness would evaporate? Let's consider this. God's resurrection power *can* be applied to your life, and when you realize this is so, you'll also realize that:

- your situation is not hopeless
- when you seek God, he will provide a way
- with God, your future is amazing

Your Situation Is Not Hopeless

Ten years ago, my friend Julie's sixteen-year-old daughter died in a horrible accident on the freeway. Recently, I was able to sit down with Julie and talk about her loss. Julie shared that when Anna died her own grief was so relentless that she'd seriously considered suicide.

"What stopped you?" I asked.

Julie said, "I decided that despite my hopelessness and grief I would live for the sake of my son."

"Are you glad you decided to live?" I asked.

Julie nodded and opened her arms to her sweet eighteen-month-old grandson, who had toddled into the room. He climbed into her lap, and she kissed him on top of his yellow curls. Then she said, "I still miss Anna terribly. But I wouldn't trade this precious time I'm having with my grandchildren for anything."

Do you suppose that somehow Julie was able to apply God's resurrection power to her life? Yes. Not only did God help Julie find a reason to live, but he also gave her joy even in her pain.

Julie still misses Anna. Yet, she knows that one day, on the day God appoints, she and her daughter will be wondrously reunited. But until that day, Julie has work to do. She has to make a difference in the lives of her grandchildren. She has to fulfill a higher calling—to love and to be loved.

I'm sure that when the Julie of ten years ago tried to imagine her life today all she could see was hopelessness and pain. But God saw his plans for her, plans for good, plans for hope, plans he fulfilled with both his purpose and his joy.

It's the same for you. Perhaps you can't imagine surviving the hopelessness you are currently experiencing, whether it's loneliness, the death of a child, a dashed hope, a rocky marriage, a careening career, a cheating spouse, a broken dream, or something even more alarming. There's no doubt that these things are difficult. Yet, God's resurrection power can grant you hope and a future too. All you have to do is yield to his power and trust him to do the rest. Your situation is not hopeless.

Dear Lord,

Sometimes when I look at what appears to be the darkness of my future, I tremble beneath the weight of hopelessness. However, you are the Lord who warned his children not to fear, you are the God who restores the hopeless, you are the God who resurrected

Jesus from the dead, and you are the God who still moves in resurrection power today. So, Lord, I yield to your resurrection power in my marriage, my future, my relationships, my job, my purpose, my dreams, and, most importantly, my relationship with you. I will stand fearless before hopelessness because you are my hope. My trust is in you.

In Jesus's name, amen.

When You Seek God, He Will Provide a Way

The next time you face what looks like a problem that cannot be remedied, I want you to think about my puppy Max, who ran headlong into trouble that could very well have meant the end of his life, yet he was able to sail above the problem.

That's how it is when you are in relationship with God. Just when it seems as if trouble is set to destroy your hope, future, or family, God's resurrection power can help you rise above it all. But to activate God's power, we must seek God himself. It's like Charles Stanley is fond of saying, "We must remember that the shortest distance between our problems and their solutions is the distance between our knees and the floor."[1]

> *Just when it seems as if trouble is set to destroy your hope, future, or family, God's resurrection power can help you rise above it all.*

When you rely on God, his resurrection power will guide you out of hopelessness and into a hope-filled future.

Let's pray:

Dear Lord,
Like Linda's dog Max, teach me how to sail over my problems with joy. Teach me how to look beyond my difficulties to you.

Show me how to trust you as you provide a way through my troubles in your power.
In Jesus's name, amen.

With God, Your Future Is Amazing

A friend of mine owned a condo that had been trashed by a renter. She needed to put the condo on the market, but it was in no condition to sell. When I walked through the place with her, I was appalled by all the pet hair that blew through the air vents, not to mention the nauseous smell of cat and dog urine. The carpet was black with grime and dotted with cigarette burns. The walls and stove were covered with spaghetti sauce, and the former tenant's trash was scattered throughout the unit. If this wasn't bad enough, there was a large stain on the ceiling where the upstairs toilet had overflowed. Cindy looked at me with tears in her eyes. "Who would want to buy a place like this?" she asked.

Jesus changes our hearts from a slum to a palace fit for his presence.

I felt my shoulders droop, and I shook my head, unsure of how to answer. This place was a hopeless mess, and I figured my friend was stuck with an unlivable unit.

How wrong I was. A couple of weeks later, after the professional cleaners and the drywall, paint, and carpet people had done their work, the condo was no longer a slum but a beautiful space. The realtor who had valued the property at well below what nearby units were selling for returned to put it on the market at a 30 percent markup.

Why the change in value? Someone had taken the time and effort to clean the place up.

This is exactly what happens when Jesus walks into our lives. Jesus changes our hearts from a slum to a palace fit for his presence.

Let's pray:

Dear Lord,

You are my majestic God, my restorer, the one in whom I trust.
With your resurrection power, you bring me up from the depths of
the earth. You inspire me to hope, and so I do hope. I hope in you.
In Jesus's name, amen.

The Story of Peace Continued

This biblical story tells of one man's journey from hopelessness to
a life transformed by the resurrection power of God.

I was a man who could hear God's voice. I was also a man who
liked to do things his own way. My stubbornness is why I'd booked
passage to Tarshish, though God had clearly directed me to go in
the opposite direction, to Nineveh.

As I settled down for a nap below deck, I muttered to myself,
"Nineveh! That place is certainly not for me." You see, I'd heard
the stories that came out of this city of Gentiles, stories of people
who were caught in a lifestyle that, well, personally disgusted me.
In fact, I'd despised everyone I ever met from that place. So when
God told me to go to these vermin and to tell them that God was
reaching out to them, giving them a chance to set things right, I
simply wasn't interested.

I settled in with the cargo as the boat set sail, smug that I would
not be responsible for leading these heathen to God. Those Ninev-
ites deserved every bit of wrath God could give them.

I must have fallen asleep, because the next thing I knew the
boat was in a violent storm. The sailors woke me, insisting that I
draw lots with them to see who among us had given God cause to
drown us. I went along with their game of chance. So was it any
surprise the lot fell to me?

The sailors looked me up and down as if I had two heads. "Who
are you?" the captain bellowed above the winds.

"I am a Hebrew, and I worship the LORD, the God of heaven who made the sea and the dry land."

The men looked one to another, fear building in their eyes. "What have you done?" the captain cried, knowing full well I was on the run from the Almighty.

I let the sky answer with great flashing booms. The captain asked, "What shall we do with you to calm this storm?"

I was resigned to my hopeless fate. "Throw me overboard," I told them. But they refused. Instead, they did something I'd so far failed to do. They turned to God. They begged him not to let them suffer for killing an innocent man.

But God and I knew I wasn't so innocent. And even when they grabbed me by the shoulders to toss me into the churning waters, my heart was still set against God. I expected death but was surprised by an open mouth of a great fish that swallowed me whole. There inside that whale, bathed in rotting fish and stomach acid with only enough putrid air to keep me alive, I experienced a living death.

I was so stubborn that it took three whole days before my heart changed, before I could tell God, "Lord, though I am losing my strength, I turn back to you. I worship you and promise to do what you ask, for you are the one who saves."

Suddenly, the fish shook with a violent spasm, and I was thrust into the surf along with the whale's vomit. I thrashed my head above the water and sucked sweet air into my lungs. The surge of the sea pushed me toward the shore, and soon my knees and palms slid into the gritty sand of the beach. The children who had been dancing in the waves went screaming for their mothers as I stood to my feet, bleached white by the whale's digestive juices and smelling like death.

It was so like God to use even my rebellion, once overturned, as part of the message that caused the people of Nineveh to listen to my words, the words of a resurrected man.

I struggled to accept the people's reconciliation with the Almighty, as my prejudice against them ran deep. But I am now glad my mission was accomplished. It just goes to show that with God there is hope for the hopeless, including me (based on the book of Jonah).

If you are struggling with feelings of hopelessness, consider whether your feelings exist because of your own rebellion. If so, consider that God might be trying to get your attention so that you finally turn to him, finally do what you know he has called you to do. What is the last thing God told you to do? Is it something simple like loving your family or being a friend or something more complicated like forgiving someone who hurt you or performing a task or a mission that you've so far refused to do? Whatever it might be, take the first step toward God and tell him, "I turn back to you. I will do what you ask of me, but I will rely on you to help me and empower me."

If you are trying to discern God's voice and direction, relax and remember that God will never cause you to do something that goes against his Word. And know that when you say yes to God he will meet you right where you are. He will empower you and guide you to the place where you can complete the task he's called you to do.

But perhaps your feelings of hopelessness have nothing to do with rebellion against God. If you are caught up in situations beyond your control, the solution is not figuring out *how* God can save you; it's trusting that he will. As Max Lucado explains, "Trust God. No, *really* trust him. He will get you through this. Will it be easy or quick? I hope so. But it seldom is. Yet God will make good out of this mess. That's his job."[2]

> *If you are caught up in situations beyond your control, the solution is not figuring out how God can save you; it's trusting that he will.*

Shine the Light of the Word

The secret to having a hope that never dies can be found in 1 Peter 1:3–5:

> Let us thank the God and Father of our Lord Jesus Christ. It was through His loving-kindness that we were born again to a new life and have a hope that never dies. This hope is ours because Jesus was raised from the dead. We will receive the great things that we have been promised. They are being kept safe in heaven for us. They are pure and will not pass away. They will never be lost. You are being kept by the power of God because you put your trust in Him and you will be saved from the punishment of sin at the end of the world. (NLV)

Say this simple prayer: "Open my eyes to your truth as I read 1 Peter 1:3–5 again."

Write down your thoughts and impressions regarding how this Scripture passage might apply to you:

Review what you gleaned and thank God for these truths.

Yielding Prayer for the Hopeless

If you need to regain your hope in any area of your life, it's time to pray.

Shine the Light

Dear Lord,

Please turn on your light of truth over me and my ability to hope in you. Help me to yield any areas of hopelessness in my life to your resurrection power.

List the areas the Lord is revealing to you now:

_____

_____

_____

Yield

Put your hand over your stomach and pray the following:

Dear Lord,
I yield all these things to your peace as well as all of my feelings of hopelessness to you through your Holy Spirit.

With your hand still on your stomach, take deep breaths and start to relax as you repeat the prayer above until you feel God's peace drop into your spirit.

Forgive

Dear Lord,
I'm not strong enough to let go and forgive myself, you, and those who have caused me distress in any of these areas. Still, I choose to forgive. Therefore, I ask that you, through your Holy Spirit inside me, forgive all. I acknowledge that you, Lord, are without sin. Though you may have allowed these difficulties, you will use them as seeds for miracles. Thank you!

Give It All to God

Dear Lord,
I cast my hopelessness at the foot of the cross. I turn my concerns over to you. Thank you for setting me free from these concerns so I can trust you.

Pray for Healing

Dear Lord,

Please heal the pain caused by my feelings of hopelessness. Thank you for your supernatural peace.

Exchange the Enemy's Work for God's Peace

Dear Lord,

Please forgive me for giving in to hopelessness. I close all the doors I have opened to the enemy in this area. In addition, I cancel any plans the enemy has for my life. I also cast out any power or influence from any evil spirits trying to give me feelings of hopelessness. I pray this in the power of the name and blood of Jesus.

I exchange the enemy's work for God's peace. Send the river of your peace not only to me but also to those with whom I've shared my hopelessness. I pray this also in the power of the name and blood of Jesus.

Praise God—You Are Free!

Thank you, Lord! I'm free!

Pray this prayer whenever you need a redo.

7

Offended

Finding Relief from Hard Feelings

But now is the time to get rid of anger, rage,
malicious behavior, slander, and dirty language.

Colossians 3:8 NLT

Many summers ago, I, along with two thousand other speakers, attended a National Speakers Association convention in Dallas, Texas. I have to admit, I was mesmerized by our incoming president Naomi Rhode—a charming woman who used the platform to do what she does best: exude the love of God.

Naomi shared the platform with a hilarious comedian by the name of Dale Irvin. He would lie in wait until a break in the program, then spring to the microphone to give one of his sidesplitting "reports," a rousing parody of the speakers' messages.

The crowd howled with laughter and stomped their feet at Dale's comedic spin. But the speaker who became the brunt of many of

Dale's jokes was dear Naomi, who handled Dale's jabs with grace and good humor.

Then came the evening when those who'd been so thoroughly roasted by Dale got to take the stage to roast him back. When Naomi walked across the platform in her sparkling silver gown, the audience members held their breath. How would she respond now that she had control of a microphone aimed directly at Dale?

She started by telling of her recent visit to Broadway to see *Les Miserables*, a musical set in postrevolutionary France. She told how Jean Valjean stole a loaf of bread to feed his family, then paid for the crime with nineteen years of hard labor.

Upon being paroled, Valjean faced rejection and hunger until he happened upon the home of the bishop of Digne, the only person to show Valjean compassion. The bishop invited Valjean to his supper table to give him a message of hope before giving him a warm bed for the night. But that evening, Jean Valjean did the unthinkable. He stole the bishop's silverware and slipped into the night.

He was soon captured by the police and thrown at the bishop's feet. But instead of condemning Valjean, the bishop extended grace and even agreed with Valjean's claim that he'd been given the silverware. Then the bishop did something unexpected. He reached for the silver candlesticks still sitting on his table and told Valjean, "But, my friend, you left so early you forgot I gave these also. Would you leave the best behind?"

Naomi said, "The bishop's motive? He wanted Valjean to know what it meant to receive grace."

Naomi called Dale to the platform and then presented him with a beautifully wrapped package. Dale opened it to reveal a pair of silver candlesticks.

The crowd was amazed that Naomi, instead of responding with barbs, had extended Dale grace. What a moment—a moment that left this quick-witted comedian completely speechless.

I recently caught up with Naomi, and she talked about the incident with these wise words: "I can choose to be offended or not. So when it came to Dale's parodies of me, I chose not to personalize his words or to let them offend me." She chuckled. "In fact, Dale's barbs toward me became a well-recognized association joke."

I can choose to be offended or not.

I also spoke with Dale about his exchanges with Naomi, and he explained that his comedy is never meant to offend but to commend. He added, "I say nothing mean and mean only to be entertaining."

My hat is off to both Naomi and Dale, and their examples lead me to ask you, "How often do you choose to take offense at things that were never meant to offend?"

Perhaps, if you're like me, you'll want to resolve to do a better job at extending grace to those whose remarks unintentionally upset you.

Still, you might be wondering, *What about those jabs that were meant to sting me? What do I do with those?*

Once again, you have the power to choose whether or not to be offended. If an offense has already taken root, you still have the power to make a choice, the choice to forgive.

Silver-candlestick living is based on Proverbs 19:11, which says, "Sensible people control their temper; they earn respect by overlooking wrongs" (NLT). Consider also the wise words of my friend Joy Schneider, who believes it's possible to find some benefit in offense. As she explains, "Opportunity lurks at the door of offense." In other words, if you can look past an offense, you may find an opportunity to make a friend, build a bond, share a goal or a cause, retrieve information you need, learn a lesson, lend or receive a helping hand, laugh at yourself, or have a happier day.

If you're not sure if this is true, check it out for yourself. The next time you feel the sting of offense, instead of snapping, pouting, or even counting to ten, say a quick prayer like, "God, what are you trying to show me? What opportunity is hiding here?"

When I take the time to do this, I often discover amazing opportunities I might have easily missed, including a ministry connection, a sweet friendship, or a healing discussion.

That's all well and good, you might be thinking, *but what about the times when offenses are so serious that they can't be overlooked and I'm left to deal with bitterness and rage? What then?*

I'd say it's time to seek the power of God so that you can supernaturally forgive the offender, not because they deserve it but because you deserve to walk free and clear of the pain and trauma of the hurt you've been trying to live with.

But watch out! When it comes to the business of forgiveness, there are pitfalls to avoid. It's as author Pam Farrel once said:

> There is a lot of confusion over forgiveness. We all know we should do it. But we're not sure what "it" looks like. . . . People think forgiveness is sweeping the offense under the rug with the phrase, "Let's just not talk about it," and pretend it never happened. That isn't forgiveness; that's denial. Sometimes we don't forgive because we think forgiveness means we must reconcile. But forgiveness and reconciliation are actually two separate acts. Forgiveness is a vertical act, a private prayer that takes place between you and God in response to a person's actions. Reconciliation is a horizontal act that involves forgiveness on the part of the person who was offended and true repentance by the person who did the harm. It is extremely difficult and unwise to reconcile unless you have first experienced the vertical act of forgiveness with God.[1]

In other words, when an offense cannot be overlooked because it's too serious to brush aside or too dangerous to ignore or deny, you can still deal with it through a vertical conversation with God like the following:

Dear Lord,
You know what _____ did, and it's not something
I can overlook or pretend never happened. Please give me wisdom

on how to respond because I want to be free from my pain and bitterness. Therefore, I'm doing the only thing I can. I'm giving this offense to you. Please do not count this offense as sin against my offender but shine your truth over their heart and mind as you bring them to repentance. But even if repentance never happens, I am still willing to let go through your power. I am also giving you my trauma and asking you to heal me of my pain.

In Jesus's name, amen.

After praying such a prayer, you may still want to ask God to guide you into reconciliation, for as Matthew 5:23–24 says, "If you take your gift to the altar and remember your brother has something against you, leave your gift on the altar. Go and make right what is wrong between you and him. Then come back and give your gift" (NLV).

Just note that reconciliation may not come easily, quickly, or even at all if the other party does not want to repent for their part in the difficulty. Still, why not start the reconciliation process and pray:

Dear Lord,

I ask that in your perfect timing you will give me the opportunity to miraculously reconcile with _____. Shine the light of your truth in this matter so that misunderstandings can come to light and repentance can be achieved, even if it turns out that I am the one who needs to apologize. If I need to repent, show me, and show me how. If through my repentance you call me to reconcile, go before me and with me and give me the words to speak to the one I offended.

Help me not to miss an opportunity of reconciliation if and when it should come. In the meantime, help my heart to be free of bitterness so that I may enjoy your peace that passes understanding.

In Jesus's name, amen.

As you continue to learn how to work through offenses, let me offer you some tips that will help you:

- live in supernatural love
- learn how to let go
- draw closer to God

Live in Supernatural Love

When it comes down to it, living a silver-candlestick life means that we must live a life filled with supernatural love. This is the kind of love described in 1 Corinthians 13:4–7:

> *When it comes down to it, living a silver-candlestick life means that we must live a life filled with supernatural love.*

"Love is patient and kind. Love is not jealous or boastful or proud or rude. It does not demand its own way. It is not irritable, and it keeps no record of being wronged. It does not rejoice about injustice but rejoices whenever the truth wins out. Love never gives up, never loses faith, is always hopeful, and endures through every circumstance" (NLT).

Evangelist Bill Bright once said of this passage:

> As you read those words, you might think, *This describes an impossible love. I could never live up to such a standard.*
>
> And you would be correct. Who is able to love like that? That is why our only hope is to cast ourselves completely upon Him and invite the Holy Spirit to fill and empower us to love in a supernatural way. In humble faith, we will be filled with a love that is far above the natural, worldly variety. It will be a love against which the world can have no defense, for it confounds all expectations. It will overcome any barrier.
>
> Through such a love as this, God will accomplish supernatural goals through you. And believe it or not, you can love anyone in this way—by faith.[2]

If you need to tap into the kind of faith that will lead to supernatural love, try praying:

> *Dear Lord,*
>
> *I have a few people in my life I'm having trouble loving, including* _____. *Please empower me with your Holy Spirit to help me become aware of the supernatural love you're constantly giving me in an endless supply. Then shine this love through me on to those I've been unable to love in my human strength. I ask that you give me your compassionate perspective as well as your ability to love the difficult.*
>
> *In Jesus's name, amen.*

Learn How to Let Go

Hebrews 12:15 says, "Look after each other so that none of you fails to receive the grace of God. Watch out that no poisonous root of bitterness grows up to trouble you, corrupting many" (NLT). When we read such passages, we know that our God calling is not to become angry, bitter people. But that said, how do we let go of offenses?

I recently found myself struggling with this very issue as I waited with a group of friends at an airport. One of my friends seemed to purposely turn her back to me, blocking me from joining in the conversation. After forty-five minutes of trying to break through the wall, I felt shunned, angry, and hurt. Later, back in Colorado, I went to bed with the sting of the shunning on my heart. The next morning, I told the Lord, "I am trying to let go of this offense, but it still hurts."

He whispered to my heart, "Give the pain to me."

So I prayed, "Here you go, Lord," but it was to no effect.

The Lord told me, "You need to let go."

"I'm trying."

"Then quit trying and let go. It's as simple as that."

In my mind's eye, I saw myself holding a beach ball. The Lord coaxed, "If you are 'trying' to let go, you are still holding on. Just let go."

I saw my hands open so that the ball fell to the ground. Then, in my spirit, I dropped the offense, just as I'd dropped that ball. I felt God's sweet presence. I felt refreshed as if a shower had washed away yesterday's grime. The Lord spoke to me again. "You do not need to go into today wearing yesterday's dirt. You have the power to let go and to come to me so you can be clean."

> *You do not need to go into today wearing yesterday's dirt. You have the power to let go and to come to me so you can be clean.*

Without the offense in my heart, I was soon able to reengage my friend in a meaningful way. I never cornered her and demanded an apology or an explanation for her behavior because I no longer needed one. Today is a new day, a day to enjoy the blessing of the friends God has placed in my life, a day to brush aside yesterday's offenses and move forward in love.

Perhaps you are rolling your eyes at my illustration, saying under your breath, "Linda, the offense you let go of is petty compared to what I'm struggling with."

Even so, the process of letting go is the same. If you are ready to be free from your pain, pray:

Dear Lord,

I've had a difficult time letting go of certain offenses, including _____. Help me to see that in my trying I was only clinging to the very thing that offended me. Give me the power and the strength to let go.

I declare that I am letting go. I am dropping the offense. It's falling from my grasp. It's gone. This is the end of my pain and the beginning of peace. I am refreshed and clean before you. Thank you, Lord!

In Jesus's name, amen.

Draw Closer to God

Do you think it's any accident that Jesus said, "Bless those who curse you. Pray for those who hurt you" (Luke 6:28 NLT)?

Neither do I, for there is a blessing in living a silver-candlestick life. In fact, author Karol Ladd writes, "When we begin to pray for our enemies, our hearts begin to change. Anger subsides as we begin to give our hurts to the Father and sincerely pray for those who hurt us. I want to encourage you to try it and then watch what God begins to do in your heart."[3]

I absolutely agree with Ladd. Praying for our enemies and pushing beyond the offenses we encounter will change our hearts and, most importantly, draw us closer to God.

Let's pray:

> *Dear Lord,*
> *Please bless my enemies and help those who have hurt me, including _____. I also ask that you would draw us closer still to you. I praise you for your great love and forgiveness, not only for me but also for those who have offended me. I pray that the truth will set us all free in forgiveness, love, and reconciliation.*
> *In Jesus's name, amen.*

The Story of Peace Continued

If you're curious to see the power of forgiveness, read my take on what happened to a man who was forgiven of more than most of us could ever imagine.

My friends guided me as I stumbled into the inn. Though the day was bright, all I could see was the whiteness that had suddenly blinded me. I was not a man struck by lightning but a man who'd struck the ground when a heavenly being had blocked my way and called me by name. "Saul! Saul! Why are you persecuting me?"

As I'd lain on the ground, I'd choked with both dust and fear. Still, I managed to stammer, "Who are you, Lord?"

"I am Jesus, the one you are persecuting!"

It couldn't be.

Only days ago, I had held the coats of those who had gathered the rocks and stoned Stephen to death. As Stephen's blood had splattered, he'd lifted his face toward the sky and called out, "Look, I see the heavens open and the Son of Man standing in the place of honor at God's right hand!"

I had felt rage at his words of blasphemy, the same rage that had given those who threw the stones energy to hasten the man's ghastly death. It was a death that had ignited my thirst for the blood of all followers of this Christ. It was in fact the very reason I'd hurried down the road to Damascus with papers giving me the authority to arrest any Christ followers I found there. And then this Jesus, this one I'd presumed to be rotting in his grave, had stood before me.

I had lain frozen in fear as Jesus, in his risen glory, had said, "Now get up and go into the city, and you will be told what you must do." My friends had seen the flash and heard the sound of a voice, but they had seen no one except me lying face down in the road.

Long after my companions left me in a room at the inn, I lay in my bed, blind, with my face turned to the wall. The innkeeper's wife could not coax me to eat her bread or taste her drink. Instead, I lay on my pallet trembling, knowing that I who had thought myself a defender of God was in fact one of his worst enemies.

What would he do to me for persecuting him? My only solace was Stephen's last words regarding those who stoned him. "Lord, don't charge them with this sin!"

After three days of terror, tears, and repentance, I had a vision. I saw a man named Ananias come into my room to lay hands on me so that my eyes were healed. So when I heard voices in the courtyard, I turned from my wall to listen.

A woman pleaded, "You mustn't go in. Can't you see it's a trap?"

A man answered, "But God said . . ."

"But would God have you walk into your death? You know this man is here to arrest you and to lead you to the same death that our brother Stephen suffered. Ananias, this is folly!"

"You must hear me, my dear wife. God said, 'Go.'"

I heard footsteps, followed by the sound of the curtain to my room sliding open. I sat up and stammered, "Ananias? Your name is Ananias?"

The man might have nodded. I don't know. But I do know he put his rough hand on my head and began to pray. "Lord, it is your good pleasure to heal this man and to open his blind eyes, so in obedience, I am asking that it be so. In the mighty name of Jesus."

As the scales that had blinded me fell away, I saw him, the man who had dared to face his own death for the sake of obeying the Lord Jesus.

He gave me a smile and patted my shoulder, but I was impressed by his courage to push past any fear or offense I had caused him. He would be my inspiration to say yes to Jesus, no matter what he might ask of me. And like Ananias, I would prove to be a man of my word. How grateful I am that first Stephen, then Ananias, through the mighty power of Jesus himself, had forgiven me so that I could share this good news of God's forgiveness with the world (based on Act 7:51–8:1; 9:1–19).

Saul became the apostle Paul, the man who wrote thirteen books of the New Testament. Besides Jesus Christ, he's considered the most important figure of the early church.

Saul was on a mission to snuff out those who followed Jesus, but God was on a mission to lead Saul to become not only a Christ follower but also one of the most influential evangelists who ever lived.

But just think, if Ananias had refused to forgive the offense of a man who had come to town to take him and his loved ones to their execution, our world would not know Paul or his writings.

Ananias probably did not know how influential Paul would become to the body of Christ. So why did he accept God's call to minister to this man who had sworn himself his enemy? Though Ananias may not have liked the idea of going to his enemy to pray for him, he did it because God told him to go. It was as simple as that.

You'll never know what miracle may be waiting at the door of your offense unless you push through it.

So if you are holding back, determined to keep a pet offense all to yourself, consider this. God is also telling you to go! So go and obey him. Go and forgive. And if need be, go and apologize and offer to reconcile. You'll never know what miracle may be waiting at the door of your offense unless you push through it.

Shine the Light of the Word

Jesus gave us clear instruction on how to handle offenses in Luke 6:27–31 when he said:

> I say to you who hear Me, love those who work against you. Do good to those who hate you. Respect and give thanks for those who try to bring bad to you. Pray for those who make it very hard for you. Whoever hits you on one side of the face, turn so he can hit the other side also. Whoever takes your coat, give him your shirt also. Give to any person who asks you for something. If a person takes something from you, do not ask for it back. Do for other people what you would like to have them do for you. (NLV)

Say this simple prayer: "Open my eyes to your truth as I read Luke 6:27–31 again."

Write down your thoughts and impressions regarding how this Scripture passage might apply to you:

_____

_____

_____

Review what you gleaned and thank God for these truths.

Yielding Prayer for the Offended

If you need to regain your freedom in this area of your life, it's time to pray.

Shine the Light

Dear Lord,

Please turn on your light of truth over me and my ability to sidestep offenses, bitterness, and unforgiveness. Help me to yield all my past and present offenses to you.

List the areas the Lord is revealing to you now:

_____

_____

_____

_____

Yield

Put your hand over your stomach and pray the following:

Dear Lord,

I yield all these offenses as well as my feelings of bitterness to your peace through your Holy Spirit.

With your hand still on your stomach, take deep breaths and start to relax as you repeat the prayer above until you feel God's peace drop into your spirit.

Forgive

Dear Lord,

I'm not strong enough to let go and forgive myself, you, and those who have caused me distress in any of these areas. Still, I choose to forgive. Therefore, I ask that you, through your Holy Spirit inside me, forgive all. I acknowledge that you, Lord, are without sin. Though you may have allowed these difficulties, you will use them as seeds for miracles. Thank you!

Give It All to God

Dear Lord,

I cast my offenses at the foot of the cross. Now they belong to you, not me. I know you will set not only my offenders free but me as well. Thank you that I can walk in your freedom.

Pray for Healing

Dear Lord,

Please heal the pain caused by my feelings of being offended. Thank you for your supernatural peace.

Exchange the Enemy's Work for God's Peace

Dear Lord,

Please forgive me for entertaining offenses. I close all the doors I have opened to the enemy in this area. In addition, I cancel any plans the enemy has for me. I also cast out any power or influence from any evil spirits of rage, offense, and bitterness coming against me. I pray this in the power of the name and blood of Jesus.

I exchange the enemy's work for God's peace. Send the river of your peace not only to me but also to those with whom I've shared offense. I pray this also in the power of the name and blood of Jesus.

Praise God—You Are Free!

Thank you, Lord! I'm free!

Pray this prayer whenever you need a redo.

8

Anxious

Finding God's Bliss

For God has not given us a spirit of fear, but of
power and of love and of a sound mind.

2 Timothy 1:7 NKJV

Perhaps you sometimes feel like Indiana Jones in the 1981 movie *Raiders of the Lost Ark*. In this fast-paced adventure set in 1939, Indiana is an archaeologist looking to find the lost ark of the covenant before the Nazis do. But on his quest, Indy has to face his worst fear as he and his friend Sallah look down into the dark, ancient ruins of the Well of Souls. Sallah asks, "Indy, why does the floor move?"

Indy grabs Sallah's torch and drops it onto the floor several feet below. The glow illuminates a pit of slithering vipers, and Indy flinches. "Snakes. Why'd it have to be snakes?"

Sallah's response includes a line that I like to tell God whenever I'm bringing him what appears to be a fearful situation: "You go first." God does go before us, as Psalm 59:10 explains: "My God on whom I can rely. God will go before me." But still, even knowing that God will go into difficulties with us doesn't mean that fear can't sneak up on us, as it did to me when I was a nineteen-year-old college student at the Glorieta conference center in New Mexico.

I awoke at dawn and decided to take an early morning walk in the beautiful prayer garden. While walking up the wide stone stairs next to a cascading fountain, I happened to notice something coiled just inches beneath my uplifted sandaled foot—a foot poised to step on that location in the next second. I froze and stared down at the now rattling diamondback snake beneath me. With my foot still held aloft, I jumped backward, just out of striking distance. I watched as the rattler uncoiled itself and slithered into a crevice under one of the stones.

I scurried back down to the base of the fountain, where I met up with a group of my friends. "Be careful," I told them as I pointed up the hill. "I just saw a rattler!"

My friends took this news in stride. In fact, one of the girls handed me her camera. "Linda, could you take a picture of us by the fountain?"

"Sure," I said, as they posed. Trouble was, I had to crouch low to get everyone in the shot. Just as my finger started to snap the picture, one of the boys said, "Hey, Linda, is that a rattlesnake behind you?"

My finger clicked the picture as I screamed and leapt straight into the air.

The boy grinned, and I realized I was a victim of a practical joke. Though there wasn't a second rattler, I did get a nice shot of my friends' expressive reactions to my unbridled fear.

But consider this. There are thirty-seven hundred species of snakes in the world, and approximately eight thousand people are bitten annually by venomous varieties, which results in fifteen fatalities.[1] With so much slithering danger, shouldn't we all just stay home?

But are you safe from snakes at home? I'm wondering because I once saw a garden snake slither into my house through an open door in our mud room, a room piled with supplies for my daughter's care. Trouble is, I never found where that snake went. So what should I do? Wear tall rubber boots in the house in case a snake is hiding beneath my couch?

I'm laughing at this thought because in the ten years that have passed since this snake-on-the loose incident I've never found any signs of that snake, which probably slithered back outside. (I left the door open so it would.) Besides, I think the raccoon that used to get in through the dog door would have eaten it by now. Now I shut the dog door at night, and I don't worry about that snake. I long ago decided this concern is just another opportunity to trust God, snake or no snake.

If my snake stories left you feeling a little queasy, I hope that I'll soon convince you to attempt to live a fearless life, regardless of the kinds of snakes (two-legged or not) you might encounter.

Yes, there may be snakes, but so what? Jesus said in Luke 10:19, "I have given you authority to trample on snakes and scorpions and to overcome all the power of the enemy; nothing will harm you." If we have that kind of power over snakes and other hostilities, why should we be afraid?

The answer is simple. We fear because we are human. But the trouble is that when we give in to fear it will stop us from having the courage to say yes to God. Max Lucado says:

> When fear shapes our lives, safety becomes our god. When safety becomes our god, we worship the risk-free life. Can the safety lover

do anything great? Can the risk-adverse accomplish noble deeds? for God? for others? No.

The fear-filled cannot love deeply. Love is risky.

They cannot give to the poor. Benevolence has no guarantee of return.

The fear-filled cannot dream wildly. What if their dreams sputter and fall from the sky?

The worship of safety emasculates greatness. No wonder Jesus waged a war against fear.[2]

Lucado's remark reveals a great truth. We cannot live a full life in Christ when we let fear—instead of God and his great love—rule our hearts.

So what will help us break free from anxiety? We need to join the war Jesus waged against fear and its twin sister, worry. If you want to trade your anxiety for God's bliss, you will need to learn how to:

- break the stronghold of fear
- break the stronghold of worry

Break the Stronghold of Fear

Author Neil Anderson explains the fear stronghold this way:

Fear is a thief. It erodes our faith, plunders our hope, steals our freedom, and takes away our joy of living the abundant life in Christ. Phobias are like the coils of a snake—the more we give into them, the tighter they squeeze. Tired of fighting, we succumb to the temptation and surrender to our fears. But what seems like an easy way out becomes, in reality, a prison of unbelief—a fortress of fear that holds us captive.[3]

The Bible tells us many times not to fear with admonitions such as "Do not be afraid," and "Fear not." But even though Jesus himself told us to "fear not," he did make what sounds like a contradictory statement when he said, "Dear friends, don't be afraid of those who want to kill your body; they cannot do any more to you after that. But I'll tell you whom to fear. Fear God, who has the power to kill you and then throw you into hell. Yes, he's the one to fear" (Luke 12:4–5 NLT).

I respond to Jesus by saying, "When you put it that way, I want to tremble and then to thank you for rescuing me from such a terrible fate through your death and resurrection!"

But to you, dear reader, I respond by saying that we are not to be afraid of the devil, for the real power to destroy comes from God himself, who is indeed awesome and mighty. However, you were designed to trust Jesus, not only with your present difficulties but also with your hereafter.

I believe God wanted me to be sure to drive this point home, as my reading today in *Jesus Calling* said, "I want you to know how safe and secure you are in My Presence. That is a fact, totally independent of your feelings. You are on your way to heaven; nothing can prevent you from reaching that destination."[4]

We who are under the blood of Christ have a blessed assurance that we belong to him, and being aware of his love for us is actually the key to banishing fear. First John 4:18 reminds us, "There is no fear in love. Perfect love puts fear out of our hearts. People have fear when they are afraid of being punished. The man who is afraid does not have perfect love" (NLV).

But when we lose our focus through distraction or rebellion, fear can slither into our lives. Sue Falcone, in her devotional for women, says, "Fear always comes when we leave God out of our lives. Throughout my life I can look back at the times when I lived in the most fear. My pattern shows I was running from God, thinking I could handle my life."[5]

Don't pull a Jonah and run away from the fear God is calling you to face. Remember who is going into the fearful situation with you: the Lord of the universe, the God who loves you, who will give you strength, and who will see you safely through in his peace. Psalm 29:11 puts it this way: "The LORD gives strength to his people; the LORD blesses his people with peace."

Still, I have a warning for you. Beware of the fear the enemy uses to sabotage your walk with God. The enemy tries to stir up fear in your life through false reports or imaginations, and it can hit you when the enemy would like nothing more than to distract you from deepening your relationship with God or what God has called you to do.

Consider what happened to me today as I set to work on this chapter. Because I had some catching up to do on my writing, I decided to stay home to write while my husband and his friends set out for the Triple Bypass, a 120-mile bicycle ride in the Colorado high country from Evergreen to Avon. This ride is a true test of strength because it encompasses several mountain passes and a gain of over ten thousand feet in elevation.

I was worried about this year's ride because it coincided with monsoon conditions, so before my hubby left for the starting line, I blessed him to have a great and, of course, safe ride.

Periodically, I checked on Paul's progress with an app on my smartphone that showed me his location by the minute. Later that afternoon, when I stopped for my coffee break, I wondered how the men were faring with the rain-slicked mountain passes. This time when I checked Paul's location, the app showed he was in a hospital.

I suddenly felt fear as I thought of all the things that could have gone wrong—a dive over a mountain edge, an accident, exhaustion, or even a heart problem. With a shaking finger, I dialed Paul's number and was relieved when he picked up. "So what happened?" I asked.

"What do you mean?"

"Were you or Mitch hurt? Why are you at the hospital?"

"What are you talking about?"

"The satellite shows you're smack in the middle of the hospital in Frisco!"

Paul laughed. "We're actually a mile away, eating sandwiches. We're all fine and having a great ride."

What a relief. It seems I'd been misled by a satellite beam bouncing off a low-hanging cloud.

So no matter the report you get, check in with God, just as I checked in with Paul. "Lord, did you hear that? Is it true? How do you want me to respond? Will you walk with me through this?"

The answer is yes he will. What the enemy uses to distract you from God's presence or purpose God uses to keep you closer to him than ever.

> *What the enemy uses to distract you from God's presence or purpose God uses to keep you closer to him than ever.*

With Jesus's help, we can wage war against fear. Let's pray:

> *Dear Lord,*
>
> *I am so relieved that I can trust in you, no matter what is going on in my life or in the world. It's like Psalm 56:3–4 says: "When I am afraid, I put my trust in you. In God, whose word I praise—in God I trust and am not afraid. What can mere mortals do to me?"*
>
> *Lord, help me to stay aware of your presence and to turn to you in every situation I face, for you go into my difficulties before me, and you turn my troubles into stepping-stones of miracles. Therefore, I give my fear to you and exchange it for the recognition of your love and faithfulness.*
>
> *In Jesus's name, amen.*

Break the Stronghold of Worry

Worry is the twin sister of fear, and a lot of the fear-defeating principles described above also apply to worry.

What benefit does worry provide? It's like Jesus explained in Luke 12:25–26: "Who of you by worrying can add a single hour to your life? Since you cannot do this very little thing, why do you worry about the rest?"

It's not that there aren't plenty of things to worry about. But most of the things we spend our time worrying about never happen. For example, despite the fact that I've disturbed several venomous snakes in my lifetime, I've never been bitten. So would it be wise for me to worry myself sick about being bitten by a poisonous snake when I walk outside to check the mail? Well, no, especially when you consider the statistics on snakebites I cited earlier. Despite the fact that there are seven billion people on the planet, only fifteen will die from a snakebite this year, which makes for pretty low odds that I will die from a biting viper on the way to retrieve a bill.

Of course, I'm not advocating pitching a tent in a venomous snake pit, but I am giving you permission to enjoy your patio and to leave your fear of grass snakes behind, which of course aren't venomous anyway.

Worrying about snakes or other troubling things is a waste of time. Still, worry is a hard habit to break, and we may find ourselves in need of divine help if we want to be free from it. I recently underlined my *Dear Jesus* devotional when it addressed this very topic. "Beloved, you do need my help, because trying to fight this battle on your own has been so counterproductive. Now you're worrying about worrying! Your best strategy is to stop focusing on this problem and to put your energy into communicating more with me."[6]

That said, I think it's time to pray:

Dear Lord,

I've racked up quite a list of worries that I'd like to now present to you. My worry cannot change the outcome of any concern. But you can! Therefore, I want to talk to you about my worries and to ask that you orchestrate the outcomes for your purposes and my good. I ask that your healing and miraculous touch would be over _____ and that your presence in these circumstances would make all the difference. Now my worries belong to you. Thank you, Lord!

In Jesus's name, amen.

The Story of Peace Continued

Remember when I advised against pitching your tent on a viper pit? Well, sometimes, despite our best intentions, we end up in the very place we tried to avoid, leaving us to ask, like the Bible character below, "Why'd it have to be snakes?"

What can I say? I may have been the first to grumble against God and Moses. I was having a bad day, and I was tired of the sand and the traveling, always the sand. We'd walked from the Red Sea to the Promised Land and now back to the Red Sea because we were serving another forty years in the desert because our tribes had refused to take the land God had promised us. We were walking, pitching camp, and then walking some more. In the past few weeks, our nation had been attacked, some of us even kidnapped.

Now we had to skirt the wilderness shortcuts because the kingdoms of the desert refused to let us pass through their lands, terrified that what we'd done to the city of Hormah we'd also do to them. So on this day, a day I felt such deep discouragement, I blurted to my friend Amaras, "What was God thinking when he told Moses to bring us out of Egypt? Was it so we could die in the desert? There is no bread! There is no water! And I detest this miserable sand!"

Amaras agreed with my feelings and even repeated my complaints to her husband. The words I'd muttered to a friend were soon the talk of our nation, as one voice after another joined with mine. The clamor of our complaints rose to God's ears.

That night my husband, Seth, and I tried to set up camp. I'd busied myself with unpacking the tent when the screams started. I lifted the flap and peered out just as Amaras, who'd also been making camp, joined her screams with the others.

It was past sunset, but there was still enough light to see that my friend had a red viper attached to her arm. Her husband grabbed it by its tail and snapped its head against a nearby rock. But Amaras had two large puncture wounds on her arm. I ran to her, and as I did, the ground began to slither. Scales slid upon scales, creating a sort of sizzling that grew louder by the moment. The screams of our tribes continued to build, but I fell quiet. I stood spellbound, staring into a pair of yellow eyes. The snake before me lifted its head, then without warning the creature flung itself through the air in an upward motion. As my screams joined the others, the snake's fangs sunk deep into my thigh.

My screams continued as the pain of the viper's fiery poison began to flow into me. I watched as Amaras fell to one knee. "No!" I yelled, watching as another sidewinder lunged at her. Her husband pulled her from its reach just in time, then carried her to their tent. But her tent was as perilous as mine, as the scaly creatures slithered around us in the night. My husband, Seth, kept his sword ready, slamming his blade on the snakes that slithered into our abode. As for me, I knew I was slowly dying. First, my flesh began to rot away from the fang marks as my belly began to cramp. Then I started to bleed from my nose. By dawn, the snakes had for the most part slithered back into their holes and crevices, so I stumbled back to Amaras's tent. "How is she?" I asked Gabor, who was cradling his wife in his arms. He looked up at me with tears mixed with blood. "I couldn't keep the snakes away from her. She's gone."

I put my hand to my mouth and watched as he stroked her head with his own snakebit hand. I turned to find Seth standing beside me. I told him, "You must go to the tribal council and beseech them to ask Moses to pray for us."

As evening drew near, my husband came with Moses's answer. God had instructed Moses to make a bronze snake and to put it up on a pole. Seth told me, "Anyone who is bitten and can look at it will live."

I clasped my hands. "How soon before it's ready?"

"Moses began his work early this day, so maybe in the morning."

"If I should live that long," I said as Seth helped me back to the tent. I was glad that my daughters, their husbands, and their little ones had survived the night. I knew because their tent was close and my grandchildren had checked on me throughout the day. So as the clouds began to turn into dark shades of gold, I was surprised when little Talia, my five-year-old granddaughter, came running into my tent. "Grandmother, I have been praying for you," she said.

"You should be at home now. The snakes could appear at any time."

I watched as Talia turned to run the way she'd come. She made it a few steps before a viper lunged, striking her arm. She screamed and tried to shake it off as Seth ran to her. He knocked the snake away before carrying her back to our tent.

I didn't mind death for me, as I'd accepted my fate. But I did not accept it for Talia. She was too young, too innocent to pay for the sins of our tribe.

I spent the night holding her in my arms as I wept, watching as Seth sliced the heads off the vipers that tried to enter our tent. Somehow I must have dozed and was surprised to see the dawn. I looked down at my granddaughter. Talia was now so very pale. Blood dripped from her eyes and streaked down her cheeks. "I'm dying, Grandmother," she solemnly whispered.

I wiped the blood from my mouth and kissed her cheek, knowing that we would die together.

Suddenly, a trumpet sounded in the camp. Seth pushed the flap to our tent open. "Dawn is here," he said. "The snakes are gone. It's safe to come out."

He carried Talia in one of his strong arms and helped support me with the other as I followed our neighbors. The healthy ones buzzed with the names of those who had died in the night, while the sick, including Gabor, stumbled with the crowd to the tabernacle.

There stood Moses, who said, "God sent this plague of fiery snakes because you grumbled against him and against me. But I have prayed for you and followed God's command to make a bronze snake on a pole. God says that anyone who has been bitten who looks at this snake will live."

When we look to Jesus, instead of concentrating on our worries and fears, Jesus will give us his peace as our worries and fears fade away.

I let my eyes follow the crook of Moses's finger, then gaze upon the bronze snake. Immediately, I felt life begin to surge back into my body. I turned to Seth. "Can you get Talia to open her eyes?"

He shook his head. "You try," he said as he handed me Talia's limp body.

Fear flowed through my being as I coaxed, "Talia, my sweet child, open your eyes. Look, look at the pole."

Talia's eyes cracked, and I pointed at the bronze snake. "Look at the snake," I encouraged.

Her eyes were opening wider now. "I see it," she whispered as she lifted her head. Color returned to her cheeks. "I see it, Grandmother."

I hugged her neck and said, "Because of God's mercy, we will both live" (based on Num. 21:1–9).

Jesus talked about this story in John 3:14 when he said, "Just as Moses lifted up the snake in the wilderness, so the Son of Man must be lifted up." Jesus was referring to himself. Jesus became the snake on the pole when he died on the cross. Because we've all been snake bit with the poison of sin, we all need to look to

Jesus for the forgiveness of our sins. Looking to Jesus is the same cure for our worries and fears. When we look to Jesus, instead of concentrating on our worries and fears, Jesus will give us his peace as they fade away.

Shine the Light of the Word

The cure for anxiety can be found in Jesus's words, "Peace I leave with you; my peace I give you. I do not give to you as the world gives. Do not let your hearts be troubled and do not be afraid" (John 14:27).

Say this simple prayer: "Open my eyes to your truth as I read John 14:27 again."

Write down your thoughts and impressions regarding how this Scripture passage might apply to you:

_____

_____

_____

Review what you gleaned and thank God for these truths.

Yielding Prayer for the Anxious

Let's take some time to pray against worry now.

Shine the Light

> *Dear Lord,*
> *Please turn on your light of truth over me and my fear and worry. Reveal any areas where I'm focused on my fears and worries more than I'm focused on you.*

List the areas the Lord is revealing to you now:

_____

_____

_____

_____

Yield

Put your hand over your stomach and pray the following:

Dear Lord,

   I yield all these things as well as my feelings of fear and worry to your peace through your Holy Spirit.

With your hand still on your stomach, take deep breaths and start to relax as you repeat the prayer above until you feel God's peace drop into your spirit.

Forgive

Dear Lord,

   I'm not strong enough to let go and forgive myself, you, and those who have caused me distress in any of these areas. Still, I choose to forgive. Therefore, I ask that you, through your Holy Spirit inside me, forgive all. I acknowledge that you, Lord, are without sin. Though you may have allowed these difficulties, you will use them as seeds for miracles. Thank you!

Give It All to God

Dear Lord,

   I cast my worries at the foot of the cross. Now they are your worries, not mine. Thank you for setting me free from my worries so I can better trust you.

Pray for Healing

Dear Lord,
Please heal the pain caused by my feelings of fear and worry.
Thank you for your supernatural peace.

Exchange the Enemy's Work for God's Peace

Dear Lord,
Please forgive me for giving in to my worries and fears. I close all the doors I have opened to the enemy in this area. In addition, I cancel any plans the enemy has for my life. I also cast out any power or influence from any evil spirits of fear and worry. I pray this in the power of the name and blood of Jesus.

I exchange the enemy's work for God's peace. Send the river of your peace not only to me but also to those who have shared my worries and fears. I pray this also in the power of the name and blood of Jesus.

Praise God—You Are Free!

Thank you, Lord! I'm free!

Pray this prayer whenever you need a redo.

9

Negative

Finding the Secret to a Good Mood

Have this attitude in yourselves which was also
in Christ Jesus.

Philippians 2:5 NASB

It had been a long trip, and after my plane landed at DIA, I made it through baggage claim and caught the crowded shuttle to off-airport parking. Once safely in my seat, I took a deep breath, readying myself for my dive into my purse to retrieve my keys and a tip for the driver.

But as I searched the dark cavern, shoveling the contents this way and that, I could not find my keys.

I felt a bead of sweat pop out on my forehead. I was forty miles from the house, and my husband was off riding his Harley with his Christian motorcycle friends. He wouldn't be available to rescue me until late that night. I felt my eyebrows knit together. I was in a pickle.

I looked up from my search to see that for the first time in history my car would be the very first shuttle stop in the parking lot. I shot off a quiet prayer. "What do I do, Lord?"

I felt the peace of his presence. "Trust me," he seemed to whisper.

With the other passengers staring at me, I said, "My keys seem to be missing."

The driver said, "Maybe you left them on the shuttle when you parked. I'll call the office to see if anyone turned them in. What do they look like?"

My cheeks suddenly felt hot. "Uh, the keychain is a plastic square with a book cover on it."

The woman next to me said, "You're an author?"

I gave her a sheepish nod. "What's the title?" the driver asked.

This time I laughed. "Well, it's *When You Don't Know What to Pray*."

"Sounds like you'd better do a little praying now," the woman suggested.

"I'm on it," I said with a grin.

The driver dropped off the other passengers, but I was still fumbling in my purse when the driver drove back to my car. "Maybe we'll be able to see your keys through the window."

Good idea, only they weren't there.

I reboarded the van and kidded with the driver as he drove me to the office so I could do a purse dump and maybe try to call for a ride home.

Once in the office, with the entire contents of my purse piled high on the table, I stared into the deep, black hole of my purse. My keys weren't there, and I shook my purse to prove it. Was that a jingle I heard?

I carefully ran my hand against the interior walls of the purse until I discovered a huge hole in the lining of a zippered pocket. When I pushed my fingers through the hole, I touched my keys!

I happily boarded the van again, and the driver took me back to my car. He said, "You're not like most who lose their keys around here."

"What do you mean?"

"You were laughing and cracking jokes, but my last lady was crying hard."

"Oh no!"

"One man was furious. But it wasn't that he lost his keys; he lost his Lexus. He had me and the manager drive him up and down the rows searching for it for hours. Just before he called the cops, he decided to call home. That's when his wife reminded him he'd driven the station wagon."

So what had made my attitude different from that of the other unfortunate travelers with missing keys and cars? I had called out to God and felt his presence. In that moment, he'd asked me to trust him. I could relax regardless of my difficulty.

I guess you could say that my attitude was both a calling and a choice. We all have the same calling to trust God, and we all can make a choice to stay calm, peaceful even, especially when we know God is with us.

Leadership author John Maxwell writes:

I read a funny story about President Abraham Lincoln that shows the relationship between our choices and their effect upon who we are. An advisor to Abraham Lincoln recommended a particular person for a cabinet position, but Lincoln balked at the suggestion. He said, "I don't like the man's face."

"But sir," said the advisor, "he can't be held responsible for his face."

Lincoln replied, "Every man over forty is responsible for his face."[1]

In other words, what you see in the mirror could very well be a reflection of your attitude, as it says in Proverbs 15:13, "A glad heart makes a happy face; a broken heart crushes the spirit" (NLT).

I know my face often says more about my feelings than I want it to. On days I think I'm secretly feeling sorry for myself, some kindly stranger standing in line at the post office will pat my arm and say, "Cheer up, dear, things will get better." Difficulties beg the question, When our circumstances are difficult, are we doomed to a bad attitude?

Maxwell says, "It's not what happens to you, it's what happens *in* you that counts."[2]

Maxwell's words ring true. You *can* overcome your negative attitude and even replace it with a good mood if you:

- learn to be content
- keep your heart open to the love of God
- take better care of yourself

Learn to Be Content

The apostle Paul talked about contentment in Philippians 4:11–13: "I have learned to be content whatever the circumstances. I know what it is to be in need, and I know what it is to have plenty. I have learned the secret of being content in any and every situation, whether well fed or hungry, whether living in plenty or in want. I can do all this through him who gives me strength."

"I have *learned* to be content." Those were important words to my friend and author Lindsey O'Connor, who as a young wife and mom lived in cramped quarters with her rambunctious brood. Lindsey admits, "I latched onto that phrase. If Paul had learned, then maybe I could too. He didn't say he *was* content in his circumstances; he said he *learned* to be content in them."[3]

And the best part of the passage is that God himself will give us the strength to be content. If you haven't already asked for it, now's the time. Just say, "Give me your strength, Lord, to be content," and he will.

Did someone just sigh because they're wishing I would provide a passage on how to be in control instead of how to be content?

The truth is that God didn't call us to replace him; he called us to trust him. When our negative attitude comes because we don't like where we are or what we have, we need to do a "will" check: God's will versus our will. Take a deep breath and pray along with me:

Dear Lord,

The hard truth is that I'm not in control because if I were things would be a lot different. Did I really just say that to you, Lord? Sorry, I forget sometimes that I am not the Creator but the creation. But I'm your creation. Please be gentle with me and, in your loving way, guide me to where you want to take me. Sometimes I forget that we are on a journey together. And sometimes I have a hard time realizing that the more I fight to have my own way the more you try to teach me the hard lessons of letting go. So in many cases, I've sabotaged myself with stress and unhappiness by clinging to my will instead of reaching for yours. That's why I've decided to say to you, right here, right now, "Your will be done in my life—not mine."

Help me to remember I prayed this so I will trust you along the road ahead, for as I learn to surrender to you, I learn to find contentment in your presence and love. I declare that I trust you to work out everything in my life for the good.

In Jesus's name, amen.

Sometimes we're not in the will of God because we seek the wrong things. A friend of mine told me that she was often on her knees insisting in prayer that God unite her daughter in marriage with a young man she knew from church.

"How do you know he's God's best for your daughter?" I asked her.

"He's perfect! Yet, it's like he doesn't even seem to notice my daughter. I'm going to pray that God will make him marry her."

I soon led my friend in a prayer in which she was able to ask for God's will in the matter. She prayed, "If it be your will, could my daughter marry this young man I've picked out for her? If this man is not your will for my daughter, could you lead her to the man you've picked?"

I'm happy to say that God answered this mother's prayer. No, the daughter did not marry the young man the mother picked out. Instead, the daughter married the man of her dreams, the man God had for her all along, a man who wasn't in the picture when her mother was busy praying for the wrong groom. So you see, asking to be in God's will is a good thing, a thing that can even protect us from a lot of misery because you can't be content if you are not in God's will.

My friend Bill Myers and I recently chatted about our ministry projects. Bill told me, "It's about getting your will aligned with God's will." His remark came just after he'd finished delivering a speech in which he'd shared that his success in both publishing and Hollywood came because a speaker had once challenged him always to say yes to God. That's why he'd left the Midwest as well as his dream of becoming a dentist. That's why he'd moved to Hollywood to make movies.

Though Bill's journey had a few detours, as Bill explained, any frustrations he encountered only caused him to go deeper with God and made him more ready to accomplish the assignments God gave him.

> *Living in God's will means always saying yes to God.*

Living in God's will means always saying yes to God. It may not mean you're going to Hollywood, but it may mean you *are* going places you never expected. Just keep in mind that you're not going alone. Jesus is not only guiding this adventure but also sharing it with you.

Keep Your Heart Open to the Love of God

I have a feeling a lot of negative attitudes arise because of love blocks—times we block God's love because we're tired, frustrated, disappointed, or angry. This kind of blockage can lead to soured feelings that can spill onto others. When such an acid spill happens, we are no longer operating in the love of God. It's like 1 Corinthians 13:2 says: "If I had the gift of prophecy, and if I understood all of God's secret plans and possessed all knowledge, and if I had such faith that I could move mountains, but didn't love others, I would be nothing" (NLT).

You don't have to live as if you're nothing because you are something; you are loved by God! Jeremiah 31:3 says, "I have loved you, my people, with an everlasting love. With unfailing love I have drawn you to myself" (NLT).

Stormie Omartian says:

> An angry, dour, unforgiving, negative person can get that way for various reasons. He stays that way because of a stubborn will that refuses to receive God's love. The Bible says we have a choice as to what we allow in our heart . . . and whether or not we will harden it to the love of God or not. . . . . We choose our attitude. We choose to receive the love of the Lord.[4]

Let's use prayer to open your heart so you can receive and feel more of God's love for you.

> *Dear Lord,*
>
> *Sometimes when I am tired, frustrated, disappointed, or angry, I can't feel your love for me. That makes it difficult for me to love others. Please forgive me. When I am tired, remind me to rest so I can be refreshed. When I am frustrated, remind me that despite how things seem you are working in ways that will benefit my life as well as my relationship with you and others. Help me to know that through you everything is going to be all right. When I am disappointed, remind me that I don't have your perspective and that I need to trust you. When I am angry, forgive me for any anger I've directed at you and teach me how to forgive. Remind me how great and wide your love is not only for me but also for those in my life.*

*If I am treated unkindly, remind me that you've been there
too. Remind me that the unkindnesses that have been directed
my way are no reflection on your great love for me. Open my
eyes to see your love. Open my heart to receive more of it than
ever before.*

In Jesus's name, amen.

When you feel the warmth of the Father's love, your negative
attitude will melt. You'll take to heart the

> *When you feel the
> warmth of the Father's
> love, your negative
> attitude will melt.*

apostle Paul's instruction to "be kind to
each other, tenderhearted, forgiving one
another, just as God through Christ has
forgiven you" (Eph. 4:32 NLT).

When you keep your heart open to
the love of God, God's love will flow in
abundant supply not only to you but also through you.

Take Better Care of Yourself

It's hard to ward off negative attitudes and bad moods when you
don't feel your best. And it's hard to feel your best when your
attempts to take care of yourself do anything but help you feel
better. For example, if you've ever skipped lunch while sipping a
diet soda in an attempt to lose weight, you may have learned that
this particular diet plan not only doesn't work but also robs you
of energy. If you've ever tried to count getting your heart pumping while sweating through rush hour traffic as aerobic exercise,
you may have noticed that this exercise plan doesn't make you fit.
And if you've ever tried to catch up on your rest by falling asleep
on the couch while watching your favorite show, you may have
noticed that those extra winks did little to make you feel refreshed
the next morning.

So what does it take to get your body in balance?

It may be time to try a few lifestyle changes, namely in diet, exercise, and rest. Be sure to talk to your doctor before starting a new program.

To make these changes, you'll need to:

- decide on a few healthy meals to cook, make a list of what you need, and head to the grocery store
- keep a set bedtime with a plan to get at least seven to eight hours of rest each night
- decide on an exercise plan

Exercise, even if you hate jogging? Well, if jogging is out of the question, no sweat. Lysa TerKeurst says:

> Running may not be your thing. So find what is. My Mom loves to say that the best kind of exercise is the kind you'll do. I agree. And while I fully realize my temple may not be God's grandest dwelling, I want to lift up to the Lord whatever willingness I have each day and dedicate my exercise as a gift to Him and a gift to myself. This one act undivides my heart and reminds me of the deeper purposes for moving my body.[5]

I hope you'll take some time to consider these ideas because the better you take care of yourself, the better you'll feel, and the better you feel, the better your mood.

The Story of Peace Continued

Has a bad attitude ever killed someone? The Bible tells of a man with an attitude so terrible that it almost brought death to his entire household.

"Yaakov is here to see you," my maid Urit whispered to me.

I'd been busy setting the table for the feast that my husband and I held for our men during sheep shearing time. Now that the wool of our vast flocks had been sheared and sold to the wool merchants, it was time to celebrate.

But this interruption by our lead shepherd was curious. I set a roasted mutton on the banquet table and turned to Yaakov, who was waiting in the doorway. I wiped my hands on my apron and said, "What is it?"

"We have a problem, Mistress."

"You couldn't go to my husband with it?"

Yaakov shook his head.

"Then tell me quickly," I said, crossing my arms. "The feast is almost ready, and I still have much to do."

The man's brown eyes glistened, and he swiped away a bead of sweat that trickled down his face. "David and his men are on the way to kill us all."

My hand rested on my throat. "For what cause?"

"First, I should tell you that the other shepherds and I often saw David and his men out in the far fields. They were good to us. They protected us from raiders and didn't lay a hand on our flocks."

I nodded. That sounded like the David of the legends, a giant killer who refused to slay an unjust king.

"How noble of David," I said. "So why is he coming to kill us?"

"Just a few moments ago, ten of David's men were with your husband, Nabal, at the tavern, asking him if he would be so kind as to give supplies to David's troops as payment for the work they did to protect our flocks."

"The tavern? So Nabal is already drunk?"

Yaakov only nodded.

"So how much did David's men ask for?"

"Their fee was whatever Nabal felt was fair."

I frowned. "Admirable. How did my husband answer this request?"

Yaakov dropped his eyes. "Nabal said, 'Who does David think he is? In my eyes, he's only a slave on the run from his master, Saul. Should I take my bread and the sheep I've slaughtered for my shearers and give it to a band of outlaws?'"

I felt the blood drain from my face. How could my husband have given such insults to David, not only the leader of a powerful army but also a man who would soon be king? Was my husband so consumed with a purse full of gold that he failed to value his life or the lives of those in his household? Was his attitude so foul that he was too foolish to know when to give honor its due?

I sat down in a chair and stared at the marble floor. "You are right, Yaakov. David's armies will soon arrive with their swords drawn. Our blood will soak into the ground unless . . ."

I looked at the food that my maids and I had placed on the banquet table, then back at Yaakov. "Call the shearers and the shepherds. They must help me and my handmaidens carry this feast to David. If we hurry, we can meet David on the road."

"There could be bloodshed, Mistress Abigail."

"Perhaps, but death is certain if we don't at least try to make amends for the insults of Nabal."

When my servants and I crested the hill not far from town, we almost collided with David and four hundred of his men. David readied his sword to strike, but I placed my basket on the ground and fell facedown into the dirt. I called to the bloodthirsty warrior before me, "Forgive my foolish husband, my lord. Punish me instead. But first, you should know I have brought you a gift and your men provision."

David motioned for silence as I pointed to my frightened servants, all of whom trembled beneath their heavy burdens. "I've brought two hundred loaves of bread, wine, raisins, and roasted mutton, as well as an apology."

David still stared down at me, so I said, "David, you are like a treasure to the Lord. Even though Saul chases you to seek to kill you, you have never done wrong. Because the Lord will fulfill all his promises to you and crown you king of Israel, be careful. Don't commit sin against the Lord. Don't let the slaughter of my clan be a blemish on your record or conscience."

David lowered his sword and reached down to help me stand before him. He said, "Abigail, thank God for your good sense! Bless you for keeping me from murder and from carrying out vengeance with my own hands."

The next morning, when I told the now-sober Nabal what his rank words had almost wrought, he was so shocked that it was as if his heart turned to stone. My husband died ten days later. Some days after that, David asked me to be his wife (based on 1 Sam. 25).

It's clear that Nabal was not the only one with an attitude problem. After hearing Nabal's insults, David was ready to spill the blood of many. It wasn't until Nabal's wife, Abigail, and her servants met David and his men with their fast-food delivery that David calmed down. But it wasn't only Abigail's delivery service that persuaded David to tuck his sword into his belt. Abigail's persuasive words about David's relationship with God also helped.

As his reward for his attitude change, David received the provision of God. In the end, David married Abigail and inherited Nabal's three thousand sheep and his properties.

The lesson is clear. When our attitudes are off the mark with discontent, rage, bitterness, hate, or selfishness, we need to remember God and his love for us. This remembrance will refresh our attitudes and help us honor God and treat others with kindness.

Shine the Light of the Word

What is the secret of improving a negative mood? It can be found in Philippians 2:14–15: "Do everything without complaining and arguing, so that no one can criticize you. Live clean, innocent lives as children of God, shining like bright lights in a world full of crooked and perverse people" (NLT). And Philippians 4:8–9 says, "And now, dear brothers and sisters, one final thing. Fix your thoughts on what is true, and honorable, and right, and pure, and lovely, and admirable. Think about things that are excellent and worthy of praise. Keep putting into practice all you learned and received from me—everything you heard from me and saw me doing. Then the God of peace will be with you" (NLT).

Say this simple prayer: "Open my eyes to your truth as I read Philippians 4:8–9 again."

Write down your thoughts and impressions regarding how this Scripture passage might apply to you:

_____

_____

_____

Review what you gleaned and thank God for these truths.

Yielding Prayer for the Negative

It's time to transform your attitude to the attitude of Christ.

Shine the Light

> Dear Lord,
> Please turn on your light of truth over me and my attitude.
> Reveal to me the attitudes I need to give to you.

List your attitudes about people or situations that the Lord is revealing to you that need improvement:

_____

_____

_____

_____

Yield

Put your hand over your stomach and pray the following:

> Dear Lord,
>   I yield all my negative attitudes, including the things I've listed, to your peace through your Holy Spirit.

With your hand still on your stomach, take deep breaths and start to relax as you repeat the prayer above until you feel God's peace drop into your spirit.

Forgive

> Dear Lord,
>   I'm not strong enough to let go and forgive myself, you, and those who have caused me distress in any of these areas. Still, I choose to forgive. Therefore, I ask that you, through your Holy Spirit inside me, forgive all. I acknowledge that you, Lord, are without sin. Though you may have allowed these difficulties, you will use them as seeds for miracles. Thank you!

Give It All to God

> Dear Lord,
>   I cast my bad attitudes at the foot of the cross. Now my attitudes belong to you. Show me if my diet or lack of sleep is causing my negative feelings and show me how to correct my lifestyle issues. Thank you for setting me free from my negativity and leading me to freedom.

Pray for Healing

> Dear Lord,
>   Please heal the pain caused by my bad attitudes. Thank you for your supernatural peace.

Exchange the Enemy's Work for God's Peace

Dear Lord,

Please forgive me for giving in to my negative attitudes. I close all the doors I have opened to the enemy in this area. In addition, I cancel any plans the enemy has for my life. I also cast out any power or influence from any evil spirits of lies, trauma, anger, frustration, false expectations, dissatisfaction, and lovelessness. I pray this in the power of the name and blood of Jesus.

I exchange the enemy's work for God's peace. Send the river of your peace not only to me but also to those with whom I've shared my bad attitudes. I pray this also in the power of the name and blood of Jesus.

Praise God—You Are Free!

Thank you, Lord! I'm free!

Pray this prayer whenever you need a redo.

10

Distracted

Finding Your Focus

Our eyes look to the LORD our God.
Psalm 123:2 ESV

It was a sunny December day in New York City. My friend Eva and I were in town to do on-location research for a novel, so we were ready for a day of exploring. I'd come prepared with my huge, blue tote bag, which I'd slung over my shoulder after stuffing it with everything I might need: an umbrella, my coat, snacks, bottles of water, all piled high on top of my wallet.

Eva and I caught the subway from our hotel so that we could walk down Canal Street to take in the sights. We browsed through the faux designer purses and fingered the bright wool scarves and smirked at the fake Rolexes on display. As we strolled, we were caught in a throng of tourists who flowed down the street like a slow-moving river.

As I walked along gawking at the sights around me, a pretty, young woman appeared beside me. She turned to face me, and with her arms opened wide, she side-skipped to my steps as if she were trying to block me from turning right and walking past her. *What in the world is she doing?* I wondered. I craned my neck for a better look, and she seemed to disappear. *Where'd she go?*

Suddenly, I snapped my head to the left, and there she was, her arm rammed deep into my tote bag as her fingers groped for my wallet. I instinctively jerked my tote away from her, and she disappeared into the crowd.

It seemed I'd been preyed upon, unsuccessfully, by a New York City pickpocket. But what struck me about the experience was the pickpocket's maneuver to distract me—to cause me to take my focus away from my tote and to place it in the opposite direction so that she would be free to snatch my wallet.

This business of distraction is the exact strategy the enemy (Satan) uses against us. Distractions, whether constructed by the enemy or produced by our ordinary struggles, can cause us to look in the wrong direction. When this happens, we shift our focus from God to our troubles. Such a shift can cause us to lose our peace, our joy, and our ability to trust in God.

The devotional *Moments of Peace in the Presence of God* explains that distractions can cause us to wonder if God has moved. Yet, as one of the writers says, "God hasn't moved; your focus has—and you must turn your attention back to him. Because he's *still* bigger than your problems and he will certainly help you."[1]

To counteract the distractions that can turn you from God, you need to:

- remember that God can use evil for good
- work through your distractions
- focus on Jesus

Remember That God Can Use Evil for Good

Recently, in one of my quiet times, I heard God's voice in my heart and jotted down these words: "The unseen world is alive and watches you. Your every move is calculated, analyzed, and considered in an effort to create evil schemes against you. But the closer you are to me—the more your focus is on me—the less effective are the plans of the enemy, plans that will evaporate in the presence of my Shekinah glory."

The closer you are to me—the more your focus is on me—the less effective are the plans of the enemy, plans that will evaporate in the presence of my Shekinah glory.

Not sure that the enemy is scheming against you? Then consider that we are in a war. The apostle Paul says in Ephesians 6:12, "For we are not fighting against flesh-and-blood enemies, but against evil rulers and authorities of the unseen world, against mighty powers in this dark world, and against evil spirits in the heavenly places" (NLT).

But even if the enemy means evil toward you, God means it for good. It's like what happened to Joseph, a young man who dreamed God-given dreams of a rosy future in which even his own brothers would bow down to him.

But these dreams of his did little to help him win his brothers' affections; instead, his dreams inspired their intense hostility toward him. Then one fateful day, when Joseph stopped by the far field where his brothers were tending sheep, his siblings decided to kill him. But because none of the young men could actually stomach killing their brother, they decided to sell him as a slave to the first caravan of merchants heading for Egypt.

This was not the rosy future Joseph had anticipated. To make matters worse, he was soon demoted from slave to prisoner on the power of a false charge.

The turnaround came the day a former prisoner of the jail in which Joseph was still incarcerated recommended Joseph to

Pharaoh, billing Joseph as the only man in the kingdom who could interpret Pharaoh's dreams. The next thing Joseph knew he was standing before Pharaoh, the most powerful man in the known universe, explaining that Pharaoh's dreams about hungry cows and shriveling stalks of corn signified a coming famine. Pharaoh was struck by Joseph's wisdom and made him not only the head of the famine preparations committee but also his second in command in all of Egypt.

God used the evil deeds committed against Joseph by his brothers to save Joseph's people from famine, for when the famine hit Canaan, Joseph's brothers journeyed to Egypt to buy grain. Joseph had the chance to tell his repentant brothers, "But as for you, you meant evil against me; but God meant it for good, in order to bring it about as it is this day, to save many people alive" (Gen. 50:20 NKJV).

And the best part about this story is that even in the face of so much betrayal and discouragement Joseph kept his eyes on God, always making the best of every situation. Think of how much more Joseph would have suffered if he'd focused on his problems instead of trusting that God would not only transform his troubles but also fulfill the dreams God had put in his heart when he was only a boy.

Charles Stanley explains God's ability to transform the purpose of troubles this way: "But the Father never allows difficulty just for the sake of difficulty—there is always a higher purpose involved. The problem is we cannot always identify God's higher purpose in the midst of our trials. That's when we must exercise our faith by waiting on His word to us."[2]

Stanley goes on to tell a story about a real estate broker who experienced a seven-year period of financial failure. The broker's thoughts as well as his prayer life became consumed with his finances, and he often wondered why God didn't move to turn his fortune around. Stanley explains that the broker finally realized he had substituted financial security for God. Stanley concludes:

The Father wanted to be recognized as the Source of all things in my friend's life. As he began renewing his mind spiritually and yielding his rights to the Lord, my friend gained a new freedom in his attitude toward finances. He started a new career and found greater financial blessing than ever before.

God had a great and mighty lesson to teach my friend—a lesson more important than keeping him comfortable. And God kept him uncomfortable until he took his eyes off his circumstances and sought God's mind in the matter.[3]

Stanley's friend had been so distracted by his circumstances that he had failed to seek or focus on God, forgetting that all things work together for good for those who love the Lord (Rom. 8:28).

Does the fact that God can take even the evil plans of the enemy and use them for good mean we should never take a stand against the enemy? Absolutely not. Even Jesus taught us to ask God to "deliver us from the evil one" (Matt. 6:13).

Our comfort is that no matter what happens, or who caused the trouble, we know that through God everything is going to turn out all right. But in the meantime, let's ask for God's deliverance from evil right now:

Does the fact that God can take even the evil plans of the enemy and use them for good mean we should never take a stand against the enemy? Absolutely not. Even Jesus taught us to ask God to "deliver us from the evil one."

> *Dear Lord,*
>
> *I am seeking your face, knowing that you are making everything come together for good. The closer I get to you, the more the strategies and purposes of the enemy evaporate in the light of your glory. Thank you, Lord, that I can trust you and that I can ask you to deliver me from evil and into victory. I cancel the evil purposes of the enemy to steal, kill, and destroy and yield to your*

good purposes of love and life instead—in Jesus's name and through
the power of his blood.
In Jesus's name, amen.

Work through Your Distractions

We have to learn how to overcome distractions lest we live our
lives as though God isn't involved. The easiest way to recalibrate
our focus is through prayer, as explained in 2 Chronicles 7:14: "If
my people, who are called by my name, will humble themselves
and pray and seek my face and turn from their wicked ways, then
will I hear from heaven, and I will forgive their sin and will heal
their land."

There are three steps God asks us to take to help us pray so
that we can turn our focus back to him and so he can respond to
us by forgiving our sin and healing our land. To start this prayer
process, we must:

1. Humble ourselves—According to this Scripture passage, we
   humble ourselves by looking to God for help.
2. Pray—Notice that a list of specific prayers to pray was not
   provided with this verse. I think this is because God is simply
   asking us *to* pray.
3. Seek his face—The way you should seek God's face is the
   same way you would search for a lost child. Desperately!

If you want to push past your distractions so that you can better
focus on God, pray the following:

Dear Lord,

I come to you humbly as I look to you for help. For you are the
God who wants me to talk to you, to have a personal relationship
with you. How amazing that you would want my attention. So I
gladly give it to you and say thank you for being who you are, my
loving God. I praise your holy name. Lord, I want to know you

more; to desperately seek your face. Reveal yourself and guide me!
In Jesus's name, amen.

Focus on Jesus

We want to stay focused on Jesus not only because he is powerful but also because he *is* our power. As the psalmist sang in Psalm 16:8, "I keep my eyes always on the LORD. With him at my right hand, I will not be shaken."

We want to stay focused on Jesus not only because he is powerful but also because he is our power.

If we shift our eyes from Jesus to our difficulties, we are asking for trouble. For example, if we focus on our lack, each bill that arrives in the mailbox will make our heart the poorer. But when we keep our eyes on Jesus as our provider, bill or no bill, we are rich in the confidence that God will provide.

Not only is God our provider, but he also walks on the water of our every storm, just as he did for his bobbing band of followers on the Sea of Galilee. When Peter saw Jesus walking across the storm-tossed lake, Peter called out to him and Jesus answered, "Come!"

But notice that Jesus didn't freeze the water and provide ice skates so Peter could zip on over. Neither did Jesus still the waves so Peter could swim the distance. Jesus didn't even create a moonlit path so Peter could follow it without getting distracted by the lurching waves. With a little intervention from Jesus, Peter could have avoided falling into the drink altogether. So my question is, Wouldn't calming the storm have been more productive than calling Peter to walk across the angry swells in a rain-drenched wind?

The answer to that question is this. Perhaps Jesus chose this turbulent miracle to teach Peter to trust him not in the absence of a storm but through it.

When you focus on Jesus, you will learn to trust him deeply, as Proverbs 3:5–6 instructs: "Trust GOD from the bottom of your heart; don't try to figure out everything on your own. Listen for GOD's voice in everything you do, everywhere you go; he's the one who will keep you on track" (Message).

Let's pray:

> *Dear Lord,*
>
> *I want to look at my circumstances through you, with eyes of trust, so that even when you call me to walk through storms I will not go under, but over, as I continue my walk to you. Thank you that you are the one who keeps me on track.*
>
> *In Jesus's name, amen.*

The Story of Peace Continued

Do you think there is a correlation between "meek" and "focused"? Max Lucado believes this is true. " 'Blessed are the meek,' Jesus said. The word *meek* does not mean weak. It means *focused*. It is a word used to describe a domesticated stallion. Power under control."[4]

The power of those focused on God comes from God, but it's power under his control—power to overcome, power to defeat enemies. And speaking of meek, how would you like to walk a mile in the shoes of three men who meekly withstood the authority of a king?

When the Babylonians attacked Judea, they killed our king and his sons and took my friends and me captive. We, the sons of Judean nobles, were stripped of our manhood, ensuring we could never father children of our own. We were forced to study the Babylonian religions and ways. Our captors even changed our names as tribute to their sun and moon gods. But my friends and I agreed that though they could change our names they could not change our devotion to Jehovah—the one and only God.

One day King Nebuchadnezzar had a disturbing dream and put his sorcerers to the test, demanding that they not only explain his dream's meaning but also tell him what he had dreamed in the first place. When his sorcerers failed this test, they were put to death. However, our friend Daniel was brave enough to call on God's power to help him know and understand the dream. Nebuchadnezzar was so pleased with Daniel's skill that he promoted Daniel to the governorship of the whole province of Babylon. Daniel then asked the king if his three friends could serve with him.

So that's how we, four Judeans, became rulers over a province that worshiped everything except our wonderful God. But we remained faithful, staying focused on our worship of Jehovah—even when the king built a nine-story-tall golden idol, a giant replica of himself.

Daniel was away on business during the idol's unveiling, leaving myself, Meshach, and Abednego to attend the ceremony. After much fanfare, the king announced that whenever his royal orchestra played his royal song everyone who heard the music had to bow and worship his idol or else be cremated alive in the very smelter that had been used to forge the idol.

My friends and I looked at one another as the harp and other instruments began to play. We watched as the throng around us dropped to the ground to worship the golden image. However, our hearts were so focused on our God that we could not bend even a knee.

Our enemies, who happened to be the officials who were unseated by our sudden rise to power, rushed to tell the king of our disobedience. Nebuchadnezzar was livid and called us to stand before him.

He announced, "How dare my governors not do as I commanded? But I am a patient man. Perhaps you didn't understand the penalty. I will give you another chance to make this right and to bow before my idol. If you do not bow, who will rescue you from my hand?"

I, Shadrach, spoke for the three of us when I said, "Nebuchadnezzar, if we are thrown into the fire, the God we serve is able to save us from your hand. But even if he does not, we want you to know,

O King, that we will not serve your gods or worship the object of gold that you have set up."

The king was furious and called for the fiery furnace, already on display for the throng, to be heated seven times hotter. He then called for his strongest soldiers to bind us and drag us to the mouth of the flames. As the soldiers threw us in, they were overcome by the heat and died in agony. But my friends and I did not feel the blaze, only a cool breeze that enveloped us in the heart of the flames. That's when I saw him, his loving eyes, his outstretched arms. My friends and I ran to his embrace.

The voice of the king rose from outside the smelter. "I called for three men to be thrown into this furnace. Why do I see four, one like the Son of God?" Then he called directly to us, "Shadrach, Meshach, and Abednego, servants of the Most High, come out! Come here!"

One by one, we stepped out of the furnace and over the fallen bodies of the soldiers. The king and his people were amazed, for we didn't even smell of smoke. We stood before them without one hair singed and with our clothes unscorched.

The king praised our God for saving us and praised us because we'd withstood his threats. He then forbade anyone else from threatening us because of our faith. But as for me, I will always remember the peace I felt in the furnace, peace I continue to feel as I keep my focus on my God, the One whose very presence can change the atmosphere from death to life (based on Dan. 2–3).

These three friends demonstrated the power of focusing on God. Such a focus helps us to become powerful yet meek as we submit everything to God.

Shine the Light of the Word

Hebrews 12:1–4 encourages us to live a life of focusing on God with these wise words:

Therefore, since we are surrounded by such a huge crowd of witnesses to the life of faith, let us strip off every weight that slows us down, especially the sin that so easily trips us up. And let us run with endurance the race God has set before us. We do this by keeping our eyes on Jesus, the champion who initiates and perfects our faith. Because of the joy awaiting him, he endured the cross, disregarding its shame. Now he is seated in the place of honor beside God's throne. Think of all the hostility he endured from sinful people; then you won't become weary and give up. After all, you have not yet given your lives in your struggle against sin. (NLT)

Say this simple prayer: "Open my eyes to your truth as I read Hebrews 12:1–4 again."

Write down your thoughts and impressions regarding how this Scripture passage might apply to you:

_____

_____

_____

Review what you gleaned and thank God for these truths.

Yielding Prayer for the Distracted

Lift your eyes unto the Lord and yield your focus to him.

Shine the Light

Dear Lord,

Teach me how to focus on you in every area of my life so I can experience your peace for my soul. Reveal to me the things I let distract me, the things that I focus on more than you.

159

List the things the Lord is revealing to you now:

_____

_____

_____

_____

Yield

Put your hand over your stomach and pray the following:

Dear Lord,
  I yield all these distractions to your peace through your Holy Spirit.

With your hand still on your stomach, take deep breaths and start to relax as you repeat the prayer above until you feel God's peace drop into your spirit.

Forgive

Dear Lord,
  I'm not strong enough to let go and forgive myself, you, and those who have caused me distress in any of these areas. Still, I choose to forgive. Therefore, I ask that you, through your Holy Spirit inside me, forgive all. I acknowledge that you, Lord, are without sin. Though you may have allowed these difficulties, you will use them as seeds for miracles. Thank you!

Give It All to God

Dear Lord,
  I cast my distractions at the foot of the cross. Now they belong to you. Thank you for setting me free from my distractions so I can better trust in you.

Pray for Healing

Dear Lord,

Please heal the pain caused by my not staying focused on you. Thank you for your supernatural peace.

Exchange the Enemy's Work for God's Peace

Dear Lord,

Please forgive me for not focusing on you. I close all the doors I have opened to the enemy in this area. In addition, I cancel any plans the enemy has for my life. I also cast out any power or influence from any evil spirits of torment, distraction, worry, and unbelief. I pray this in the power of the name and blood of Jesus.

I exchange the enemy's work for God's peace. Send the river of your peace not only to me but also to those who have shared in my distractions. I pray this also in the power of the name and blood of Jesus.

Praise God—You Are Free!

Thank you, Lord! I'm free!

Pray this prayer whenever you need a redo.

11

Depressed

Finding Real Joy

The Lord is my strength and my safe cover. My
heart trusts in Him, and I am helped. So my heart
is full of joy. I will thank Him with my song.

Psalm 28:7 NLV

My daughter Laura has no fingerprints. That's because in order to have fingerprints you must have busy hands. Laura's hands are warm to the touch but have little movement due to her paralysis. Still, her hands are far from useless, as I find that they are perfect for holding. Clasping my fingers around one of Laura's warm hands often brings a smile to her face, a smile I love to receive, a smile I reflect back to her. When I hold her small, misshapen hands, I feel as though I'm holding love itself, a love so pure it brings tears to my eyes. You would think that with all the difficulties my daughter must daily face she would be devastated by her condition. Yet, my daughter never complains. Instead, she sings—happy, wordless songs of praise to a God she knows and loves. She sings out of the joy of her heart.

Thursday afternoons are special because a dear friend, Karis, always stops to give my daughter a fresh coat of colorful nail polish, decorating Laura's nails with swiggles, bright colors, stickers, and designs. Though Laura can't raise her hands to admire her nails, she still loves to have a new coat of polish. She also loves it when we lift her arms, bringing her hands to her face. That's when a little miracle happens—Laura extends her fingers to look at her nails as she giggles in delight.

I'm always amazed by Laura's joy, a joy she gladly shares with all in her life, a joy that comes from a heart close to our heavenly Father. Her heart sings when we play hymns of praise and ushers in the holy presence of God.

How I want to live like that—always in the presence of God, never mind my lack, my frustrations, or my fears because God is near and my trust in him is complete.

In other words, Laura has taught me to strive to be like her, to continually invite God into every area of my life. I love to seek God, to fill my home with songs of praise, and to daily remember that God's love is covering me as I purpose to stay aware of his constant presence.

Not only does God want us to practice his presence, but he also wants us to treasure him above all else, even above our abilities, our health, and our bank accounts.

It's a practice I've not yet perfected. I have good days and bad days, but the more I practice, the sweeter God's presence.

Not only does God want us to practice his presence, but he also wants us to treasure him above all else, even above our abilities, our health, and our bank accounts. Sarah Young's devotional *Dear Jesus* puts it this way: "Many of my children view devotion to me as a duty, and they look elsewhere for their pleasures. They fail to understand that the Joy of My Presence outshines even the most delightful earthly joy."[1]

To find joy in the Lord, we must yield ourselves to his presence. As David sang, "Give me happiness, O Lord, for I give myself to you" (Ps. 86:4 NLT).

Why wouldn't we want to yield to the God who invented joy? Max Lucado says:

> Think about God's joy. What can cloud it? What can quench it? What can kill it? Is God ever in a bad mood because of bad weather? Does God ever get ruffled over long lines or traffic jams? Does God ever refuse to rotate the earth because his feelings are hurt?
>
> No. His is a joy which consequences cannot quench. His is a peace which circumstances cannot steal.
>
> There is a delicious gladness that comes from God. A holy joy. A sacred delight.[2]

Stop wallowing in depression and steep yourself in joy. The best way to accomplish this is to:

- keep God first in your life
- choose joy
- develop an attitude of gratitude

Even if you are clinically depressed, these action steps may give you a boost. But if they don't seem to make a noticeable change, continue to strive to follow these steps, even while you follow your doctor's orders.

Let's bring our quest to understand these concepts to God in prayer:

Dear Lord,

I'm ready to step out of my depression. Teach me how to see you as my treasure and to experience your joy. Help me to keep you first, to seek and choose joy, and to develop an attitude of gratitude. Thank you that the more I give myself to you the more I feel your joyful presence. I give my difficult emotions to you. Please heal them and teach me how to live in your joy.

In Jesus's name, amen.

Keep God First in Your Life

King David wrote, "Take delight in the LORD, and he will give you the desires of your heart" (Ps. 37:4).

When you let other things compete with your delight in the Lord, you make those things your treasure and therefore your idols. A. W. Tozer once said, "The man who has God for his treasure has all things in One. Many ordinary treasures may be denied him, or if he is allowed to have them, the enjoyment of them will be so tempered that they will never be necessary to his happiness."[3]

> *The more you have of God, the more your blessings will pale in comparison to the joy you've already found in Christ. You may enjoy your blessings, but you will enjoy the source of your blessings even more.*

The more you have of God, the more your blessings will pale in comparison to the joy you've already found in Christ. You may enjoy your blessings, but you will enjoy the source of your blessings even more.

Don't let depression or the world or its temptations compete with God for the first-place position in your heart. Instead, renew your mind with the Word, worship, and fellowship with other believers while trusting that God will take care of you in every way. As Matthew 6:33 says, "But seek first his kingdom and his righteousness, and all these things will be given to you as well." Let's pray:

Dear Lord,

I give myself to you because you are my treasure. You are the key to my happiness because nothing can compare with you. Give me more of you and your presence so that my joy may be complete.

In Jesus's name, amen.

Choose Joy

I often think of how much my daughter, who was disabled at eighteen months of age, has in common with Helen Keller, who when she was eighteen months old suffered from an illness that left her blind and deaf. For five years, Helen lived in a quiet world of darkness in which she was unable to communicate until her teacher, Anne Sullivan, entered her life. It was Anne who turned on the light of understanding in Helen's mind.

Helen had a lot of reasons to be bitter about her condition, but as David Jeremiah says of Helen, "She never pitied herself; she never gave up. She once said, 'The marvelous richness of human experience would lose something of rewarding joy if there were no limitations to overcome. The hilltop hour would not be half so wonderful if there were not dark valleys to traverse.' "4

Don't you think that if Helen and Laura can find joy in their circumstances, then perhaps you can also find joy in yours?

Joy is not based on your circumstances but rather on your choice to be joyful. It's just as Max Lucado says in his book *When God Whispers Your Name*: "I choose joy. . . . I will invite my God to be the God of circumstance. I will refuse the temptation to be cynical . . . the tool of the lazy thinker. I will refuse to see people as anything less than human beings, created by God. I will refuse to see any problem as anything less than an opportunity to see God."5

When you shift your thinking and begin to see problems as opportunities, you can choose to trust God. You can choose joy.

I can tell you from a recent experience of sitting in a waiting room waiting to hear a doctor's opinion concerning a loved one that instead of waiting in fear and turmoil it's much better to wait with a deep trust in God. It's better to wait knowing that no matter what happens it will create yet another opportunity to see more of God in difficulties.

So instead of sitting in that waiting room swatting away my tears, I put on my headphones and listened to praise music. I felt calm, peaceful, and even joyful in the knowledge that God's presence was with me and that everything was going to be all right.

We are all in the waiting room of life, all waiting to hear opinions, outcomes, revelations, diagnoses, and prognoses. But happily, we do not wait alone. We wait with a God who is already at work in our situations.

So when a problem presents itself, don't go to pieces. Instead, rest in the peace of God as you count it all joy. As James 1:2–4 says, "Dear brothers and sisters, when troubles come your way, consider it an opportunity for great joy. For you know that when your faith is tested, your endurance has a chance to grow. So let it grow, for when your endurance is fully developed, you will be perfect and complete, needing nothing" (NLT).

Let's pray:

> Dear Lord,
>
> I invite you into my circumstances. Even when my way is filled with pain, I choose to trust in you. I choose joy. Trouble will give me the chance to grow and to endure, and even when I struggle, you are with me. You are my life preserver. In you I trust. Give me your strength to live in joy no matter what.
>
> In Jesus's name, amen.

Develop an Attitude of Gratitude

Are there days your family wishes you checked your depression or even your bad mood at the door?

"I can't help it," you say. "There are a lot of crazy-making influences in my life beyond my control. Just be glad I've read your book this far and stop meddling with me!"

I too have had both sadness as well as my inner grump steal my joy, so I really do understand. But what if I suggested that we don't have to live the life of despair? It's time to take our joy back. Let's begin by reading Colossians 4:2: "Pray diligently. Stay alert, with your eyes wide open in gratitude" (Message).

Did it really say gratitude?

Yes, it did. So think of three things you have to be thankful for and write them down.

1. _____
2. _____
3. _____

If you can't think of anything, then I have two words for you: try again. Still can't think of anything? Then try this exercise. Write down your three biggest problems.

1. _____
2. _____
3. _____

Okay, now without delay, thank God for them.

No, I'm not crazy. I'm on a mission to demonstrate a powerful secret that can transform your mood from sad to grateful—and it's all based on 1 Thessalonians 5:18, which reads, "Be thankful in all circumstances, for this is God's will for you who belong to Christ Jesus" (NLT).

How can you be thankful in "all circumstances" when some of the circumstances you're facing are serious or even tragic? How can you be thankful when all you want to know is why? Why did it happen? Why did God allow it?

David Jeremiah writes about a woman whose heart was crushed by a tragedy that happened through no fault of her own. One day she told her pastor, "Your advice to stop asking *why* helped a lot." Then, referring to herself and her husband, she added, "And your sermon yesterday helped to make us able to say, 'We will,' and leave it in God's hands. We will let him use even this, till his plan is perfected."[6]

God miraculously moves in any circumstance we give to his care, and the quickest way to give a circumstance to his care is to thank him for it. If you can learn to stand on this concept, you won't fall. Instead, you'll begin to trust that God is up to good.

Have I tried this exercise myself? Yes, believe it or not, I've actually thanked God for my daughter's situation. Looking back at the first difficult year, as well as the years that have since passed, I can see that our circumstances were full of blessings. Let me take a moment to jot down three of our blessings so you can see them for yourself:

1. Laura is living her divine purpose—to love and to be loved—better than anyone I know.
2. A website that shares her story, www.GodTest.com, has seen over three hundred thousand people come to faith, making my daughter one of the top female evangelists in the country.
3. Her precious spirit has touched the many people she has come in contact with, making a profound difference in their lives.

When I was a brokenhearted mother hovering over her baby in a coma, I would never have dreamed anything good could come out of our predicament. But there came a day I was able to thank God anyway.

When you can live this concept of gratitude, you can live the life my friend and bestselling author Lysa TerKeurst describes:

The reality is that sometimes life is hard. Yet, the Bible says that each day is a gift from God we should rejoice in (Ps. 118:24). Daily adventures with God will add an excitement to your life that will change your whole perspective. No longer is your day just one boring task after another, but rather a string of divine appointments and hidden treasures waiting to be discovered.[7]

So if you haven't already done so, try my experiment and thank God, in an act of trust, for three things you wish were different.

Dear Lord,

Paul says in Philippians 2:5, "Have the same attitude that Christ Jesus had" (GW). Help me to find and have this attitude of Christ. Help me also to have gratitude, especially regarding the three problems I am bringing to you now.

1. _____

2. _____

3. _____

As an act of faith, I'm thanking you for these problems because I know you will use them for miracles. Open my eyes to see these miracles and to receive them, even if they are miracles I wouldn't have expected or picked. Thank you, God, that you are in charge and that you are moving in these situations.

In Jesus's name, amen.

The Story of Peace Continued

Ingratitude is a difficult place to be, a place that Paul and his buddy escaped from, as you'll see in his story below.

I've never known a man to change the way Paul, my friend and fellow Roman citizen, changed after his trip to Damascus. One minute he was caught up in the cause to eradicate all Christians from our Jewish community, and the next minute he'd joined those same Christians in their mission to spread the good news of Jesus Christ. The change was so startling, and his story so compelling, that I too became a believer committed to spreading this good news to others—first with Peter, as I helped him transcribe his letters, and now with Paul in his travels.

Paul and I had journeyed to Philippi to conduct meetings down by the river, telling all who would hear that Jesus is the Messiah. Things were going well until Satan sent a slave girl with a dark gift of fortune-telling to follow us wherever we went. She constantly shouted, "These men are servants of the Most High God, and they have come to tell you how to be saved."

Though her message was true, the enemy was using her to put us in a dangerous situation. Not only was she attracting the wrong kind of attention, but she was also setting herself up as a false believer, a weed in our wheat field. As we were there to build a church that we would soon leave behind, we were worried that she would influence it with Satan's destructive purposes.

Finally, Paul had enough. He turned to the girl and said to the demon within her, "I command you in the name of Jesus Christ to come out of her." Instantly, the demon left.

Her masters had tolerated, even encouraged, her earlier displays toward us, as they'd felt it was a clever way to drum up more customers for their fortune-telling business. But when her powers left her, so did their income and their hospitality toward us. They dragged us into the marketplace before the chief magistrate and charged, "These Jews are throwing our city into confusion!"

At the mention that Paul and I were Jews, the crowd went into a frenzy, calling for us to be beaten. After our brutal beating, we were thrown into prison, and our feet were fastened in painful stocks.

Paul and I sat in the darkness of night, unfed, our raw wounds untended. We weren't alone in this place that smelled of sewage. The prison was filled with other prisoners of the magistrate. Paul and I began to pray aloud, first for our freedom, then for the other men to find freedom in Christ. As Paul prayed, a joy filled my soul. A melody of praise began to rise in my spirit, and I began to sing a psalm of David. "Call out with joy to the Lord, all the earth." Paul's rich baritone voice joined mine. "Be glad as you serve the Lord. Come before Him with songs of joy" (Ps. 100:1–2 NLV).

Suddenly, the ground jerked, twisting our bonds so they broke open. The violent shaking also swung open the doors of our cells. In the raining dust and debris, the jailor stumbled out of his house, just next door. His sword was drawn, and it was apparent he assumed we had already escaped because he pointed the blade at himself. He knew the Romans would torment him before executing him anyway.

But Paul called out, "Stop! We are all here!"

Trembling, the jailor fell on his knees before us. He cried out, "What must I do to be saved?"

I said, "Believe in the Lord Jesus and you will be saved, along with everyone in your household."

Soon the jailor brought us to his home, where he washed our wounds as we joyfully shared the good news of Jesus Christ, news he gladly received (based on Acts 16:16–34).

When we praise, God moves. But more than that, praise causes our hearts to fill with joy when we learn the art of praising God in every circumstance.

Shine the Light of the Word

Paul and Silas were able to find joy in a devastating situation because they chose to praise God in the midst of that situation. Psalm 89:15–18 expresses the result of such a decision:

> Happy are those who hear the joyful call to worship,
>> for they will walk in the light of your presence, LORD.
> They rejoice all day long in your wonderful reputation.
>> They exult in your righteousness.
> You are their glorious strength.
>> It pleases you to make us strong.
> Yes, our protection comes from the LORD,
>> and he, the Holy One of Israel, has given us our king.
>> (NLT)

Say this simple prayer: "Open my eyes to your truth as I read Psalm 89:15–18 again."

Write down your thoughts and impressions regarding how this Scripture passage might apply to you:

_____

_____

_____

Review what you gleaned and thank God for these truths.

Yielding Prayer for the Depressed

It's time to yield your depression to God so you can experience the joy he has been waiting to give you.

Shine the Light

> *Dear Lord,*
> *Please turn on your light of truth over me and my depression and difficult moods. Reveal any areas of rebellion or depression I need to trade for your joy.*

List the areas the Lord is revealing to you now:

_____

_____

_____

Yield

Put your hand over your stomach and pray the following:

> *Dear Lord,*
> *I yield all these sorrows, sadness, and depression to your peace and joy through your Holy Spirit.*

With your hand still on your stomach, take deep breaths and start to relax as you repeat the prayer above until you feel God's peace drop into your spirit.

Forgive

Dear Lord,

I'm not strong enough to let go and forgive myself, you, and those who have caused me distress in any of these areas. Still, I choose to forgive. Therefore, I ask that you, through your Holy Spirit inside me, forgive all. I acknowledge that you, Lord, are without sin. Though you may have allowed these difficulties, you will use them as seeds for miracles. Thank you!

Give It All to God

Dear Lord,

I cast my sorrows, difficult moods, and depression at the foot of the cross. Now they belong to you. Thank you for setting me free from my sorrows, difficult moods, and depression so I can experience your joy, regardless of my circumstances.

Pray for Healing

Dear Lord,

Please heal the pain caused by my sorrows, difficult moods, and depression. Thank you for your supernatural peace.

Exchange the Enemy's Work for God's Peace

Dear Lord,

Please forgive me for allowing myself to be overcome by sorrows, difficult moods, and depression. I close all the doors I have opened to the enemy in this area. In addition, I cancel any plans the enemy has for my life. I also cast out any power or influence from any evil spirits of sorrow, depression, despair, stress, anger, and unhappiness. I pray this in the power of the name and blood of Jesus.

I exchange the enemy's work for God's peace. Send the river of your peace not only to me but also to those with whom I've shared my despair. I pray this also in the power of the name and blood of Jesus.

Praise God—You Are Free!

Thank you, Lord! I'm free!

Pray this prayer whenever you need a redo.

12

The Peace That Passes Understanding

Peace I leave with you. My peace I give to you. I
do not give peace to you as the world gives. Do
not let your hearts be troubled or afraid.

John 14:27 NLV

When my daughter was in a coma, whenever I tried to rest
at night, I'd wake up in a cold sweat with the same question pounding in my heart. *When will it end?* I'd sit up and blink
at the darkness and wonder, *How? How will it end?*

Over twenty years have passed, and I still don't know the answers to these questions. However, I rest easier in the knowledge
that whatever happens at the end of my paralyzed daughter's life,
God will see us through. After all, Laura spent a year in heaven the
year she spent in a coma, and I know she'll return to Jesus—who
is our final destination.

The first time I asked Laura if she'd seen Jesus while she was "sleeping," she beamed a smile so bright that her face glowed as she lifted her hands above her head in worship. (A pretty good trick for a person who has no purposeful movement.)

As she slowly lowered her hands, I said, "And Mommy believes you sat in Jesus's lap too." Once again, Laura glowed as she lifted her face and flung her hands above her head.

Wow. My daughter *has* been with him, Jesus, the Prince of Peace. Though I can only imagine what her life was like in heaven, I can testify that Laura came back with a peace so deep that it would be hard to believe she hadn't been with the Lord.

Peace. I know you've figured out that peace is the solution to our stress dilemma. Rhonda Rhea says this about peace: "The secret to successfully living in peace is actually no secret at all. A deep, vital relation with the God of peace. Pursue it. Continue to learn about him and grow in your love for him."[1]

Peace is about going deeper in God. It's about trusting him and yielding our worries and fears to the Holy Spirit— who is already at work inside us. It's about placing our focus heavenward instead of fixing our focus on our struggles.

Rhea is right. Peace is about going deeper in God. It's about trusting him and yielding our worries and fears to the Holy Spirit—who is already at work inside us. It's about placing our focus heavenward instead of fixing our focus on our struggles. Colossians 3:1–2 advises, "Since you have been raised to new life with Christ, set your sights on the realities of heaven, where Christ sits in the place of honor at God's right hand. Think about the things of heaven, not the things of earth" (NLT).

Even Jesus taught us to pray, "Your kingdom come, your will be done, on earth as it is in heaven" (Matt. 6:10 ESV). Why did Jesus want us to pray like that? Because in heaven there is no death, no fear, no tears, no anxiety, and certainly no stress. So if we pray for

God's will to be done on earth as it is in heaven, we'll be blessed indeed.

A lifestyle of peace includes:

- knowing God
- trusting God
- yielding to God
- resting in God's presence

Knowing God

Who is this Jesus we serve? I love how Max Lucado reveals the answer to this question through the many people Jesus came in contact with during his earthly ministry:

> "My Lord and my God!" cried Thomas.
> "I have seen the Lord," exclaimed Mary Magdalene.
> "We have seen his glory," declared John.
> "Were not our hearts burning while he talked?" rejoiced the two Emmaus-bound disciples.
> But Peter said it best, "We were eyewitnesses of his majesty."
> His majesty. The emperor of Judah. The soaring eagle of eternity. The noble admiral of the Kingdom. All the splendor of heaven revealed in a human body. For a period ever so brief, the doors to the throne room were opened and God came near. His Majesty was seen. Heaven touched the earth and as a result, earth can know heaven. In astounding tandem a human body housed divinity. Holiness and earthliness intertwined.[2]

And now, through God's miracle of heaven on earth, God's Holy Spirit has entered our clay temples, once again intertwining holiness and earthliness.

Dear Lord,

I know you are the King of kings and Lord of all. The Holy Spirit has intertwined with my spirit, making me a new creature in you. Not only are you the great and powerful God who created the universe, but you are also the healer of my past, the forgiver of my sins, the comforter who abides in me, and my great and only hope. How can I ever thank you enough? I love you and praise you.

In Jesus's name, amen.

Trusting God

Perhaps you're still having difficulty finding God's peace in your storms. My friend Debbie Alsdorf says:

> If there was never rain, there would not be flowers in the garden of your life. Rain, though soggy and annoying, is a beautiful expression of God's provision. The harsh times in life are the same—though difficult and discouraging, they will prove to be the change agent we need . . . to trust God with everything.[3]

Young Bethany Hamilton learned this lesson despite the fact that heartache was something she never thought she'd experience in the sunny surf of Hawaii. But one day, when she was thirteen, Bethany and her best friend, Alana, lay on their surfboards just off a beach on Kauai's north shore when a fourteen-foot tiger shark silently glided beneath her. As Bethany and Alana waited for the perfect wave, the shark suddenly sank his razor-sharp teeth into Bethany's arm, and the waters around her turned red with her blood.

Though Bethany lost her arm in the attack that day, she did not lose sight of God's will for her life. She overcame her disability by learning to surf competitively again, and she also founded a nonprofit organization called Friends of Bethany that helps other amputees. She even got the chance to play herself in the surfing scenes in the movie *Soul Surfer*, the story of her rise from tragedy.

The loss of her arm made Bethany wise beyond her years, and we can all learn from these words she wrote to teens:

Maybe you've had something happen in your life you didn't plan on: Your parents divorced or someone you loved died. Maybe you've gotten sick or injured or lost your home to a natural disaster such as a hurricane. Guess what? It's all part of God's plan and he'll use you through it if you are willing. Willingness means letting God's plan become your own, whether it's losing your arm in a shark attack or simply listening to his voice.[4]

God will use whatever happens to you as stepping-stones to his wonderful plan for your life if you are willing to trust him through your pain. Are you willing? If you are, you will see miracles begin to unfold around you, miracles of a nature and magnitude that you might not expect.

Perhaps God is referring to *you* in Jeremiah 29:11: " 'For I know the plans I have for you,' says the LORD. 'They are plans for good and not for disaster, to give you a future and a hope' " (NLT).

> *Dear Lord,*
> *Whom else can I put my trust in but you? For you are the One who makes all things come together not only for the good but also for eternity. Thank you that your plans, even when they include what seems like a disaster. These things are only part of the journey to a wonderful future and hope in you. Thank you!*
> *In Jesus's name, amen.*

Yielding to God

Romans 6:13 says, "Neither yield ye your members as instruments of unrighteousness unto sin: but yield yourselves unto God, as those that are alive from the dead, and your members as instruments of righteousness unto God" (KJV).

Billy Graham once explained:

In the original Greek language the words that are translated "yield yourself to God" in the King James Version have a beautiful meaning.

The thought has been translated various other ways by other versions: "Put yourself in God's hands" (Phillips); "Offer yourself to God" (NIV); "Present yourself to God" (New American Standard Version). However the fullest meaning of the word "yield" is to "place yourself at the disposal of someone." In other words, when we yield ourselves to Christ, we do not simply sit back and hope that God will somehow work through us. No, instead we place ourselves at his disposal—we say, in effect, "Lord, I am Yours, to use any way You want to use me. I am at Your disposal, and You may do with me whatever You will. I seek Your will for my life, not my own will." "Put yourself at the disposal of God" (Rom. 6:13 NEB).[5]

We can yield not only our will and our lives to God but also our emotional baggage—our sin, pride, bitterness, worries, anxiety, cares, fleshly desires, and, yes, even our stress. But the beauty of this is that as we yield these emotional toxins to God he trades them for his peace. What a blessing!

Graham reminds us that in this process of yielding "we can hold nothing back,"[6] to which I ask, with the kind of deal God is offering us—peace in exchange for pain—why would we *want* to hold anything back?

> *The more we yield our will, pain, and turmoil to God, the more we become the new creatures he designed us to be —creatures who though fully human have yielded themselves to him.*

Living the yielded life is a process. We have to continually surrender our minds, will, and emotions to God, because life is not a still photograph. Rather, life is like a movie with plot twists and dark moments and times we say, "I didn't see *that* coming!"

But through it all, God is with us. The more we yield our will, pain, and turmoil to God, the more we become the new creatures he designed us to be—creatures who though fully human have yielded themselves to him. The truth is that because our spirits are infused with God's Spirit we've become eternal creatures. The life we live now is only temporary. We are only visiting this world while we look forward to the next—our future life in heaven. It's as Jesus explained in John 18:36: "My Kingdom is not an earthly kingdom. If it were, my followers would fight to keep me from being handed over to the Jewish leaders. But my Kingdom is not of this world" (NLT).

Paul said, "Those who use the things of the world should not become attached to them. For this world as we know it will soon pass away" (1 Cor. 7:31 NLT). Our goal then should be to continue the yielding process, living unattached to worldly things but living attached to God and the souls he has given us to love, nurture, work beside, help, and befriend.

It's not always easy to live with the eternal in mind. In the now, we have betrayal, sorrow, pain, and stress. We don't always see a way to live above our heartaches, desires, and longings. Debbie Alsdorf says:

> Truth is, when I am in a meantime place, I often excuse my behavior because I am upset. I suppose that because most people live this way, I have not stopped to realize that God wants so much more from me than living from freak-out to freak-out. I like the idea of living from peace to peace or from glory to glory as I am being conformed to his image one moment at a time.[7]

By continually conforming to God's image, we can break free from our "freak-outs" and live in peace. Galatians 5:22–23 says, "But the fruit that comes from having the Holy Spirit in our lives is: love, joy, peace, not giving up, being kind, being good, having faith, being gentle, and being the boss over our own desires. The Law is not against these things" (NLV).

Dear Lord,

As Billy Graham once advised, I pray that I am yours to use any way you want to use me. I am at your disposal, and you may do with me whatever you will. I seek your will for my life, not my own will.

I know you are making me stronger so that I can endure the race you have set before me, not just so I can stumble across the finish line but so I can hear you say these words to me: "Well done, my good and faithful servant."

Give me the will and the strength to continue to yield everything to you.

In Jesus's name, amen.

Resting in God's Presence

David Jeremiah says:

> Analysts tell us that at any given moment there are numerous wars taking place somewhere in the world. Twenty-four hours a day, 365 days a year, people are fighting with each other. Those statistics are sad, but here's something that's worse: there are other wars taking place that we rarely hear about.
>
> The heart of every human being is a battlefield where fear attacks faith, and flesh wars with the spirit; despair attacks hope, and hate battles against love. Fortunately for us the Bible says that all of those personal battles can be won by the Prince of Peace who stands knocking at the door of our heart.
>
> Restful hearts are free to face life's battles confidently and fearlessly.[8]

Perhaps one of the best benefits of surrendering ourselves to the Prince of Peace is learning to *live* in his blessing of peace.

In my book *When You Can't Find God*, I tell the story of the time my four-year-old son collapsed at my feet during a late night of Christmas shopping. He wrapped his arms around one of my snow boots, looked up at me, and said, "Mom, I can't go on. Could you drag me for a while?"

"No," I told him, imagining how dirty he'd get if I dragged him through the shopping mall. "But I can carry you." I leaned down and scooped him into my arms. Then I held him next to my heart as I carried him to the car.[9]

This is exactly what God wants for us. He wants us to yield to him so he can scoop us out of the muck and carry us next to his heart while we rest in his arms.

Rest your weary head on God's chest. Let him do the heavy lifting. Let him carry your burdens. Let him carry you through your trials with his peace. Philippians 4:7 says, "The peace of God is much greater than the human mind can understand. This peace will keep your hearts and minds through Christ Jesus" (NLV).

Dear Lord,
    My arms are not only lifted to you in praise but also lifted to you in surrender. I surrender to your presence. Teach me how to rest in your presence and to let you do the heavy lifting. Carry me through my trials in your peace, which is greater than I can understand, a peace that will guard my heart and mind in you.
    In Jesus's name, amen.

The Story of Peace Continued

From the moment the angel stood before me and told me not to be afraid, I was filled with questions. I, a virgin, had been chosen to give birth to a son? What would Joseph say, or my parents, or our neighbors?

After all, I was only a teenaged girl whose name meant bitter. My parents were bitter that I had not been born a boy because as a woman it was certain I could not be the Messiah our people so longed for. However, no one had understood that a woman would usher our Messiah into the world.

So I could hardly believe I was gazing up at a beautiful angel who had told me I was highly favored by God and would be the mother of the Son of the Most High.

I could only stammer, "I am the Lord's servant. May it be done to me as you have said."

Shortly after the angel left, I escaped the prying eyes of my village and rushed to see my aunt Elizabeth. Even though I hadn't told her my secret, my aunt said, "Blessed are you among women, and blessed is the child you will bear!"

My situation was harder for Joseph to accept, but the angel appeared to him in a dream and told him that my pregnancy was of the Lord and that my son would save many from their sins.

Though I knew God was with me, many parts of my journey to become the mother of the Messiah were difficult—from hearing the whispers of the town gossips, to the journey to Bethlehem on the back of a donkey, to the birth of my son in a dark cave that served as the innkeeper's stable.

But there were blessings too, like the joy of watching Jesus learn carpentry from Joseph, and his first journey to the temple, where he proved to the scholars that he had a greater understanding of the Word than they did. The one thing I knew about my son was that he was always about his Father's business.

When Jesus put on the mantle of a rabbi and began to walk the countryside with the twelve he called his disciples, I was often in the crowds that gathered to hear him teach. I saw his mighty miracles. The blind could see, the deaf could hear, and the lame could walk. Was there any doubt that my Jesus was the chosen one of God?

I have to admit that when Jesus started his ministry I felt entitled to his attentions. Once his brothers and I stood outside the crowd he was teaching. We had come to Jesus on an important family matter, but instead of stopping his sermon, Jesus gave the crowd the honor of being equal to us, his own family, by saying, "Whoever does my Father's will is the same as my brother, sister, and mother."

His words were hard for me to understand, but harder yet was the ordeal of his arrest the night of the Passover. This is not how I expected things to be!

I stood in the throng at the governor's palace and saw Jesus after the Roman guards had beaten him. I barely recognized him with his precious face so bloody and swollen. He wore a ghastly crown of thorns on his head and stood silently before the mob as they began to cry, "Crucify him!"

My screams of, "Dear Lord, no!" were lost in the death roar surrounding me.

I followed Jesus as the soldiers made him carry his own cross. I fell to my knees weeping as they pounded nails into his hands and feet, then lifted him up on that cross. His body sagged as he struggled to lift himself by his wounded hands and feet every time he needed to take a breath.

My aunt and I held each other as we watched my son slowly die. He looked down at me, and though he was in agony, he said, "Woman, your son," indicating his disciple John. And to John he said, "Here is your mother." John immediately came along beside me and led me away. I leaned heavily on him, especially as we neared the bottom of the hill. Darkness suddenly fell, and the ground beneath our feet shook. Then I heard Jesus's voice call out, "It is finished!"

Jesus was dead. How could this be? The One who came from God to save us from our sins was dead!

Three days later, I was with John and the disciples in the upper room when the women who had gone to bring fresh spices to the tomb pounded on the door. When John opened it, the women poured into the room, crying and laughing at the same time, saying, "He is risen! Jesus is risen from the dead!"

The disciples didn't believe, but I did. I slipped out behind Peter and made my way to the tomb. There I found the stone had been rolled away. Could it be? Hope surged through me. Hadn't Jesus said that the Son of Man had to be put to death before coming back to life three days later?

Late that evening, two of our friends returned from a brief trip to Emmaus to tell us Jesus had appeared to them. Even as they were talking, Jesus suddenly stood before us. My son! Alive from the dead!

His first words? He told us, "Peace be with you."

Jesus had many things still to teach us, many things we still needed to understand. And for the next forty days, we followed him, watching him heal the sick and proclaim that through his death and resurrection he had set us free from our sins.

On that last day, we followed Jesus to a high place that overlooked the city of Jerusalem. While he was still talking, he began to ascend into the sky. We stood with our mouths hanging open as Jesus disappeared until two men, glowing like the sun, suddenly appeared and said, "Why are you standing there looking up at the sky? This Jesus, who was taken from you into heaven, will come back in the same way that you saw him go."

Somehow, I always knew that Jesus would return to God his Father, and the words he had so often said to us rang in my heart. "Peace I leave with you; my peace I give you. I do not give to you as the world gives. Do not let your hearts be troubled and do not be afraid" (John 14:27) (based on the Gospels and Acts 1).

These words of peace that Jesus taught in his earthly ministry are also for you. Your first step in receiving them is to believe that Jesus is the Prince of Peace. Then open your heart to trust him even in times of hardship and trouble.

Shine the Light of the Word

Trusting God is a key to experiencing God's peace, as Isaiah 26:3–4 explains: "You will keep the man in perfect peace whose mind is kept on You, because he trusts in You. Trust in the Lord forever. For the Lord God is a Rock that lasts forever" (NLV). Say this simple prayer: "Lord, open my eyes to see your truth as I read Isaiah 26:3–4 again."

Write down your thoughts and impressions regarding how this Scripture passage might apply to you:

_____

_____

_____

Review what you gleaned and thank God for these truths.

Yielding Prayer for God's Peace

Shine the Light

> *Dear Lord,*
>
> *Please turn on your light of truth over me and my stress and fears. Reveal any trust issues that I have toward you or your plan for my life. Reveal to me my self-induced stressors, including a poor diet, a lack of exercise, a lack of fellowship with other believers, and a lack of quiet time and rest.*

List the areas the Lord is revealing to you now:

_____

_____

_____

Yield

Put your hand over your stomach and pray the following:

> *Dear Lord,*
>
> *I yield all my stress to your peace through your Holy Spirit.*

With your hand still on your stomach, take deep breaths and start to relax as you repeat the prayer above until you feel God's peace drop into your spirit.

Forgive

Dear Lord,

I'm not strong enough to let go and forgive myself, you, and those who have caused me distress in any of these areas. Still, I choose to forgive. Therefore, I ask that you, through your Holy Spirit inside me, forgive all. I acknowledge that you, Lord, are without sin. Though you may have allowed these difficulties, you will use them as seeds for miracles. Thank you!

Give It All to God

Dear Lord,

I cast my fears and stress at the foot of the cross. Now they belong to you. Thank you for setting me free from my stress so I can live in your peace that passes understanding.

Pray for Healing

Dear Lord,

Please heal the pain caused by my stress. Thank you for your supernatural peace.

Exchange the Enemy's Work for God's Peace

Dear Lord,

Please forgive me for allowing myself to be overcome by stress. I close all the doors I have opened to the enemy in this area. In addition, I cancel any plans the enemy has for my life. I also cast out any power or influence from any evil spirits of lies who say your peace isn't for me, in the power of the name and blood of Jesus.

I exchange the enemy's work for God's peace. Send the river of your peace not only to me but also to those who have shared my stress. I pray this also in the power of the name and blood of Jesus.

Praise God—You Are Free!

Thank you, Lord! I'm free!

Pray this prayer whenever you need a redo.

Conclusion

Finding God's Peace

Thank you so much for traveling with me on this journey to leave our stress behind as we go deeper into the peace of God. What a journey it has been. We've learned to yield our feelings of being overwhelmed, stuck, frustrated, burdened, hopeless, offended, anxious, negative, distracted, and depressed to Jesus, the Prince of Peace, by the power of the Holy Spirit.

This skill of yielding to the peace of God is a skill you've practiced as you read through the pages of this book. It's also a skill you can continue to master throughout your walk with God.

So now, at the first signs of stress, take a deep breath and begin to yield your burdens to the Lord as you also yield to his peace. As Jesus told his disciples, "Peace be with you" (Luke 24:36).

Now enjoy and practice God's peace no matter what your circumstances.

God bless you![1]

1. A study guide for *The Stress Cure* can be found at www.StressPrayers.com.

Notes

Introduction: The Problem of Stress

1. www.psychologytoday.com/blog/the-race-good-health/201212/4-healthy-ways -cope-stress.
2. Ibid.
3. www.webmd.com/balance/stress-management/stress-management-topic -overview.
4. http://en.wikipedia.org/wiki/Stress_(biology).
5. http://dictionary.reference.com/browse/stress?s=t.

Chapter 1: The Key to Peace

1. Max Lucado, *A Gentle Thunder: Hearing God through the Storm* (Nashville: Thomas Nelson, 1995), 68.
2. Ibid., 70.
3. Billy Graham, *The Holy Spirit: Activating God's Power in Your Life* (Grand Rapids: Zondervan, 1978), 113.

Chapter 2: Overwhelmed

1. http://dictionary.reference.com/browse/overwhelm?s=t.
2. Sarah Young, *Jesus Calling: Enjoying Peace in His Presence* (Nashville: Thomas Nelson, 2004), May 10.

Chapter 3: Stuck

1. Phillip Keller, *A Shepherd Looks at Psalm 23* (New York: HarperCollins, 1970), 54–55.
2. Sarah Young, *Dear Jesus* (Nashville: Thomas Nelson, 2007), 121.

3. *Nature, International Weekly Journal of Science*, January 4, 2012, "Demonstration of Temporal Cloaking," http://www.nature.com/nature/journal/v481/n7379/full/nature10695.html#/contrib-auth.

4. Katie Drummond, "Pentagon Scientists Create Time Hole to Make Events Disappear," January 4, 2012, http://www.wired.com/dangerroom/2012/01/time-hole/#more-68739.

Chapter 4: Frustrated

1. Max Lucado, *Life to the Max* (Nashville: Thomas Nelson, 2011), http://tinyurl.com/akjxw24.

2. Ibid.

3. Billy Graham, *Dealing with Doubt: A Thomas Nelson Study Series Based on The Journey by Billy Graham* (Nashville: Thomas Nelson, 2007), 4.

4. Ibid.

5. Stormie Omartian, *Just Enough Light for the Step I'm On: Trusting God in the Tough Times* (Eugene, OR: Harvest House, 1999), 41–43.

6. Ibid.

Chapter 5: Burdened

1. Janet Holm McHenry, *Daily Prayer Walk* (Colorado Springs: WaterBrook, 2002), 175.

Chapter 6: Hopeless

1. Charles Stanley, *Handle with Prayer: Unwrap the Source of God's Strength for Living* (Colorado Springs: David C. Cook, 1982), 11.

2. Max Lucado, *You'll Get through This—Hope and Help for Your Turbulent Times* (Nashville: Thomas Nelson, 2013), 201.

Chapter 7: Offended

1. Pam Farrel, *Fantastic after Forty* (Eugene, OR: Harvest House, 2007), 172.

2. Dr. Bill Bright, *The Joy of Supernatural Thinking* (Colorado Springs: Victor, 2005), 80–81.

3. Karol Ladd, *Thrive, Don't Simply Survive: Passionately Live the Life You Didn't Plan* (New York: Simon & Schuster, 2009), 109.

Chapter 8: Anxious

1. http://pediatrics.about.com/cs/safetyfirstaid/a/snake_bites.htm.

2. Max Lucado, *Fearless: Imagine Your Life without Fear* (Nashville: Thomas Nelson, 2009), 10.

3. Neil T. Anderson and Rich Miller, *Freedom from Fear* (Eugene, OR: Harvest House, 1999), 25.

4. Sarah Young, *Jesus Calling: Enjoying Peace in His Presence* (Nashville: Thomas Nelson, 2004), May 19.

5. Sue Falcone, *Lighthouse of Hope: A Day by Day Journey to Fear Free Living* (Kindle Edition) (Lighthouse Publishing of the Carolinas), May 11, 2012.

6. Sarah Young, *Dear Jesus* (Nashville: Thomas Nelson, 2007), 106.

Chapter 9: Negative

1. John Maxwell, *Your Road Map for Success: You Can Get There from Here* (Nashville: Thomas Nelson, 2002), 51.

2. Ibid.

3. Lindsey O'Connor, *If Mama Ain't Happy, Ain't Nobody Happy!* (Eugene, OR: Harvest House, 1996), 102.

4. Stormie Omartian, *The Power of a Praying Wife* (Eugene, OR: Harvest House, 1997), 150.

5. Lysa TerKeurst, *Made to Crave: Satisfying Your Deepest Desire with God, Not Food* (Grand Rapids: Zondervan, 2010), 94.

Chapter 10: Distracted

1. Lila Empson, ed., *Moments of Peace in the Presence of God: Morning and Evening Edition* (Bloomington, MN: Bethany, 2004), 657.

2. Charles Stanley, *Handle with Prayer: Unwrap the Source of God's Strength for Living* (Colorado Springs: David C. Cook, 1982), 10.

3. Ibid.

4. Max Lucado, *Grace for the Moment—Women's Edition: Inspirational Thoughts for Each Day* (Nashville: Thomas Nelson, 2007), 263.

Chapter 11: Depressed

1. Sarah Young, *Dear Jesus* (Nashville: Thomas Nelson, 2007), 96.

2. Max Lucado, *The Applause of Heaven* (Nashville: Thomas Nelson, 1990), 13.

3. A. W. Tozer, *The Pursuit of God* (Rockville, MD: Serenity Publishers, 2009), 20.

4. David Jeremiah, *Turning toward Joy* (Colorado Springs: David C. Cook, 2006), 40.

5. Max Lucado, *When God Whispers Your Name* (Nashville: Thomas Nelson, 1994), 71–72.

6. Jeremiah, *Turning toward Joy*, 42.

7. Lysa TerKeurst, *What Happens When Young Women Say Yes to God* (Eugene, OR: Harvest House, 2014), 166.

Chapter 12: The Peace That Passes Understanding

1. Rhonda Rhea, *Whatsoever Things Are Lovely* (Grand Rapids: Revell, 2009), 218.

2. Max Lucado, *God Came Near* (Nashville: Thomas Nelson, 1986), xv.

3. Debbie Alsdorf, *A Woman Who Trusts God: Finding the Peace You Long For* (Grand Rapids: Revell, 2011), 14.

4. Bethany Hamilton, *Soul Surfer Devotionals* (Nashville: Thomas Nelson, 2006), 1.

5. Billy Graham, *The Holy Spirit* (Grand Rapids: Zondervan, 1978), 119.

6. Ibid.

7. Alsdorf, *A Woman Who Trusts God*, 19.

8. David Jeremiah, *1 Minute a Day* (Nashville: Thomas Nelson, 2008), 123.

9. Linda Evans Shepherd, *When You Can't Find God: How to Ignite the Power of His Presence* (Grand Rapids: Revell, 2011), 167.

Linda Evans Shepherd is the author of over thirty books, including *How to Pray through Hard Times* (which won the 2012 Selah Christian Life Award), *Experiencing God's Presence*, *When You Don't Know What to Pray*, and *When You Need a Miracle* (which won the 2013 Selah Christian Life Award).

An internationally recognized speaker, Linda has spoken in almost every state in the United States and in several countries around the world. You can learn more about her speaking ministry at www.GotToPray.com.

Linda is the president of Right to the Heart Ministries. She is the CEO of AWSA (Advanced Writers and Speakers Association), which ministers to Christian women authors and speakers, and the publisher of the magazine *Leading Hearts*, found at LeadingHearts. com. Linda has been married to Paul for over thirty years and is the mother of two.

To learn more about Linda's ministries, go to www.LindaEvans-Shepherd.com. Follow Linda on Twitter @LindaShepherd or on Facebook at www.facebook.com/linda.e.shepherd.

Also check out her ministry's website at www.FindingGodDaily. com as well as her suicide outreach at www.ThinkingAboutSuicide. com and invitation to know God at www.GodTest.com.

To find more information about this book, or to view the study guide questions, go to www.StressPrayers.com. Or use the QR code below.

Connect with
Linda
Evans Shepherd

 Linda Evans Shepherd

LindaShepherd

Visit
www.sheppro.com
to book Linda to speak at
your next event.

GOD WANTS TO HEAR FROM YOU—BUT HE ALSO WANTS YOU TO HEAR FROM HIM

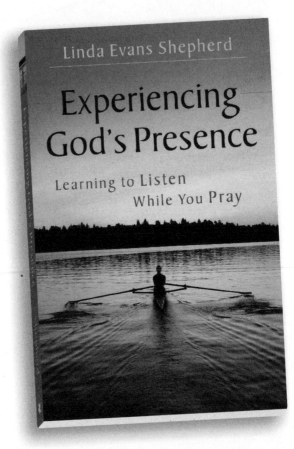

"If you long for a relationship with God that is deeper, richer, and more intimate than you've ever known before, read this book."

—**Carol Kent,** speaker and author, *When I Lay My Isaac Down*

NO MATTER WHAT THE HURT, THERE IS ALWAYS, *ALWAYS* HOPE

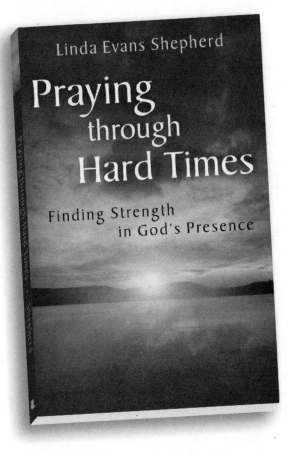

With compassion born from her own experiences with tragedy, Shepherd offers you practical strategies for surviving difficult times, giving your worries and sadness to God, praying through the pain, and finding peace, hope, and joy once more.

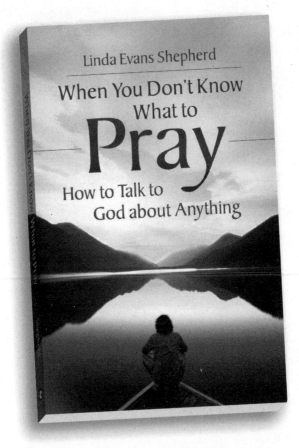

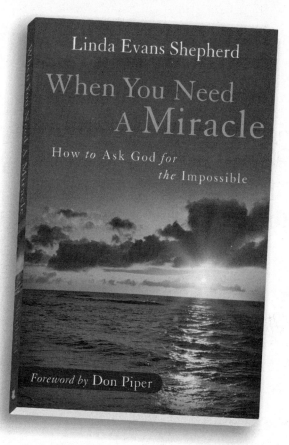